THE ORDWAYS

Books by William Humphrey

THE ORDWAYS

HOME FROM THE HILL

THE LAST HUSBAND
AND OTHER STORIES

A TIME AND A PLACE

FARTHER OFF FROM HEAVEN

HOSTAGES TO FORTUNE

THE
ORDWAYS

William Humphrey

A LAUREL/SEYMOUR LAWRENCE BOOK

To Dorothy

A LAUREL/SEYMOUR LAWRENCE BOOK

Published by
Dell Publishing Co., Inc.
1 Dag Hammarskjold Plaza
New York, New York 10017

A portion of Part One, in somewhat different form,
first appeared in *The Saturday Evening Post* under
the title "The Monument and the Shadow."

Laurel ® TM 674623, Dell Publishing Co., Inc.

ISBN: 0-440-36713-1

Printed in the United States of America
First Laurel printing—November 1984

For their efforts in recovering the manuscript of this book, left aboard the Rome–Milan Express on March 15, 1963, the author wishes to thank the Italian National Railways, and in particular Capostazione Michele Fortino of the Stazione Termini in Rome.

CONTENTS

PART ONE: *In a Country Churchyard*   1

PART TWO: *The Stepchild*   99

PART THREE: *Sam Ordway's Revenge*   147

PART FOUR: *Family Reunion*   325

In a Country Churchyard

CLARKSVILLE is in Texas—but only barely. Take a map and place the index finger of your right hand on Clarksville, your middle finger will rest in Oklahoma, your ring finger in Arkansas, and your little finger in Louisiana. It lies fifteen miles south of the Red River, on the road from the ferry which transported the first colonists to Texas. Standing on the edge of the blackland prairie, it was the first clearing they came to out of the canebrakes and the towering pines which choke the broad river bottom. Southerners, those first settlers were, and in the towns of northeast Texas, such as Clarksville, the South draws up to a stop. Mountain men, woodsmen, swampers, hill farmers, they came out into the light, stood blinking at the flat and featureless immensity spread before them, where there were no logs to build cabins or churches, no rails for fences, none of the game whose ways they knew, and cowered back into the familiar shade of the forest, from there to farm the margins of the prairie like a timid bather testing the water with his toe. The Texas of cattle herds and cowboys, of flat little sun-swept towns with low sheet-iron buildings strung out along a single main street, the Texas of the West, lies farther on, in time as well as space. The shady streets of Clarksville radiate from a spacious square, from the plaza in the center of which, bedded in wild roses, rises a tall marble shaft surmounted by a Confederate foot soldier carrying a bedroll on his back and a canteen at his side, resting his musket, and shading his eyes to gaze over the rooftops towards the southwest, in which direction the view is almost limitless.

The first colonists, and some later immigrants like my own great-grandfather, who drew back appalled from those vast and lonely prairies, went no farther, but settled in the town and in the farm hamlets which cling like children to its skirts. They felled timber and planted cotton and some brought in slaves while others did their own picking, and before long they were calling their town the long-staple-cotton capital of the world. Two blocks north of the public square they laid out another, and raised, of imported yellow stone, a courthouse eight stories high which to travelers on the oceanic prairie looked like a lighthouse, in the plan of a Greek cross topped by a tower with a tapered spire carrying on each of its four sides a great white clockface that could be read for miles, this in turn capped by a belfry from which on the quarter hour the bells rolled out over the town like a peal of thunder. After that there was no disputing that Clarksville would be the seat of Red River County. West of the courthouse they built a large jail and north of it a cotton compress and storage shed and a railway depot and a sawmill to finish the logs brought out unendingly from the river bottom.

Thirty years ago, when I was a boy there, Clarksville was already an old, old town. In fact, thirty years ago, before the discovery of oil nearby, Clarksville was an older town than it is today. Shoals of autos thronging the streets now fill with bleat and roar the square where then the rumble

of ironbound wheels on bois d'arc paving bricks was heard
and the snapping and crackling of a wagon bed carried like
rifle shots around the four sides. Seated along the tailgate
of the wagon with their legs dangling, the country children,
stolid, neuter creatures all with the same homemade Buster
Brown haircut, bobbed up and down like corks riding the
waves. Now high in octane, the air then was spiced with the
tang of fresh-cut pine, and in ginning season, when cotton
lint lay in drifts against the curbs like snow, with the ap-
petizing aroma of fresh-pressed cottonseed meal. On Saturday mornings the farmers hunkered in groups on the corners
of the square, whittling. Asked to carve something other
than shavings from his billet of wood, one of them would
have looked at you as if you had asked him to bake you a
cake. At noon, when they folded away their knives and stood
up and brushed off their laps, it looked as if a sheep had been
sheared on the spot, the shavings as curly and fine as wool.
Market Square—where one went with one's mother to buy
fresh vegetables from out of the farmers' wagons, and where
it was a common sight, if there were many younguns in a
family, and there always were, to see a pallet spread on the
ground in the shade of the wagon bed and a row of them,
crawling with flies, napping there—is a parking lot now.
It occupied the large empty area in front of the county jail,
and when business was slack the farmers would often hear
the mournful wail of a French harp (harmonica, that is)
from high up in the hard-faced old jailhouse. The bars were
spaced too closely for any heads to be thrust out, but late in
the day when the sun sank low in the west and sent a raking
light into the dark interiors of the cells, then the farmers
could see the prisoners' faces, striped with shadows. Conversations were often carried on between those behind the
bars and those beside the wagons, and not infrequently the
visit, though loud, had a familial intimacy. The rooftops are
trellised with TV aerials now, and from studios in Dallas
come the revival meetings and the medicine shows which

thirty years ago were staged on the courthouse lawn on Saturday afternoons.

Then too an old custom, an annual rite, was still observed. The less well-to-do of Clarksville—which included the Ordways—were at most one generation removed from the farm, and all had country kin; and once a year, in late October, after crops had been gathered and after the first frosts had brought hog-killing time with presents from the farm of fresh pork sausage and sorghum syrup, after the west winds sweeping in off the prairie filled with the rustle of dry cornstalks and the rattle of empty cotton bolls had stripped the trees and dumped a blizzard of yellow leaves upon the streets before blowing themselves out, there came a Saturday when we got up early, and finding the weather clear and still, put on old clothes, packed a lunch basket, and drove out of town to our ancestral homes for graveyard working day. In our case it was to Mabry, where among the cedars and the now bare-branched elms beside the small white clapboard church my father's people all lay buried.

For some, those from whose family circle an accustomed face was missing, in whose burial plot was a raw dirt mound on which as yet no grass had grown, no weeds to be plucked, but instead a browned and weathered wreath of flowers with weathered, faded ribbons to be removed and taken down back of the graveyard and thrown upon that common heap of dried bouquets and wire skeletons with colorless shreds of matter left clinging to them, for such as those, I say, graveyard working day was a time of sorrow and lamentation. On meeting they fell sobbing and wailing into one another's arms. For most, however, graveyard working day, though tinged with melancholy, was not so mournful an occasion as the name might suggest. The greater number found themselves reunited without recent loss. Old friends met, and though their conversations were weighted with sighs, though their eyes grew misty as they recounted the year's toll among their common acquaintance, though they said they too must soon follow after and doubted that they would meet again until they met in heaven, they were glad to be there and pleased to see one another. Younger grave-tenders were not noticeably oppressed by the thought that others would someday do the same office for them. Many a mating in the community, later solemnized in the church, had had its beginning as boy and girl pulled weeds side by side on graveyard working day, and among the grove of trees behind the schoolhouse was one tall beech in the bark of which, high above my head, was carved a pair of hearts joined by an arrow and monogrammed with my father's initials and those of my mother's maiden name.

We children were licensed to run and play as usual (though actually it was more fun to help with the work, where little pitchers with big ears might overhear, from the lips of relatives or from visitors to the family burial plot, the most intriguing anecdotes and reminiscences of their ancestors), were encouraged to, in fact, without restraint; as I remember it, even that dire warning not to step on any graves arose from our own superstitiousness rather than from any parental admonishment. One knew which families were in mourning, and play was steered away from them. As much piety was expended upon our right to enjoy our animal spirits, indeed our powerlessness to resist them, as upon the dead. "They don't know any better," was the statement frequently heard. "They'll learn soon enough. Let them be happy while they can."

For our family, at the time I am writing about, graveyard working day was a time of quiet rejoicing. My father was one of ten children, not counting two half-sisters and one half-brother, all then still living. Year after year (minus always that one half-brother, who was "out west" and unable ever to get home for this or any other of our family reunions) they had all met there with none missing from their ranks. It was thirty-five years since any Ordway had died, and that last was one whose death, even had it been more recent, we

were not expected to mourn, not one of "us"—by which I
mean my father's side of the family. This was my grandfather's first wife, Agatha, the mother of my Aunts Winifred
and Beatrice and of that dim, distant half-uncle of mine
whose name was Edward and who would be a man of thirty-
five (born the day his mother died) but who for some reason
was always referred to (the rare occasions that he was mentioned) by the double diminutive Little Ned. But he had
been gone a long time, so long he was all but forgotten—in-
tentionally, I seemed to sense, and already I had learned that
I was not to question too closely into the circumstances of
his leaving home nor the reasons for his prolonged absence.
In any case, he was not missed, nor did Agatha Ordway
cast any shadow upon our day—not even, I am sorry to say,
upon my grandfather's day. Poor soul, she appeared to have
been taken at her word, which, engraved upon her tombstone, was: "Weep not for me, but be content." Aunt Winnie
and Aunt Bea could hardly be expected to remember their
mother; they were only children when she died. As for my
grandfather, well, he could hardly be expected to grieve for
his first wife after all those years; still it used to embarrass
me to hear him, in saying grace over our dinner spread on
the ground just a few feet from where poor Agatha Ordway
lay buried, thank God for having spared him *all* those whom
he held dear, and rejoining him with them all once again.

As though the prairieland had been a pool into which the
town was dropped, Clarksville was ringed with low wavy
hills, flattening, growing fainter as they spread away. Mabry,
ten miles due west, sat on the outermost ripple; beyond
stretched Blossom Prairie, endless, treeless, smooth as water.
The settlement consisted of just four buildings: the store and
the house of its owner squatting along the narrow dusty
road, and behind them, thrown down like a pair of dice
upon the faded green baize of their yard, the one-room
schoolhouse (in which my grandmother, years ago, before
she married my grandfather, had once taught for a time)

and the church. Lacking a bell, they shared between them a large iron-rod triangle suspended between two wooden trestles, of the kind sometimes to be seen outside farmhouse kitchen doors by which the men are summoned from the field for dinner. The length of rod for beating the triangle was kept inside the schoolhouse, the temptation to bang out a triplet or two being more than passing boys could be expected to resist. Tempo quickening as schoolmarm or preacher got into the swing of it, like a locomotive accelerating from a dead stop, its ringing tricornered clang grew hexagonal and finally circular, rolling westward unobstructed into infinity, and long after the beating had ceased the triangle went on vibrantly humming to itself. The church, simple as a child's drawing, the architectural semblance of the elemental creed it housed, needed only a span of oxen yoked on in front to pass for one of those prairie schooners which had brought its builders to the spot, and, lent a footloose and somewhat reckless air by its poverty, appeared to be sniffing the wind blowing in its face from off the wide open land stretching before it, and thinking of trying its luck farther on. Inside, the walls were as bare as outside. A rusty potbellied stove sat on a tattered zinc mat in the center of the room; supported by wires dropped from the ceiling, the rusty, flaking stovepipe ran overhead and out the flue at the rear. The benches were each the handiwork of a different member of the original congregation, in a variety of woods and workmanship, heights and depths, uniform in one thing only, the perpendicularity of their backs. The altar was a kitchen table, the altar cloth a yellowed lace doily. On it always stood, one inside the other, the two wooden collection plates lined with faded and motheaten purple felt into which one dropped one's penny, then passed it on down the row, where at one end my grandfather and at the other Mr. Bartholomew, the elders, stood waiting with abstracted mien to receive it. On the back wall behind the rickety low pulpit hung a notice board with replaceable

letters whereon, beneath the chapter and verse of the day's
sermon text, was published the attendance and the always
miserably small collection which had been taken up on the
preceding Sunday, or rather the last Sunday on which services had been held, for, being so poor, Mabry was obliged
to share its preacher in rotation with two other settlements
—a forced economy which did not much sadden me when
later on I went to spend the summer with my grandparents
on the farm. A small parlor organ completed the furnishings.
It required pumping by hand, a job which, performed by
some strapping farm lad, made the little building rock like
a churn. The congregation's aim was not to sing with the
organ but above it, and I can still see my grandfather, his
chest expanded, neck stretched forward, and his elbows out
at his sides as he held his hymnbook, like a rooster about to
flap its wings and crow, waiting to come in on the beat with
"When the roll is called up yonder." When one got done singing he stood with his eyes fixed straight ahead, waiting for
the others each to finish, then all sat down together.

Mabry people all had small farms, large families. To get
a start in life many of their children had had to leave home.
Many had left the land altogether. Not all had been drawn
into Clarksville; with the coming of the automobile some had
gone as far away as the distant cities, Paris, Sherman, even
Dallas and Fort Worth. On graveyard working day they all
came home. To see the country folks reunited then with their
grandchildren from the towns was to see evolution in action.
They might have belonged to different epochs, different
strains, the farmers with flaming cheeks and red ears and
leathery brown necks, work-swollen hands, slitted eyes from
squinting at the sun, with wrinkles at the corners so deep
they seemed to have been drawn on in warpaint; the women
bent like the rare prairie trees beneath the prevailing wind,
gnarled, sinewy, dry, with pale, wind-cracked, chapped and
peeling lips, more than one of them with that lichenlike
splotching of the skin which denotes Texas sun cancer, and

which may end by eating away the septum of the nose right up to the very bone. From long seething in caustic home-made lye soap, and from a lifetime of scrubbing the overalls of a family of working men against a washboard, their hands looked as if they had been cooked, and when they extended them in one of their shy, faint handshakes, they felt feverish to the touch. They spoke a different language, too. Slow-talking, unused to having to shout to make themselves heard, speaking little in any case, they spent their hoarded and antiquated words as my grandfather in town in the stores counted out his old-fashioned Indian-head pennies and his nickels and dimes from deep in his long stocking-shaped purse and stacked them in neat deliberate stacks on the counter. Alongside their grandchildren they presented a picture of wild flowers, more like weeds than flowers, stubborn, tenacious, tough, and a domesticated seedling of the same species, shade-grown and delicate.

Though Mabry itself was small its graveyard was quite large. It served a numerous community scattered among the piney woods and the red hills to the north and east, and out on the prairie, who, while they preferred not to be jostled by neighbors in this life, craved close companionship in death, or else feared they might be overlooked on Judgment Day unless they were found in God's own crowded back yard. They had been burying there for a long time. One passed under a roofed gateway where, on those drizzly days that funerals are always held on, the coffin rested on sawhorses while the service was read. Down the path, padded when we used to go there on graveyard working day in the fall with brown pine needles, on the left, beneath a broad knotty oak which peppered them with acorns, lay the Jervises, whose care and upkeep devolved upon the community, the family having "died out." Beside the burial plot of this extinct clan, though strongly impelled to hurry past, I used often to linger, trying to give features and a voice to the host of spirits who hovered there, beseeching me, on that day when

all the dead were resurrected by the memories of those who
had known them, to grasp their hand and save them from
sinking deeper and deeper into oblivion. Hastening on, one
passed the Leonards, a son of which tribe on one memorable
graveyard working day was to disabuse me of the notion that
I had nothing to learn from country boys, to teach me the
most unsettling things about myself, and to make it hard for
a time for me to look any girl in the face. Then came the
Claibornes, all, according to their tombstones, asleep in
Jesus, a state of repose which I never could succeed in pic-
turing to myself. The next large plot on the right was ours.

The monuments in Mabry graveyard reflected the poverty,
and the taste, of the survivors of the dead. Small, with mini-
mal inscriptions. In many plots there were no stones but
instead homemade wooden crosses, the hand-carved legends
full of quaint misspellings and highly personal abbrevia-
tions. On some graves stood upended fruit jars, purplish
through exposure to the sun's rays, inside which, through
beads of moisture, one saw bouquets of faded crepe-paper
flowers. Children's graves were numerous, and on them were
often to be seen china dolls, perhaps one of those pistol-
shaped bottles filled with colored candy pills, a celluloid
fish or duck, on the still humbler ones simply a glass or porcelain doorknob or a few marbles, sometimes a teething ring,
a pacifier. Among some family plots one saw, left over from
Memorial Day and by October bleached, color-run, and tattered, the flags of three nations: the Republic of Texas, the
Confederacy, and the United States.

We used to arrive early, first among our own family and
among the first of those car-borne, before work had begun,
oftentimes before sunup, when Mabry was a sketch in
grisaille upon the immense blank canvas of sky, at an hour
when it was truly as if the dead, as so many of their monuments testified, lay asleep—still forms beneath patchwork
quilts of leaves drawn up to the chins of their headstones.
Wagons and buckboards stood in the road and in the school-

yard, their nodding teams hitched to the fence palings, the beds piled high with baskets of food, thermos jugs, cushions and old blankets, campstools, rakes, brooms. From scattered parts of the graveyard came the steady grate of files on hoe blades, and the long-drawn slash of a whetstone down the edge of a sickle or a scythe. The country folks—among them my grandparents, he in overalls and jumper and a collarless shirt, she in a mother hubbard, for protection against the briars, which allowed only her head and her hands to show, and a poke bonnet of flowered gingham, the ribbons tied underneath her chin—chatted in groups while awaiting their children and grandchildren from the towns.

I loved both my grandparents dearly, but of the two I loved my grandfather more, despite the fact, or possibly because of it, that he liked me least of all his grandchildren, whereas I was my grandmother's favorite. This difference was always marked in their respective greetings. She gave me a big hug and kiss and made a great fuss over me, while my grandfather not only suffered with visible impatience the shy, fervent, and hopeless kiss which I implanted on his wrinkled cheek, just at the tip of his wiry mustache—he hardly bothered to conceal his disapproval of my grandmother's affection for me. It was not merely that, being a man, he was less demonstrative. Towards others of his grandchildren he was affectionate enough. He just did not care for me.

"Silly boy! Whatever put that foolish notion into your head?" my mother cried when finally, unable to suffer in silence any longer, I spoke to her about it. "Why, of course your grandpa likes you! He loves you!"

"He loves me, all right," I remember saying. "I'm his grandson and he has to love me. But he doesn't like me. If only he did! Oh, if only he liked me as much as Grandma does, how happy I would be!"

To understand the reaction which this produced in my mother the reader must know that, along with the rest of

their sons- and daughters-in-law, she was devoted to my
grandfather, somewhat less than devoted to my grandmother. Ever ready to leap to my grandfather's side in the
rare and insignificant differences between his wife and him,
she would attack my poor father, who sought to maintain a
strict neutrality and who knew how unimportant his parents'
quarrels were, as if he had automatically taken his mother's
part. My mother's cause was fraught with frustration because my grandfather would never stand up for himself.
The soul of discretion, he retired from the field as soon as
battle was joined. He would rather be wrong than wrangle;
what was more, it did not bother him not to have the last
word, even when he was in the right. This placidity of temper, which was precisely what she loved him for, used to
provoke my mother to exasperation.

After giving an angry snort, shaking her head, jumping
up from her seat, and pacing rapidly around the room, my
mother sat down again and drummed her fingernails on the
table, looking hard at me. I no longer recall her exact words,
but this is the gist of the little family secret which she decided to let me in on that day. She did not say that my grandmother loved me less than she appeared to—this was merely
implied in the way in which she said that my grandfather
loved me a great deal more than he showed. It was my misfortune always to be the first of the grandchildren to arrive
at any family gathering.

Knowing that his wife suspected him (quite unjustly) of
a preference for her stepdaughters, and thus of her stepdaughters' children, and also because he wished to counter-
act the flagrant partiality which she showed among her own
children and her children's children, my grandfather always
determined beforehand to be unimpeachably equal in the
warmth of his welcome to each and every one. In practice this
worked out to mean equally cool to all. Quite possibly—for
he was like that—he was particularly on guard against being
driven by his wife to favor those whom she favored least—

which would include my father, and therefore me. But being affectionate by nature, he was able to sustain this pose only through the first two or three arrivals, unbending all the while, until finally he dropped it altogether. As I came first, I felt the full brunt of his fairness; those of my cousins who came later not only got their proper share of his affection, they got my share as well. My grandmother, on the other hand, knowing how he disapproved of her favoritism, was always resolved for once to show none, with the result that she effused most over those for whom she cared the least. My grandmother had her fixed and permanent favorite (my Uncle Ewen, her first-born son); after him she valued her children in proportion to the distance by which they were separated from her and the worry they caused her. We lived closest by of all, and so, not having far to come, we gave her no particular concern, and were therefore less precious to her. The kiss I got from her, so unlike that unrequited one of mine on my grandfather's cheek, had more light than warmth in it; those she bestowed on my cousins who had had to travel farther to get theirs were too heartfelt for outward show.

On graveyard working day, as at any family gathering, as one by one her children came home, my grandmother grew more and more fretful over those still missing. As the number narrowed, instead of taking comfort she merely transferred the anxiety released by the arrival of the latest one onto those still to be accounted for. Other families were already assembled and at work. Scythes hissed in the dry grass, the rhythmical chopping of hoes was heard on all sides and the scratching of rakes among the papery leaves. Already brush fires had begun to crackle and the air to thicken fragrantly with smoke.

While waiting for the rest to arrive, my grandfather would bring those of his children who lived outside the range of ripples from Mabry up to date on the chronicle of deaths since last graveyard working day. Fetching a sigh, he might

declare, "What us folks hereabouts will do for fish now, I
don't know. We buried poor old Dora Exom in July."

"How's that? Is Aunt Dora Exom dead?"

"Dead and yonder in her grave. Yes, Dora is wetting her
line now where the big ones bite every day."

"I reckon you mean to say she's in heaven. I don't gainsay
it. But I expect Aunt Dora wouldn't have any trouble filling
her stringer down in the other place."

"I never seen anything like it," my grandfather said.
"Many a summer afternoon I've set on the creek bank alongside of that old woman, used the same bait, same size hook,
set my bobber to the same depth as she set hers, and she
would be hauling in fish like that boy yo-yoing there, and I
would never get a nibble. Why, in clear water—now you
all may not believe this, but in clear water I have seen fish
steal her bait and sneak off to eat it, then just give up and
turn around and come back and swallow the bare hook!"

"Wonder did she hand on her secret to anybody before she
passed away?"

"If you ask me I don't believe it was a thing she could have
handed on to anybody else if she'd wanted to. She let on to
have some secret formula, but I never believed it. I once
heard her say that her mamma honed after fried fish all the
while she was carrying her. Don't you expect that might've
had something to do with it?"

"Them Exoms sure et the fish! Pile of old fishbones out
back of their house big as a haystack."

"Wellsir," said my grandfather, "she give away just as
many as she fed her own family. You would hear a racket
'long about sundown and look out the window: there'd come
Aunt Dora Exom stomping down the road in her gum boots
and her old sunbonnet, wet gunnysack over her shoulder
and about seventy-leven cats tagging along behind her mew-
ing and meowing and yawning and licking their whiskers.
'How'd you folks like a little fresh fish today?' she'd say.
And she would reach in her sack and feel around, picking

out the very nicest ones for you. That good old soul must
have give away a boxcarful of fine white perch in her time.
'Now you take and roll these in yellow cornmeal, honey,'
she'd say, and have your grease good and hot and fry them
till they're brown, and you just tell me if they ain't good!'
Bless her old heart! 'Now watch out for them little bones,'
she would always say. Ah well, Aunt Dora and old St. Peter
ought to be able to swap some good lies. He was a fisherman
too, so I've heard tell."

My grandmother, meanwhile, if she heard any of this, what
with fretting and fidgeting and glancing surreptitiously up
the path every five seconds, sat thinking, "Oh, devil take old
Dora Exom and her fish! How can he sit there and chatter
away so unconcerned when right this minute his own child,
our darling Ellis (or our Herschell, or our Florence) may be
lying dead on the highway somewhere for all he knows to
the contrary? Oh, my precious, my love, where are you?
Why don't you come? If it was his Winnie or his Bea we
wouldn't be hearing about Dora Exom and her old fish!"

Having so often been told that her fears were foolish, my
grandmother enjoined upon herself a strict silence, which
she was totally incapable of observing. "What do you suppose could have held them up like this?" she would ask when
she could stand it no longer, which was very shortly, trying
in vain to sound merely curious, or else pretending uncon-
vincingly to be mildly annoyed with the tardy ones for keeping her waiting.

Those were the days when something was always going
wrong with automobiles. Roads were bad, detours frequent,
long, and rough. None of the children had been married
long, all had young families, these youngsters had to be
caught and dressed and herded into cars, along the route
had to be stopped for every few miles and treated for car-
sickness, taken behind the bushes, etc. In short, there were
dozens of good reasons for any delay. My grandmother took
them like pills, sucked the sugar coating off, and found them

all bitter inside. "Oh, why don't they come!" she would cry out then. The worst thing that could be done at this juncture was to remind her how often in the past she had gotten herself worked up like this, only to have the missing son or daughter turn up at the next moment, safe and sound and full of apologies. Yet someone, which is to say my grandfather, was sure to do it. Recognizing his tone, she shuddered in anticipation.

"Now, Hester," he would say, "don't be a fool. You're getting yourself all worked up over nothing. There! What did I tell you? There come Florence and Cecil now. That leaves just Ewen."

"Just Ewen!" my grandmother thought. "As though Ewen is any less precious to me than Florence. Just Ewen! Always my pet, as he very well knows. Is he throwing that up to me now, when the poor boy may be lying at death's door, without even his mother at his side to ease his pain?"

"Now, please," my grandfather continued, "try to remember that your children are not babies any more and don't have to have you to hold their hand every time they take a step" (an observation, a truth, which gave my grandmother no comfort whatever—rather the reverse). "He'll be along directly. They've all always showed up before, haven't they?"

This my grandmother was bound to admit, though just how it was any assurance that they would all show up this time, she never could understand. On the contrary. And even to mention it seemed to her to be tempting fate. She was convinced that she was destined to be bereft of one or more of her children, and the fact that she had gotten them all ten up to an average of thirty did nothing to allay her fears; it only brought ever nearer the day of reckoning, and made it all the harder to give them up. Whichever of her sons or daughters got home last, instead of being made to do penance for the anxiety he had caused her, was assured of being all day long the object of her special tenderness. But, as my grandmother was forced to acknowledge, the laggard did turn up at last, was scolded for the apprehension he had caused their mother by everyone but her, and work could begin.

There was much to be done. For although, as I have said, it was thirty-five years since any Ordway was buried, ours was the biggest, that is, the most populous plot in the entire graveyard, containing as it did every Ordway who had ever died in the New World, most of whom never in their lives set eyes on Mabry. In addition to his own, his wife's, his first-born son's, and his daughter's, there were the graves of all his ancestors and kin whose bones and moldering remains old Thomas Ordway, my ghoulish great-grandfather, in flee-ing Tennessee and vowing never to return, had disinterred and brought to Texas with him. Fondly spoken of in the family by nicknames conferred upon them by the various kegs in which that all-too-filial son had packed their relics for the journey, these reached as far back as old "Blackstrap" Dismas Ordway, my great-great-great-grandfather, and Amy his wife, known with affectionate irreverence as "Old Sour-mash." And Dismas begat Aubrey, called "Old Tenpenny" on account of his ossuary, a nail keg, and Aubrey took to wife Genevieve, whose dust had come west in a cask which lent her the title "Granny Blackpowder." These and many others, courtesy great-aunts and great-granduncles whose precise relation to one another and to me must needs be re-estab-lished each graveyard working day, lay awaiting their yearly maintenance like so many patients in a hospital ward the coming of the nurse to make their beds, and while so doing to reassure them that they had not been altogether forgotten in the world outside.

The gray stone faces of my ancestors—how clearly I see them still! Bearded with moss, freckled with fungus, bathed in tears when the rain fell, inclining this way and that as though in whispered conversation with one another. Each had, for me, taken on the aspect of its owner: here a high

bald dome, pinched features formed by the cramped and
scanty epitaph, here a crack like a scar across a cheek, a
pair of small round old-fashioned spectacles formed by a
double O in the text: my family album in stone. Barely
legible by now, I suppose; even in my childhood some of the
older ones could scarcely be made out, effaced by those
prairie winds which, laden with grit, are like a sandblast—
yet carved upon the tablets of my memory as with a chisel.
My people, my dead, with each of whom, I was taught to
believe, and in those days still did, I should one day sit down
and converse. To them I owed my features, my voice, the
strengths and weaknesses of my mind and body. Their mi-
grations had determined that I was born where I was and
not some other place. Before I could become myself, as according to the biological law, ontogeny recapitulates phy-
logeny, I would first have to live through the lives of those
who had produced me.

With each was associated some story, which, as his or her
mound was raked, the weeds cleared away, the fallen stone
set upright, was once again retold. Yearly repetition did not
dull these tales; on the contrary, we looked forward to them
as, seated in the concert hall with program in hand, one
anticipates the opening notes of a favorite piece of music,
and we would have been disappointed if, for instance, the
tending of Great-uncle Hugh's grave had not elicited from
my grandfather the story, known to us all by heart, of Uncle
Hugh and the lady's corncobs. Honest, blunt, plainspoken
Hugh Ordway, the enemy of all pretense and pose, whose
epitaph stated not that he had "passed away" or "fallen
asleep" but that he had died on a day in March 1858, had
once been among the guests at a supper party, back in
Tennessee. The menu included roasting ears, and to the
problem of what to do with the unsightly cobs, the hostess
had worked out this delicate solution: the white-gloved
Negro butler (borrowed for the occasion) would go around
the table with a big silver platter (likewise) and collect them

from the guests between servings. From right to left he went, and as our Uncle Hugh happened to be seated on his hostess's left, by the time it got to him the platter was piled high. As he had done with the dishes of food all evening, the butler stood with his platter at Uncle Hugh's elbow. Noticing him at last, Uncle Hugh inspected his soggy offering, and in his broadest back-country accent said, "No, thank you just the same, don't believe I'll have any."

Bachelor Great-granduncle Giles was extremely absent-minded. Once he bought himself a horse and buggy, the first he had ever owned, to go on a trip to Knoxville, a three days' ride. His business there concluded, he took the train home. About a week later he remembered his horse and buggy, and went to the depot and bought a round-trip ticket to go and get them. Uncle Giles was never known to refuse a chew, yet he never became a slave to the weed. A heavy chewer once marveled at this. "I like tobacco," Uncle Giles responded. "There's nothing I like better, and I wish I could get the habit. But unless somebody reminds me I just can't seem to remember it." However, it was not really absent-mindedness: Uncle Giles had a lifelong preoccupation. When he was young he had overheard someone assert that the lifetime of man was not long enough for him to count to one million. "What!" he had snorted. "Well, we'll just see about that!" and commenced counting. "Giles, how's it coming? How far along are you now?" people would ask. "Three hundred and eighty-six thousand, four hundred and twelve —make that thirteen," Uncle Giles would reply—until, latterly, he became secretive about his total. Just how far he did get no one ever knew. For though he was vouchsafed twelve years more than his allotted three score and ten, and did hardly anything else towards the last, his dying words were, "Tell them that fellow was right. It can't be done. I only got up to—" And there Uncle Giles stopped counting.

Dismas, the Columbus of our line, was the youngest of three sons of a coal-and-timber merchant in Leeds, England.

A born American in spirit, young Dismas, just turned fifteen, proudly refused when his eldest brother commanded him one day to black his boots. His brother beat him; still Dismas refused. He ran away from home. He walked to London. There he took passage on a boat to Savannah, Georgia, earning his fare as a cabin boy. From Georgia by stages he worked his way west to Tennessee, and there chose the tallest hill he could find, where the soil was of the meagerest, but where nobody could look down on him. His English accent, which he never lost, was a source of great entertainment to Amy, his wife, and to succeeding generations of his offspring. Once he went into a hardware store and asked the clerk for a hax andle. Another time he told his son Aubrey to go throw them ogs over the fence some hoats. "Amy," he was forever saying, and among us there was no other way of saying it, "w'ere is me at?" To which the reply, after Amy, was, "At the moment, Mr. Hordway, you are standing in the all." He once had an encounter with a man named Arrison. "Man named what, Mr. Ordway?" asked Amy. "Arrison," said he. "An odd name, Mr. Ordway," said she. "Odd? Nothing odd about Arrison," said he. "How do you spell it?" said she. "Haitch hay harr harr hi hess ho hen. If that don't spell Arrison then wot the ell does it spell?" said he. We employed that saying for all sorts of occasions. It was one of the very few not-quite-nice expressions which even the children in the family were permitted to use. When I solved the last problem of my homework at night and shut my book, "There! If that don't spell Arrison," I would say, "then wot the ell does it spell?"

There was my Great-granduncle Wesley and his wife Caroline. She outlived him by forty years, never ceasing in all that while to lament him in these words, "Such a good man! Such a good husband and father! Never drank, never smoked nor chewed, never dipped, never diced nor gambled, and never used language." So that in our family it became a byword, and we could never hear the catalogue of virtues of some pattern of them all without appending to it, "And she never used language."

Not all the stories were amusing.

There was Inez Ordway, my grandfather's second cousin. One of her babies was eaten alive by a sow. For days the poor distraught mother refused to accept the fact and went about searching for her child in unlikely places and calling its name, asking the neighbors and even passing strangers if they had seen it. Then her mind cracked and gave way. She was hopelessly insane for months, never fully recovered. She would hum tunelessly without stop, even in church. Another baby was universally prescribed for her, but after the calamity she could never have another. In her later years she came to fancy that she herself was her own child, her own mother.

Then there was Dorcas Ordway. Listening to my grandfather recount her pathetic history, I used to thrill with indignation. The man she had been about to marry was shot dead on the very church steps by the suitor whom Dorcas had rejected for him. Within a week the killer was shot down by a kinsman of the slain man. Instead of being pitied, Dorcas Ordway was blamed by the community, led on by the women who had always envied her beauty, for these acts of madness which had cost the lives of two of its young men. She was accused of having cast a spell over them. Bitterest of all were the mother and sisters of her bridegroom. Cursed and shunned when she went out, she kept to the house. It became the rule, whenever a cow went prematurely dry or a person fell mysteriously ill, to expect signs painted on their door, rocks thrown through the windows. Her old father braved these attacks as well as he could, and her brothers fought many fights in her defense. Dorcas Ordway wasted away and died of unhappiness at the age of twenty-eight. A revulsion of feeling thereupon swept the community, all of whom came penitent and ashamed to her funeral. "You have hounded her into the grave with your unkind-ness," said her father as the dirt was being shoveled in upon her. "May God forgive you. I never will, and I hope and pray that your consciences, if you have got any, will never stop tormenting you until you are all where my poor dear girl is now."

In the entire history of the Ordways only Willis, my great-grandfather's eldest brother, was ever musical. Though no one had told him, he knew the name for a fiddle the first time he ever saw one, and how it was to be held and bowed. He could play any instrument, sang like a bird. Hearing him, they would ask what was that lovely tune, they could not remember ever hearing it before, and Willis would blush and admit that it was something he himself had just made up. Willis Ordway, born frail, died at twenty-three of galloping consumption. Only then did they realize that they had had another Stephen Foster in their midst. They tried to recall, to preserve his songs. In vain. They were too unmusical to reproduce them, and all were lost to the world forever.

But these were distant kin, and all that was long ago and far away, and nothing lasts forever, not even unexpiated wrong. Time redresses many grievances, the rest it wears out in sheer weariness, and even the most vexed and ill-used wraith lies down at last with a sigh—especially if removed to a second grave far to the west of the scenes of its unhappiness. Ours, like the lettering on their tombstones (also transported from Tennessee by my great-grandfather), grew dimmer with each passing year. Their characters flattened by time like flowers pressed between the pages of a book, they had become types, useful to point a moral, but powerless to scare. Progress and enlightenment, by rendering so needless their fates, so old-fashioned their attitudes and stances, had made them all quaint, slightly unreal, even faintly comical. Disappointed lovers nowadays seldom shot their rivals, certainly not with such a melodramatic flair for the setting. Today's tough-minded young women seldom perished of community opinion, nor did their fathers make brave speeches at their biers. The eating of an infant by a hog was horrifying, but it was too grotesquely rural to affright the modern mind, even the modern child's mind. These old ghosts had accepted the changes in the world, and no longer harrowed their kin.

The custom was for friends to assist one another at these family seances, in session throughout the graveyard that day. One rested from his labors by dropping in on others' plots, lending a few minutes' help with the weeding, and leaving behind a little wreath of remembrances of their dead. Something amusing, in a respectful way, by preference, or else sweetly sad—some saying or doing which revealed an endearing bias of character, or, overlooking all faults, which trained a light on the good side of his or her nature, something to bring a smile to the lips, followed by a meditative sigh. This my grandmother did—spent the entire morning doing, in fact, dispensing consolation wherever she went. My grandmother had few living enemies, no dead ones. She buried her enmity with the person who had earned it, and never afterwards could be brought to speak an unkind word of him. For her the good which men did lived after them, the evil lay interred with their bones. To one family on her round of visits she would recall some small characteristic act of kindness which she had once received at their mother's hands, sinking all mention of a long-standing feud between them, and would say, if any of us remonstrated with her afterwards for her hypocrisy, "Mavis Mahaffey and I may have had our little differences. But I was no doubt as much in the wrong as she was" (a concession which you needed to be dead in order to win from my grandmother). "In any case, I no longer even remember what the quarrel was about. She was a good wife and mother and an excellent housekeeper, and for my part, if the Lord forgives Mavis then I certainly do." Cowardly herself—or so, despite having borne ten children in a farmhouse bedroom attended by a doctor whose preparedness for emergency consisted of eighteen months' training at a frontier medical academy fifty years before, she believed—she admired silent endurance of pain, and on graveyard working day liked to recall to survivors the patience and the fortitude with which their departed had sustained the illnesses which claimed them at the last. She would gladden a lonely widower (a class towards which she felt especially drawn) with praise of his dead wife, and stooping unseen, would pluck from her grave the one weed which he had overlooked, as during a sick call she might have plucked a loose thread from her invalid friend's skirt.

Repaying us these courtesy calls was not so easy for the friends of our family. None of course had known any of those old long-dead Tennessee Ordways, nor the tenant of our smallest grave (who would have made such a suitable text for the sort of homilies that were wanted that day), little Dexter Ordway, my grandfather's brother, who on the ninth of October 1863 had been recalled to heaven at the age of five. Agatha the Unwept was still remembered by many, but hers was a ghost deemed best left to lie. Some few professed to be able to recall my grandfather's sister Helen; but as she had died at twenty-six, and had been so self-effacing as hardly to have any character of her own, they could only nod over her grave, remember her devotion to her poor father and her usefulness to her mother, and sigh over the brevity of her life. That left my great-grandparents. There were still a good many old-timers who remembered them, but it was not possible to recount any amusing anecdotes of either of them, nor anything even tolerably melancholy. Only one thing kept the remembrance of Ella Ordway from being unbearably depressing, and that, an ambiguous sort of mitigation, was her own unconsciousness of anything especially hard about her wretched life. One might have admired her enormously, even have marveled at her adventures (I did), but those who had known her, and seen her wonder at their admiration, had ended by

accepting her intrepidity, her endurance and self-sacrifice
at her own low estimation. Her patient and obliging spirit
would come when summoned on graveyard working day, as
she herself had always come when called, and unlike *his*,
would go away when sent; but it seemed to say that the
afterlife was just as cheerless and exacting as this one.
There were few solacing reflections to be drawn from her
story, none whatever from my great-grandfather's.

From the time he settled in Mabry until his death twenty-
five years later, Thomas Ordway was an all-too-familiar
figure in and around Clarksville. He was a specter haunting
the town, a reminder of events which everyone wished to
forget, the symbol of their common defeat, an object of
universal pity and of unconquerable aversion. Watching
him, his boy leading him by the hand, drag himself along
the sidewalk like a half-crushed insect, each slow deliberate
step seeming to require a separate resolution and the re-
marshaling of all his shattered faculties, hearing the tap-tap-
tap of his cane on the pavement and smelling that odor
arising, despite the twice-daily changing of the wrappings,
from his suppurating legs, men shuddered and turned their
heads. Time passed more slowly in those days, brought
fewer changes, hardly seemed to pass at all, and forty years
later, standing over his grave, they shuddered afresh as that
old lazarus of their youth rose up before their mind's eye.
My grandfather, down on his knees tending his father's
grave as in life he had tended the helpless man, was only
repeating what as a boy he had overheard from them, when
he said, "Better if he had never been born." Even for
me, who never knew him, who came long after, my great-
grandfather cast a shadow (I am speaking literally) on my
town, and I could not cross the square, as I did every morning on my way to school, without seeing it.

We lived across town from the grammar school. It was a
long walk and I was usually behind time, often late. I was
too young to own a watch and the bells of the courthouse

clock were not much use to me; they measured time in
gross quarter hours whereas I was either late or on time for
class by minutes, and a minute was as good as an hour for
earning a demerit from Miss Addie Dinwiddie. But I had
my own way of telling time, at least on clear days. The
square was my sundial, its needle the monument rising
from the plaza in the center. My way lay diagonally across
from the northeast to the southwest corner, and the moment
I entered the square I always knew by where the shadow of
the statue fell in relation to the doorway of, depending on
the season of the year, Athas's Confectionery or the Duke
& Ayres store or the Gas Company on the west side, whether
to walk or to run, or, since one might as well be hung for
a sheep as a lamb, to dawdle. It was instinctive for me then,
whether betimes or tardy, to cast a glance up at the soldier
on top of his column. High above the workaday world, attended by swifts and swallows, he stood bathed in morning
sunlight, proud, erect, unscathed. But in the twisted shadow
which he cast upon the pavement his rifle became a stick to
lean on, the pack on his back a symbolic burden of pain and
tribulation, and the hand with which he shaded his eyes to
scan the far horizon a hand held over sightless eyes to shield
them from the view of others.

Thomas Ordway's war against the Union was over almost
as soon as it began. Hit by shrapnel in the first day's fighting
at Shiloh, he had been blinded on the spot, and both his legs,
which were never to heal, so shredded they had looked like
boiled soup shanks. He had been a dirt farmer, had tilled
the same small stony hillside plot that his father and his
father's father had tilled, in Tennessee, before the war. In
Clarksville he made a living caning chairs, my grandfather
being put when he was old enough, which is to say before
he was old enough, to gather and to peel the willow wands
he used and to split the hickory splints. He wove baskets,
plaited buggywhips, netted seines which were highly prized
by fishermen up and down the river. He knitted: sweaters,

socks, stocking caps. He became quite a knowledgeable man, and there were those who would have braved that odor for the pleasure of his conversation; but he took their overtures for pity, to which he was even more hyper-sensitive than to the repugnance he knew he aroused, and repelled them gruffly. Uneducated, barely literate, he turned in his blindness to books, and at night after Ella and the boy were asleep Helen would read to him until she began to drowse and lose her place. His reading added to the reputation which blindness had automatically conferred on him among the simple-minded of being somewhat of a wizard. Water-witching powers were attributed to him, but always out of his hearing, for he rejected the imputation with scorn and anger. His learning was fragmentary (which may have helped to make it seem oracular), broken by odd gaps, limited by the range of books available to him in the few private libraries of Clarksville at that date, and the fact that often the owner of a certain work possessed only three or four of the six or eight volumes of a set. Someone in town, taking the precaution to do it anonymously, had made him a gift of the one thing he was ever heard to wish aloud for, a dictionary. At first, instead of a key to other books, it was a joy in itself and he loved having it read aloud to him. But becoming discouraged at the number of words he did not know, he discontinued. His favorite reading was the Bible (which he was wildly credited with knowing by heart and being able to recite from any set passage on to the end), his favorite books Chronicles and Psalms. His greatest consolation was music—strange consolation, as even the sprightliest tunes saddened him—his greatest regret that he could play no instrument, nor even carry a tune (the family defect), for he would never permit himself to go where music might be heard, not wishing to spoil the pleasure of others by his presence.

He was not so hideously disfigured by his wounds as he imagined—though the first sight of him was always a shock

—and the worst of them, that to his eyes, did not immediately show. Outwardly they were unimpaired, seemed in
fact to have been miraculously spared by that shell fragment
which had deeply gashed his forehead; and as his hearing,
in compensation, had grown extra sharp, so that he turned
with unerring accuracy towards every sound, it was possible
for strangers to hail him, only to find that the bright brown
gaze turned upon them was blind. The extreme instance of
this dated from the time in Arkansas, on their way to Texas,
when a chivalrous man on the gallery of a crossroads store
where they stopped for a moment had offered to thrash him
for letting a woman in his wife's condition lead their team
while he sat in the shade on the wagon seat, not realizing
until too late that he was blind, and never realizing that in
his blindness he was ignorant of his wife's condition. Old
Thomas Ordway was said to have been amused by the recollection of this incident, perhaps because it was a tonic to
the pity, piety, and abhorrence with which, like the broken
idol of a discredited creed, or as if he were the victim of a
blood sacrifice that had been botched, he was generally
treated.

Consideration for the feelings of others could not keep
him from attending Clarksville's annual Memorial Day services. There his wounds entitled him to the place of defer-
ence. It was he, blind and lame, who set the pace of the
veterans' parade. This used to start from the square, where
in their grays and butternuts, brushed napless, smelling of
cedar chests, the old soldiers gathered to await the com-
mencement of the day's ceremonies. There was still no
monument to their honor there at that time. From the square
they marched, limped, straggled out south, over the bridge
to Washington Street, where they did a right turn up the
hill and past the tabernacle to the cemetery for the speech-
making and the wreath laying.

Intended as a day of mourning for the war dead, Memorial Day, in the South, had quickly become a day for

celebrating, rather, the glorious cause for which the dead had fallen. Orators, for whom the occasion was not without bearing on the next elections, fanned more and more patriotic fire out of the ashes of sorrow, and they began to find the presence of Thomas Ordway there in the front row of seats, a ring of vacant ones setting him apart, with that fixed and empty gaze of his, an accusation and an embarrassment. So did the other, unwounded veterans. They had come to think of the day as their annual get-together rather than one to honor their dead comrades-in-arms, and to their reminiscences of youthful highjinks and derring-do they found that broken, groping, stinking figure a hindrance. They suspected him of subversive reservations as to the truth and beauty of what they had done, even of doubts as to the justice of the cause for which they had fought. They did not know that to those speeches which his presence alone was enough to render tawdry and indecent, no heart among them swelled more enthusiastically than his. That when a man has given everything to a cause he cannot disavow it, but must cling to the last to that which has betrayed him.

When the war memorial was unveiled Thomas Ordway was present, and it was this, his last appearance in public (he died shortly after), which lingered in the memory of many of our visitors on graveyard working day.

A motion to commission and erect a monument had been made, seconded, and, with one abstention, unanimously approved at a meeting of the Board of Aldermen several years before—in fact, at the very first meeting following the departure of the district Federal commandant and the return of the town to self-government. A committee was appointed to investigate and make recommendations. After a year's study they reported a wish and a will among all classes of the people for a memorial to commemorate the fallen and to honor the survivors of the conflict. That there was a general readiness to bear whatever costs were encountered.

That, as to the most suitable location for a memorial, this question was no sooner asked than answered: in the most conspicuous spot in town, the center of the public square. The committee envisaged a raised plaza, or small floral park, circular in form and perhaps enclosed by a draped chain. A pedestal rising from the center. The horse rearing to charge. The rider with saber drawn, symbolizing the indomitable—

"Horse?" said one alderman—the original abstainer, and the only former infantryman on the Board. A man not born to rule, but who had become a power to reckon with in the town and county just during the past few years, and who retained a certain amount of the enlisted man's rancor against his former mounted officers. "Rearing to charge? I reckon you mean, charging to the rear."

And so for some years nothing came of the proposal. For though overruled by his colleagues, the one old foot soldier let it be known to his former comrades throughout the county that they were being asked to buy a brass horse for a brass lieutenant or captain or worse to prance on in the middle of the town square, and the motion went unimplemented. And there the matter might be resting to this day had the westbound train not stopped one morning in the fall of 1884 and let off a passenger. This in itself was an event, the stranger was a marvel. He wore a cape, a furry soft hat with a wide floppy brim, a yoke collar, a ribbon tie, and carried a thin gold-headed cane, although he walked without a limp. He spoke a language which none of the usual half dozen men lounging on the platform waiting to watch the train throw off the mail sack could understand (it was English) and he produced a calling card which rendered illiterate even those among them who were not. As they could not make out where he wished to go, they took him to the courthouse, which in fact was where he had asked to be taken, though as they could have told him, he found no one at work in that vast edifice but one aged female, the town clerk. The stranger succeeded in making her understand that he wished to see His Honor the Mayor. She directed him to the place where except for one morning a month His Honor was always to be found, keeping store. By now there were about three dozen men outside on the courthouse grounds, and they accompanied the stranger on this second leg of his quest. The Mayor had been born to better things than keeping store, as had many another whom the war had brought still lower than feed-and-grain, and could even get a piece of his tongue around the name engraved on the stranger's calling card:

MAESTRO MICHELANGELO PADELLA
DELL' ACCADEMIA DI SAN LUCA

A meeting of the Board of Aldermen was called to announce that the very first Italian sculptor ever to visit the town had come, at which meeting the old dispute between former officers and former enlisted men was settled at long last. An equestrian statue would cost five thousand dollars, an unmounted soldier could be had for one fifth the cost and in one fourth the time. The Maestro spent the rest of the day seeing the sights of the town. He climbed to the top of the courthouse tower and stood for some time looking westward. From there the railroad tracks could be seen winding over the prairie and out of sight like the trail of a man who has disappeared into the desert. So when he left the following morning it was back on the eastbound train. He promised to submit a design. In due course this arrived, was approved without abstention, and the formal commission and a deposit of half the fee sent off. A year passed. Then one day the westbound train pulled into the depot, uncoupled the last boxcar and shunted it onto the siding, and out of the coach came the Maestro. The aldermen were summoned and when all were there the boxcar door was unlocked and they all disappeared inside, from whence issued the sound of crowbars and the screech of nails being drawn, then

silence, then hammering. Everyone came out smiling and
nodding, and the next day the Maestro took the train back
the way he had come and was never seen again.

A good many years were to pass before anybody from the
town made the same trip (those who left went west, and did
not come back) and returned to report that there was hardly
a town of monument-aspiration size along the railway line
from Clarksville to Atlanta—which was as far as that particular eastbound traveler had gotten—without its copy of
our soldier. Still later, in the piazza of many a small Italian
town, the touring descendants of that generation were to be
reminded of home by the statue commemorating the march
of Garibaldi and his Thousand. But at the time of the un-
veiling (which was three years after the delivery of the
statue, one for the erection of the plinth and, prior to that,
two years before the Board of Aldermen would give in to
the fact that the only place from which a column of marble
of that size could be had was Vermont) no one knew this.
The entire county, black and white, young and old, was there
that day. From the platform on the plaza, draped in Confederate flags, visiting dignitaries made dedication speeches
lauding those who had made the supreme sacrifice, and
those there present, more fortunate but no less courageous,
who had survived the crusade. Then the rope was pulled,
the veil came fluttering down, the applause went up, sub-
sided, and as the first of many pigeons alighted on the
soldier's head, a solitary off-key voice accompanied by the
tapping of a stick on the wooden paving bricks began to
sing:

> In Dixie Land where I was born in,
> Early on one frosty mornin',
> Look away! Look away! Look away! Dixie Land.

Often we were joined at our work by strangers. Along
would come a man in a collar and tie and town suit who,
after a glance at the name on our tombstones, would salute

my grandfather with a "Good morning, Mr. Ordway," in
which the joviality was edged in black, and would pitch in as
if he were one of us, as if he were that long-lost son and
brother returning to claim kin and catch up in one day on
his lapsed duties to his dead. Such feverish work could not
be kept up for long; they soon tired, then they introduced
themselves, said what office they were running for, and
solicited my grandfather's vote. (Not my grandmother's;
female suffrage had been won, but country women still
thought it was not ladylike, nor properly respectful towards
their husbands, to exercise the right.) For graveyard working day always fell just a week or so before elections, and
candidates used to make the rounds of the country churches
and bid for support by pulling weeds.

Then the children were called in from play, the women
stacked their rakes and brooms, the men climbed down out
of the trees where they had been sawing off dead limbs, the
fires of brush and leaves were allowed to die, and between
the graveyard and the cars and wagons streams of women
and children carrying food plied back and forth like ants.
Campstools, car cushions, blankets were brought, tablecloths
were spread, the baskets opened and the food set out. This
was before the days of luncheon meats and bottled cheeses.
Knowing that one of these Saturdays would be graveyard
working day, the women had cooked each Friday for weeks
in possible readiness, and among those in our family there
was keen emulation. There were whole baked hams and
roast joints of beef, fried chicken, cold turkey, fried squirrels. There were great crocks of potato salad and macaroni
salad and chowchow; brandied fruits, and pies of every sort:
chocolate, pecan, lemon meringue, coconut custard, banana,
sweet potato, peach, berry cobblers—each the best of its
kind, the product of that one of your aunts known for that
dish, and you had to have a little of each for fear of offending any one of them. You were allowed to pass up only the
things your own mother had brought. When it was all laid

out we bowed our heads and my grandfather asked God's
blessing on us and thanked Him for His bounty and for
bringing us all together again another year.

We Southerners are accused of living in the past. What
can we do? The past lives in us. And not just that single
episode which those who accuse us have in mind: the Civil
War—but all of the past. If the Civil War is more alive to
the Southerner than to the Northerner it is because all the
past is, and this is so because the Southerner has a sense of
having been present there himself in the person of one or
more of his ancestors. The War forms merely a chapter—
the most vivid single chapter, it is true, but still just one
chapter—in his book of books, the bible of his family—
which is not to say the family Bible, but rather that collection transmitted orally from father to son of proverbs and
prophecies, legends, laws, traditions of the origins and tales
of the wanderings of his own tribe. For it is this, not any
fixation on the Civil War, but this feeling of identity with
his dead (who are the past) which characterizes and ex-
plains the Southerner, which accounts for his inflexible
conservatism, his lawlessness and love of violence, his
exaggerated respect for old age, his stubborn resistance to
change, his hospitality and his xenophobia, his legalism and
his anarchy. It is with kin, not causes, that the Southerner
is linked. Confederate Great-grandfather lived in stirring
and memorable times, but he is not remembered by his
descendants for his (probably undistinguished) part in the
Battle of Bull Run; rather, the Battle of Bull Run is remembered because Great-grandfather was there. For the Southerner the Civil War is in the family, and if he belongs to
the generation now forty or older, then he was in time
to hear about it from the lips of elderly relatives who had
lived through it. A man, or men, had fought in it who bore
his own name. That very blood which stirred in his veins
had been shed at Shiloh, at Chickamauga, at Gettysburg.

"Well now, the men who fought on the other side in that old war had families, left descendants, too," says one of them, a friend of mine. "You didn't lose it without our help. It was our war, too. As the winners we cut a pretty sorry figure by comparison, no doubt; but please remember that though the poetry be all on your side, we *were* there. I heard those old Civil War tales too when I was little. Us Yankee boys had great-grandads the same as you-all. But we never thought the world began at—where was it? Appomattox? Why should you think it ended there? For Christ's sake, did all your clocks stop down there that day? My great-grand-father! May the old gentleman rest in peace, but what has he got to do with *me*?"

Now that is a question which a Southerner could never ask. He might wish to, might envy the man who can (while despising him for it at the same time), but he could never do it. He is conscious of his great-grandfather as a constant companion through life. He will seek his counsel in moments of moral perplexity, his guidance in the choice of a career (if the family tradition leaves him any choice), will borrow courage from him on going into battle and will expect to join him in eternity in whichever place he and the majority of the family men (the women are one and all in heaven) are judged to have gone. No, the clocks of the South did not all stop in 1865; they have gone on ticking; but they are all grandfather's clocks.

Scotch, in good likelihood, by blood, the Southerner has retained the Scottish clan spirit. It is inculcated in him from birth. At his numerous family gatherings the stories told are of his ancestors, who in the retelling are purified of all superfluities and become heroes, and like figures out of legend, beyond good and evil. The manner in which they deceived or in whatever way triumphed over their and their family's enemies is the important thing; that they may have been the ones originally in the wrong is lost sight of. Mark Twain is dead serious—and dead right—when he suggests that reading Sir Walter Scott helped condition Southerners to fight the Civil War, but he got the reasons wrong why this was so. In Scott they read of the exploits of their own clansmen—or the clans they liked to claim kin with. What is more, they knew from Scott's tales of the border wars that they were destined to lose—another inducement, given their contrary and quixotic turn of mind, to fight. They had an affinity for lost causes.

Conscious of a long and vigorous lineage, the Southerner is assured of a long continuity to follow him. Meanwhile in his time he is the priest of the tribal scripture; to forget any part of it would be sacrilege. He treasures the sayings of his kin, and "As my grandaddy always used to say . . . As my poor father would say if he were here . . . As dear old Aunt Pris (God rest her soul) was fond of declaring . . ."—these expressions and others like them will preface his remarks to an extent hardly to be observed anywhere else. If he forgets them, he will be forgotten. If he remembers, he will be remembered, will take the place reserved and predestined for him in the company of his kin, in the realm of myth, outside of time.

The usual sort of selective genealogical pride, which seats certain relatives below the salt, others in the kitchen out of company's sight, has no resemblance to this clan feeling I am trying to define, which is all-embracing, all-forgiving, catholic, disowning none, welcoming alike the sinner and the saint, the pirate and the patrician, all who can claim the indissoluble tie of blood. Indeed, with his innate love of violence and his disrespect for the law (also Scotch, also exacerbated by a sense that the laws are not of his making but imposed upon him by conquerors), the Southerner will boast of ancestors whose memory another man would hide at the back of the highest shelf in his family skeleton closet. He will not only exhibit to view that particular limb of his family tree from which a horse thief dangles by the neck; he will cheerfully charge his ancestor with more horses than he was hanged for the theft of. The Southerner is like those ancient Hebrews who preserved and recounted and gloried in the stories of double-dealing and the bloodymindedness of their untrammeled forebears, and in his own rather frequent outbreaks he is emulating the exploits of his family heroes whom he has heard about all his life, who lived in freer and more manly times. When a Southerner sighs and says, "We are not the men our fathers were" (an expression often on his tongue), he means to say we are more civilized; he is lamenting the fact.

Undoubtedly the Southerner clings to certain outmoded social attitudes and resists changes, which for his own part he knows he could learn to live with, because they are unacceptable to Great-grandfather, whose voice, should he think one moderate thought, he hears accusing him of capitulation, of cowardice, of betrayal, of unworthiness of the name he bears in trust. To appeal to his reason does no good: he admires foolishness above all qualities—in the sense one intends when saying, a fool never changes his mind, a fool never knows when he's licked. "That's the kind of fool I am! A damn fool!" he will proudly assert. This is why telling him that the old cause, Great-grandfather's old cause, is doomed, already lost, is the surest way to harden his resistance: those are precisely the odds which appeal to his imagination, the odds which Great-grandfather fought against, which are calculated to win Great-grandfather's esteem. Tell him he is on the winning side, he loses interest and quits the field. This is not because he does not like to win, but because he does not like to have a side. He sees himself as the stubborn lone remnant, conquered but unsubdued, unreconstructed, he and Great-grandpa, ready to grapple with the very winds of change.

Great-grandpa, by a huge statistical probability, not only did not own any slaves, he hated the institution of slavery as

only a poor man can hate the symbol of a leisure to which
he will never attain. What is more, he believed not only that
for his sins he was under the curse to eat his bread in the
sweat of his face, but that it was sinful not to do so, and
that those who lived off the sweat of others were storing up
damnation for themselves. Certainly he did not go to war to
defend slavery, no more than his opposite on the Union side
went to war to end it. For love of country, then? What
country? A confederation some few months old with a flag
still new and stiff as a dime-store bandana, perverse in its
origin, negative in purpose, comical in its maladministra-
tion, composed of states with nothing more in common than
an indefensible and unpopular and even already demon-
strably uneconomical institution, a union of disunion which
had it survived would have had to fight at least eleven wars
of secession of its own? The Southerner no more identified
himself with the Confederacy than he did with the Union;
both were abstractions. In the final analysis even Alabama,
say, or Mississippi, was filled with too many people not his
relatives for him to feel much sense of common purpose
with them. He was as hypersensitive to his own state's en-
croachments upon his precious liberty as he was towards
those of the federal government upon states' rights. He was
still in the primitive tribal stage of social evolution. Clan-
nishness was and is the key to his temperament, and he went
off to war to protect not Alabama but only those thirty or
forty acres of its sandy hillsides or stiff red clay which he
broke his back tilling and which was as big a country as his
mind could hold, whose sanctity to him came from the fact
that in it were buried the bones of his own blood kin. He
went because he had a taste for violence, because in it he
found release and serenity, because it was the one orgiastic
outlet sanctioned by his Calvinist creed and peace had raged
for as long as he could stand it; because he resented any
interference by outsiders, even in reforms which he was
ready and even eager to make on his own, because it prom-

ised comradeship and adventure, a holiday from cotton chopping and a chance to shine, because he believed he would come through it unhurt, and most of all because his family ghosts all urged him to it. As for ideology, good or bad, he went with about as much of that in his kit bag, or awareness of any on his enemy's side, as most soldiers go off to fight most wars. He fought not out of conviction but out of pride, and wounded pride was what he nursed in his defeat. While the G.A.R. member convinced himself that he had fought for a cause, and that his cause was just, the Confederate veteran told himself, and his sons, that it was all the finer to have fought without a cause, and all the harder then to have lost.

"Oh, for heaven's sake, Tom! That was all a century ago," my Northern friends exclaim when they hear me in this strain. Alas, no (though it wouldn't matter if that were true), it is still only about twenty years ago. It is not much more than that since Southerners sat on their grandfather's knee and listened to him tell again of Great-grandfather's wasted courage and his wounds, the desolation of the land and the loss of the farm, the hunger, the humiliation. But, as I always tell my friends, have patience, there is hope. Not even a Southerner's memory lasts forever. I reckon the active life of a Southerner to extend three generations past his death. He lives on in full vigor in the minds of those who as children heard about him from those who knew him in the flesh. As mine is the last generation to whom the Civil War is a told story remembered in the accents of familiar and kindred voices, I calculate that it will come to an end when the last of us is gone.

As it exists in my mind today the story of Thomas and Ella Ordway is a series of stereoscope views, like that trayful of them in my grandfather's house with which I whiled away many evenings of my childhood. In black and white (my memories belong to the pre-Kodachrome era), speckled, yellowed, the subjects staring self-consciously at the photographer, above them a filterless, bald, overcast gray sky. Our viewer likewise was pre-battery-lit, pre-pushbutton-plastic: an antiquated and clumsy apparatus with a hood for the eyes and a cutout for the nose, a large wooden handle, and a track along which the card holder slid. You put one of the cards into the rack and moved it back and forth until it swam into focus, and you beheld twin ladies seated on twin cliff edges. Then you waited, and after a time (it was a little like sobering from drink) this slightly sickening double image began to merge, the two pictures became one. Simultaneously the picture space opened inward, the flat vista behind the now single young lady plunged into perspective and the perilous chasm gaped beneath her feet. So it is now with my collection of mental views—older by some thirty years, faded, spotted, curled with age; yet if I wait the scene will come into focus, and those old pictures first printed on my mind by my grandfather as we lingered over dinner on the ground on Mabry graveyard working day sharpen, open inward, and as it was then with the stereoscope, it is as if I have been drawn bodily through the lenses. . . .

Eight days afterwards the battlefield at Shiloh was still strewn with corpses and with the carcasses of horses with bloated bellies, their stiffened legs sticking out like toppled equestrian statues. White-clad stretcher bearers wearing white face masks carried corpses to wagons which, when loaded, lumbered away drawn by teams of six mules in tandem, to be replaced by others returning empty for more. Meanwhile, in the area not yet cleared, black-clad women wearing bandanas over their mouths and noses revolved among the bodies, bent as though gathering firewood or picking cotton, and, like cotton pickers, crooning a steady low lament, broken occasionally, as a body was turned face up, by a wail of recognition. Flies were thick and buzzards hung overhead in the soft spring sky like kites on strings.

Ella Ordway also remembered and later told her son, and
when she herself was a memory he told her great-grand-
children of a man seen hanging by the neck from a limb
of a tree and slowly spinning, with, pinned on his chest, a
sign which read, "He was caught robbing the dead." She was
told that a number of bodies had been discovered with the
ring fingers missing. The women searchers formed a posse.
They had surprised him the day before Ella's arrival in the
act of extracting a gold tooth from a corpse's mouth, and had
lynched him on the spot.

And even on the eighth day afterwards the line of wagons
waiting outside the commandeered cotton shed where Ella
Ordway was told to go was like the line outside the compress
at the height of ginning season. Some, like hers, with one
mule where there ought to have been two harnessed to the
tongue, and equally wobbly; others sound, tight, painted,
drawn by well-fed teams, all driven by those who had been
left at home, fathers too old to fight, wives and mothers,
some with infants at the breast. Nor was she the only one
to have thought to provide herself, figuring they would be in
short supply, with a coffin.

The relatives were not allowed inside the shed. Soldiers,
two by two, took the coffins inside—those who had not
brought their own were given one—six returned with it on
their shoulders and slid it onto the wagon bed. There the
parents or the wife was allowed to view the body; when they
nodded the carpenter nailed the lid down. As her turn
neared and her wagon drew closer to the door, Ella could
see inside as the soldiers went in and came out. The bodies
lay in rows on the floor, covered with blankets, except for
those which had been sewn into cottonsacks coated with
paraffin wax. Of these bundles some bore only a semblance
of human shape; some among them were only half length.
The old man ahead of Ella Ordway had apparently seen that
he was being given one of these cottonsacks. When his
coffin was brought out it was already nailed shut. Ella

Ordway overheard him say to the soldiers, "Men, are you sure? I don't ask to be shown, but are you sure it's my boy in there?" So when her turn came and her coffin was taken inside and she heard hammering on the lid and it was brought out, she signed the receipt without a word. She was sent to another barn, where she was given his effects, his watch and her last letter to him, all that was found on him. The officer in charge there insisted on having her wagon filled with hay for her mule. A native of Nashville, he recognized the address on the envelope and knew the length of the trip home which lay ahead of her. He also insisted that she take a loaded horsepistol, almost as big as she was, to defend herself with.

In planning his death Thomas Ordway had overlooked two things, or rather three. First, that he belonged to an army drawn from a race of idolaters of the dead like himself, that never since the early Greeks had any body of fighting men lost more opportunities to pursue and harry a retreating enemy in order to gather and identify and notify the next-of-kin of, and render obsequies to, their fallen comrades; and that even had his wife appeared another week later they would promptly have detailed a squad to go and dig him up for her, to be taken home to lie among his kin. Only it was not necessary. He had not been buried yet. There were too many of them, and as he had been among the first casualties, and his telegram had gone out in the first batch, and as she lived within the state, she was expected. Second, his wife—that the very devotion which he sought to escape a lifetime of indebtedness to, would surely bring her, by day and by night, and even if it killed one mule, a mere three hundred and fifty miles to fetch him home, knowing he would never rest peaceful until he was laid beneath the dove-haunted cedars on that knoll down back of the house where every other known and remembered Ordway lay. Even so, he might have gotten away with it but for the watch, and an impostor be lying in that grave in Tennessee, and his descendants would never have sat above his bones in Mabry graveyard listening to the tale of how they came to be there. And even so, he almost did get away with it, because Ella Ordway was halfway home again before she looked at the watch, having instantly conceived the notion that it had stopped running when he died, that if she should open it (it was one of those with a closed face, a hinged cover released by pressing the stem) she would see the hands pointing to the exact moment of his death. So instead she waited until sometime during the third night, when lying in the hay alongside the coffin she awoke with no sense of the hour and in the dark opened the watch and moved the hands and wound the stem and set it going. And even after seeing that it was not her husband's watch—which was the following morning when she stopped a man on the road and asked him the time—Ella Ordway still drove on towards home, saying to herself, they must have made a mistake back there in that office. Putting herself in that officer's place and thinking, with so many to sort out and label and keep track of he must have gotten two watches mixed. Wondering how she was going to get it back to him. Telling herself then that maybe since leaving home her husband had swapped watches with some man. Not daring to admit the thought already pounding on the door of her mind, she urged the mule on still harder, the coffin jouncing on the bedboards. He had my letter on him, she said. She felt for it in her pocket. It was there. Then saying to herself finally, if I don't look I'll never know the difference. If I just go on home and dig the grave and bury it then it will be too late to do anything about it, too late to worry about it. If I find it's not him I'll have to take it back, and then I'll have nothing. Then I will never know where mine lies buried, or even if he does. But if I go on home and bury this coffin then I can always believe I have him. If it's not him I'll never know. And what I don't know won't hurt me. Believing it's him in time will make it so.

Meanwhile Thomas Ordway lay in his bed in the impro-
vised hospital secure in the knowledge that he was safely
buried by now, and that the unknown soldier whose memory
had been destroyed along with his sight, and whose breath
he drew, would not be long in following. For he did not know
that in the darkness (his own, his personal and private darkness: to the rest of the world, as he had learned from overhearing the conversation of two orderlies who were carrying
away those who had died in the night, it was morning, broad
daylight) he had gotten the two watches confused. They
were indistinguishable to the touch, and he had had to
hurry. While they were carrying away the dead man on his
right he had put his letter from Ella in the hand of the one
on his left and exchanged watches with him. Or thought he
had. Instead he had returned his own watch to his pocket
and the dead man's to his.

He also did not know that the brevet major in charge of
the casualty records (he who had given Ella Ordway her
husband's effects), when those who had been turned away
at the cotton shed, then had searched the battlefield without
success, came to him, took them to look at this patient, first
warning them what they were about to see, and admonishing
silence. Around this one patient's bed a screen of blankets
had been hung, for as he refused to eat, he had to be force-
fed: the screen was to protect the other patients from this
sight. Around himself the man had hung a curtain of
despondency which nothing, not even yesterday's news that
his legs would not have to be amputated after all, could
draw aside. No identification had been found on him, nothing but a watch of ordinary make and middling value, and he
could not remember who he was or where he came from.
The people who were brought to look at him one and all
shook their heads and the curtains were dropped and they
turned away, whether disappointed or relieved would have
been hard to say.

The brevet major had argued with him—or, rather, at him. To despair like this was wrong, he maintained. Things would not look so black, he said, conscious too late of the pun, when he was once more among his own people. They would restore his memory, and with it his will to live. Under the loving care of his mother, sisters, a wife if he had had one, the shock would gradually wear away. If it was earning a living that worried him, he was sure to be pensioned. Nor was his own usefulness at an end; there were lots of things he could still do. All the brevet major's arguments met with silence. The young soldier's face never changed expression, that is to say, never assumed any: it was like stone. And so these sessions always ended the same way, with the brevet major coming out from behind the curtains and ordering the patient to be fed. It took three men to do it.

At noon that day the little woman who looked hardly big enough to open a sardine can without help pulled up at a farmhouse gate and asked the man who came out and stood staring at the pine box riding amid the hay, soaked with water to keep it cool, for the loan of a crowbar.

"It ain't just curiosity, mister," she said. "I have got reason to doubt." She heaved a sigh and said, "I ought never to have taken it without first making sure. I ought to have made them open it back there at that cotton shed. Here I've come all this way towards home. I can't go no further till I know, one way or the other. There ain't no getting around it."

"Little lady," the man had said, "it ain't likely they would make a mistake like that."

"You wouldn't think so, would you?" she said. "But with so many of them, you can see how it just might happen."

The women of the house stood looking on from the doorway, an older one, the farmer's wife, and a young one with a baby on her hip, his daughter-in-law or his own daughter come home to stay while her husband was away.

"I expect they just give you the wrong watch," the man suggested. "Or like you yourself say, maybe he swapped watches with one of his buddies since leaving home."

"I'm hoping that's all it is," she said.

The man studied her for a while, looked again at the coffin, then darting a glance up and down the road as if afraid of being observed, and impatiently motioning his women indoors, he told her to drive around back into the lot. He opened the gap for her and she drove through. He went into his toolshed, emerged carrying a rusty crowbar and a claw hammer. He came to the side of the wagon and stood looking over the sideboards at the coffin, at the rim of its lid studded with bright new nails. He shook his head. "I'm liable to split them boards," he said.

"I never meant for you to do it," she said.

"Be a shame," he said. "I don't see how I could help but split them with this dang crowbar."

"I'll be much obliged to you," she said.

Next I imagine—remember—see the wagon crawling along the road, headed east once more, away from Mabry, the one undersized and undernourished mule hitched to the tongue, on the seat holding the reins the tiny woman in the sunbonnet and the rusty black dress. Behind her a stretched tarpaulin forms a pup tent over the forward section of the wagon bed. The mule's gait is spastical. The wagon creaks, the bed rocked like a boat by the regular-irregular turning of the wobbly wheels, the worn eccentric hubs grating and screeching on the dry ungreased axletrees and flinging the light little woman about like a rag doll. Yet despite this shaking, her head nods steadily lower, and as hers does, so does the mule's. Then when a wheel rides over a bump and the wagon groans and then settles with a crash and from underneath the tarpaulin comes a human groan, she jerks awake, casts a quick glance over her shoulder, then shakes the reins and the mule starts and lunges into the traces.

Gradually her head begins to droop again, again the mule nods with her, his pace slackening like a wind-up toy running down. Once he comes to a dead stop. For some time the wagon sits in the road, the mule asleep in the traces, the woman asleep on the seat. Then she comes awake, casts a hurried and frightened look beneath the tarpaulin, then slaps the reins, turning the mule aside and off the road. She climbs stiffly down, planting her small foot carefully in the spokes of the wagon wheel. She goes to the rear of the wagon, lets down the tailgate, fills her arms with hay and returns and throws the hay down in front of the mule. She gathers sticks and a handful of dead grass and carefully strikes one of her few matches and blows up a flame. From underneath the wagon seat she takes a blackened pot and from her pocket extracts a large black iron spoon. She sets the pot on the fire and slowly stirs the contents, the spoon making a dull clatter against the sides. For a moment, lulled by the sound and the flames, she relaxes the taut grip she has kept on her face, her eyes glaze, her lips part, and over her features spreads an expression of dumb resignation, bleak hopelessness. She sighs, or starts to sigh and catches herself, gives her head a shake, and the pot having begun to steam, lifts it by the bail with the handle of the spoon. She goes to the rear of the wagon, darts a look up and down the road, finds it empty and lifts her skirts and clambers into the wagon bed. Underneath the tarpaulin a man lies in the hay. A bloodstained bandage like a turban is wrapped around his head. His trousers are slit and both legs wound in bloodstained bandages. His eyes stare unblinking at the sunlit white cloth overhead. She crouches, raises his head, dips the spoon in the broth, and holds it to his lips. His mouth clamps shut. She holds the spoon there. After a while she spills that spoonful back into the pot, refills the spoon, and again holds it to his lips. His mouth remains shut tight. She lays him back in the hay, rises and goes to the rear of the wagon and climbs down and puts the gate up again. She eats,

mechanically, a few mouthfuls herself. She scatters the fire
and climbs back on the wagon seat, shakes the reins, and
once again the mule lunges into the traces and resumes its
stagger. The wagon creaks. From underneath the tent the
man begins to speak, his voice worn and dry, like the sound
of the hubs grating on the worn axles:

"You're a young woman still. After the war is over you'll
get married again, a man that can look after you, provide for
you and the children. If you loved me you would. It would
be a kindness. I beg you. I'm not asking you to do it yourself.
Just leave me something in reach, something I can do it with
myself. It would be done in a minute. No one else need ever
know. If you loved me as you say you do . . ."

She sits erect and impassive on the wagon seat, bouncing
and swaying violently with the motion, dry-eyed, her lips
set, shaking her head, turning finally to say, "Hush, now.
We're coming to some people on the road. You don't want
them to hear you taking on thisaway. Try to rest. It won't
be much longer now before we're home. Ssh. Hush, now.
Just lie quiet and try to get a little sleep." At the word "sleep"
her own eyes close longingly. But when shortly the road
begins to climb, she gets down from the seat (as if her
weight made any difference) and walks alongside the slowly
turning, grating wagon wheel.

Women must feed us. At the breast, with the spoon, at
table. Food is their medium, their meaning; rejection of it
therefore strikes at their deepest urge, denies their function,
and thus arouses their determination, calls up all their stra-
tagems. Not only Ella Ordway but soon a conspiracy of all
the menless women on the mountainside was bent on getting
the invalid to eat. Never, even in the best of times, with
much to spare beyond the needs of their own families, they
nevertheless came bearing tempting gifts, whatever art and
cunning could contrive of the sparse and simple materials
at hand: baked bread, still smoking from the oven, which

made the children swallow hard; hot honeybuns, savory
soups, spiced meats. When it became known that his fast
was broken every woman felt a share in the triumph, and
a vindication of her kind.

When they were unable to aid her in any other way the
neighbor women gave Ella Ordway a morning's or an afternoon's work in the garden or in the field, or helped get out
the wash, knowing she was tied indoors. For she seldom let
him out of her sight, never out of the girl's easy call. She
did not fool herself. She did not trust him. She hid his razors
and refused to shave him. She hid the knives, even hid her
sewing scissors. At night she slept on a pallet on the floor
in the hall outside his door.

Meanwhile the war went on. There were scarcities in the
stores. Prices soared. With the able men away the crops
were thin, and that portion of them which ought to have
been set aside for seed was eaten. Since February, Nashville
had been under enemy occupation. Rumors of Federal requi-
sition parties caused stock to be killed out of season, the meat
quickly crammed into hungry mouths before it could go
bad in the heat. And with each such alarm the lonely women
whispered among themselves tales of rape.

Ella Ordway got him up at last, set him to sun himself
on the porch, and smiled for the first time in months at her
accomplishment. The bandages were removed from his
head. His legs improved to the point that he could get about
a bit. And so it vexed her especially that just as his appetite
was improving the food should begin to give out. Then she
awoke to realize that in her concentration on him the children had been neglected, had grown thin as two shadows.
She felt their round hungry eyes following her as she carried
the tray into their father's bedroom. And as the food worsened he developed a convalescent's finickiness. Visitors,
hearing that he was up, came to call. He dreaded being seen.
They tried not to notice the smell. The war had come closer
and they could not keep it out of their conversations. If

they tried to avoid it he noticed the effort. It was going slowly. At the mention of each reversal he seemed to shrink, as if he felt personally responsible, as if he knew that the sight of him must be dispiriting, a portent of defeat, something which might happen to their sons and husbands. As his strength returned he grew restless. His capacity to do himself mischief increased. It was more and more difficult to keep him under surveillance.

Unleavened bread, yes; they were unused to any other kind. But it was not the paschal lamb that the Ordways slaughtered before the flight from Tennessee, it was the family mule.

The milch cow had already been eaten. That was early in the fall, when Thomas Ordway had still to be watched over constantly, could not be trusted alone with himself, the ten-year-old girl relieving her mother at the post in full awareness of what she was on guard against, freeing Ella to go out to the barn to milk, out to the shed to split wood for the cookstove. Then the scrawny cow went dry and no bull was left in all the countryside to breed her to. So Ella Ordway sent down and got a neighbor who in exchange for the hide and one forequarter came up and killed and butchered her.

But in the spring she was ashamed to ask the man to come up again, or even send down and beg the loan of his block and tackle. For he knew there was only one animal left on the place. She was further ashamed, ashamed for her neighbor this time, foreseeing that he might offer to do the job for her on the same terms as before.

The crows had settled thick and bold upon the meager stand of corn. They perched upon the scarecrow's head and laughed. The boy was put to frighten them off, came home crying with humiliation for the contempt they showed for his size. What the crows did not get went for cornmeal for the table, the poor mule got none. By February its ribs were showing like a washboard and it had begun to gnaw the wooden railings of its stall.

Nobody loves a mule, and a farmwoman loves no animal, except perhaps her cow. But she knows that upon the family mule depend their crops and their transportation. But now the Ordways faced starvation. Ella's pantry, her root cellar, her smokehouse were bare, no longer even smelled of food. One night after serving a supper which wrung her heart with shame, Ella Ordway made up her mind. Terrified of that long horsepistol which that brevet major had given her, she spent the following morning at the grindstone sharpening a new point on the kitchen knife which she had deliberately broken off. That night after a still more wretched supper, and after the house was asleep, she got up and slipped outdoors. She took from underneath the washstand outside the back door the things she had secreted there earlier: the knife, two raw turnips, and one wrinkled apple. She went out to the barn. She fed the mule the turnips and the apple and listened to him munching in the dark. She waited until he had finished, then as he nuzzled her begging for more, she felt along the bony ribs until she discovered the beat of the heart. She placed the knife between two ribs and shoved with both hands, then fled from the barn and ran to the house, where for the rest of the night she lay shivering on her pallet on the floor. Next morning she found herself spattered with blood.

The children bowed their heads over their plates and closed their eyes, relishing the odor of hot meat, not only for itself but because it relieved that other odor which they spent their lives trying not to notice, not to flinch from, because already his hearing told him whenever anyone averted his head in speaking to him, that odor which was the War and her childhood to Helen Ordway. No grace was said. It was years later, in Texas, before Thomas Ordway thanked God for another meal. They had looked up after a time, and my grandfather could recall his sister telling how the tears ran down from her father's sightless eyes, and years later, and a thousand miles distant, remembering that sliced mule meat on her dinner plate and her father's dead eyes swimming in tears, she still wept. Retelling it to us on graveyard working day would bring tears glistening to my grandfather's eyes.

"I won't live in a country where things have come to such a pass the folks have to eat their mules," Thomas Ordway said.

It was the first indication he had given that he meant to live in any country. So when he pushed away his plate and pushed back his chair and got up from the table and felt his way to the door and out of the house, and Helen rose automatically to follow, to trail him, her mother motioned her back into her chair. "Eat, children," she said. And they did.

"What, Grandpa? Eat *mule*! Phew!" we would exclaim, sitting over the remains of our feast.

And my grandfather would say, "Ah, you-all have never known what it is to go hungry. May you never know! Your Great-aunt Helen, poor soul, there she lies, used to say she never in her life ate anything that tasted half as good to her again as that old mule."

When a man decides to pull up his roots and set off in search of a new life, he instinctively heads west. No other point of the compass exerts that powerful pull. The West is the true magnetic pole. Ever since his expulsion from the garden to a place east of Eden, man has yearned westward as towards a state of remembered innocence, and human history is one long westward migration—or was until just the other day, when with no more West to go to, we began to look towards the moon. What housebound Northerner peering through his frosted windowpanes at the slushy street with its pack of shuffling, shivering humanity has not felt his thoughts turn, following the sun, westward? Has not longed to get away from self-searching and soul-twisting, away from factions and parties and monthly installments and jury duty and female equality and starched collars and business suits and steam heat and sinusitis and the subway rush hour and the dog's nightly walk around the block, to go West and get out of doors, doing a man's work among men? What Southerner, be he a South Carolinian or a southern Italian—for the South is the same the world over—has not yearned to escape his oppressive long hot summer and his long oppressive history and go where the wind blows free across the high plains and where a man is his own man? To escape the rigidity of his life, the sense that all his efforts are foredoomed, his place marked out for him unalterably. Away from that oppressive hospitality, that chronically inflamed sensitivity to slight and affront, that vendetta mentality, that all too well grounded political cynicism, that paternalism, that orgiastic religiosity, that hedonistic puritanism, away from those morose, mistrustful faces with their eyes slitted from squinting at the merciless sun. And which way does he turn? What Easterner has not longed to follow where the young and the adventurous have already gone, to be free to employ that exhilarating and patronizing phrase "back East"? Where everybody does not know everybody else's business and the sins of the fathers are not visited in perpetuity upon their children. To shake off the dust of age and overrefinement, to escape that worn-out land and its worn-out people. To go West! The West is the one unfixed pole of the compass. It has moved with man, always retreating before him. What was once the West is now the East. The West lies on the other side of that last range of hills, where the day still lingers, where the sun is still shining after it has set in the East, where there is still another hour to correct one's mistakes or begin a new project before nightfall. The West is where people go to start over, or to start out, the land of losers and beginners, of promise and of recovery. The West is unfenced, unfettered, unencrusted with history. Where never is heard a discouraging word and the sky is not cloudy all day. A man's country. God's country. Lit by a glow which even a blind man might see.

At that moment when old Thomas got up from the table that day we Ordways ceased to be Tennesseans. Five minutes more and it was settled that we should become Texans. This, however, was not Thomas Ordway's decision, it was Ella's, made as, unable to choke it down herself, she watched her children devour that proscribed meat which she had provided for them and hold out their plates to her for more. Had it been left to Ella, we Ordways would have been more Texan than we were, would never, once past Clarksville, have turned around and gone back. She wanted, as she was later to tell her son, to get clean out of mule country into cow-horse and cattle land. He, that son, was an added incentive for this. She knew about him before leaving home, claimed to have known from the start that he would be a boy, for like his brother and unlike his sister he announced his presence with immediate daily and violent spells of morning sickness. The time before, these had continued right up to the last; consequently she expected them to do so again, and so they did, from east Tennessee to Texas; notwithstanding this, she kept them from her husband's knowledge, fearing that he might think it a reason to postpone, or once underway to interrupt, possibly never to resume, the trip; to her it was reason the more to set off, to push on.

It took some time to find a buyer for the farm; meanwhile they made their preparations, made them in the knowledge that they were leaving not just a home but a life. On credit, pending the sale of the place, they bought a new, rather a newer wagon. It was delivered with a team of his own by the man from whom they had bought it. To avoid questions or any odd looks, they had him unhitch and leave it in the lot; then, lacking a mule, they themselves drew it down to the family burial ground. They attacked the graves with spade and grubbing hoe. The stones were uprooted and laid on the floor of the wagon, bedded in straw. Thomas Ordway was proud of those stones, all the Ordways had been, proud to the point of offending their neighbors, for there, as later in Mabry, real dressed marble tombstones with engraved lettering were an enviable mark of family piety. Their combined strength not being equal to that of a half-grown boy, they got them into the wagon bed by inching them up an incline. When the stones were out the graves were opened, the remains exhumed, packed, the containers labeled and stowed in the wagon. The children, watching forbidden from their hiding place, lost interest after a time and returned to their games.

No doubt the lingering aftertaste of that roast joint, along with the look of reproach which she read in the eyes of every mule, influenced Ella Ordway to spend half the money they got from the sale of the farm on a yoke of oxen. Gaunt, spectral white, draped in their ill-fitting hides, with deep dewlaps that swung like cowbells to their rolling gait, they looked, and were, half starved; still they represented a ton of butcher's meat, and by then the Ordways were not the only ones to have had a taste of mule. This was all they were waiting for, and so in mid-April (it was hot, and about his head already hovered the escort of blowflies which, in warm weather, was to accompany him for the rest of his days) the Ordways set out, afoot all of them, to lighten the load, she with the boy trudging in the rear, he on his stubborn festering legs and blind as a bat, leading the way. Oxen must be led; they stray from the track unless guided by frequent nudges and taps with the goad. They are too unintelligent to respond to reins. Patient creatures, an eternity of servitude in their yoke-bowed necks, their plodding gait. And he, asserting his mastery, his independence of her oxlike devotion, plodding alongside them, fleeing his darkened land and groping his way along the sun's path, a young man still, but one who looked and moved like the figure of Time and

about whom there clung the odor of death and decay, leading the bony oxen and being led himself by the bony barefoot little girl.

Their body of red water would come later. They would
have it to cross, and for them the waves were not to part,
but in their case this was to come at the end of the trek.
For the Ordways stumbling out of the mountain fastness
of northeast Tennessee it was downhill at the start, and for
a long way, so steeply downhill much of the time that in
order to keep the wagon, with its ballast of tombstones, from
overrunning the team, the brake levers had to be lashed
down and the pads soaked regularly to keep them from
bursting aflame. The wet brake pads steamed from the friction. The stiff-kneed oxen were pushed forward by their
horns by the yoke. On these roads it was a good day when the
Ordways made four or five miles, and including time out
for rain, and more time after the rain had stopped, waiting
for the road to dry, waiting even after other wagons were
moving again, because those stones caused them to bog
down in places where others got through, it was five weeks
from the time of their leaving home that the Ordways
reached Nashville.

The creak of any wagon whatever along the road sufficed
to bring farmwomen, townwomen too, to their front doors,
to straighten the backs of plowmen in the fields alongside,
to draw upright men leaning in chairs against the wall
along the porches of stores: a hush ran before the passage
of the Ordways and lingered in their wake. Women lowered
their eyes and shooshed their children, men got to their
feet and bared their heads and sometimes then held their
hats over their hearts as is done whenever the flag or a
funeral passes by. Storekeepers wherever they stopped
pressed candy and cakes on the children. Helen Ordway was
to remember this as the time of her life when she had eaten
them the most, and to wonder what people meant when they
recalled the scarcity of sweets during the war. Ella tried

at first to refuse them. The craving in the children's eyes forced her to relent—that and the craving in the eyes of the storekeepers to be allowed some outlet for the feeling which the sight of her husband aroused. She tried then to ration them. But the war had weakened her discipline, especially over the boy, had sapped her strength to say no, to deny them any little pleasure when they were denied so much already. The boy had learned to wheedle, and though she sighed that he would ruin his teeth, he got his way. Later she was glad he had. At least he had had that, and she took comfort in her last years in the picture she retained of him sitting on the tailboard of the wagon or else trotting along beside her in the road, his cheek rounded with a jawbreaker like the pouch of a squirrel.

It was a country of women, children, and old men through which they passed. Even boys of late adolescence—the "Seed Corn of the South"—were being called up now. To these fathers, mothers, and wives Thomas Ordway personified the calamity which they too had known, or the calamity which daily threatened them. That his blindness might have been congenital, or sustained in some private manner, seemed to occur to no one; he was taken automatically for a casualty of the war. Perhaps it was the conjunction with his limp, or the redness of the scars on his brow—more likely it was the times: there were others, few so badly hurt as he, but others like him in most communities now.

Stopping by water in the late afternoon, they would make camp for the night. The oxen were hobbled to graze. Ella and the children gathered wood. Two fires were built. Over one his bandages were boiled, then these were hung to dry overnight on bushes out of sight. Over the other fire supper was cooked. As they stopped rather early in the day, the evening was long, and sometime during it they could generally expect a call from the owner of the land, or from his wife or widow. They came, especially the women, bearing gifts, more sweets for the children, and almost inevitably

one of the dead husband's shirts or a pair of socks that had
been knitted for him or a new pair of boots which he never
got to wear, with an accompanying tale of how these articles
had been saved by hiding them from Yankee pillagers. To
refuse these things was hard, was all but impossible. In the
morning they would sometimes find hanging from a nearby
limb, like a stocking on a Christmas tree, hung there out
of reach of night-prowling animals, a sack containing more
donations. Sometimes at their campsite, come to pay their
respects, would arrive a whole congregation of people,
especially when bad weather kept the Ordways on the spot for
longer than one night and word of their presence spread into
the surrounding countryside. Ella even found people there
already when she got up in the morning. When she peeped
out through the flap in the wagon cover, there they would
be, men mostly but occasionally women among them too,
standing patient as trees in the dripping rain or squatting
silent and solemn and Indian-faced around a fire which they
had gathered and started. Seeing her they would gravely bare
their heads in wordless greeting. They too came bearing
gifts. Jugs of corn liquor, combs of wild honey, twists of
home-cured tobacco, bags of nuts, small dark close-grained
hickory-smoked hams from half-wild razorback hogs as lean
as marble. These could not be refused. The spirit in which
these offerings were made was not charity, not propitiation,
not even compassion. This was veneration. These pilgrims
belonged to the timeless and universal tribe—especially
numerous in the South—of leper-lickers and shaman-wor-
shippers who see in affliction a sign of the special favor of
God; in blindness vision, in witlessness wisdom exceeding
the normal mind's, in epileptic seizure an orgasm of the soul
in union with the otherworld, and they came to sit at the holy
man's feet and listen to his oracles. Had he but cared to ex-
ploit his handicap Thomas Ordway might have gone far in
his native land as a faith healer or a phrenologist, a preacher

or a politician. Smartly handled, even that odor he gave off
might have been made to pay during all those years when his
adopted town wore him about its collective neck like a bag of
asafoetida.

This was in the beginning. After their adventure with one
community on the road between Knoxville and Nashville
the Ordways began to get up and even in bad weather eat
their scanty breakfast in haste and yoke up and move off
their campsite, fugitives from commiseration. A sudden
storm had forced them one afternoon to stop on the outskirts of the town they had just passed through. As usual,
their passage had been noted, and the next morning when
the rain continued unabated they received the usual call.
So confident was she of receiving it by this time that Ella
Ordway, despite a particularly severe attack of her nausea,
had tidied her temporary home as best she could in expec-
tation. In midmorning, during a letup in the downpour,
three ladies, the wives of the three local ministers, drove
out from town in a covered surrey. Ella Ordway invited them
into her tent kitchen, apologizing for the muddiness of the
floor and for the lack of seats. Led by Helen, Thomas Ordway appeared. He seemed to feel a compunction to satisfy
the morbid curiosity of people to see him, perhaps a morbid
urge to show them more than they had bargained for, which
alternated, and was always to do so, with an unwillingness
to be seen. Satisfied that the travelers were decent, though
poor, the ladies offered to take the children into their homes,
suppressing by a common impulse the offer they had come
prepared to make, to take in the entire family. The offer was
declined, as was the basket of food which they had brought,
and the ladies drove back into town.

The Ordways continued on the spot in the unabating rain,
and as their predicament worsened, they saw themselves
pass by stages from being a care which concerned the town
to being an anxiety which engrossed it. One day brought the

husbands of the three ladies, another day a doctor, still
another day the county sheriff and with him a second doctor, who was also the district medical officer, and who told
the Ordways that they could not stay where they were any
longer.

"We are not breaking any law," said Thomas Ordway.

"Now did we say that?" the sheriff demanded. "You never
heard us say nothing like that. No. What we are here for is
to say—"

"We don't intend to stay no longer than we have to," said
Thomas Ordway. "Just as soon as this rain lets up we'll be
moving on."

"Who said you had to move on?" asked the sheriff.

"Man, you are in no condition to move on anywhere,"
said the doctor. "What you need is rest. Your wife too. Your
children too, for that matter. Now we have got a hospital
in this town, and while you're there your wife and your
children will be taken in and looked after, and later on, well,
we'll see. Maybe—"

Thomas Ordway had protested for a while, then he gave in.
They said they would come for them tomorrow. That night
the rain came on harder than before, and under cover of the
darkness and the rain they pulled out. To elude pursuit they
left the main road and traveled down rutted, back roads all
that night, where the wagon wheels sank in the mud and the
oxen grunted and wheezed and the flat heavy stones on
which lay the thin flat mattress which she shared with her
little brother heaved and bounced and Helen Ordway lay in
the darkness listening to the bones rattle in their kegs like the
seed inside a gourd.

Their route ran from one extreme corner to the other of
the parallelogram which is Tennessee. As far as Nashville,
Ella knew the way. She had come by that same road the
year before to fetch him home. Out of Nashville they would
take a slightly less southerly, more westerly route than the
one she had taken, in order to reach Memphis.

Traffic along the main thoroughfare of Nashville stopped or turned aside as for a funeral at their passage, wagons reining up at intersections and a platoon of blue-uniformed soldiers being halted by command of their corporal at one corner to let them go by; for here too he led the way, having ignored her suggestion that perhaps they might get through the city more quickly if she were to lead the team. Nor would he allow her even to ask for directions. Turning the team off the street and parking the wagon in an empty spot at the curb following Helen's instructions, he bade Ella wait there with the boy and set off down the walk to make inquiries. He stopped a man approaching him and said, "Mister, could you—" He broke off as the man took his hand, the free one, the one she was not holding, and Helen Ordway never forgot the sight of her father staring down at it as if he could see the coin, a Yankee half dollar, which shone in his open palm. As he stood there bemused another passerby stepped aside from her path, approached, and, with a barely perceptible *chink*, carfully laid a second half dollar on top of the first one.

And so he had to ask Ella, after all, the way to Pittsburg Landing. The very information which she herself had sought at this same point almost exactly a year earlier. At that time Nashville people had all been asking themselves where the place was. Until just that week few had ever heard of it, and some she asked still could not tell her how to get there. But now, and forevermore, anybody in Nashville could have told you how to get to Pittsburg Landing. Or rather, no. Shortly the name would disappear again, this time for good, absorbed into that of the hamlet consisting of nothing but a one-room log meetinghouse just outside this village on the Mississippi border, near the Alabama state line, where the battle of Shiloh was fought. She neither argued nor questioned. She supposed he must know what he was doing, that it must be a strong urge, too strong to deny, which would drive him back there again. So she told him, or rather told

Helen, and went back to the rear of the wagon, where she slogged along, fighting down her nausea, and where the boy tugging on her arm wearied her with endless questions about all the strange and wonderful sights through which he was passing.

Told one day that the bridge ahead of them is out, blown up to prevent its use by Yankee raiders, they are sent down a detour. This is long, sparsely settled, and somewhere on it they take a wrong turning; a few miles farther on the road suddenly comes to an end in a cow pasture. The land ahead being clear, however, and unfenced, they proceed. After a time they come to a creek, which they ford. Beyond the creek the land has recently been burnt over, not that very day, for it is cool, but no longer ago than the previous day—set afire by those same Yankees, as they will learn on coming out on the other side. Hayfields, these had been; now a layer of fine, soft, fluffy soot covers the ground like a fall of black snow. Stirred by their passage, it rises and hangs motionless upon the hot, still, windless air. The Ordways have to tie bandanas over their noses. Up the legs and wattles and up the bellies and the sides of the oxen the blackness spreads until all that remains is a white stripe down their backs like that of a skunk, then this closes and they are solid black, all but their polished white horns. To their own sweaty faces too the soot sticks, and the Ordways appear to be a family of Negroes.

Another day they ride all afternoon towards a storm. No clouds are visible anywhere in the sky but they can hear the rumble of steady thunder and when darkness begins to fall they can see the flashes of heat lightning low on the horizon. There comes one clap which shakes the ground they stand on, and against the evening sky bursts a flare which is not lightning but flames, illuminating the smoke billowing above them, and then they know that this is no storm but a town beleaguered. All night long the glow burns

steadily on the horizon, is still glowing when they awake before dawn, and Thomas Ordway, told of it, says (as he is to
say again more than once before he dies), "There are times
when blindness is a blessing. Maybe I have been lucky."
And Ella, as she is always to do, whispers, "Ssh. The children. They may be listening."

For Grant's drive down the Mississippi has entered its
final phase. New Orleans has long ago fallen, Memphis is
theirs, Natchez has surrendered without a shot being fired,
only Vicksburg still links the Confederacy east and west,
and now, in June, after thirty days of round-the-clock shelling, the people there are living on mule, some say on rats,
the mules all eaten now, thousands of them having been
driven out of the city into the encircling enemy lines at the
start of the siege for lack of fodder to feed them. "Them two
beeves of yawls'd set you up for life in Vicksburg now," a
man tells the Ordways. "If you was to live for life, that is.
Fetch you," he adds, looking at the team as if he can taste
them, "a right fair price here, for that matter" (*here* being
the town of Selmer, Tennessee, not far from Pittsburg Landing) "in case you was thinking of selling?" And that night,
all night long, columns of soldiers in blue march past their
campsite headed south down the Corinth Road, on their way
to reinforce the besiegers of Vicksburg.

For me, as for every Southern boy, it was learning that
the Civil War was lost which started it all over again; from
that time onward each battle had to be refought. The finality
of it being inadmissible, my mind drew up short, clinging
to that last moment when there was still time. For me it was
always noon of July 2 at Gettysburg, and now that the cost
of delay was clear, Longstreet would delay no more. Pickett's
charge still moved forever up Cemetery Ridge, and at Chan-
cellorsville meanwhile there was still time to warn that
sentryman that the figure on whom he was drawing a bead

was his own beloved general, Stonewall Jackson. But of course it was not still noon at Gettysburg, and Longstreet had waited until too late. Pickett's charge had nobly failed, and Stonewall Jackson had crossed over the river to rest under the shade of the trees. I had to lose each of these heart-breaking battles not once but countless times. So it must have been for my great-grandfather. Each day as the sun rose he must have had to lose his sight anew and reconcile himself again to the loss. Listening to the story of his return to Shiloh, I felt I understood him. He could neither accept nor deny his fate, and he went back there out of an irresist-ible, childish, forlorn hope of either retrieving that terrible day, or of ending it once and for all. The minuteness with which he was said to have toured the battlefield resembled that of a latter-day Civil War "buff." He was searching for some flaw in the sequence of events which would cancel it, which would declare that day void and bring it back to be played over again. He was hoping that on that spot where he had lost it, his sight would be restored to him by a miracle. Lacking that, he was hoping to learn to cease hoping.

That no step of his on that fateful day might go unre-traced, the Ordways camped overnight on the same spot where his brigade had camped the night before the battle. Souvenirs of that earlier stay still littered the site a year later, and in the morning the children were left to collect them. They found a rusty bayonet, a rusty broken-bladed knife, a leather cartridge pouch, weathered and cracked. Meanwhile Ella, following his directions, led him over the route of his former march.

Thomas Ordway's brigade, the 52nd Tennessee, under the command of General Chalmers, had been ordered up early that Sunday morning, April 6. They were sent north along a creek towards a line of bluffs below which, on the low ground between yet another creek and the Tennessee River, a regiment of Yankees was encamped, their tents pitched amid a peach orchard then in full blossom. Down these bluffs and upon the waiting Yanks they were ordered to charge. At the first volley the brigade broke, turned and ran. Thomas Ordway saw it happening; for a moment he faltered, half turned, himself. The attack was repulsed and they were drawn back, and the 52nd Tennessee was ordered ignominiously from the line, denied any further share in the day's fighting. Two companies, for their soldierly conduct, were exempted from this dishonor and sent back into battle, one of them Thomas Ordway's. Let by the hand now back to the spot, he stood where by turning and running with the rest, he might have saved his eyesight. He wished that he had run, and the wish troubled him with not one twinge of shame. With his whole soul he wished that he had run.

The hardest fighting of the entire first day at Shiloh had taken place around an abandoned sunken road running from the meetinghouse down to the river, in which a Yankee regiment, falling back, had found cover. The approach to this natural fortification was uphill through a tangled thicket overlooked by enemy artillery which poured, in addition to the musket fire from the entrenched infantrymen, cannonballs, canister, and shrapnel upon the attackers as they tore their way through the underbrush. It was in one of the many assaults upon this position, just past noon, that Thomas Ordway had been hit, and it was there that he directed Ella to lead him. But no such thicket as he remembered could Ella find. Indeed, there was none any more. For the Yankees caught in the sunken road had held out until evening of that day, and in that time the thicket had disappeared, cleared as though by fire by the shelling from the guns. Laid open to the red clay subsoil, the raw ground looked as if it had been picked by the buzzards still hovering overhead a year later, and the crows bickering in the woods along the creek bottom.

For a long time Thomas Ordway stood upon that spot which was the last he was ever to see. The unexpected miracle did not come. What came instead was an inkling of what he had been turned into. He wished again that he had run when he might have; as he had not, he found himself obliged to take pride in the courage, or that variety of fear called courage, which had blacked out his life past and to come and transformed him into a running sore. That was the worst part of wounds like his, that the only way to live with them at all was to end by cherishing them. They left you nothing else. They were all you had, all that you were. They became you, and made of you at last a kind of disfigured blind Narcissus, in love with your own ruination.

He had lasted, had forced himself on, as far as this; at Shiloh his legs gave out. From there to Memphis, a distance of one hundred miles, Ella led the team while he lay in the heaving wagon bed biting his lip to keep from groaning. Told that he had walked on those legs from northeast Tennessee, the doctor in Memphis snapped, "Well, sir, you may have walked your last step!" The infection was in the marrow of the bones, he told Ella. Asked if this meant a renewed threat of amputation, he said it could not be ruled out. Thomas Ordway went into the hospital demanding of the doctor, whom the question exasperated, how soon he could come out, and what was to become of his family while he was there, and what was to become of his team of oxen?

During that time Ella Ordway and the children camped around the outskirts of Memphis, moving as the oxen ate down the grass and before they should become a burden upon the charity of any one neighborhood. Her husband, everyone said, was eligible for a pension; Memphis being in Federal hands, unfortunately, Confederate pensions were blocked. In the first flush of freedom the former slaves had quit the land, and Ella was able to earn a little money hoeing cotton. The children herded the oxen as they grazed, their helplessness serving as a guarantee against theft. From their campsite every evening after work she walked into the city to visit him. Having been warned of his suicidal tendencies, the hospital staff kept him under close surveillance. Up to a point, soon reached, his legs showed improvement. At the end of ten weeks he was discharged as incurable.

By then her pregnancy had begun to show. Coming up from the ferry landing on the Arkansas shore, she leading the team, he, his eyes shaded by a hat brim, sitting on the wagon seat stiff as an idol in a procession, their passage provoked a murmur of sympathetic disapproval from people at the sides of the road. In their general tackiness now, the family looked like the kind of white trash of which the man lazes while the woman does all the work, and the swarm of flies buzzing round his head, and his indifference to them, added to the impression of his shiftlessness. He appeared to think it only fitting that he should sit at his ease in the shade while his pregnant wife trudged along in the dust and heat. The inobservance which was owing to his blindness was taken for a sullen disdain. Remarks, meant as sympathy for her, were uttered against him. Fortunately these were vague; decorum forbade too direct a reference to her condition; and if he heard them, sunk in apathy, he envinced no curiosity. But she dreaded lest something more open be said.

At bedtime that first night in Arkansas their mother joined the children where they slept, separated from their parents by a partition formed of casks, in the forward section of the wagon. They made a place for her between them. Their father was restless, she said. The following night again she slept with them. Thereafter for the rest of the journey she shared their bed; their father slept alone.

She could not spare his feelings. Should he discover that she was expecting, he would insist that they stop wherever they were. Once stopped, they might never get going again. She had not come this far only to stop short of her goal. She was set on Texas, or rather on that place in her mind to which she gave that name, and which she envisaged

as a vast, windswept blank, a place without landmarks, too
wide for the plow, where this son she now carried would
be born to something better than following behind a mule.
Little was needed to estrange her husband, alerted as he was
for just such a movement. He had watched in the darkness
for any indication that she had withdrawn to her side of the
narrow mattress they shared, had strained to catch any
hesitation, any stiffening as she changed his bandages in
the morning and the evening. The morning being the time
when the queasiness was always upon her, he had not
failed to detect such signs; then he had shriveled like a
salted snail. Inside the darkness which enclosed him his
feelers were out in constant agitation like the flutter of his
fingertips as he felt his way around a room. Especially in
bed he had watched with all his remaining senses for any
sign that she came to him out of duty and against her inclination. In the beginning, back home, when she first got
up off her pallet and returned to their bed, he had repulsed
her, refusing this as he had refused food. He may even
unwittingly have hoped to find that he disgusted her. The
unstilled longings of his wrecked and repellent body filled
him with shame, and with a sense of disloyalty towards the
death he had tried to die. At the least suspicion that anyone
had shrunk from him (and in his darkened mind these
suspicions bred like germs) he would retreat into that death
and the scarred features of his face set like incisions in stone.

Still she could not spare him. The rate of their progress
had been slow and Texas was still far away. From what
information she picked up about the distance, she figured
she would just about make it; she only hoped they would be
there before he discovered her condition. There would be
time then to salve his wounded feelings. Meanwhile, under
cover of his blindness, careful never to brush against him,
in constant anxiety lest somebody say something to give
her away, she drove them all on. The days were long, the
weather dry. She got them up before daybreak, fed them a

skimpy breakfast, yoked the team, and set off, her secret nausea forcing her to hang on to the yoke for dizziness.

They were in the cotton belt now, where slaves, more than ever they had seen in Tennessee, worked the broad fields. The bolls were opened full and the white fields shimmered in the glare of the sun. This white landscape with black people in it was like a photographic negative, or like that image which comes just before the loss of consciousness in a sunstroke, when everyone turns black, outlined by a glittering aureole of light. Ella Ordway's thin cotton dress, soaked with sweat, clung to her figure, accentuating her belly. The Ordways were stared at now fully as hard as they had been when he led the team.

It was during this time that the man seated on the porch of a country store where they stopped had taken it upon himself to interfere on her behalf. Their approach to the store had, as always, been studied from afar, and now this man watched the hot, dusty, pinched, and gravid little woman climb the creaky steps and cross the sagging, creaky porch in her thin shapeless dress, her worn and dusty shoes, waited until she was inside, spat out into the road, and said to his companions at large, "Now ain't that a sight to make you ashamed of being a man? Big lazy good-for-nothing taking his ease up there in the cool while that poor little woman has to walk along poking them oxen!" His tone was one almost of raillery. You might have thought he was baiting an old friend.

If Thomas Ordway heard this, and would have liked to hush the man for his own sake, it was already too late; there was nothing he could have said. In any case, he did not speak, and this must have seemed to the man on the porch like more of the same disregard which had been so provoking to begin with. "I'm talking to you," he said.

As Thomas Ordway sought to locate the voice, his unseeing gaze passed without acknowledgment over his assailant.

"Here I am," said he, stepping to edge of the porch and

squinting against the glare. "It's me that's talking to you. I'm an old man but not too old to tell you—and to prove it on you, too—that any man who would sit on that wagon seat and let his wife, in her—"

At that point Ella returned. But before she could intervene the man gasped, uttered a strangled, horror-stricken sob, turned, and slunk along the porch and around the side of the store, a look in his eye as if he were bent on hanging himself. It was the closest call she had had. Thereafter, hot as it was, and though dizzy already with nausea, Ella Ordway wore her overcoat—which drew stares, too, but hid her condition.

In Little Rock they heard rumors of another threatened invasion like that of U. S. General Banks from New Orleans up the Red River shortly before. They would, they also learned there, have to cross that Red River. They were told of a ferry above Clarksville. Preferring redskins to Yankees, they decided to cut across the southeast corner of Indian Territory. Travelers who had been there assured them that the Indians of that section—Choctaws and Cherokees—differed only in color from folks everywhere: lived in houses, dressed in clothes, farmed small holdings, went to church. The savages were civilized, it was the white riffraff you had to fear in the Indian Territory. And even with them the Ordways' helplessness and their poverty seemed a guarantee of safe conduct.

From Little Rock they went to Arkadelphia, from Arkadelphia to De Queen, where they entered the Territory, arriving in Broken Bow on the second day of October. They had been on the road for not quite six months, and had come nine hundred miles from home. Their money was gone. Now Ella bartered with storekeepers for supplies, beginning with the things they had been given, then dipping into their own meager possessions. Piece by piece she spent her mother's silverware. Picture frames, china, the mantelpiece clock of imitation ormolu: all these were traded away. No longer could they rely on the hospitality of the countryside. The

Arkansawyers had been poor, the Indians were even poorer. Their veneration of the blind was great, and when they came in their wagons to call, they solemnly extended their welcome through a translator, one of their children or grandchildren who had had government schooling. Still, they were more used to exacting petty tribute from travelers passing through their territory than helping them on their way. They took Ella's mirror, her cameo brooch, her sewing scissors, the brighter-colored articles of her clothing. One anxiety of hers she was able to lay aside. With the Indians her obvious secret was safe. They saw nothing remarkable, much less reprehensible, in the fact that the pregnant squaw should walk with the team while her man rode; nor would they, had he been in full possession of his faculties. Neither were the few white men here the kind to challenge a husband's mistreatment of his wife. As the temperature now hovered in the 90's, it was a relief to shed that overcoat.

The Ordways were asked if the war was over. They replied, not so far as they knew. Why? Well, they were the first folks to be seen coming through headed for Texas since shortly after the war began.

They turned south. Down into the red bottomlands, where out of stagnant sloughs cane-legged blue cranes rose creaking into the air and alligators sank from sight and mud turtles and fat water moccasins dropped off logs at their approach. Where in small stump-dotted patches Indian farmers snatched a crop of cotton between risings of the river which backed water inland for as deep as five miles, leaving in the forks of trees higher than a man's head tufts of matted trash like squirrels' nests. Then into the dark, cool, and fragrant pine forests: trees as thick as hair, with occasional clearings hacked out of them where loggers had operated, and in the clearing a mound of sawdust blackened at the base, growing yellow as cornmeal at the top. On into the brooding stillness, and then their first glimpse of the river. Impossibly red, silent, sluggish, it was as unlike water

as anything could be. It looked simply like a crossroad to
the one they were on. Thick, motionless, semi-solid, it might
have been a fresh-poured concrete highway; you felt that
just by waiting overnight you would find that it had set, and
you could walk across to Texas.

And you found that you might have to do just that. The
ferry had shut down. Had not run for nearly a year, the
owner having gone off, beaching his boat over on the other
side. This was told the Ordways by the half-breed farmer,
market hunter, trapper, who lived in the last cabin. Where
the next nearest ferry was he had no notion. He did not ask
if the war was over; it was doubtful that he knew there was
one going on.

Though hope of crossing there was gone, they were drawn
irresistibly down to the ferry landing. There for the first
time the Ordways beheld Texas. Dividing them from it were
only a few hundred yards. After coming a thousand miles,
to be balked by so little seemed intolerable.

Ella unhitched the oxen and led them, yoked, down to the
water to drink. Dexter took her hand and padded along
beside her in the deep red dust. Helen remained with her
father, who leaned against the wagon looking towards the
river. The oxen shied at the strange water, sniffed it, blew
in it trying to clear it. While they drank Ella stood resting
her hands on her stomach, gazing across to the opposite
shore. A wall of black-green pines rose there with pointed
tops as regular as the palings of a fence. At the base of this
wall, between it and the red water, which lay as flat as
though it had been smoothed with a trowel, stretched the
thin gold stripe of a sandbar. The woods were parted by a
fine line where the ferry road ran, until lost in the shadowy
depths. Ella's eyes brimmed suddenly with tears. After this
tantalizing glimpse to have to turn back, retrace their route
to Broken Bow, and push on westward—who knew how far—
through poor, inhospitable country until they learned of
another ferry, that too perhaps shut down—the disappoint-

ment was too cruel. Frightened by his mother's tears, the boy commenced to whimper.

A crash in the woods at their back made the oxen toss their yoked heads. Out of the trees a deer broke, streaked across the bar, and plunged into the river. Instantly it sank from view, leaving only its head above water. Straight out it swam, cutting a wake in the slow surface. It reached the middle, and there the current must have run stronger than appeared, for the deer was swept steadily downstream. It disappeared from sight. Ella caught her breath. Had it gone under? Was it drowned? Anxiously she scanned the surface, the opposite shore. Nothing could she see. Over the sullen river a desolate stillness hung, and seized by a fit of despair she let out her breath in a sob. Then Dexter cried, "Yonder he is! Yonder!" Far downstream the deer rose slowly from the water, silhouetted against the golden strand. Head hanging wearily, it hauled itself out. Bit by bit it drew erect, dark with wet, distinct against the shining sand. Then it was gone, vanishing into the darkness of the woods.

That night over supper the Ordways considered their predicament. Their money was gone, most everything they had was gone. It was October; before much longer the weather would begin to turn cold. And Texas lay just across the water, not a quarter of a mile away!

Thomas believed the river could be crossed. Her misgivings angered him; he ascribed them to fear of his helplessness. She pondered whether to tell him of her condition. The consequences were vivid to her. This poor, half-savage country was not the birthplace she had dreamt of for her child. With winter coming on they could not travel far with a newborn baby. Though near destitute now, they would have still less to travel on next spring, after a winter spent keeping alive in this place. It was not a very big river: only a quarter of a mile wide, if that; and quiet, hardly rougher than a pond. Once across it, and they were there. . . .

The cover was removed from the wagon, leaving the four

hoops sticking up in the air like an arbor on which no vines had yet grown, spread on the bank, and freshly coated with waterproofing compound. Overnight this dried and next morning the canvas was given a second coat. Slits were cut in it for the four axletrees. Then it was spread underneath the wagon and drawn up over the sides. The seams were tacked to the sideboards and sealed with the last of the waterproofing compound. Inside the box a rope was passed through the grommets and the tarpaulin tied down all round. All was ready. Only then did Ella broach the question which had troubled her mind from the start. "Just one thing worries me," she began, speaking across that space which she kept always between them.

He said nothing, did not even nod, though it was plain from the set of his face that she would not even need to name it, that his mind was made up, was not to be budged. He is a man, said Ella to herself; he understands such matters better than I do. He must know it is safe, reasonably safe. Proud as he is of those stones, he would not endanger us all for them. She heaved a sigh and said, "It would be a shame to leave them behind here, after bringing them all this way. Worse than a shame," she added, meeting with her own his fixed, unblinking gaze, "be a sin." She rubbed her tar-stiffened hand along the side of the wagon. "Three feet," she mused. "That ought to be deep enough to float a pretty heavy load." Still getting no response from him: "Well," she concluded, "there is one way to find out!"

Thomas Ordway sat with a child on either side of him on the wagon seat. Ella, barefooted and stockingless and with her skirt tucked up to where it barely covered her big belly, prodded the oxen, and the wagon rumbled down the bank. At the water's edge the team drew up. They had not balked; it had not yet penetrated to their brains that they were expected to enter the water, to swim that river; they just stopped, and when they felt the goad they turned upon Ella a patient look from out of their big lash-lidded liquid eyes, then lowered their heads to take a sip to drink. She stung the near one with so sharp a jab that it started, giving the wagon a lurch and taking itself and partner knee-deep into the water. Finding themselves there, they at once began backing out. But already the wagon wheels had begun to settle in the mud. Ella waded in after them and jabbed both in the rump. They balked. They would not go ahead, they could not go back. She prodded them until they set up a lowing, and tossing their heads, made the yoke clatter against their horns. Ella waded farther out, and reversing the goad, snapped the swivel in the nose ring of the inside ox. She gave it a twist. The ox bawled with pain; still he would not budge. The water now lapped their sides. Ella herself was in up to the armpits. The warm water was the color of coffee thickened with cream.

"Stubborn creatures!" Ella cried, and she gave the goad another wrench. Again the ox bawled, but it only set its hooves deeper in the riverbed. From its nose blood began to drip, spattering as though on solid ground on the surface of the water, red on red.

"Ella!" her husband called. "Stop." She had already. She was about to say that maybe the oxen knew best what they could and could not do. "Listen now, and do as I tell you. Take Helen, and the two of you go back up to the woods. Gather all the dry brush you can find and bring it here."

The brush was laid in two large piles on the bar just behind the wagon, one on either side. This done, he ordered them back into the woods with instructions to gather pine boughs, dead but with the needles still on. These he wanted in the wagon. He had Ella set fire to the brush piles. Then she climbed over the tailgate.

The fires began to crackle and the oxen to shake their heads. Torn between two fears, they could neither go ahead nor stand still. They rocked the wagon forward and back, rolling their eyes behind them at the fires. These were now burning at their pitch, snapping and popping, almost igniting the wagon. Still the oxen shifted and hesitated. Striking a match to one of the pine boughs, which roared aflame, Thomas Ordway dropped it across their backs.

With a deep double bellow like twin blasts from a steamship's stack, the oxen bolted, jerking the wagon so violently that Ella was flung flat, Thomas Ordway thrown off his balance, and the two children, both crowing with delight at their father's cleverness, sent flying backwards off the seat. The wheels tore free of the mud, the wagon shot from shore, and promptly sank. Sank to within six inches, that is, of the tops of the sideboards. To that level, but no higher, the waterline rose. They were afloat.

But the oxen, when they had swum out some fifty feet and began to recover from their fright and found themselves where they were, swung about and headed back towards the Oklahoma shore. Directly in their path another blazing branch was tossed. This turned them, but then they swung completely around the other way. To right and to left of them Thomas Ordway threw his burning boughs, while both children jumped for joy and begged to be allowed to throw one. Ella was kept busy with a pole preventing the boughs from washing into the wagon.

Resigned at last to crossing over, the oxen pushed out towards midstream. They swam scared, but powerfully, straining into the yoke, which rode far down their necks. Then, about a hundred yards out, they struck the current. Those in the wagon felt it. It came with no sudden jolt; to look at, the river here was hardly faster than inshore. But against the side of the wagon it bore down with tremendous pressure, like a bed of lava in its slow inexorable advance. They had their ballast of tombstones to thank that they were not tipped over. It was as if the water were rapidly congealing, and the oxen, rearing themselves in leaps, their humps breaking water like fishes' fins, appeared to be strug-

gling to extricate themselves from some thick and sticky
fluid. They began to lose headway and were borne irresistibly downstream. The landing, the road between the trees on
the Texas shore, slipped behind. Yet the wagon still did not
pitch, scarcely rocked, and although the waterline now
lapped up to within a scant two inches of the top, inside all
was dry.

Midway across, maybe a bit farther, the oxen faltered.
They sank back. The yoke rode up their necks until it caught
on their horns. When this happened the wagon was spun
round, astern to the current. Its broadside relieved of pressure, it rose, and with it, floundering helplessly, rose the
oxen. They shot downstream. Throughout all this, and all
that followed, hardly a sound broke the stillness. Like molasses, the smooth brown river flowed heavily on its way,
indifferent to its passengers, and along both wooded shores
a drowsy stillness reigned.

The oxen tried to break out of the current. When they
veered aside (and the Ordways were willing now to let them
choose their bank) the strain bowed the wagon tongue. Then
could be seen how powerful the silent and scarcely visible
current was: breaking over the bent and quivering wagon
tongue the water rippled like shot silk, drawn taut. For an
instant then the wagon would hang broadside in the current,
shaking, while the team churned up and down, getting no
place; then they would fade, sink back, spent, wheezing for
breath, tongues lolling, drift helplessly around, and again
be sped downstream.

After about three quarters of a mile of this they were
carried around a bend. There the banks rose, the river narrowed, and the current quickened. Into this narrows (actually the banks were still two hundred yards apart, but to
Ella they seemed to be rushing together, closing upon them)
they shot as into the neck of a bottle. Presently the river
took another, reverse bend. Here the main current ran not
in midstream but close inshore. Still in that dreamy silence,

wagon and team swung in a wide, accelerating arc towards
the deeply undercut and overhanging bank along the Oklahoma side. Now the oxen dangled uselessly, held afloat by
their yoke. The speed was dizzying and Ella closed her eyes,
expecting to be dashed against that red wall. They were
swept around this bend as though on rails, and when she
opened her eyes Ella found herself clear across the river,
close to the Texas side. She caught a glimpse of what lay
beyond. From between the tall bluffs the river emptied into
a broad shallows. It was lighter in color there, and from the
Texas shore it ran far out in a flat stretch, as calm as a plate
of soup. Then she became aware of the fact that she was
standing halfway up to her knees in water. Over the back
it was pouring in and the wagon was filling like a bucket.
Mattresses, pots and pans, kegs were rising off the floor,
floating. Up front on the elevated spring seat neither the
children, whose legs were too short to reach, nor her blind
husband, his braced against the dashboard, was yet conscious of what was happening to them.

With a final shove the wagon was shot out of the fast
water into the calm, where it plunged to a dead stop. Ella,
as she went down, saw Dexter slip, sweep under the seat,
saw Helen shoot upward, saw her husband clutch at the
gaps in the air where the instant before the children had
been sitting. The wagon took a last gulp, filled, brimmed
over, and sank. A rectangular swell conforming to its outline
rose momentarily upon the surface, then flattened away in
outgoing ripples. The oxen went down rearing, their forelegs
pawing air, until over them too the dark waters closed.

Saved by the same thing which sank it, those stones, the
wagon settled upright and as gently as a bucket in a well,
the four wheels coming simultaneously to rest upon the
riverbed, in eight feet of water, leaving the three cover hoops
above surface, looking like croquet bails. While Ella Ordway,
her open eyes useless to her in that red opacity, searched the
inside of that flooded box for her children, for her blind

husband, the kegs containing all the dead Ordways, strung out like stumps in a field, sailed slowly downstream. At a certain point the first one stopped, hung on something. Down floated the second one, and it too caught, just a few feet away, on the same thing. The third, the fourth one floated down and they too stopped. Then at a distance of some thirty feet from where they had gone down, the oxen, horns first, broke water. They clambered up the rising river bottom. The top of the wagon box emerged. Three of the Ordways, all but Dexter, came up for air. They stood up and found themselves in a brimming boxful of water, but above the surface of the river. By then all but one keg, which had floated past and out of sight, were strung in a line not far downstream, a line which bellied slightly in the middle, gently bobbing.

"That trotline that them kegs with all you-all's dead kinfolks in them caught on was ours."

Uncle Dave Crenshaw is the speaker. Uncle Dave (no kin: everybody's Uncle Dave), an old-timer who, when I was very young, used to turn up regularly at Mabry graveyard working, claimed to have been on hand that day in October 1863 to see my great-grandparents' entry into Texas. Beyond question, he was old enough; but as he *was* that old, and the story pretty well known thereabouts, it is possible that Uncle Dave was confused. Perhaps, poor lonely old soul, he had made up his tale in payment for the invitation to partake of our dinner which my grandfather always pressed on him. Though why I should doubt him now I don't know; I didn't then.

"We was staying on the ferry road down near the river," said Uncle Dave. "As near as you dared, that is. Trying to make a crop between flood stages. How old I was at the time I can't exactly say—old enough to know I was just too little to go off and join the fighting with my big brothers. One day —it was towards the end of cotton-picking time—we heard a wagon coming up the road from the river. We dropped our sacks and run to look, for they wasn't no ferry running and hadn't been for the past year. Up the road come a wagon dripping water like an ice wagon, drawn by a pair of oxen. Leading them was a little bitty woman who oughtn't to been on her feet. Sopping wet she was, and her dress sticking to her showed her to be about seven months gone with child. Setting on the wagon seat where she ought to been, was a man. Walking along behind the wagon was a barefoot little girl dripping water in the dust of the road. They pulled up at our gate.

" 'Where does this road go to?' the man called down from his wagon seat. He never said mister, nor please, nor even hidy, and his look had a way of missing you by just about a head, then when he lowered it, of kind of stopping just before it reached you, as if not wanting to soil itself, which brought the blood to my pa's face. Pa had been going to ask them to come in, maybe offer them a bite to eat. He was certainly curious to know how they had gotten across that river. But Pa was a quick-tempered man, and when his temper was up it put even his cur'osity down. 'I reckon that depends,' he said, 'on how long you stay on it.'

"Meantime I sidled up to that little girl and said, 'Yawl got kind of wet crossing over, didn't you?' I grinned, but she commenced to cry. 'Well, don't cry about it,' I said. 'This ain't no time for that. Here you are, safe on dry land. You have made it across.'

"She sobbed and said, 'Yes, but poor little Dexter, he never.'

"Taking that for the name of a pet, I said, 'Was Dexter your puppy dog?'

"She said, 'Dexter was my little brother, and now, poor thing, he's dead. You can look at him if you want to.'

"I stood on tiptoe and looked in the wagon and seen a little dead boy.

"I said to comfort her, 'Well, don't carry on, sweetheart.

You're fixing to have another one soon to take Dexter's place. That, or you a little baby sister.'

"She quit crying and looked at me big-eyed through her tears. Maybe she is younger than I took her for, I thought. The woman was the same. I mean, but for that little girl you might have suspected she didn't herself know that she was in the family way. They don't sometimes. It was enough to make you rub your own eyes, the way she acted like they wasn't a thing in this world to see down there at her waist.

" 'Honey,' said my ma to her, giving Pa a dirty look, 'wouldn't you like to come in the house and lay down and rest yourself a little?'

" 'Oh, no!' she cried. 'No, thank you just the same, I'm fine! Just fine!' You'd have thought she swum the Red River every day just for the fun of it. And then she bust into tears.

"The man said, speaking to Pa, and you had to remind yourself (remind him, too, it seemed) that he had just lost a child, for even in thanking you he had a tone to his voice that rubbed your fur the wrong way, 'We haven't got no time to waste. I would be obliged to you for one thing. We lost something overboard. Something worthless to anybody else but precious to me. A keg is what it was, a nail keg. It floated off down the river and my wife wasn't able to recover it.'

" 'Your *wife* wasn't able to!' cried Ma.

" 'A nail keg? And it floated?' said Pa.

" 'It had something else in it besides nails,' said the man.

" 'It's Great-grandpa,' said the little girl to me.

" 'Huh?' I said.

" 'In that keg,' she said.

" 'Little girl,' I said, 'what are you talking about?'

" 'We got all the rest of them back again but him,' she said.

" 'What on earth are you talking about?' I said.

" 'I'll tell you something I bet you don't know,' she said.

" 'What?'

" 'My papa,' she said, 'is blind.'

"I looked down. By then they had made a regular mud puddle in the road in front of our gate.

" 'If you or any of your neighbors find such a keg,' I heard the man say, 'just hold on to it. I will send you a letter as soon as we get settled. Maybe then I will be able to offer a reward. One thing more. If you do find it, do not open it.'

" 'I bet your papa still don't know,' said the little girl. Then in the middle of a smile she bust out crying again harder than ever. Then they set off down the road towards Clarksville, the woman poking the oxen with her stick and the man setting on the wagon seat and the little girl, still wet, following along behind, her thin little shoulders shaking as she cried. When I told Pa, he said he thought he noticed something the matter with that man's eyes. Ma said the same. We never talked about nothing else for days but that blind man and that big-bellied little woman crossing the Red River in a wagon. About a week later we was running our line when we seen something caught in the bushes along the bank. It was that lost keg. Painted on the lid was some letters. I couldn't read them and neither could Pa. Pa, he shaken it and it rattled, and then I told him what that little girl had told me was in it. He said, why didn't I tell him that before he shaken it? He wouldn't let that keg in the house but kept it out in the hayloft until one day about three months later them folks came back to ask if anybody had ever found it. They come in the same old wagon, only this time instead of oxen a span of mules was hitched to it. They had a new baby with them.

" 'What did I tell you?' I said to the little girl.

"She grinned, then went red in the face.

" 'Brother or sister?' I asked her.

" 'Little brother,' she said. 'We call him Sammy.'

"That time again, even knowing now that he was blind, Pa come close to losing his temper with the man. That was

when he took out his billfold and commenced taking out
bills. He took out three and asked his wife what they were.
She said it was three ones. He held them out in the air and
asked, 'Is that enough for your troubles?' Pa set the keg in
the wagon and told him to put his money back in his pocket.
He took out two more bills and asked his wife what them
were—two more ones, she said—and held out the five and
said, 'Will that cover it?' Pa just backed out of range. The
woman thanked him. I come to know your daddy later on,
Sam, and he was like that, proud, despite his blindness, or
maybe I ought to say, on account of his blindness. It went
hard with him to accept a favor. And there the old gentleman lies," Uncle Dave concluded somewhat unexpectedly,
nodding towards Old Tenpenny's grave, " 'longside the rest
of his folks, where he belongs."

Clarksville, as I began by saying, is only barely in Texas,
and originally Thomas Ordway stopped there—or rather in
Mabry—for cemetery plots, even small ones, in the town were
not to be had on credit and he refused the offer of a patch
in the potter's field—only long enough to bury Dexter, then,
mothlike in pursuit of that flaming sun, pushed on beyond.
How far beyond they never knew; far enough for the sounds
and smells of things to turn unfamiliar and frightening to
that lost veteran of a lost cause. Out of the woods they came
and onto the plains, where the wind blew not in gusts but
endlessly, unintermittently, coming unchecked, out of nowhere, with nothing to rustle on its way. The earth stood
still all day and crackled beneath that burning sun. The
rattle of thunder was distant and dry; rain, when it fell, was
preceded for hours by a smell arising from the hot earth as
if rain had already fallen; when it came, it fell with a noise
like water galloping from a bottle, splattered in great warm
clots against your face, rattled like buckshot on the hard-
baked ground, and then abruptly ceased. In that parched

and alien soil, would the bones of his ancestors take root
and flower? It was a place without echoes, and when at
times the wind died, you could hear forever—hear nothing.
Then in his darkness, listening, Thomas Ordway knew that
he had crossed a line. He had stepped beyond the bound of
recorded time, into a land waiting for history, into the long
unbroken hush of antiquity. And there came to the blind
cripple then a realization of his place in the record of things.
Men like himself had bled and died unknown in battles since
the dawn of time; but behind him at least were pages in
which the dates had been preserved; and there was consolation, he found now, in that anonymous immortality, in
knowing that though the battle might have been lost, the
cause itself lost, the wrong cause, perhaps, from the start
and one's own part in it insignificant, that the day which
had cost a man his eyes would not be forgotten, but would
go down in history. Here there was time for an army, a race
to have fought and died, but no tongue to remember
them in. Listening to that ancient silence, Thomas Ordway
seemed to hear, seemed almost to feel brush past, a throng
of ghosts: the unrecorded legions of the nameless, unlet-
tered dead. Then after a long space of silence he came again
among living men and heard them speak. It was Spanish,
and he shrank back as if a second bomb had burst, blinding
his ears. Then while coyotes howled about him in their
moonlit night, he, in his, turned, lonely and frightened and
fumbling, to his wife, and found her big with child.

In his later years Thomas Ordway's son Samuel often
imagined that night on the plains when his father's groping
hands first found him in his mother's ripening belly. And
that other, earlier, related night in Tennessee, when Thomas
Ordway had turned to his wife and she had not flinched,
though he thought she had, but, clumsy, fumbling, noisome
as he was, had taken him to her breast.

No man wants his children to be born foreigners. One of
his strongest desires is that his sons have the same boyhood,

the same memories, only maybe happier, as his own. The following morning Thomas Ordway turned and retraced his faltering steps to Clarksville, where already the only absent member of his whole clan lay buried.

And there we were still, we Ordways, above ground and below, where old Thomas had brought us, our wanderings over; and once a year, on graveyard working day, that son whom he never saw but knew only by touch, now grown old, would, like a Jewish patriarch at the Passover *seder* answering the questions of the youngest male child, recount our exodus, led by that blind and crippled Moses of our tribe. The tale told, work was resumed. But I, from an early age, was always left feeling restless and dissatisfied by the way the story ended, and would wander off by myself to the churchyard, there to stand with the wind in my face gazing wistfully towards the country which had almost been my birthplace.

To grow up a boy in Clarksville in my time was to be a double dreamer. For there where the woods joined the prairie was the frontier where two legends met. At one's back one heard the music of a banjo and the strains of "Dixie," the tramp of marching men, the roll of drums and bugle calls, the rattle of musketry, the thunder of cannonades. A boy gazing in that direction saw proud, tattered ensigns streaming above the haze of battle; saw burst from the clouds of gunsmoke gray-uniformed figures waving sabers and long horsepistols, shouting the rebel yell, grinning at death, glory-bent and beckoning him to follow. Those wooded hills rang all the way back with the names of Jeb Stuart and Stonewall Jackson and Texas's own Albert Sidney Johnston and the hapless but courageous John Bell Hood, and the sonorous Miltonic roll of place names where battles were fought: First Manassas, Antietam, The Wilderness, Chickamauga, Chattanooga, Shiloh.

In the other direction stretched Blossom Prairie, the vastness alone of which would have drawn out the soul in vague yearnings, even if beyond it had not lain a place already fabled as a land of romance and the home of heroes. What the ocean is in that once-famous picture of the boy Raleigh shown sitting on the shore with his knees drawn up to his chin and his eyes fixed on strange distant lands below the horizon, my prairie was to me. Except that I knew what lay beyond my ken. Just beyond the range of my vision the prairie became the plains, and there another world commenced. It was a new world, and in it a new man had come into being, the most picturesque the world has ever produced: the cowboy. There was no place there for old men or for women. Life was spiced with danger there. A man wore his law strapped round his waist out there. Strong, fearless, taciturn, the cowboy was a natural aristocrat, chivalrous towards women, loyal to his friends unto death, reserved towards strangers, relentless towards his enemies, a man who lived by a code as rigid and elaborate as a medieval knight's. The cowboy was a man whose daily occupation was an adventure, whose work clothes a sultan might have envied. A man lifted above the plodding pedestrian world: a horseman—just the best ever known. On that wind which blew in my face off Blossom Prairie I seemed to catch the lowing of vast herds of cattle and the strumming of a guitar to the tune of "The Old Chisholm Trail," and along that flat rim where the earth met the sky there would sometimes appear in silhouette a lone rider sitting tall in the saddle, wearing a broad-brimmed sombrero and chaps, a bandana knotted round his throat, the sunlight glinting on the pearl handle of the pistol slung low on his thigh.

Lee surrendered to Grant on April 9, 1865. The news was two months reaching Texas. I did not hear about it until 1931. I learned by reading on to the end of my school history book. Before that time I had sensed that we were in for a long struggle, but I had no idea that things were going that bad. We had suffered setbacks—that was war; but we had given as good as we had gotten, and, no one having told me any different, I supposed that the fighting was still going on. Suddenly at the age of ten I not only had snatched away from me any chance ever to avenge my great-grandfather and redeem our losses and cover myself with glory on my country's battlefields, I had to swallow down my pride and learn to live with the chronic dyspepsia of defeat.

Nothing had prepared me for this. My knowledge of American history up to that point had conditioned me to the habit of success and leadership. I had theretofore identified myself with my country's eminence and expansion, and as a Southerner I had belonged to the dominant party. The founding fathers, the early generals, the great presidents, were Southerners. In the War, as presented to me, we had fought the better fight. At the point at which the account of it had always previously left off, we were winning. Now all of a sudden it was over, and we had lost. For me, a Texan (which is just another word for "proud"), this was even harder to accept than for most Southerners.

I say that, yet is it true? The moment when he discovers that the Civil War is lost comes to every Southern boy, and proud Texan though I was, it was perhaps less shattering for me than for most. I had, right on my doorstep, another myth to turn to. When the last bugle call went echoing off into eternity and the muskets were stacked and the banners lowered and that star-crossed flag hauled down—in short, when Appomattox came to me and I was demobilized and disarmed and returned home, filled with wounded pride and impatient with peacetime life—like many another veteran—I began to face about and look the other way, towards Blossom Prairie, where the range was open and the fancy free to roam. In my fashion I was repeating not only the history of my family, but of the country. For the West provided America with an escape from the memory of the Civil War.

In one of its sons the Ordway clan had realized its manifest destiny. Somewhere out there I had an uncle—half-uncle, that is to say, and provided he was still alive. Rancher? Wrangler? Roustabout? Rustler? What was my unknown western uncle? By this time I knew, in bare outline, the true story of Little Ned. Unwilling as my father and all my aunts and uncles were to talk about it, my mother was nothing loath, for to her it showed my grandmother in a blameworthy role and my poor innocent grandfather suffering at her hands—with which interpretation, though my mother did not know it, my grandmother agreed entirely and my grandfather entirely disagreed. Without assigning any blame myself, I would have liked to comfort my grandfather for the loss of his son, to let him know, as we stood side by side gazing silently off into the distance (for he too used to leave the cemetery after dinner, drawn to the churchyard and its view), that after all these years of enforced silence he had in me someone to whom he might open his heart and speak of Little Ned. But I was shy with him, and it was such a sad story that I was afraid to remind him of it. So we stood there sighing, he for his lost youth (I only thought it was for his lost son), I for I did not know what. For a Shetland pony and saddle. For adventure. For my interminable childhood to be over and my life to begin.

Actually my grandfather joined me in the churchyard to get away from the sight of his wife at her grave-cleaning chores.

Though it was hardly to be expected that my grandfather would still mourn for his Agatha after thirty-five years, especially as her death had given him the opportunity to marry my own dear grandmother, it went without saying that he felt the care and upkeep of her grave to be his responsibility, his duty, and that he had taught their two daughters to feel the same. So you would think; but sad to relate, none of those three ever went near that grave on graveyard working day, the weeding of which was left year after year entirely to the one person who might have been excused for neglecting it, namely my grandmother. In a man of such patient disposition, so forbearing, so utterly unvindictive as my grandfather, and in whom the day otherwise awoke a host of tender memories, this dereliction could be explained only by supposing that Agatha had been a wife whom he was not sorry to have lost. Still it was surprising in him, who took forgiveness almost to a fault, and who was ordinarily incapable of nursing a grudge even overnight. I loved him no less for it; indeed, I pitied him, for even a child could see that it mortified him to be unable to render the outward forms of honor to the memory of a woman he had once been married to, who had borne him children, who, in fact, had died giving birth to one of them. But, seeing my grandmother down on her knees unselfishly plucking weeds from her predecessor's grave (she did a thorough and conscientious job, leaving not one unsightly stalk), I admired her all the more. I agreed with the Maynards and the Claibornes, the families whose burial plots adjoined ours, who called her, to her face, a saint. I admired her still more for the frown of unfeigned displeasure with which she always received the compliment. Even when it was a case of being lauded for her goodness in remembering the woman whom she herself had displaced in his heart, and that was what this amounted to, my grandmother could take no pleasure in anything in which was implied the least dispraise of her husband. How many women in her position but would have rejoiced in the evidence that her husband had so completely forgotten his first wife? My grandmother not only did not, she maintained his fidelity to Agatha's memory to the point that sometimes she had to break off in confusion, sensing that if all she claimed was true, then he ought never to have married *her*.

Imagine my astonishment, my indignation, the first time I heard my grandmother accused, by her own children, my father among them, of jealousy of the dead Agatha Ordway! What could they mean? Had they not seen her, as I had, on

graveyard working day, down on her hands and knees tending that grave the care of which belonged by every right,
custom, and duty to others, whom she was the last to be
expected to look after, which but for the goodness of her
heart would have been waist-high in weeds, a scandal to the
neighbors and to the whole community? Then I saw that it
was a joke (a very poor one, I thought); my grandmother
herself joined in the pretense.

Her children thought, as children will, that they themselves had superseded their parents' love for one another.
Deep mutual affection, of course, they were supposed still
to feel, and mutual trust—not to say, a mutual taking of
one another for granted. Passionate love at their age was
unthinkable; passionate jealousy would have been ridicu-
lous, almost indecent. They were merely having a little fun
with her.

Which, I wonder now, was more painful to my grandmother—to be accused of jealousy, or to be accused of it in
a manner which made it seem a joke? Which implied that
jealousy at her age was such an improbable, even such a
comical thing that one might tease her with it without fear
of being taken seriously? For, alas, my poor grandmother
was more in love with her husband now than ever, though
prevented from showing it as she would have liked because
she too believed that at her time of life it was unseemly. Left
alone with him now that the last of the children was married
and gone from home, she was more than ever dependent on
reassurances that he loved her. My grandfather, that gentle
soul, that devoted husband, gave her all the reassurances
any man could, but she admired him too much to believe in
them. That is to say, she prized constancy above all qualities,
and as he was her model for all the virtues, he was also her
model for that. She knew that thirty years of living with
another man would never have altered her love for him; she
feared that thirty times thirty years could never abate his
love for Agatha, who, having died young, and who being dead

was placed beyond all rivalry, remained eternally young while she herself grew old and even plainer.

Now jealousy was simply not in my grandfather's nature. He was utterly incapable of it. He did not even despise it. Instead of sharing the world's contempt for that ignoble and degrading passion, he profoundly pitied anyone afflicted with it—or would have, that is, if he had known anyone so afflicted. Consequently he was incapable of imagining that he might inspire it in anyone.

Thus those loud sighs which she would heave at night after supper, when he was settled down with his copy of *The Dallas Morning News* (there was rural free delivery in Mabry now), were all lost on him. "Mr. Ordway?" she would have to say at last.

"Mmmh."

"Mr. Ordway, if I was to die . . . Are you listening, Mr. Ordway?"

"Yes, dear. What was that you said?"

"I said, if I was to die—"

"Oh, don't talk like that!"

"But if I was to?"

"Well, you're not going to anytime soon, let's hope."

"But if I was to, would you miss me, Mr. Ordway?"

"Miss you? Why, of course I would miss you! What a foolish thing to ask."

"Well, why don't you ever say so then! Would you" (this after a momentary pause) "get married again?"

"What! At my age?"

"If *you* were to die and *I* was to remarry, you wouldn't like that, would you?"

"On the contrary, my dear. It's exactly what I would want you to do. I wouldn't like to think of you all alone."

There the conversation would come to a halt. He would resume his reading, she her sewing. After a time she would say:

"Mr. Ordway?"

"Dear?"

"Mr. Ordway, you do love me, don't you?"

"Love you? Well, what a silly thing to ask!"

"You're not ever sorry you married me?"

He would lower his paper, and peering over his glasses, would crane around the back of his armchair and say:

Well, in fact, he would not say anything. For before he could: "Are you sorry you married me?" she would demand. What she really meant, what in thirty-five years he had never understood that she meant, was: Are you sorry Agatha died?

"My dear! Of course I'm not sorry I—"

"Then why don't you ever say so!" she would cry, and flinging her sewing behind her, the wooden darning egg bounding across the floor, would jump up from her seat and storm off to bed.

"But what did I say?" he would call after her, chasing the darning egg.

"Nothing! Nothing!" she would call back. "You never say anything!"

True, on one occasion his second wife had revealed her jealousy of his first wife in a manner unmistakable even to him. But that was long ago; Hester herself had remorsefully confessed it; she had seen what calamity it could lead to (though he blamed himself for that calamity more than Hester); he had pointed out to her the foolishness of being jealous of a dead person, and she had promised never to be jealous again. Hester's tending of Agatha's grave he looked upon as her little yearly act of atonement for that one old injury. Little yearly act of atonement it was indeed, but for a jealousy which after thirty-five years still burned with a flame like a blowtorch. None of her children suspected that what they treated as an endearing little foible, which perhaps they even sought to encourage so as to prevent her discovering that she had grown old and incapable of passion, was a nagging torment, and that she endured their teasing and smiled the arch and roguish smile which was expected of her while writhing with anguish that they should treat it as a joke, and at the same time trembling with fear lest they discover the ravages which her affliction had made upon her soul, as a sick person will dissemble the extent of his illness from those who love him.

My grandfather had his own reasons for being just as glad to leave the care of Agatha's grave to someone else, and never, as I have said, went near it. Thus he was unaware of one result of Hester's long loving upkeep. In selecting his wife's tombstone my grandfather had unfortunately forgotten the pressing necessity he even then lay under of taking a second wife and providing a foster mother for his three children, and in the stonemason's yard in Clarksville had given way to his feelings and picked a monument with this inscription, ready-carved:

> *Weep not for me, but be content.*
> *I was not yours, but only lent.*
> *Wipe off those tears, and weep no more.*
> *I am not dead, but gone before.*

In appointing herself sole custodian of her rival's grave, my grandmother, hardly noticing what she was doing, had encouraged the mound to rise over the years until now all that was visible was the top line. She had succeeded in fooling everyone but herself; for she, and she alone, knew that, like an iceberg, the dangerous three quarters of the verse lay below the surface.

My grandmother's one remaining wish was that she might predecease her husband. To get to heaven and have it out with Agatha before he got there. (She was to outlive him by fifteen years—too ornery to die, as she would say; fifteen years of agonized suspicions of how he and Agatha were carrying on up there in her absence.) For she was as certain

as that she was alive on this earth that there was a life to
follow this one. Certain too that if Agatha's childbed martyrdom were not enough, then the very fact that she herself
wronged her daily in her thoughts would have secured for
Agatha a place in paradise. She was certain that she herself
would go there too. For though, unlike her children, and her
husband, she believed jealousy to be a sin, and her own a
very great sin, she believed it had caused her enough hell on
earth to open the gates of heaven to her when she died. Not
that in this she found much consolation. Even if she got
there before he did, she was still uncertain what her rights
would be. She foresaw the possibility that she would be
given a shanty on the outskirts of heaven and have to rear
all thirteen of their combined children by taking in wash
through eternity, while across town Mr. Ordway and Agatha
lived in a towered and turreted mansion like those lining
Silk Stocking Street in west Clarksville.

The shame, the guilt, the remorse one feels for doing something wrong can be genuine and deep without in the least
restraining one from doing it again: such was my grandmother's state of soul as she cleaned her rival's grave on
graveyard working day. Having borne (in the same room)
ten children herself, and come near death in at least one of
her deliveries, she pitied the poor girl who had died in childbirth at the age of twenty-seven. A girl who, moreover,
sinned against her only in having loved the man whom she
believed the whole world ought to love as if married to him.
For nearly thirty-five years her conscience had been in pawn
to the woman, the mother, who lay beneath that mound.
But for her resentment of him, the child whose coming had
put Agatha Ordway in her grave would be here today, not—
if he were even still alive—separated from his father, his
whereabouts unknown. It was like Mr. Ordway to say that it
was not her fault, that he was more to blame than she was.
Like him too never afterwards to reproach her, to avoid
as far as possible all mention of Ned's name out of con-

sideration for her feelings, to relinquish to her, in misplaced trust, the care of Agatha's grave. She knew whose fault it was. And even so she could not only continue to be jealous, but could suspect and resent the fact that he had never allowed any of the six sons that she had given him to take the place in his affections of that one he had been deprived of through her antagonism.

PART TWO

_____

The Stepchild

AFTER the long spring rains the road was rutted as deeply as the furrowed fields alongside, and the wagon, drawn by a lean, mincing mule and a flat-footed, one-eyed mare, swayed and lurched, axles groaning, tongue, sides, and dry weather-warped bedboards popping and cracking as if ablaze. While my grandparents, she clutching the baby with one hand and the rattling egg basket with the other, jogged along on the spring seat, Winnie, Bea, and little Ned, the dead Agatha's children, sitting along the tailgate with their legs dangling, were flung from side to side and bounced up and down like Mexican jumping beans. The Ordways were going into town, all except Ned, who at two going on three had never yet been taken, and all were dressed for the day, my grandmother in her good green calico, my grandfather in fresh faded overalls and a collarless shirt fastened at the throat with a bone stud and striped like the paper that a barber wipes his razor on, the girls in sunbonnets and full, ankle-length slate-gray dresses, high-button shoes, and

coarse coffee-colored cotton stockings that gave them the
look of a pair of miniature nuns. Ned, towheaded, whey-
faced, solemn little Ned, also wore a dress, one similar to
his sisters'; in fact it had been Bea's, to whom in turn it
had come down from Winnie. In the wagon bed rode two
empty barrels lashed with plowline to the sideboards. Underneath the seat sat a wet cedar firkin covered over with a
damp white cloth. It contained butter, and as the sun broke
over the low hills away to his left, my grandfather reached
down and felt to make sure it was sitting in the shade.

In the lee of the hills, shaggy with pines, dogwood blossomed in white puffs and redbuds flamed amidst the fresh
green of sweetgums and oaks and the pale inconstant
smudge of willows. Below the hills the land flattened;
covered now with bright young cotton, it seemed to lie under
a sheet of clear shallow water. Westward to the right of the
road the land stretched away unbordered to the skyline.
No hedgerows separated the road from the plowed ground
here, and over these fields now rippled the shadow of wagon
bed and elongated spokes, of mule's ears and bonnet wings.
A wheel would ride up out of the rut, the wagon would tilt,
protesting in every joint, then settle with a crash which
flushed sparrows and mourning doves and once a booming
covey of quail out of the roadside drainage ditch. The team
plodded on, heads bobbing. From time to time my grandfather slapped them gently across their rumps with the
slackened reins and clicked his tongue at them, and the
mare would half turn and roll her one good eye at him.

They were still half a mile away when the clatter of the
wagon brought Mrs. Vinson out onto her front porch. My
grandfather saw her and saw out of the corner of his eye
that my grandmother had seen her, saw the quick irrepressi-
ble little toss of the head with which, as he had learned, his
wife betrayed her dislike. Mrs. Vinson, her Felix toddling
ahead of her down the flower path, came to the gate and
stood waiting for them, shading her eyes as she watched

the wagon's ponderous and creaky progress down the road.

My grandfather felt deeply obligated to his neighbors the Vinsons, and the coolness which had come between them since his remarriage pained and embarrassed him. It was Mrs. Vinson, whose Felix was at the breast at the time, who had taken the newborn motherless Ned home with her and nursed him along with her own. She had offered to take the girls home with her too, only Winnie, then barely eight, not only would not go, she would not let them take Bea, and if only she could have found a way to inspire milk in her own flat little bosom she would never have let them take her new baby brother either. Mrs. Vinson was one of those broad-breasted, patient, cheerful, tireless, almost mindless women made for breeding and bringing up children, to whom, as she said now whenever my grandfather apologized for always putting Ned off on her for the day, one more—she might equally well have said half a dozen—did not matter. During that spring and summer and fall when he was going it alone, a widower with a crop to make and gather and two little girls on his hands, she was forever sending over some baked dish or a dress she had whipped together for Bea or for Winnie or for both. And one day he had gotten caught up on housework and the wash and gone down to turn under the last few acres of his cover crop of rye, and had found the job finished and done. Will Vinson, incapable of accepting thanks for any favor he ever did you, had steadfastly denied knowing anything about it, insisting that Sam Ordway had more friends than he realized. And he had no call on the Vinsons. They were neighbors to be sure, but only of short standing, and prior to their taking the place next door down the road, my grandfather had not even known Will Vinson, who came from some some other, distant part of the county. He still did not know him, after all the man had done for him. Picking side by side in the cotton rows as Vinson helped him gather his crop, eating side by side with their backs against a tree on the edge of the field, sharing the doughnuts or the fried pies of which Mrs. Vinson had sent one for him, they called one another, if by any name at all, Mr. Ordway and Mr. Vinson, having gotten started that way and having gone on until it became impossible for either to say to the other, call me Sam, or call me Will. Vinson was a shy, untalkative man by nature, so for that matter was Sam Ordway, or perhaps it was not nature in either of them but rather a lifetime spent following a plow, hoeing, dragging a cottonsack over the silent, empty fields; but now he had placed weights on his already heavy tongue out of consideration for his neighbor's grief. So to this day the only thing that either man knew about the other was the only thing which mattered to either of them to know about a man, that he could work, and that in time of need he would not even have to be called on for help. There had been an extra-good crop of cotton that season, the picking and ginning and baling of which, even with his neighbor's help, had put off until late in the year, almost November, the time when my grandfather could begin to look around for a new wife, shortened the already brief period before next planting time during which to woo and win her. Again it was Mrs. Vinson who by minding the girls had freed him to go looking, and it was she who had made him presentable, trimming his hair and mending his suit and sewing on the buttons which, because it was to go courting her a stepmother, my grandfather felt shy of asking Winnie to sew on his shirts for him. All this was known to Hester; still she could not conceal her dislike of her neighbor.

"Now, son," said my grandfather, "be a good boy and mind Mrs. Vinson."

"Ned always minds me," said Mrs. Vinson, accenting the "me," as she handed him down from the wagon bed.

"That's more than he does me," said my grandfather. If she heard the remark Hester did not let on. But sensing that she had gone too far, Mrs. Vinson said, "Ned minds me better than any of my own." To which her Felix, peeping out from behind her skirt, grinned corroboratively.

"We'll bring you back a play-pretty from town, Ned," said Winnie. And with an uncertain glance up front, where her mother used to sit and where for a time she herself had sat as the little woman of the family, and where now her stepmother sat on the seat beside her father, "Won't we, Pa?"

"We'll see," said he. And he again told Ned to behave himself.

My grandfather looked at his watch. It was just six. You had to get an early start if you were to get into Clarksville and attend to everything you had to do there and get back in time to milk again at evening. He asked Mrs. Vinson if there was not something they could bring back for her. Thank you just the same, Mrs. Vinson said, or rather shouted, for the baby, little Florence Ordway, had begun to cry again: she had cut her first tooth only the day before; thank you just the same, they would be going in themselves next week. In those days farm folks like the Ordways and the Vinsons went into town just once a month.

Then my grandfather flicked the reins and snicked to the team and the wagon lumbered off. The girls bounced along on the tailgate, waving back every now and again to their little brother. You could see a long way there on the edge of the prairie and it was a quarter of an hour before you went over the first hill. Ordinarily Mrs. Vinson turned back into the house after a short while, but that morning she stayed until the wagon was going over the rise and held Ned up to wave a last goodbye. The girls waved and he waved. And then at the last minute, just as the wagon was dipping down out of sight, Ned struggled out of Mrs. Vinson's arms and started running after them. According to Winnie and Bea, at any rate. Seated backwards at the tailgate of the wagon, they were the last to see him, and as the legend

grew in later years, so they always maintained in telling of
that morning, the seventh of May 1898.

A breech delivery, the doctor had called it in explaining
the failure; the words often echoed in Sam Ordway's mind
when looking at his motherless son. He had come hind-
foremost into the world and he seemed framed, at three
seemed almost resigned, determined to go through it that
way. An awkward child, always underfoot, by turns stubborn and sniveling, with round reproachful eyes and a lower
lip triggered permanently for a pout. He was a constant
reminder of his mother's death, of obligation to the neighbors, and now he was a source of tension, unspoken but
unremitting, between his father and his stepmother. But
whenever my grandfather found himself losing patience
with him he had only to remember that if he had lost his
wife through his coming, Ned had lost his mother, and that
he had gotten himself a new wife.

The one he had gotten was a good one, though she had her
faults of course, like everybody else. Sam Ordway felt lucky
to have found any woman who would have him, a poor
widower with three small children and no counter-attrac-
tions. To say, though, merely that he might have done
worse was to do Hester an injustice, and certainly it came
nowhere near expressing my grandfather's appreciation of
her. A better wife could not be found, nor, on this side of the
angels, a better stepmother. She took excellent care of her
predecessor's children and she did it ungrudgingly. If
only little Florence had been a boy! Then perhaps she would
have been a little less resentful of Ned.

She was a jealous woman by nature, a discovery which
at first had rather flattered him, yet for which he pitied her
at the same time. It was a trait of which he himself was
blessedly free, could scarcely comprehend, and he pitied anyone who suffered from it. Alas, though he did everything in
his power to spare her, Hester's situation was ready-made

to exasperate a jealous woman, coming as she had into a house still redolent with the memory of a rival who was all the more formidable through having escaped beyond rivalry, beyond comparison.

He himself did not compare the two of them. One was one, the other the other, and they were as different as two women picked by the same man could be. Aggie, for instance, had been a placid and easygoing sort of person, seldom carried away and just as seldom downhearted, quiet and even-tempered in her affections as she was in all things. Hester on the other hand was as changeable as the weather, and required constant encouragement and reassurance. He could tell that his neighbors the Vinsons thought he was fonder of Hester than he had ever been of Aggie, and seemed to reproach him for it. He was not; he was fond of them in different ways and in their turns. And Aggie had not needed the open demonstrations of his affection that Hester had to have.

It had been hard on Hester, coming into a house already made. A woman liked to set up housekeeping with little things of her own choosing instead of ironing curtains made by the dead hand of the previous mistress of the house, finding on the backs of shelves months after taking possession scraps and tatters of things saved by the other, sleeping in another woman's bed beneath quilts patched from another woman's discarded garments, the very bed in which that woman had died giving birth to your husband's child, above all raising the other one's children. In the case of Ned she was not to be blamed for resenting a child of whom she had had everything but the joy. Without having conceived him, borne him, nursed him, named him, before her own marriage was yet consummated, stopping by on the way home from church, in the graveyard of which her husband's first wife lay beneath a still grassless mound, she had put her bridal wreath under the wagon seat and taken him, just weaned, squawling, from Mrs. Vinson's arms, home to the house waiting pre-equipped by her predecessor, whose dresses, waiting now to be made down for the children, still hung in the closet, still diffusive of her personal scent. The girls had ducked their heads and said hello, and climbed up on the tailgate, where they sat bouncing, clutching hands.

For Winnie it had been a demotion, going back to the tailgate of the wagon. She had sat, a diminutive replica of her mother, in her mother's place on the spring seat alongside her father, until that day. Already an accomplished needlewoman, expert at the churn, she had been quick around the house as she was quick at school, following like a duckling at her mother's heels, so that she knew without ever being taught how to mix biscuits, how to bake cornbread, how to pluck and singe and draw a chicken. At hog-killing time in the fall she stuffed sausages and rendered lard, helped make the harsh brown sudsless lye soap with which later, every Monday morning before she started school, standing on a bench over a tub alongside her mother sousing the heavy overalls and the bedsheets, she had scrubbed them up and down against the washboard until her knuckles were skinned and red, breaking off only to prevent her little sister, whose self-appointed guardian she was, from falling into the washpot where the clothes bubbled and boiled over a fire for which she herself had collected the kindling and toted the wood. Hardly big enough to lift a flatiron, she knew to lift one and lick her finger and touch the iron and listen with her ear cocked to the hiss of her spittle and judge the heat accurately before touching it to cloth. And so on the day following the funeral she had gotten up in the dark of the morning and dressed herself, and instead of going to school had started a fire in the range and mixed a pan of biscuits, set coffee to percolate, sliced bacon and put it on to fry in the skillet, and when the meat was done, standing on a chair above the stovelids, had dusted flour into the sputtering grease and added milk and stirred it into white gravy and had it all on the table and her little sister washed and combed and the beds made when her father came in from the barn. When the Vinsons rode over later to get the two girls and take them away she had met them at the door in her apron, her sleeves rolled above her knobby elbows and her hands and forearms clotted with dough, a smell of boiling greens and pork wafting out from the house behind her, and sent them home again. "Pa needs somebody to look out for him," she said. "Ma wouldn't want me to leave him alone." Thereafter she would get her little sister ready for school, to which she was admitted ahead of time out of consideration for Mr. Ordway's difficulties, even more for Winnie's, and walk her the two miles there because she was afraid of the Vinsons' dog and walk back home and take her basket and go down to the garden and pick the vegetables that her mother had planted, would return and shell the peas and peel the potatoes and the onions, then go to the smokehouse and choose meat and make her father's dinner and set it to cook and sweep the house and dust, and in the afternoon go fetch Bea, and in the evening help her with her lessons. "What about your own schooling, Winnie?" the teacher, Miss Duncan, asked her once when she came to meet her sister. "I'll catch up, Miss Duncan," she replied. "Soon as Pa has found us a stepmother." In town in the store she would gravely advise her father what things she was low on, and would frown when the grocer grinned fatuously at her over the countertop. But she would accept his gift of candy, and coming home seated beside her father in her mother's place on the seat, holding on to her little sister, would studiously suck lemon drops as if she had but this short while to be a child in before getting home to her chores again. Then it was she and her father who did the week's wash together, while she broke off now and again to shoo Bea away from that washpot, which exerted a fatal fascination upon the child, and it was she who instructed him, pursing her lips in repressed impatience for his clumsiness as they scrubbed side by side at the tubs or wrung out a sheet together, and he would sometimes catch in those wise, already worn, women's eyes of hers a look of pity for him, a man reduced to woman's work.

Fall came at last, freeing him, or rather forcing him to go in search of a wife.

Going courting again, spending all that time just getting into town and back, idling on the corners of the square inspecting the girls who passed in review there on Saturday afternoon, going to dances and cutting a figure, to grave-yard workings and over the still-unflowered mound beneath which his wife lay, striking up a courtship with another woman, going to call on her under the watchful eyes of her father and her brothers, provided he was able to find one who encouraged him that far, and squiring her to church suppers and play-parties. Sam Ordway had thought he was done with all that, at thirty-three felt foolish even to think of himself in the role, had no heart for starting life all over again. He was used to one woman's ways, she to his; now he would have to learn a new woman, train her to his ways. And he was afraid of making a mistake in his choice, especially as he had so little time in which to make it.

He would have preferred a young widow woman. Such a one, herself tried by loss, would better understand and appreciate his predicament, his frame of mind. The first bloom rubbed off her own passion, she would not be disappointed to find his gone from him. Trained already in being a wife, she would fit right off, broken in, comfortable, not pinch and cramp like a new pair of shoes. If she had a child, or better still two, of her own, that would be all right, that would be all the better. The risk that she would favor her own, he was willing to run, to try and cope with; he would feel less beholden to her for taking on the care of his three.

Hester Duncan was not a widow. In fact she was, at twenty-eight, an old maid. She was a plain woman, though no plainer than many a one who had found herself a husband. Sam Ordway was no beauty himself, and did not expect to find one, did not want one, who might think she was wasted out here in the country. Hester Duncan was country-born and -raised, and not afraid of dirtying her hands, though at the time he first met her they were employed in nicer work. And though she was an old maid, being a schoolteacher she understood and liked children. She had come to teach the Mabry school just that year. She had taught before, in Clarksville, but when her old mother was struck helpless she had given it up and come home to take care of her. Her father was long dead and the farm run down and triple-tied in mortgages, and when during the previous spring her mother died, she had sold what little equity remained to her in the old place and taken the vacant job at Mabry's one-room six-grade schoolhouse.

That was Winnie's first year in school. She liked it and she liked her teacher. She would set off in the morning with her books and the lard pail containing her lunch, which she as well as her teacher called her dinner, looking in her bonnet and ankle-length dress like a spry little old woman setting off down the road on a visit. Unlike other girls, she never ran or skipped but walked with a dignified matronly tread. On the papers that she brought home from school was written in a fine, careful hand, "Good." She was quick and studious, and after Christmas, just before the mid-term vacation, Miss Duncan had come over one afternoon to visit Mrs. Ordway and compliment her on her clever child and to offer, if closer inspection of the family and its circumstances seemed to warrant, a suggestion about her future. In those days, at the first sign of intelligence in a little girl people began asking her if she meant to be a schoolteacher when she grew up. The age of eight was not thought any too young to begin preparing for such a career, as it was often entered upon at the age of fifteen or sixteen. Moreover, it was a solemn step, rather like pledging a daughter to take nun's vows, for state law forbade teachers to marry.

Most promising girls were taken out of school after just two or three years as little sisters and brothers began to multiply. Three years' schooling was considered by many farm families quite enough. In many cases it was three years more than either parent had had. It was to judge if this was likely, and if possible to prevent it in the case of bright little Winifred Ordway, that her teacher came over that afternoon to praise her.

It was not the first time that Sam Ordway had ever seen Miss Duncan. She rented a room and took her board with the people who owned and ran the Mabry store. Saturday, unless something urgent came up, was the only day of the week when the Ordways ever went to Mabry, or past it on their way into Clarksville, and school was out then, so during the past months they had sometimes seen the new teacher cleaning out the schoolhouse, which was part of her duties, but which she looked the tidy, conscientious sort to have done whether it had been stipulated or not, or hanging out her skimpy virgin's wash on the line (though never her undergarments; these she apparently hung inside the house to dry, out of sight of the farmers who on Saturday gathered to pitch washers alongside the store across the road. And every third Sunday they had seen her regularly at church, where once already she had passed them a compliment on their Winnie.

It was wintertime and my grandfather not in the field but at home, and after giving the women a while to talk between themselves, he had come in from the tool shed. It had been a pleasant visit. It was flattering to hear one's child called clever, and he had vowed to see that Winnie went as far in school as she wished to go. The child who was to be Ned was already beginning to show on Aggie. My grandfather had pitied Miss Duncan for having to interest herself in other women's children instead of having a child of her own. The next time he saw her Aggie was dead and in her grave.

It was in the churchyard that they met, or rather in the field below the churchyard, after services every third Sunday. Below the burial ground lay a hollow where wildflowers flourished in almost macabre profusion, phlox and swamp pinks, verbena, Indian blankets, which went largely unpicked, most survivors preferring to bring garden flowers from home to decorate the graves of their kin. This year for the first time around the Ordway house there were no flowerbeds, and so it was down to the hollow that my grandfather and the girls would go after church to pick a bouquet for Agatha's grave. There they found Miss Duncan, who also had no flower garden of her own, picking a bouquet for the grave of her mother. She had been devoted to her mother and missed her terribly. The note of loneliness which sounded in her voice struck in Sam Ordway, like the second tine of a tuning fork, a sympathetic vibration.

This was during the summer and into the fall, before he had undertaken his quest for a wife, while he was still just thinking about it, or rather putting off thinking about it, dreading it.

It was the girls who brought them together. Winnie had been the teacher's pet. "Are you picking flowers for your mother's grave?" she asked. "So are we." In an impulse of motherliness Miss Duncan had hugged the two orphans to her. At the appearance of their father she grew flustered. However, she quickly regained her composure.

Once started, Sam found it easy to talk to her. It was not like talking to a woman. She had resigned herself to life as an old maid schoolteacher and expected to pass unnoticed by men. Thus she was unguarded and without airs and coquetry and he could talk to her simply as to another person. Meeting there on a common errand of sorrow, they were unembarrassed by their encounters. Shortly Sam Ordway began to visit his wife's grave also on Sundays when there were no services. Miss Duncan too came regularly. Once she was sick and did not appear. That day he picked an extra bouquet and put it on her mother's grave. The following Sunday she found it there and met them at the gate and warmly thanked the girls for it. On a Sunday in September he did not appear in the hollow. Winnie and Bea were there and they told Miss Duncan that their father was busy putting up a tombstone on their mother's grave. He had picked it up in town the day before and brought it home in the wagon. That morning he had come in overalls and with pick and shovel, and instead of going to services had planted the stone. When she and the girls came up from below he had it finished. The girls invited her to come and look. She said it was a beautiful stone. She was still standing over her mother's grave when he gathered up his tools and left. Her loneliness struck him as never before, and it occurred to him to wonder who would put up a stone for her when her time came, and to wonder if she was thinking the same.

He learned that she had a married sister living in Clarksville. She saw her seldom because it was hard to get in. He offered to take her when he went in once a month. She colored. It was with pleasure but he took it for embarrassment and wondered why. He realized she was thinking that she was a single woman and he a single man. He had not yet grown accustomed to thinking of himself as a single man, and he had not yet thought of her as a woman at all.

She was, and no sooner had he realized it than she began to seem the ideal woman for him. Her easy availability figured in his interest. She would save him the search he dreaded even to begin. He liked the fact that with her the field was clear, that he would not have to compete with other men for her attention. Her affection for children was evident. No doubt one of her own was what she longed for, perhaps at her age with not much remaining hope, but she liked them all, and had a special fondness already for one of his. The risks and disadvantages of marrying a widow became apparent to him. The time in which he had to find one was short, and he might get one who later would be forever throwing her first husband in his face. If she had children of her own she would need to be a saint not to be partial to them. He was not eager to raise another man's children.

Sam Ordway had not had much schooling himself, and did not greatly miss it; he appreciated it in a woman, though, and it flattered his self-esteem to think of having an educated wife. The idea strongly appealed to him of being able to give Aggie's girls, as well as those who were sure to come later (with boys of course this mattered less), not only an educated mother but one experienced in teaching children.

He believed he would stand a chance with her. He was no prize catch, but an old maid could not be too choosy. Unless (this struck him now for the first time, and whetted his desire to have her), unless she was an old maid out of choice, unless no man could ever hope to win her.

Though plain in a schoolmarmish way Miss Hester was not at all sour or severe, certainly not outside her classroom. On the contrary, she could be spirited and lively, and he had found she was not nearly so bossy and not nearly so infallible as he had supposed all schoolteachers to be, a discovery which it pleased him to make, as before he too had stood somewhat in awe of her. When it got so they could trust one another's devotion to his dead then they could afford to forget them sometimes, and he found that she enjoyed a quiet laugh and was capable of making him laugh. He found her natural and unaffected. He began to like her pleasant, square, unadorned face. On the basis of her plainness he made the common, and commonly erroneous, assumption that she was free of vanity. He admired her for this.

In his proposal he was forthright and frank. He told her precisely what his assets were, listing the house, his acreage, his stock, his age, the state of his health: the list of credits was not long. Indeed, whether they—house, land, and stock —belonged on the credit or the debit side of the ledger was open to question. Debits certainly were three small step-children to have to take on, and he dwelt at length on that, though pointing out that Winnie at least was remarkably self-reliant. The boy as yet was neither fish nor fowl, but the girls were good girls. He said it who shouldn't; but the credit was none of his, it was his wife's—Aggie's—Agatha's.

He knew he ought to have taken longer about this than he had. But he knew too that she was a sensible woman. She would appreciate the fact that he could not wait. He did not know that no woman likes to be told that she is sensible. Especially one who has heard it all her life.

It was coming home from Clarksville in the wagon one Saturday afternoon that he proposed to her. Even as he spoke he was conscious of the thawing fields alongside, already summoning him. The first robins were back, were busy scavenging for straw to build their nests. The sides of the road were bearded now with the first shoots of grass and patches of yellow-green fog hovering above creek banks showed where the willows had leafed out. The seed for his crops was already laid in. In the wagon bed rode a bright new plowshare.

He said he believed he could say he was as good a worker as the next man, a good provider, and that while he had his faults in plenty, at least he did not drink nor gamble and—

He stopped, turned, and found her crying, silently, bitterly, and through her tears regarding him with a look which he could not fathom. She could not tell him what was wrong. No, he had not offended her. She answered yes, and he put down her tears to joy. It never once occurred to him that what he had done was not propose to her but offer her a job, trying honestly not to conceal its disadvantages but still offering her a job, and not nearly as good a one as she already had, that he had never once said he loved her nor given her a chance to say that she loved him, no chance even to preserve her self-respect, only to say yes, she would be his wife, while saying to herself, yes, she would be any man's wife who asked her rather than go on as she was, lonely, barren, unwanted—an old maid.

Sam Ordway expected his new wife to realize that he was so hard-pressed for time that he would get around to loving her later, after he had gotten around to grieving for Aggie and gotten that out of the way. He did not phrase it to himself this way, but if he had it would certainly not have seemed unreasonable to him. Hester should realize that a part of his grieving for Aggie would have to be done, so to speak, on her time. That he had not been able to do it, farming, looking after two young children and worrying over a third, courting her.

But she could not forever walk on tiptoe, speak in whispers, as though in a shrine or a tomb. She expected him sometimes to entertain her, to be demonstrative and affectionate, sometimes gay, forward-looking, full of plans for their life together, a man whose life lay in the future, not buried in the past. She had a sense of her life's beginning, a late flowering that like a retarded spring was all the more efflorescent for having been kept back. She was determined to think of her husband as hers, resented the notion of his ever having been anyone else's, refused to share him with a memory, a ghost. She did not want a mere provider, a partner, who in fairness for his own lack of ardor excused her from showing any. He had awakened her love, and love was what she wanted in return.

She began to resent the children. Between her and Winnie things did not work out as expected. The forwardness which she had shown when she was Miss Duncan's pet pupil disappeared when Winnie became her stepdaughter. Sam grieved to see this, and believed that Winnie disapproved of the match. Winnie neither approved nor disapproved. It was simply that she continued to treat Hester with the respect and awe appropriate to a teacher, and which towards a mother seemed like coldness. For a time she even continued,

despite herself actually, but seemingly with intention of
keeping her at a distance, to call her Miss Duncan. The
child's precocity with the housework caused friction. In her
well-meant efforts to help Hester find her way about the new
house in her new role, she touched unwittingly upon a raw
spot: the former old maid brought with her into marriage
a sensitivity in the presence of any other female of whatever
age, and to her even little Winnie was not too young to
patronize her for her supposed lack of womanly skills. To
make matters worse, whenever Winnie discerned that she
had offended her by offering to help with the cooking and
the housework or telling her where something was to be
found or how she made a thing, and sought to apologize by
effacing herself, she did so by saying that she only knew
because that was how her mother had always done it.

Then there was Bea. Bea had never been quick, but as a
pupil at Mabry school she had suffered even more by comparison with a brighter older sister. This too carried over
into the new arrangement. The stepmother could not cease
overnight to be the schoolmistress, and the schoolmistress
had been one known for her impatience with slow pupils.

But none of these matters was grave, and all would in
time come to be smoothed out. It was little Ned who from
the start was the thorn in Hester's side. Though the two
events, Agatha's death and Ned's birth, were one, and neither could be thought of without the other, Sam Ordway
certainly did not blame the boy for his mother's death. It
was Hester to whom he was a living reminder of his mother's martyrdom.

She ached for a child of her own. It was as if she felt
challenged to emulate the dead Agatha, to pass through the
same trial, ached for the pain itself as for a purifying flame
to test and demonstrate her love, believing it would stimulate
her husband's love for her, that love which she would be
obliged to share with Aggie's ghost until she had done what
Aggie had done for him.

It was not just a child she longed for, not just the pain and the proof, but for a son, a namesake to give him. Then, she believed, she would come to love Ned as well. While pregnant she was noticeably more affectionate towards the boy. When hers turned out a girl so keen was her disappointment that little Florence counted in her mind almost as a fourth stepchild.

You could see a long way if, like Winnie and Bea facing backwards at the tailgate of the wagon, you were looking westward. But facing forward, as the little nucleus of the second Ordway family faced, your view was more restricted. Ahead there the land rose and broke in waves like the off-shore lapping of the sea. In the shallow valleys the soil was black, and when turned up in moist furrows by the plow, shone with a waxy iridescence like tar. Here grew cotton which when ripe blanketed the ground like a heavy fall of snow. Sloping upwards the soil changed colors, shading from black to brown to a golden red the color of bread crust. On the hillsides grew corn. A pale green fuzz upon the land now in May, it would stand taller than a tall man in August, with ears like clubs and long, broad leaves like banners.

And yet, facing forward as you went east into Clarksville, you had the odd sensation that you were going backwards. Perhaps it was just that you were meeting the sun as it went its journey in the opposite direction, giving you the sense that you were traveling counter to the course of time. Or was it a lingering sense that time and the course of history lay west, in that open space at your back towards which all the morning shadows pointed, a sense inherited from your forebears—not very remote from you in 1898—and that eastward, in the direction from which they had trekked, lay your family's past, yours and everybody else's you knew, that place of the past, the South? Whatever the cause, hearing the bells of the Clarksville courthouse clock you felt that they tolled a time already reckoned, already lived and buried, as the clock itself, though the tower rose eight stories high, lay buried in the folds of the hills.

The clock caroled every quarter hour and the notes came at you over the undulant hills like a series of balls sent rolling your way, fading as they struggled up the intervening inclines, then rushing at you two or three together as they rolled down the slopes. In a wagon you were making good time if, after you first heard them, the bells rang just twice more before you topped the hill from which you could see the belfry with its gleaming brass weathervane in the shape of a feathered arrow. By the time they tolled again you could see the pointed yellow tower rising out of the trees like an ear of corn half shucked, and the great white western face of the clock; and if just then the bells should strike again you could see the birds of the belfry from there. For the swallows that made their nests and roosted there had never grown accustomed to the noise that time makes, and every quarter hour with the throbbing of the bells they scattered out like the notes made visible on the air. As the sound died away they swooped back in.

On coming into town farm families like the Ordways drove straight to Market Square, two blocks northwest of the public square. There the farmer unhitched his team and reversed them towards the wagon bed, and if he did any truck gardening he arranged his goods and took up a stance alongside to await the coming of the Negro cooks and the housewives of the town. My grandfather was strictly a cotton and corn grower. His life was spent among hard things, things of iron, hickory, of thick unbending hide. Yet hard as they were, they were never hard enough, but were always breaking, wearing out. And so his one morning a month in town was spent in the hardware store and the blacksmith shop. Like every farmer of his time, he had a little home forge, and could shoe a horse in an emergency. But when a clevis snapped, or a whippletree, or when a colter hit a rock, then it was a job for the blacksmith. He liked going there.

He liked to watch the iron redden in the forge, enjoyed the explosive *whoosh* and the billow of steam when the burning metal was plunged into the cold tempering bath. He liked also to linger in the hardware store, making his purchases of harness, rope, nails; loved especially to buy himself a new hand tool, such as a new handsaw or a new axe, handling them all though in the end always buying a Diston saw, a Plumb axe, a Stanley plane; for his loyalty to certain brand names was religious, and went to the point of giving him an almost religious intolerance of men who swore by other makes.

Around ten o'clock he rejoined the family back at the wagon for dinner, for they ate even earlier than usual, having breakfasted earlier that day. My grandmother would have spent her morning shopping, without having bought anything. She knew just what she wanted, and spent the morning in the stores comparing prices. Then in the afternoon, having nursed the baby, she would go back to the best place for each item on her mental list, and giving her order to the clerk in a tone which discouraged any salestalk, would complete her purchases in half an hour. They ate sitting in the wagon bed: cold fried ham, biscuits, fried fruit pies.

After his dinner my grandfather liked, in wintertime, to stroll over to the courthouse and up to the trial room and listen for a while to whatever case was on the docket. In the spring now, with the court calendar recessed, he would saunter downtown, and after a turn or two around the square, join one of the groups of men on the corners, and taking out his billet of cedar, would settle down to an afternoon of whittling and talk. There the girls would find him and they were given a nickel and set free, and spent the next three or four hours going round and around the square working themselves into a frenzy of indecision over how to spend their money. Bea was to mind Winnie when they were alone, and did, according her sister an authority which, now that she was no longer the woman of the family, and now that Bea was older, she knew better than to try to assume at home, or even outside the city limits. On that particular Saturday my grandfather closed his knife at half past three by the courthouse clock and stood up and brushed the shavings off his lap and set off towards the blacksmith shop to call for the part he had left. Passing the variety store he remembered his promise to bring Ned something from town. The gift he chose, perhaps reminded of the medley of songs that had come drifting out of the jailhouse as he sat eating his dinner, was a little French harp.

Back at the wagon the team was hitched and the family drove to the grocery store, around to the loading platform on the side, where Negroes lounged, eating cheese and crackers and sardines and bananas. Haines's, with whom the Ordways had always traded, was dark as a root cellar, and even more redolent. The first thing to hit you on entering was a tingling sour smell which was not the smell of pickles but of the pickled oak of their barrel. Then coffee and the strong yellow smell of soap in unwrapped bars laid up like masonry and the slightly rancid smell, like a new copper penny, of the leathery bacon flitches hanging from the rafters, between which hung spiraling flypapers encrusted with dead and struggling flies. Beneath the long counters on each side ran rows of bins with sloping hinged glass covers containing cookies and dried fruits. On the floor, squat barrels of salt cod like flakes of slate; fat sacks with tops rolled back of beans and rice. On the counters sliced hams the color of cedar, the yellow bone like a knot in the wood. The Ordways bought flour and cornmeal in hundred-pound barrels, sugar in fifty-pound sacks, coffee in the bean, and such things that Hester could not make for herself as bluing, baking powder. While their parents gave their order the Ordway girls would bashfully peek into every bin, dragging their feet in the sawdust sprinkled on the floor.

When the wagon was loaded and while my grandfather settled his bill (he had refused for years Mr. Haines's offer of credit), the sordid side of the business which was left to the wife of the firm, Mr. Haines gave the girls their treat. They were no longer invited as they once had been to name their choice. This they had never been able to do, but were overcome with such a paroxysm of shyness that Mr. Haines used to just fill up a bag with assorted candies and force it on them. Then one day the truth came blurting out. They really did not want candy, being by that hour of the day already glutted, sometimes a little sick, on their nickel's worth. It came out that each had long suffered a suppressed passion, Winnie for dried apricots, while Bea burned secretly, shamefully for cheese. So now each got what she craved; and going home they sat on the tailgate dangling their legs, each extolling her treat and wondering loudly how the other could *stand* hers, and nibbling small so as to make it last all the way home.

The Ordways were a bit late coming back that day and by the time they turned down the road home it was past milking time. The cows would long since have trundled to the barn, spraddle-legged and rolling with each pendulous sway of their swollen bags. As milking time neared their teats stiffened and rose outward like a bunch of carrots drawn together by the tops, and oozed and dripped, and by now a puddle would be standing under each, the color of porcelain, bluey-white. But though my grandfather could see all this in his mind, still he did not whip up the team. You did not wind one animal for the sake of another.

They went up and over Latimer's Hill and the Vinson house came in sight. "Oh, Pa!" said Winnie from the back of the wagon, her voice bouncing, "I promised Ned we'd bring him something from town."

"Rather late for you to think of it now, ain't it, precious?" said my grandfather, while to himself he smiled.

Mrs. Vinson was not at the gate and for once her Felix was not out in the yard to run shouting to the house. The

Ordways drew up and sat waiting to be discovered, and my grandfather reached under the seat and drew out the striped paper sack filled with coconut bars, peanut patties, jaw-breakers, licorice sticks, and jellybeans which he always re-membered to bring the Vinson children, his way of thanking their mother for minding Ned, and which they were gen-erally at the gate waiting for. Now, however, no one ap-peared, and when the front door suddenly blew in and banged against the inner wall and echoed through the house, that brought no one out either. A bellow from the Vinson cows reminded my grandfather of his own waiting, and tying the reins to the brake handle, he leapt down from the wagon.

He went through the gate, which hung open, and around to the back of the house. No one was in sight. There was no sound.

"Hello!" he called. He waited a moment but no answer came. "Hello!" No answer. He opened the door, stuck his head in, and called, "Hello?" Just from the sound of his voice dying away through the rooms he could tell that the house was empty. He shut the door, stepped back a moment to ponder, and he heard a cow bawl.

Still carrying the sack of candy, he went out to the barn. There, unmilked, stood Will Vinson's three Jersey cows, as he had imagined his own cows waiting for him. Just fresh-ened for spring, they were heavy with milk. The knotty veins on their bags stood out like hemp ropes. Their hind hooves stood in pools into which a steady drip fell from their bursting teats. As soon as he stepped into the barn they let out a groan as if all three were having calves.

Something must have come up. My grandfather was slow in the extreme to suspect anything out of the common run, but being one himself, he knew that a farmer did not lightly go off and leave his evening chores undone. And he knew that like himself Will Vinson made just one regular trip a month into Clarksville. Something must have come up. One of the children, possibly his, hurt or suddenly taken sick? Why take along the whole family? An accident to Will Vinson, necessitating his wife's driving the wagon, which would mean taking along the children, as none of them was big enough to leave in charge of the rest? Yet why had he not met them in town or on the road?

The thing to be done now was to milk those cows. My grandfather went back to the wagon and told my grandmother what he had found; and since milking three cows was a matter of only half an hour, left her and the children there to wait. He went round to the kitchen for the milk pail. It was not on the drainboard where it should have been. He looked in the cupboards, trying to see nothing but a milk pail, for he had a horror of seeming to pry, and he looked outside to see if it was hanging on the wall. He looked in the closet and on the shelves. It occurred to him to try the springhouse. But out in the springhouse there was not only no milk pail, there was nothing at all—which seemed odd.

He could hear the cows bawling as he returned to the house and they reminded him again of his own cows. He thought of the water bucket. But though the gourd dipper hung in its place over the washstand, the bucket was gone; in the place where it was supposed to sit was a bleached circle, now quite dry. The cows bellowed louder and more insistently, and now mystified and vaguely uneasy, my grandfather spread his legs and pushed his hat forward and scratched the back of his head and wondered where else a man might think to keep his milk pail. But you could not hear yourself think for those cows. It sounded like a slaughterhouse out there.

Their noise was not like anything that my grandfather had ever heard come from cows before, and it drew him out to the barn without any pail. Inside he cast a look around in the faint hope that the pail might have been left there, and he took closer note of the udders of the cows. They were the size of washpots and, almost touching the floor, sat upon

their stiffened teats like washpots on their legs. He stooped
and touched the near one, and he jerked his hand back as
if he had burnt his fingers. He had expected to find it full
but not to find it so hot. Why, it was more like a huge running boil, throbbing with fever, than like a milk bag, and at
his touch the cow had flinched and let out a bawl that was
almost human. He stood up and in the silence heard the
steady drip of the milk into the puddles. . . . These cows had
not been milked this morning either.

Momentarily quieted by the man's presence, the cows now
let out a roar that sent my grandfather dashing out of the
barn and back to the kitchen to search again for the pail.
It was surely there. But it was not, and when he then began
searching frantically for a pot, a saucepan, anything that
would hold milk, he discovered that all such vessels as those
were missing too. Just then the front door banged against
the jamb again and, starting up, my grandfather wondered
if someone had taken advantage of the absence of the family
and burglarized the house. He dashed into the parlor, had
just time to see that everything appeared to be in order there,
when again the cows roared, and looking out towards the
barn he caught sight of the well.

He dashed back through the kitchen and out of doors and
across the yard to the well, and there he found the rope gone
and the bucket gone with it. He stared at the empty pulley.
And though the noise from the barn now sounded like three
love-crazed bulls instead of three milch cows, he did not
hear it. He peered down the shaft: his mind seemed to drop,
to plummet down, down, and to splash in the black shimmer
deep below. He seemed to have to draw it all the way back
up. . . . Had someone murdered all the Vinsons and murdered his Ned and were their bodies even now all lying at
the bottom of the well?

When the bawling of the cows broke in upon his mind
he was grateful for the distraction. But out in the barn he

found them all three now straining and heaving as if they were trying to throw up. Their tails stuck out rigid, their sides labored and fell as they wheezed and coughed. He gave them bran and meal but they were in too much distress to eat. He grabbed the stool and sat down under the nearest one. Her teats had ceased to drip, they were hot to the touch, thick and hard as ears of corn. Feeling hands upon her, she let out a grunt, a sort of grateful protest, then a querulous little groan like a child helpless and bewildered by pain.

My grandfather began milking, or rather trying to milk, for though he squeezed and tugged as never before, nothing came. The cow could not let down her milk and with each dry, unyielding tug she moaned with pain. Meanwhile the other two moaned with her and stamped and tossed their heads. At last in spurts and broken jets the milk came: viscous, clotted, and from one quarter streaked pink with blood. Then it flowed, hissing upon the straw, frothing as if at a boil, and watching it swirl with the brown stain of manure and run away into the waste, my grandfather felt like a criminal. It spewed upon his shoe tops and sprayed his trouser cuffs, welled up and foamed in puddles, and still it came, squirting with a kind of constant thud upon the sodden straw as he pumped rhythmically on. The manure trench ran brownish white as the milk, floating bits of straw and stover, drained out of the barn and into the lot outside. The cow's flank twitched against his forehead and her sides heaved and the great crooked milk vein under her belly twitched and jerked in orgasmic spasms. Her voice sank bit by bit to a hoarse sigh of pained and partial ease. The other two had commenced meanwhile a kind of tortured, ponderous dance. Rising on one hind hoof and then the other, they shifted their weight from side to side, their inner organs swishing audibly, their great distended bags swinging, the teats dragging in the puddles beneath them. They bawled only sporadically now; when they did it sounded as if they

had the croup. Sweating heavily, his face flushed from the
heat of the cow's flank, his hands and forearms knotted with
aching muscles, my grandfather could at last feel the pressure ease, could at last see the streams thin, dwindle. At last
they dribbled out. The cow could not stand on her feet to be
stripped. As soon as the milking was done she sank quivering upon the milk-soaked straw as if she had been deflated,
as if every drop of substance had been pumped out of her
body. Then my grandfather moved to the next in line, who
now seemed almost to bark, as, racking her back and straining like a cow unable to calve, she tried to bawl. Again he
drew the milk down in solid streams, until, hearing a noise
at his back and stopping like a thief caught stealing, he
turned to find Bea standing in the door.

"Whatever is keeping you, Pa?" she asked. "And whatever
is wrong with them cows!" She skipped, finding her feet wet,
warmly wet, for the barn floor was flooded white now,
steamy.

"Go back!" snapped my grandfather. "Get back to the
wagon. I'll be along directly."

But she must have seen. Must have seen the uncanny
sight of a man milking without any milk pail, for suddenly
shocked silent, she turned and crept away.

To his wife my grandfather said nothing about the missing buckets and kitchen utensils. That the cows had been
kept waiting past their time was all that he told her. They
went on home and he unhitched the team and fed them and
milked his own three cows, who by this time were in almost
as bad shape as Vinson's; and as he listened to the steady
fizz of the milk and watched the spume rise up the sides of
the pail, he puzzled over what he had found, or rather not
found, at the Vinson place. Every explanation that came to
his mind got just so far, and then tripped over those missing
vessels. Of one thing only was he sure: whatever it was, it
had happened shortly after they had left Ned there in the
early morning, before Will Vinson had even had time to

milk. Word had come of the sudden illness of some relative? Why take buckets? One of the children, or all of them, suddenly taken sick? Why take along all the kitchen utensils? And then he had it, and nodding to himself and pausing in his milking—so that the cow kicked—he said, "Yes! Now that'll hold water!" A fire. News had been brought of a fire and the Vinsons had dropped everything and dashed off to help fight it. Clever of them to have thought to take along all their pails, their pots and pans, anything that would carry a pint of water, something to cook a meal in for the family that had been burnt out. He felt much better. Not only relieved of worry but confirmed in his belief that there was always a simple commonsense explanation to everything if you just thought about it long enough. Not of course that he was glad to think that somebody had had a fire. He wondered where it was, wished he had been at home to volunteer. It must have been a big one to keep the Vinsons from early morn till night.

Well, this had been a day! he thought as he got into bed. But there was nothing strange in this world when you kept your head and looked calmly at things. And on that comforting thought, and looking forward to hearing all about it from Vinson when he went to get Ned in the morning, my grandfather bade my grandmother good night, sighed once, and fell asleep.

When the Ordways drew up at the Vinsons' gate on their way to church the next morning the place looked about as empty as it had the day before. No smoke rose from the chimney, and as he was tying the reins to the brake handle my grandfather heard the front door blow open and slam against the inner wall with a hollow boom. It occurred to him then that no dog had barked at their approach, nor had one last evening. The Vinsons had a dog to be sure, a big collie named Rex; and generally he came out to bark at you when you were still half a mile away, especially if his folks were gone from home. The Ordway girls sitting along the tailgate would draw their legs into the wagon just thinking of Rex as soon as they came over Latimer's Hill if it was a day when the Vinsons were known to be away from home. But Rex was not here now, nor had he been yesterday when they stopped.

My grandfather went round to the back door and called: "Hello! Anybody home?"

There was no answer, not a sound. He opened the door, and the first thing he saw was the sack of candy, alive with ants, on the table where he had forgotten it yesterday.

When he told my grandmother that they were still away, to his annoyance she gasped and turned pale. Why must women always jump to dire conclusions? "Something has come up," he said. It annoyed him that she, who had never shown enough concern for the boy, should now show too much. "Something has called them away and they have had to stay overnight. It'll all be explained."

"You'd think they might have left a note," said my grandmother.

"They didn't know they would be gone this long. Now you drive on to church with the children while I do the chores here. Stop and pick me up on your way back."

The cows were quiet this morning, but there was an angry snuffling of pigs from the distant pens and a squawking of hens. Last evening in his perplexity over the milking he had not even heard them. Determined not to milk onto the floor again, he found a bucket in the barn loft, a battered old thing full of rusty fence staples; but while anything from it would be unfit for human consumption, he was able to get to the pigpen before all the milk leaked out. The barn stank of sour milk.

When he was finished he went and sat on the front porch to wait for Hester. The door banged again and he got up and shut it once and for all. Coming back to resume his seat, he was struck from out of nowhere by an odd, and oddly disquieting, question. Who were the Vinsons' relatives? His or hers?

They never came to bring Ned home all Sunday afternoon. So, that evening, after his own chores were done, my grandfather went again over to their place. He was gone for nearly two hours—time enough to mean to my grandmother that he had again had to tend the Vinson stock. When he came in she broke down and cried, ran crying from the room. This time my grandfather was not annoyed. Not that he shared her uneasiness; but he was grateful, was touched that she should show so much concern, uncalled for though he believed it to be, over Aggie's boy.

At breakfast Monday morning they outdid one another in feigned lightheartedness, fluttering about and chirping like two canaries, while Winnie and Bea, making themselves small, followed them with wide, watchful eyes. Bea knocked a cup and saucer off the table and at the crash everyone exploded with held breath; yet, to her terror, she was not even scolded. My grandfather drew out his watch, and as though alluding to a brand-new topic, said, well, he wondered what Will Vinson would have to tell them when he came bringing Ned home?

In loyalty to his waning conviction he held out against going over to the Vinson place until that noon.

The house, even from a distance, looked emptier than ever. The chimney was dead, and although hereabouts, as early as May, a housewife's first thought in the morning was to pull down the window shades to keep out the heat, the panes of the Vinson house stared open like the glazed eyes of a carcass.

"They might have left a note," my grandfather muttered.

Possibly they had. In searching so singlemindedly for a milk pail the other evening he might have overlooked a note. He went into the kitchen. The hush of emptiness had begun to settle upon the house. A coating of dust lay upon the

surface of things. The disused range was beginning to stink
with the sour smell of damp wood ash. There again was that
sack of candy; from it in all directions on the tabletop, moving like molasses, slow trickles of small brown ants. He
flung it out of doors.

The kitchen contained no note. He stepped out to the hall.
Hearing something, he stopped. It was the sound of foot-
steps, of someone coming down the stairs. It stopped. He
took a step: it took one. Someone coming downstairs, slowly,
slowly, a few steps at a time, then stopping as he stopped,
listening. Then suddenly they were moving, running. He
dashed to the foot of the stairs—just in time to have a rubber ball bounce down the last few steps, land at his feet,
and going like the heart in his breast, bound across the hall
into the parlor.

Aimlessly he followed it, glanced about, was wandering
out again when he noticed something. Noticed something,
but what it was he could not grasp. Something was odd, something not quite as it should be, though, and he paused, and
then—it must have been a puff of wind outside—a long, low
sigh and the windowpanes trembled and the house gave a
shudder, and my grandfather froze, breathless, overcome by
a conviction that he was in a deserted house, that Will Vinson had run away, had fled something or somebody, had
done some awful thing, and had taken his boy along because
Ned had been a witness to the crime; or that he had been
threatened with some punishment, so swift, so terrible, that
he could not tarry long enough even to return his neighbor's
child left with him for the day.

My grandfather was not, as has been said, a suspicious-
minded man. But even the most mistrustful soul would have
laughed at his fears, as my grandfather laughed, when, a
moment later, the face of Will Vinson came up, like the full
moon, to dispel the darkness of his thoughts. To see Will
Vinson once was to know him, to know him was to trust him
with anything and to entrust him with nothing. He was

comprehended in the phrase "a good old country boy": hard-working, none too bright, softhearted, and, all in all, about as sinister as Santa Claus.

But though he did not realize it quite yet, the face of Will Vinson was precisely what my grandfather could not see when he looked about the room. What he could see, what had seemed odd before, was that on the wall above the mantel hung . . . well, nothing. A dark square of nothing. Of original, unfaded, pristine patterned wallpaper, from the upper corners of which ran two lines which met at a nail overhead. On each of the side walls a similar, smaller, dark, colorful, blank rectangle showed where other pictures had always hung, until very recently taken down. Pots and pails and pictures: on what sort of an outing would you take that queer assortment along? Then into those spots materialized the bland, bashful face of Will Vinson. In those spots had hung the family photographs, that large rectangle in the dust on the piano lid, there had always lain the family album. Gone. All gone. All the pictures by which the Vinsons might have been traced, identified.

So it was not until the afternoon of the tenth, the third day, that my grandfather came into Clarksville, to the sheriff's office—afoot, having left the wagon and his broken-winded team a mile outside of town, and in the wagon bed the frayed piece of harness strap with which he had punished Dolly and the mule for his own slow unsuspicion.

"Vinson?" said the sheriff. "Vinson? The name sounds vaguely familiar, but I don't seem able to call the man to mind."

"Well, he was a quiet sort, and never in any trouble before, I'm sure, so it's not surprising that you should have trouble remembering him. But try. Will Vinson. Local boy. Grew up somewhere in Red River County."

"What'd he look like?"

"Look like? Why, Will Vinson was . . ."

"I say—what did he look like?" said the sheriff.

My grandfather shook his head. He knew he was not a very observant man (each of his wives had found occasion to tell him he was not); he wondered, though, if anyone could have described such an ordinary old country boy as Will Vinson was. There was nothing to describe. He shook his head. "I couldn't tell you," he said, "to save my soul."

They came back out in the sheriff's buckboard. Together they went through the house. Upstairs they found the mattresses gone from the beds, found the drawers emptied of clothes, and everywhere throughout found evidence to indicate that the house had been abandoned—not ransacked, but picked over, with care, as though by plan. There no signs of struggle. They said nothing, either man, until the sheriff opined that it looked like they had left, all right.

To suspect Will Vinson of any recent crimes was not possible; there had not been any. Certainly none the consequences of which were fearful enough to make a man abscond. The sheriff said he would keep him informed. Meanwhile he would send somebody out from town with his wagon and team. My grandfather pulled the front door shut behind him. The closing of the door seemed to echo the sheriff's words through the empty house: it looked as if they had cleared out, taking his boy with them.

He ought to go home himself, he supposed. But in his perplexity he lingered. As yet his feeling was one of bewilderment so complete as almost to muffle any concern for his child. The Vinsons had been such good neighbors to him! And now he was supposed to wonder whether a murder would shortly come to light, or a robbery, or whether some husband would shortly publish his wife's infidelity, or, unable to lay violent hands on Will Vinson, do something worse to her. It was not in my grandfather to deny the ancient wisdom in the sheriff's words ("It's them quiet ones you can never tell about," he had said); and yet to try to connect Will Vinson with crime or scandal was enough to make him feel like a fool. And if flight, for whatever reason, was the man's imperative need, why had he hobbled himself not only with his own kindergarten, but added to it a neighbor's child not yet three years old?

My grandfather found himself drawn out to the barn. He was not at home in houses. Houses spoke of their mistresses, spoke to other women. He could tell as much from a man's barn as a woman could tell from five minutes alone in another's kitchen. But he could not tell from Will Vinson's barn what the man had kept hidden behind that face that seemed to hide nothing, because there was nothing to hide, to reveal nothing because there was nothing to reveal, what he had done or what been threatened with to make him snatch up a few belongings and disappear, run away, taking another man's child along with him. There was no indication of that kind of man. The tools, such as had been left behind, the plowshares and cultivators, were all sharp and sound, bright, rust-free, the handles all worn smooth by hard work. You could, as he said to himself, have eaten off the floor. The bins for the bran and the cottonseed meal were lined with zinc to keep out rats. The peanut hay in the loft was of a quality to compare with his own—and peanuts was a crop that my grandfather particularly prided himself on.

He went out into the fields. The cotton was ahead of his own, a downy green, and ahead of his own, too, in already having had a first hoeing. Will Vinson plowed a straight furrow, he would have to say that for him. But to say so was to use the very figure of speech which my grandfather used to say that a man led a straight life. What had happened? What had Will done to make him throw up everything, leave his home, his stock, and, with a crop in the ground, run off like a thief in the night, not even stopping to milk his just-freshened cows, compounding his crime by not even returning his neighbor's child left with him for the day? My grandfather turned to leave. All this had taught him nothing. And he found it hard to hate a man, any man, while standing amidst his young cotton.

During the following week my grandfather went over to the Vinson place every morning and evening as soon as his own chores were done and milked Vinson's three cows, slopped his hogs, fed his chickens, and collected his eggs. At first he brought over pails and jugs from home and put the milk in the springhouse, put the eggs in the kitchen. Soon the milk began to sour and had to be fed to the chickens, the eggs commenced to turn, there were no table scraps for the hogs, and it being spring and the corncrib getting low, my grandfather did not know what else to do but take all the animals over to his place.

Meanwhile he went into town every other day, neglecting his crops to do so, and called at the sheriff's office. No crime rose to ripple the surface of life in Clarksville, or Annona or Avery or Detroit. A report came in after about a week that a family answering more or less to the description of the Vinsons had been seen passing through Bagwell on the day of their flight; but Bagwell was only ten miles away, and so that, if reliable, was hardly a fresh clue.

It was a trying time, and people were all very kind, very considerate. A little too considerate—depressingly so. They said little, but their avoidance of the topic seemed ominous. Their looks were heavy with sympathy, and had the effect of suggesting that the child was lost forevermore, dead. All were, perhaps, conscious of a certain delicacy in my grandmother's position; perhaps that was why they hung back. As for her, she could not have taken it more to heart had it been her own child. That too was, however, taking it harder than my grandfather cared to believe was called for.

That spring he worked both his place and Vinson's. Where before he had always gotten up at four thirty, so as to milk the cows and do the chores, have his breakfast and be in the field by half past five, now he was up an hour earlier, milked his own and Vinson's three by lantern light, and was in the field by five, out till after dark. Why he did it he himself hardly knew. Somebody had to do it. Perhaps, though he would have considered this sentimental and would not have owned to it, it kept alive a hope that Will Vinson would come back. Mainly, however, he did it simply because he could not stand by and see a crop, any man's crop, rot in the ground. He knew too well what labor had gone into putting it there.

Milking six cows, he now went into Clarksville every Saturday with butter and cream to sell. The family went with him, though they could not enjoy themselves in town, and spent the time at the wagon in Market Square. Past the Vinson place they would drive in silence, while each stole sidelong glances at the house. Already in that burgeoning heat weeds overran the yard, and here and there among the burdocks and thistles a poppy or a coxcomb or some other of Mrs. Vinson's perennials had shamelessly reared its gaudy head. As the wagon drew near the gate the one scraggy hen who had eluded all my grandfather's and the girls' efforts to capture her on the morning they came to take the chickens away, and whose eggs, for a time afterwards, he would find dropped about the yard, sloshing rottenly when shaken, would fly up out of the weeds with a squawk like murder, the only sound ever heard now about the deserted house. For a while afterwards, out of their habit of stopping to leave the boy, the team would slow down there, and my grandfather's voice was husky as he growled, "Hum up."

They drove straight to Market Square and parked the wagon, and my grandfather crossed over to the jailhouse, where on the first floor the sheriff had his office. The news was always the same. There was that report, of which the sheriff seemed never to tire, that a family almost certain to have been them had been seen passing through Bagwell. However, their description had been circulated, the Texas Rangers brought in on the case, the U.S. marshals alerted, and so it was only a matter of time, said the sheriff, before something broke.

But cotton-chopping time came and went, the cotton flowered, the bolls appeared, swelled in the heat and burst white like popcorn, and it was cotton-picking time, and the news remained the same. The only difference was that now a deputy told it, my grandfather's visits being punctually on the last stroke of eight from the courthouse clock, so regular that the sheriff could quite confidently plan his absences from the office. Which, though it confirmed the lines around the corners of his mouth, did not greatly surprise my grandfather. He was a country man, and had the country man's contempt for the law.

In Texas back in 1898 people felt differently about children from the way people feel today. They loved their children, but their love had to be spread over a larger number than is usual nowadays. And they often lost them. They were resigned to this, and they buried them, and dried their tears, and had others, and forgot them. They swore they never would, and their hearts were broken and sore; but there was just not much time, while having and rearing eight or nine others, to miss the missing one. The case of Ned was a harder one than most. It was harder to resign yourself to the loss of a child who was not known to be dead but was presumed alive, somewhere, growing up among strangers, ignorant of his kin. Nevertheless, there was cotton to be hoed and picked, cows to be milked, corn to be husked; and when my grandmother told him that another child was on its way, my grandfather felt that it was being sent to take the place of little Ned.

That year, to pick his own and Vinson's cotton, my grandfather had to hire extra hands. One day in early September he was picking a row alongside a Negro woman of indeterminate age named Belle, whom he had hired for the past three or four seasons. Belle was a good picker, could keep up with him. On the tail of her sack, with its hundred-odd

pounds of cotton, rode a child of about ten pounds—
most of *that* pot belly—as waxy black as the trail of soil
which followed the cottonsack as it scraped along, and which,
two or three feet back, dried gray in the broiling sun. Like
a new-shorn lamb, the baby was bare except for a fore-knot
of wool on his crown. The two picked without straightening,
to the sound of their two sacks scraping along. When they
stopped they could hear, as the pickers in the adjacent rows
moved on, the steady faint fibrous squeak of the cotton
being plucked from the bolls, while the sweat dripped
unattended down their chins and noses. They came to the
end of the row, where my grandfather straightened his back
and wiped his face and puffed, and Belle, taking her cue
from him, straightened, wiped her oily face, turned to her
child and cried: "Boosker! Stop eatin that cotton, boy! You
want to ketch the cholera mawbus?"

Sure enough, Boosker was plugging himself with cotton,
looked like a stoppered flask of something dark.

"I don't believe you've been feeding Boosker right, Belle,"
said my grandfather. "He don't look to me like he's done
much growing since this time last year."

Belle made no reply for a moment. Then, "Mista Awdway," she said, in a tone chosen, he realized a moment later,
to spare him embarrassment as much as to spare herself
pain, "you thinkin of my last year's baby, Toodler. This here
is my this year's baby, Boosker. Toodler took the hwoopin
cawf over the winter, po little soul, and wasn't nothin nobody could do to save him."

"Forgive me, Belle," said my grandfather. "I didn't know.
Thoug̣ I ought to have taken more notice."

"Mista Awdway," said Belle softly, "you got trouble enough
of yo own on yo mind."

They were both silent for a moment, then Belle hitched
up her sack, giving Boosker a bob like a hiccup, sighed, and
said, "You don't appreciate em till they taken f'om you, an
then it's too late." Her grief had passed, like the little mo-

mentary cloud no bigger than a boll of cotton just then passing over the sun, and she was merely mouthing a phrase. But it struck home to my grandfather.

The following day was a Sunday, and he awoke with the consciousness of a duty long neglected. He did the chores and hitched the team, ate his breakfast, stropped his razor with such vigor it sounded as if he were whipping a horse out in the kitchen, dressed in his Sunday suit, the one he had bought to marry Aggie in, and drove off with his family to church. It was Mabry's day to have the circuit rider, and my grandfather vowed to listen to every word of the sermon as if he were the only person in church. His principal act of piety, however, was to be performed before services, while the children were in Sunday school, an hour ordinarily spent in gossip with friends beneath the oak trees in the church-yard.

He left Hester among the women and, not to attract her notice, postponed his mission for a few minutes, joining the men and listening, or pretending to listen, to their talk. He knew that Hester begrudged him none of his memories. Still he saw no point in spreading them out, so to speak, and fondling them while she looked on. She knew he made an occasional pilgrimage to Aggie's grave; she must know too that he made them more and more infrequently as time went by. After a while, unable to see Hester anywhere about, he drifted away from the group. He went around back of the church, behind the privies and down along the graveyard fence to the hollow.

Among the wildflowers he found a ragged aster or two left over, and a few snaggle-toothed daisies. Passing a pine tree on his way back to the graveyard, he broke off a branch and added this to his bouquet, saying to himself, evergreen for remembrance. He was creeping along the fence, trying not to notice his stealth, when, at the gate, just as he was about to slip in, whom should he meet but Hester, just coming out. She was alone, having left the baby with some woman friend to mind. In his confusion my grandfather let drop about half his flowers. As he stooped to gather them up, the warmth rising around his stiff collar, he felt a momentary resentment against Hester, not because she might resent his coming here, but because of his own unmanliness in hiding it from her. This feeling passed, his awkwardness returned, mounted, and rising—and again dropping a flower or two— he stammered, "A few flowers. To lay on poor Aggie's . . . Agatha's grave."

"Oh, no!" cried my grandmother. "Don't!"

He was too astounded to be angry. Apparently astounded at herself, my grandmother gasped, and squeezing past him, rushed out.

Then he was angry. He would go and lay a few flowers on his first wife's grave if he wanted to! It was nothing much. He was only too conscious of that. It was nothing much, after letting her child, the child she had given her life for, be taken away. And who was more to blame for that, him or Hester? And had he ever breathed one word of reproach to her? And she begrudged him coming to lay a few flowers on poor Aggie's grave!

And small cause she had for her jealousy! For look, he could no longer even remember where Aggie lay. That showed, ah, showed all too well, how little time he had spent here of late. He was torn between resentment towards Hester for not appreciating his neglect of Aggie, and guilt towards Aggie that he could longer even find her. In his search his eye fell again on the grave with the fresh little bouquet lying on it. That was Aggie's! ("Weep not for me," to his shame it said.) That was Aggie's: the one with the bouquet. No wonder he could not find her!

Who could have put that there? Who was there to remember poor Aggie but himself? The girls? But they had gone directly indoors to their Bible class. Puzzled, and vaguely irritated, he knelt and laid aside his own bouquet and took up this interloper. It had been picked—just picked, still damp—in the same place as his, for it was composed of the same flowers as his. Then looking closer he perceived that this bouquet was not, after all, quite the same as his own. For it contained a flower that his was missing, and which told him who had laid it there. Told him, too, in what spirit it had been brought. For it was a plant whose single shy syllable in the language of flowers was a pink whisper of remorse. It was a tendril, carefully twined about the daisies and the phlox, of the plant, peculiar to the region, known as shame vine.

That was what Hester had been doing in the graveyard, and the reason she had wanted him not to come. She had not put it there for him to find. On the contrary. This was something between herself and Agatha. For a moment my grandfather felt himself the husband of neither. They were together, and both beyond him: two mothers.

Forgetting the bouquet that he himself had brought, and rather untenderly returning to Aggie's earthen bosom the one that Hester had brought her, he rose to go and find his wife, tell her that she was not to blame herself, comfort her and tell her that it was not her fault. He turned and found her there behind him, hanging back, uncertain of him, eager but afraid to approach, tears trembling on her lashes, ready to fall as soon as he had shown her what kind of tears they must be. He held out his arms to her. She sobbed, ran to him, and flung herself quaking against his breast.

"Oh, Mr. Ordway," she sobbed, "can you ever forgive me? Not now, but someday? I was jealous of her, and I didn't love her child enough, but oh, Mr. Ordway, try to forgive me. If you knew how tormented I've been you wouldn't be hard on me."

"There, there," he said, patting her back, his own eyes brimming. "There now. It was nobody's fault. Certainly not yours. There's nothing to forgive."

"It was my fault!" she cried. "Oh, blame me! Blame me!

Do! Only, give me a chance to win my way back to your heart. Don't cast me off. Give me a chance, that's all I ask. I'll give you other boys—many boys—fine boys, Mr. Ordway. Oh, I don't mean that the way it sounds, for I know they won't be the same to you. But they will be yours too, Mr. Ordway. They will be yours too and you will love them too. I'll raise them so carefully and they will be good boys, and I won't expect you to love them as much as Ned. I won't expect it. But they will be good boys, and I will be a good mother to your boys, and more careful, as I should have been of poor Agatha's little Ned, and not let anybody steal one of them and run away with him. Oh, God forgive me for saying it, but why couldn't it have been mine they wanted? Or why couldn't *she* have been where I am, and I where she is now?"

Then at last my grandfather knew what Will Vinson's crime had been.

He stiffened and Hester felt it and stiffened too. His arms slackened and fell from about her and he turned his face to hide his emotion. She cried, for she misinterpreted his turning from her. The church bell, rather the triangle, rang just then. He said, "You go in. I'm not coming. I'll stay out here. Go on now. And don't torment yourself any further. I forgive you for your part in it."

He knew now what Will Vinson had been running away from. He was running away from him. He had seen the theft of his son as a mere accident attendant upon some crime, and for weeks and months had waited for the crime to come to light. Now he knew, as Hester, feeling herself, poor thing, to be an accomplice to it, had known all along, that Will Vinson's crime was the theft of little Ned. She was less to blame than himself. She had never loved the boy; but it was not to be expected that she should. And though she had not loved him, she could imagine what his father could not— that someone else might. She could blame herself and could suffer under the burden of his unspoken accusation, could credit him with kindness in not speaking it, when the truth was, he had not suspected that he had been done a personal injury.

At the strains of singing from the congregation floating out through the open windows of the church, my grandfather stirred himself and wandered away through the graves to a farther part of the cemetery. He could have borne it easier if the Vinsons had been childless. Not, of course, that that would have made him any more willing to give them one of his. But that they could love the child for himself, and not just because he was a child, made their theft of him more of an accusation than ever. They had children, they wanted this child; and to have him they had been prepared to give up everything—everything, as he remembered saying to himself before: their home, their stock, a crop in the ground, their good name, their own children's future—and fly to an unknown country still only half tamed, sooner than give him up again at the end of the day. He knew he had never loved the child that much, and it was almost enough, he said to himself, to make you let them have him.

He could see his boy clearly in his mind's eye. Clearly, for he was no foolish father. A little thing, pallid, plain, ordinary. What had the Vinsons seen in him to make them commit such folly? I don't mean that I didn't love him, said my grandfather to the gravestones, ranked in clans, his own included, that accused him with their bleak and stony stares. Only that you wouldn't think anybody else would except me, and his mother.

Thus he was recalled to the spot on which he once again found himself standing. He looked down at the grave, with its two bunches of wildflowers, of the woman who had died young giving birth to the fruit of his pleasure. At that moment the organ inside gave out with a wheezing chord. The congregation would be bowing their heads. At the foot of the grave, facing the stone, my grandfather also bowed.

"Aggie," he said, "my dear, I have two things to confess to you. The first is about Hester, my wife. I don't compare the two of you. You're as different as two women picked by the same man could be. I loved you, Aggie, in your time. But the world moves on, though you have left it. Hester is my wife now, and I have to put you out of mind.

"That brings me to the second thing. I have lost our boy, Aggie. The child whose coming put you where you lie. You mustn't blame Hester; it was more my fault than hers. I didn't appreciate him until it was too late; but, Aggie, you couldn't want me to miss him more than I do now. Please, try to forgive me. And though I must forget you, I vow never to forget our boy again, and not to rest till I have found him, Aggie, though I have to search to the end of the world."

PART THREE

Sam Ordway's Revenge

SINCE my grandfather, so many lone avengers in western romances, films, and TV serials have buckled on their holsters and mounted horse and set off across the plains in pursuit of the man who wronged them, that it will be necessary to distinguish him from the type. Sam Ordway differed in certain particulars from the heroes of television. First of all, Texan-born though he was, he was no horseman; he was an *East* Texan. The hind end of a plowhorse as he plodded behind it breaking a furrow was about the extent of his knowledge of horseflesh. Like any dirt farmer, given the choice between going somewhere on foot or riding horseback, he would have walked any day—the longer the distance, the easier the choice. It was in his creaky old all-purpose farm wagon, drawn by Dolly, his swaybacked, sluefooted, one-eyed mare, then already long in the tooth, and the mouse-gray mule whose only name was a cuss word, that my grandfather went after his man. He was not very fast on the draw either; that was another difference between my

grandfather and John Wayne. In fact, up to that time he
had never fired a shot at anybody in his life. So if I say
that he packed a pistol when he went after Will Vinson, the
reader is not to picture him taking down from its accustomed
peg his cartridge belt and holster and strapping it around
his waist and spinning the cylinder of his six-shooter; when
I say he packed one, I mean packed it on the bottom of his
gladstone bag, wrapped in his extra union-suit, so as not to
alarm his wife. Anyhow, it was too big to carry any other
way—or, I may say, *is* too big, as it lies on my desk before
me as I write: the same old percussion cap and ball horsepistol given to his mother by that brevet major on the battlefield at Shiloh. It is seventeen and a half inches long, and
tips the baby scales at six pounds three ounces. When my
grandfather took it west with him in 1898 it was still loaded
from that brevet major's hand. Caps were still available, a
good many old muzzle-loading shotguns being still in use at
the time, and black powder was still stocked by the hardware
stores, but he lacked the mold for casting balls. So those five
shots (it's a five-shooter) were all he had, and they were
thirty-six years old. Since 1862 the pistol had not been fired
nor the charges drawn. My grandfather did not know how
to draw them. Whether the gun would go off or not there was
no knowing, unless, of course, you were to test fire it once,
but this my grandfather did not bother to do, as he had no
intention of shooting anybody. Even to think of pointing
that cannon at a man he had known, worked alongside of,
like his ex-neighbor, made him feel like a fool. Just how he
was going to deal with Will—supposing he succeeding in
finding him: he had faced, or rather had glanced sidelong at
that question once or twice, but had said to himself, well,
it'll probably never come to that, the chances are I won't
find him. He took the pistol along just because he figured it
was something a man traveling in strange, out-of-the-way
places with close to three hundred dollars in cash on him
probably ought to have. And the wisdom even of this was

unclear to him. As he was packing it, "My Lord," he said, "that would sure be a lot to get down if somebody was to make you eat it!"

Nor was my grandfather, in setting out on his quest, so singlemindedly bent on vengeance, as the heroes in the movies always are. As he later said, it wasn't easy to hate a man who had wronged you by loving your child enough to steal him. A man who loved him more than you yourself ever had. "For I might as well admit," my grandfather told me, "that I didn't really miss the boy as much as I told his poor mamma's spirit I did. How could I? I hadn't had time to take much notice of him. He wasn't but two years old. A mother can love them at that age, but to a father they're not yet either fish nor fowl. In the second place, by then I was more or less beginning to get used to the idea of him being lost. In the third place, little Ned up to that time had been mainly a worry to me and little else. Not that I held his mamma's death against the poor child, you understand. But put it this way: if I just had to lose my wife, then I wouldn't have sorrowed long, I would have counted it a blessing, if the motherless child had been taken at the same time. I expect that sounds awful, but just remember the fix I was in: a man with a crop to make and two little girls on my hands. Well, the child had lived, and though it was no fault of his, had made trouble on all sides. I was obligated to my neighbors on his account, and your grandmother. . . . Well, your grandmother. . . . Naturally. Any woman would. All this is not to say I was glad to lose him, and later on I came to miss him sincerely; but at the time I was madder at Will Vinson for taking him from me than I was grieved at the loss of my boy."

Disarmingly open and full as it sounded, this admission of my grandfather's actually obscured the truth. That he had yet to learn to love his boy and long to have him back was true; but even at the outset he missed him more than he told me; he was always shy of displaying his deeper feelings,

and in telling me the story he minimized his loss. Also he
wished to spare my grandmother, even at that late date, any
self-recriminations, and to spare me having to judge her.
And secondly, he was not mad at Will Vinson, as he said;
he was mad at himself. Will Vinson had merely exposed to
public view a lifelong failing of his: a character too easily
put upon, trusting, unsuspicious, slow to anger, quick to
pardon, incapable of imagining that anyone could mean
him harm. Both his wives had found occasion more than
once to tell him that he was a regular doormat. "Without me
around," each in her turn had said, "you would let people
just walk all over you." He made frequent resolutions to
bristle more, to take exception to passing remarks—in vain.
Not until days afterwards would he find the barbs of deliberate provocation buried in his thick hide. He could never
nurse a grudge, could be joked out of anything, always saw
the other fellow's side in any argument, was absolutely not
to be stopped from admitting it and apologizing whenever
he found himself in the wrong. In another place this weakness might have passed unnoticed; it was my grandfather's
misfortune to have been born such as he was in Texas. In-
sults and aggravations there are possibly no more common
than elsewhere, but it is a place where a man, where even
a boy is expected to find quarrel in a straw when honor is at
stake. My grandfather admired men who could take fire at
a spark, who were not to be mollified by anything short
of blood, who handed down the torch of their wrath to
their descendants, but he could not emulate them. Now,
like Hamlet, he had had a cause, and been unpregnant
of it.

"Will had made me look like a fool," he said. "I had let
six whole months go by not only without doing anything, but
without even suspecting I'd been wronged. What I mean to
say is, I didn't know it was me, personally, that Will had
wronged. I felt ashamed for the world to see that another
man loved my son more than I did. And I had done some-

thing else to be ashamed of too. I'd done something I ought never to have done. Something I was going to have a hard time ever living down."

"What, Grandpa? What had you done?"

"I had gone to law, sir. This was something to be settled man to man, and I had gone to law! I suddenly saw the sheriff's failure to turn up any clues in an entirely different light. He hadn't tried. He had refrained from interfering in the matter until I awoke to a sense of my duty. If I was ever to be able to hold my head up again I had to do something to make up for that.

"While I am at it, though," he said, "I might as well also admit that I was not really prepared to search to the end of the world. That was only a manner of speaking. Nor did I believe that I would have to. Putting myself in Will's place, I figured that if I had been running to get away from me, I'd have begun to feel pretty safe after about thirty miles. So I really thought I would find Will holing up somewhere just the other side of Paris. Of course, in those days Paris was the end of the world, as far as I was concerned."

He set off after breakfast one morning in October, two days after his last bale of cotton had been ginned, with tufts still clinging in the sideboards and the cracks of the wagon bed. He left home quietly, telling no one of his plans. It was sure to leak out, but the quieter he himself had been about it, the easier it would be to return home emptyhanded. He traveled light, trusting to the luck of the road, the hospitality of people: an extra shirt, pair of socks, union-suit, a complete change of clothes for Ned, let out to allow for six months' growth. "I may not have any use for them," he had said wistfully. "You may not," Hester all too readily agreed. "But if you do, then there you'll have them." He shaved, then packed his razor and strop, brush, mug, and whetstone, and that little French harp he had bought to give Ned on the day he was stolen; harnessed Dolly and the mule, put his grip and the lard pail with his dinner in it under the wagon seat, kissed his wife and daughters goodbye, clicked his tongue at the team, and lumbered away. The baby was crying, the girls were puckered up, Hester had that now-don't-you-worry-about-us look. He did not look back until he was beyond the railroad crossing, then he turned on his seat and waved and they waved to him. A disheartening thought arose in his mind at this last sight of his family: how long would it be before he saw them again? A cold trail Will Vinson's was by now. In bed the night before, waiting for sleep, he had said, "Hester? Hester? Hester, what do you honestly think? Do you think I'll find them?"

"Well," Hester had replied, "you won't if you don't look, will you?"

Driving past the Vinsons' house, he wondered where they were right that moment. He thought of the six months' head start Will Vinson had, and Paris did not seem so very far away. Six months! How far, even with a wagonload of younguns to slow him down, Will could have gotten in that time! From the inner pocket of his jacket he drew out a folded map, unfolded a section of it, and spread it on his knees. It was a map of Texas. His gaze went from right to left. Past Bagwell lay Detroit, Paris, Bonham. Southwest of it lay Fulbright, Bogota, Sulphur Springs. He unfolded another, more westerly fold of his map and allowed his left eye to stray over into that expanse of buff-colored blankness on which settlements were as small and sparse as flyspecks on a ceiling. What a haystack to have to search through for one little needle of a boy!

It had needed no report from Bagwell to establish the direction Will Vinson had taken. Men went west. Especially those with no place to go, but rather some place to go urgently from. You would as soon have looked for the sun to turn around at noon and start back, as to expect a man striking out from Clarksville on a new life to head any other way. How far west he had gone before deciding to stop, that

was the question; and revolving it, with the map spread out
before him on the kitchen table these past few nights, it had
come to seem to Sam Ordway that he was studying a chart of
Will Vinson's imponderable soul. The question *where* Will
Vinson was became the question *who* he was. Had Will the
nerve, the daring, the madness, whatever quality it required,
to strike out into those unending, uncolored wastes? Sam
Ordway was lost. For as Clarksville was only barely in Texas,
the rest of the state stretching west of his ken, so he realized
now that he had never gotten beyond the Clarksville of his
former neighbor's character—a character which had suddenly opened out vast and blank, unmapped, unexplored.
How smart was Will Vinson? Not very, Sam Ordway would
have said. But then he would also have said that he was the
last man on earth to turn baby-snatcher and run off into
the wild West. And how brave and how smart was he himself? Again, not very, he would have said. Brave enough to
follow Will however far he went, smart enough to find him
in all that blank expanse?

At Mabry store, where his road joined the main road,
while he was lost in his speculations, the team automatically
turned left, east, towards Clarksville. It was only after the
turn was made that my grandfather woke up. He pulled on
the reins, backed the team into his road, and turned them
the other way. The mare cocked her head and rolled her one
eye at him.

Once started in that unaccustomed direction, with that
flat and far horizon before him, he wondered what would
make anyone ever stop. The road ran straight as a seam. The
barb-wire fences alongside the road, wires drawn so taut
they twanged in the breeze, ran on and on, straight as the
ruled lines of a musical stave. Housetops appeared, then disappeared, like the small boats toiling in the trough of a wave.
Beyond, the sweeping treeless terrain was furrowed in fine
regular waves like water rippled by a steady breeze. Tufts
of cotton clung in the weeds along the fencerow; and occa-

sionally on a barb of the wire, like a dirty tuft of cotton, underfeathers loosened from the plumage and ruffled by the breeze, hung the corpse of a songbird, impaled thereon by butcherbirds.

My grandfather looked again at his map, drawing his eyes back right, away from those desert-colored western sections, and gazed again at PARIS. Will Vinson was a country boy, like himself; on reaching, say, Honey Grove, after a week or ten days in a wagon, would he not have felt that the chance of news of him getting all that far back was pretty slim? Settled in some place with a name like Gober, or Pecan Gap, would he not have felt himself lost to the world? But one is never more scornful of anything than of a just-lost illusion, and Paris, which only yesterday had seemed to Sam Ordway the point at which a fugitive from him would begin to feel himself safe, now seemed the mere gateway to the route Will Vinson had taken. Bobbing about on the wagon seat as the team inched along, he thought that Hester had been very naïve in agreeing with him yesterday when he said he expected Will was hiding out somewhere in Lamar or Fannin County.

He was reminded of Hester when, unfolding a further section of his map, he found a wisp of hair lying in the crease. It was his hair, must have fallen there yesterday as he sat under the chinaberry tree out back of the house with the map on his knees while Hester gave him a haircut in preparation for his journey.

"It is certainly too bad," she had said, "that you haven't got a picture of Mr. Vinson to show people. How will you go about describing him? He stood an inch or two taller than you, didn't he?"

"Who, Will Vinson? He wasn't a bit taller than me. Inch or two shorter if anything."

"I would have said he was taller. What color eyes did he have?"

My grandfather could see Will Vinson's eyes very clearly

in his mind, the way they had of sometimes bugging at you, and he could see that they were light. But light what? Blue? Brown? "Brown, weren't they? Sort of a light brown? Hazel?"

"Keep your head down. I seem to recall that they were gray," said my grandmother. "But of course you knew him a lot better than I ever did."

As a matter of fact, he had never known him at all. If he now called him Will in thinking of him, it was a familiarity which had come in the time since he ran away, had come through frequent speculation on the man's motives, his character, his trail, his whereabouts. Five years of living as next-door neighbors had only made it awkward for them to mister one another, without getting them on a first-name basis, so that they had usually just called no names at all.

Noticing the hair lying on the map, he had said, "What color hair would you say the man had?"

"Oh, dear," said my grandmother, pausing in her clipping. "Just that common sort of muckledy-dun-colored hair, wasn't it? No color at all, really."

"I suppose that's the way to describe it. Only how can I expect anybody to remember seeing a man six months ago that they wouldn't have noticed in the first place?"

"Mr. Vinson was not the sort of man you would turn around to take a second look at, that's the truth. He wasn't tall and he wasn't short. He wasn't fat and he wasn't lean. He wasn't dark and he wasn't fair. Just middling in everything." There was a moment's silence, rather a moment's snipping, then she said, "How old would you say Mr. Vinson was?"

"That's another problem," said my grandfather. "Will was one of those fellows that don't really show their age. Two or three years older than me, I would guess. I would put him around thirty-seven, eight."

"You never were much good at judging people's ages. I'd have said he was two or three years younger than you."

"I don't know why we keep saying *was*," said my grand-father.

"Be easier to describe her," said my grandmother.

"Who?"

"Who? Why, *her*. Mrs. Vinson. Who else?"

"Oh. Why, how would you describe her? She never seemed much more noticeable than him, to me."

"That's it. Why, she was plain as a mud fence. Great big ears and—"

"I never noticed her ears being particularly big."

"Men never notice anything! Now I could never take my eyes off those ears of hers. Made her look like a horse wearing blinders. Her eyes were green. Her hair was a mousy yellow."

"Well, I ought not to have any trouble finding her," said my grandfather. After a moment or two, "Isn't it funny," he said, "how little any description helps you to really see a person?" There was silence for another few moments, then, "You know how I would describe Will Vinson? I would say he looked like the last man on earth to ever do such a thing."

"It's a good thing you've got a picture of Ned, at least," said my grandmother.

Yes, it was a good thing he had a picture of Ned. Though looking at it now, and thinking for the first time of actually showing it to strangers, made my grandfather wince with shame, so neglected, so accusing did that pinched little face look out at him. But it was a good thing he had it. For he would certainly never have been able to describe Ned. He was a little boy; when you had said that you had said about all there was to say. Oh, you could add a few touches; such as, that he was skinny, had tow hair. Which was to say that in any collection of ten little boys Ned was not the fat one nor the redheaded one, but one of the other eight. He had a photograph, yes; but would anybody have noticed his boy? The Vinsons had, to be sure. But then the Vinsons had seen

something in Ned which his own father had to admit that
he had never seen.

"Whereabouts are we, Pa?" Bea had asked.

My grandfather had pointed, and his blunt square forefinger, in touching Clarksville, had shaded Arkansas, Oklahoma, and Louisiana. Bea put out her hand, entranced at
the notion of touching the spot on the map which marked
the spot she stood on. She was eating bread and butter and
sugar, and seeing her buttery little paw, her father had
jerked the map away. Not far enough away, however, and
that was how the Panhandle area, which was covered with
nothing much else, had come to be covered with a grease
blot this morning.

"The question is," my grandfather had said, "where is our
little Ned? That is what we have got to find out."

The girls had sidled away then, as they did of late, he
thought he had noticed, whenever Ned's name was brought
up. Peeved, he had called them back. "You haven't begun to
forget your little brother, I hope, have you, girls?" he asked.

Tears had sprung to the eyes of both, and he was sorry he
had doubted them. Then Winnie cried, "Oh, Pa, don't go!
Stay home, Pa! Don't leave us!"

"But you want me to go and find our little Ned and bring
him back home again, don't you, hon? Of course you do."

"No, I don't!" she cried. "I want you to stay home with us.
Get us another little brother. Oh, Pa, I'm afraid you'll get
lost and never find your way back again."

"I won't get lost. Don't you worry about that. See, I have
a map. You just be good girls and mind your ma and help
her while I'm gone, and I'll come back, all right, bringing
little Ned with me." He had glanced at Bea then, and said,
"You believe I'll find him, don't you, Bea?"

"Yes, Pa," said Bea. And nothing yet had made it seem so
unlikely as that prompt childish certitude.

"Now you all run and play, girls," said my grandmother,
and then to him, "Duck your head while I trim your neck."

He had, and as she leaned against him he felt the rounded firmness of her belly.

"You want to take good care of yourself, Hester, while I'm away," he said.

She was anxious that he feel no sense of duty towards her, but free in his mind to search for the child that she blamed herself for the loss of. "Having a child is a lot easier than finding one," she said. From the start she had approved his plan. Not that she encouraged him to believe that he would succeed. "But you must go," she had said. "Even if you don't find him, you'll feel better for having tried. And so will I. Only . . ."

He thought she would say, "Only remember, he has three children of his own," or words to that effect, to which he had ready the reply, "He ought to have thought of that before taking another man's."

"Only, be careful," she said. "Remember you've got three other children, and another on the way."

Bea returned as Hester was shaving over his ears, with a drawing for his approval. It was a picture of a man. "Oh, nice!" said my grandfather.

"It's a picture of Mr. Vinson," said Bea. "To show to people and ask if they have seen him."

"Well, thank you, Bea! That will certainly be a big help, all right. It looks just like him! You see, Hester, we were both wrong. He's got purple eyes."

He had it with him now, had found it in his pocket when he replaced the photograph of Ned, and now he unfolded it, and smiled. He ought not to smile, though; it was better than he had been able to do. For he had tried—first making sure that his women were all occupied and not likely to walk in and catch him at it—had gotten the idea from Bea and had tried himself to draw a picture of Will Vinson later that evening. First he attempted a front-face, and produced a jack-o'-lantern. Then he tried a profile, and that had wound up looking like an orangutan.

Now as he jogged along he grew conscious of the wind strumming the telegraph wires overhead. The poles marched westward across the prairie and over the distant rim. Looking at that line of diminishing crosses, my grandfather imagined how, during the first few hours of his flight, along this very stretch of road, Will Vinson must have fancied that in that sound he could all but hear the alarms racing ahead of him down the line. How could Will, wanting the boy bad enough to do what he was doing, suppose that Sam Ordway was such an indifferent father that he was letting those critical first few days go by without taking after him in pursuit, without even suspecting anything amiss? From the map there now arose a new image of Will Vinson. My grandfather saw Will looking backwards, over his shoulder, fearfully, at him.

He unfolded the final, westernmost fold. All of Texas, from Clarksville to El Paso, lay stretched out before him. And now when fully spread, what the map gave back to him was no longer an image of Will Vinson at all, but rather an image of himself. Of Will Vinson's image of him. And along with an inkling of the enormous quest which lay before him, he felt a sickening sense of compliment unmerited, the ignominy of an enemy's esteem. As big as Texas: that would be Will Vinson's estimation, based on his own reckless love for his boy, of the scope and reach of Sam Ordway's revenge.

In Bagwell, or just the other side of Bagwell, my grandfather stopped and called on his only known informant, Mr. Ingram, the farmer who had reported seeing the Vinsons on the day of their flight. He turned out to be a good deal less positive about it than the sheriff had reported him as being. He lived on the main road, and as he now said, lots of wagonloads of folks headed west went past his door. Still, a man had stopped at his place that day to ask for water from the well, a man whose team was lathered with sweat, and who struck him as nervous, jumpy, suspicious. He fitted

grandfather's description of Will Vinson, though as my
grandfather said to himself, so did this man, so did ninety-
nine men out of a hundred. The farmer said yes, he
believed it was four younguns they had with them, but
when shown the photograph of Ned he could not say if that
was one of them or not. Scratching his head, he said he
guessed the truth was, he never took much notice of kids.
Truth was, my grandfather reflected, neither did he. Never
had. "Oh, you're old Bill So-and-so's boy," he would say. "Yes,
you take after your daddy." And he would be reminded of
some quirk of old Bill's, or of Bill's old father, and the boy
himself would be forgotten. Little boys had no names, no
identities, hardly any faces of their own. Did other men, he
wondered, take as little notice of children as this man, and
he himself?

"Going after him on your own, are you? Them law never
done you no good?" Mr. Ingram asked. He seemed to smirk,
whether from contempt for the law, or for a man who had
gone to law, or both, my grandfather could not tell.

"Yes, well I wouldn't have left it up to them, you understand, only I had my crop to make, my family to look after.
I've got three more youngsters, and another on the way."

"I know how it is. Got six myself," Mr. Ingram said with a
sigh. "A poor farming man ain't even free to get mad just
whenever the mood takes him. Well, Mr. Ordway, I wish I
could do more for you. I sure wish you luck," he concluded,
his gaze stealing westward and his head shaking involun-
tarily.

One mile past that farmer's house my grandfather came
to the first of many, many crossroads that he was to stop at
and ponder which way to take, or to pass and wonder if he
had done the right thing. He decided to keep on the main
Paris road. Now he was on his own. Now he would have to
introduce himself and tell his story. As he rode along he
rehearsed his speech. "How do you do, ma'am," he would
begin. "I wonder if you can help me?" That would disarm

right off any housewife's suspicions that he was a peddler and wanted to sell her something. "My name is Ordway?" he would say, giving it that slight interrogative inflection that removed any hint of self-assertiveness. "I'm from over in Red River County" (for he had crossed the Lamar County line now). "I'm on the trail of a man named Vinson. That is, I hope I'm on his trail. Will Vinson. He was my neighbor, and we were in the habit of leaving our little boy" (*"our* little boy," he would say; no point in mentioning Aggie) "to play with his whenever we went anywhere for the day. One Saturday last spring—the seventh of May, to be exact—when we came home from town and stopped to pick up our little Ned, they were gone." No point in anticipating the problem of describing Will unless she showed some signs of recollection astir. Just say, "Do you recall seeing a wagonload of strangers passing through here sometime around then— man, wife, four youngsters running from nine months up to three years, in a wagon drawn by a team of two brown four-year-old mules?"

A housetop rose into view. Looking about, my grandfather said to himself, well, if anybody did pass through here you couldn't miss him, unless he went through by night. You would know he was on his way a day ahead. His own approach was greeted half a mile off by a chorus of yapping dogs. He had a moment of misgiving. What would people make of him and his story? The unfortunate are so often regarded with suspicion. But one good omen: there were young children at this house, the wash on the line (it was a Monday) proclaimed them. He drew up at the gate, got down, went through the yard, giving a wide berth to the dogs, and around to the back door, conscious all the while of eyes watching him from behind window curtains. The door opened before he could call hello, and before he could get his hat off, the lady of the house, wiping her puckered sudsy red hands on her apron, stuck her head out and said, "Thank you, but we don't need nothing."

He wasn't selling anything, he told her. He wondered if she could help him? This phrase had the opposite effect from what he had expected. Her eyes narrowed suspiciously and her head commenced to shake. He told her his tale. Her reaction was to shrink from him and clutch her children to her, as if he carried some child-losing germ which she might catch if he came too close. He thanked her, went back to the wagon, and set off down the road.

The woman at the second stop had finished her wash and was now baking, came to the door wiping clots of dough on her apron. She was not so old as the woman who lived in the shoe, but like her she had so many children she didn't know what to do. They all came and gaped at the stranger like goldfish flocking to the side of the bowl. She listened confusedly, and shook her head. "None of you children saw any folks like that, did you?" my grandfather asked, and they fled like goldfish at the movement of a hand.

"Wellsir," said the ancient sitting on the front porch at the next stop, "if they went past here they just kept on going. I seen em if they did, no doubt about that. Don't n'ere a dog go down this road but I don't know about it. Been setting here in this rocker for the last two years. It's this left leg of mine. Always served me perfectly well till one day last January a year. Locked. Just froze up tight. You can't no more bend it than a stick of stovewood. They have to set me out here in the morning and take me indoors at night like a piece of furniture. This is where you'll find me every day from around the first of April till frost. So it ain't much happens along this stretch of road but I don't know about it, and the folks you say you're after, well, if they did go by then I just waved at em like I do everybody whether I know em or not, and never give em another thought in this world. Unless of course I had just dozed off. It does happen sometimes and so it's just barely possible—"

"Well, I'm much obliged to you just the same. And I hope your leg gets well real soon."

"Don't mention it. Glad to help you out, son. Low-down trick, stealing a man's boy. Your own neighbor, you say? What is the world coming to? Well, if and when you do catch him, stomp him once for me, hear? As for the leg, well, I don't know. I appreciate the thought, but if it ain't got no better in two years, why . . ."

So it went. Stopping everywhere along the road, at every farmhouse, at every crossroads store, blacksmith shop, my grandfather spoke to old and young, male and female, black and white, and not one did he find who could honestly say he recalled the folks he was looking for.

Now my grandfather made his first deduction. As he entered Paris on the evening of the second day he put himself in Will Vinson's place and pondered what he should do at this point, how, feeling the hot breath of Sam Ordway down his neck, or imagining that he did, he ought to proceed. The question was, whether to go through the town or skirt round it. Out in the country you ran less risk of being seen by anyone; for that very reason, though, anyone who did see you was more apt to remember it. In town the chances of your being seen were multiplied; but by the same token, they were lessened of your being noticed and remembered. So at this point (assuming that Will had reached this point) the clever thing would have been to plunge right in, lose yourself down these streets, amid these crowds (my grandfather was afoot now, carrying his satchel, having left the wagon and team at a livery stable, and proceeding to a hotel), and like a fox crossing water, break your trail. And because that would have been the clever thing to do, Will Vinson had done the other thing. The instinct of a country fellow like Will would have been to stay out in his own element. He knew, because he felt it himself. Will Vinson had never even approached Paris. The reason no one after Bagwell remembered seeing him was that somewhere down one of those many side roads which he had passed today, Will, knowing that Paris lay ahead of him, had foolishly turned off. He knew, because that was what he would have done in Will's place. To admit it gave him an odd momentary little sensation of fellowship with that other country boy, his former neighbor, and what was even odder, it was a not unwelcome feeling as he made his way alone through the streets of this strange city.

"Well, I wouldn't say civilized, no. That I don't reckon it'll ever be. But you don't find any more red Indians out there nowadays. I wasn't scalped. I've been like this for years. I'm told one family of Choctaws went out and had a go at sodbusting, but wound up saying give it back to the white man."

"Whereabouts was you?"

"All over. Up in the Panhandle. Out around Lubbock, Wichita Falls. All the way out to Amarillo. I was in one town called Sundown and another called Halfway and one called Pep and one called Needmore (most fittingly named place I believe I ever was in) and then when I come to one called Circle Back, I did."

"Who do you travel for, Mr. Hewlett?"

"The Good Neighbors Company. Out of St. Louis. Barbwire fencing. You?"

"I'm in the wholesale hardware line myself. Nuts and bolts. Nails."

"Nails? Then stay away from west Texas. Not much doing in your line out there. To need nails you've got to have planks, and to have planks you need trees. Why, I was to a fat-stock show once out there, and sue me if afterwards I didn't see them sweeping up the sawdust and putting it in crokersacks to use over again. No, no. West Texas is no place for you. And your friend?"

"Mr. Tullamore here is in ready-made clothing. Travels for a Birmingham, Alabama, concern. But say! Didn't none of them fence-cutting cowpunchers out there take a potshot at you?"

"Barb wire is not popular in some quarters. But you can't stand in the path of progress. The cowmen're fighting a losing battle, and they know it."

"Country opening up fast, is it?"

"Yes, well I'm in the business of enclosing it again once it's opened up. I took orders for nearly seventeen thousand ton of wire this trip. But I wouldn't hardly call it crowded yet. They say out there that when you set off to visit your neighbor you ride a pregnant mare so as to have a way of getting back home again."

"Big country."

"Too damn big."

"And hot."

"And cold. Hot and cold."

"Yet people will go out."

"Hah! When I was there I seen them coming out pushing a wheelbarrow. You won't believe that, Mr. Webb, but I seen it with my own two eyes. A wheelbarrow, or I'm not sitting here this minute. I heard of one nut going it on a bicycle. One man and woman in Wichita Falls was setting off afoot leading an Ayrshire cow. They had it figured that that cow was going to be a kind of walking canteen to get them across the great plains. What she was going to drink, well, they hadn't given any thought to that. The man had been a copy clerk up to the week before, but he'd had enough of that. Now he was going out and live next door to God. What was he aiming to do out there? Why, farm. His notion of farming was, he would stake a claim to about two thousand acres, sprinkle him a few handfuls of wheat, and in about two weeks' time it'd come up covered with blossoms in the shape of little Parker House rolls. I talked to one poor sonofabitch on his way back. He'd went out a couple of years before in a big new prairie schooner, drawn, he told me, by a fine fat span of mules. Well, he never had nor wagon nor team when I spoke with him, and he didn't have the wife and two younguns he'd went out with neither. He'd lost everything.

Wiped out. Drought. Grasshoppers. Dust. Cholera. And do
you know what the poor fool told me he was on his way to
do then? Going back—back home to Mississippi—and find
him a new woman and get him a job tapping turpentine and
save up enough money to buy a new outfit and try it again.
I seen one family going out with a big glass-doored break-
front taking up about three quarters of the wagon and
sticking up in the air about a story and a half high and I
thought to myself, now you're going to need that in a one-
room sod shanty. Well, you remember what General Sheri-
dan said."

"What'd ole Phil say?"

"Said if he owned Texas and hell he'd live in hell and rent
out Texas. And you know what? People being what they are,
he would find tenants. Won't you join us, mister?"

"Oh! Excuse me!" cried my grandfather. "I never meant
to eavesdrop on you gentlemen. I got so interested in what
you were saying I seem to have forgotten my manners."

"Glad to have you join us at our table," said Mr. Hewlett,
the barb-wire man, and he cleared some additional elbow
space among their dirty dishes.

"I will then, if you're sure you don't mind? And, mister,
I'm burning to ask you a question. Here. In your travels out
west, I wonder if you remember ever seeing a little boy that
looked like that?"

"In all my travels I've never seen any little boy that didn't
look like that," said Mr. Hewlett after a glance at Ned's
photograph.

His two colleagues looking over his shoulder at the picture
chortled, and my grandfather fetched up a smile and joined
in—though he found an unintended meaning in the words
which pained him. The three men then chased the levity
from their faces and composed them for listening to his
story. My grandfather cleared his throat and said, "The boy
in that picture is my boy."

In a chastened tone, Mr. Webb asked how he had come to be separated from his boy.

My grandfather told them. They shook their heads, clucked their tongues, and the second two shot reproachful glances at the original joker, Mr. Hewlett. He took another look, said no, he had been just about all over the West and never seen that boy. My grandfather said he really wasn't surprised to hear it, because actually he didn't believe his boy was out in the West. He expected Will had not gone much farther than right here in Lamar County.

"Don't you believe it," Mr. Hewlett said. "Once they get started they just keep on. He won't stop this side of Plainview. He'll have to go that far to find a bush to go behind."

"Can he read?" asked Mr. Tullamore.

"Read? Why, no. He wasn't but two and a half years old."

"No, no. The man, I mean."

"Will? Why, of course *he* can read," my grandfather replied.

"Then you wouldn't want to do what I was fixing to suggest."

"What?"

"Run a notice in the various newspapers throughout the western part of the state. But if he can read, why he might see it, so never mind."

"Well, of course he can read!" my grandfather said. Odd, though, that he should feel so sensitive to aspersions cast by a stranger upon his enemy.

The hardware man, Mr. Webb, now accepted the photograph from Mr. Hewlett, and to my grandfather said, "Your first, I take it."

"First boy," he replied.

"Always the hardest one to lose," said Mr. Tullamore.

"I haven't lost him yet," said my grandfather.

"'At's the spirit," said Mr. Webb. "Never say die."

"And all this happened six months ago?" said Mr. Tullamore.

"Yes, well you see, I couldn't do anything until my crops were in," said my grandfather. "I've got three other—"

"I never meant to reproach you," said Mr. Tullamore. "I just mean to say that while I admire your spirit, the same as Mr. Webb here, I wonder how much you can hope to accomplish if in six months the law had never found a trace."

"The way I feel is, it's my off season, I've got nothing to lose by trying," said my grandfather. They had piqued him somewhat, though, and privately he felt, momentarily at least, much less modest about his chances.

"'At's the spirit," said Mr. Webb.

"Had no youngsters of his own, this neighbor of yours?" asked Mr. Tullamore. "Wife barren? Case like that, was it? Figured he would need him a boy to help work the land out there?"

"No. No, they had three of their own, two of them boys, youngest child still a babe in arms, wife a perfectly sound woman to all outward appearances," said my grandfather. Then he noticed that even as he asked the question Mr. Tullamore had been studying the photograph.

"You'd think," said Mr. Webb, "that the law would've turned up something in all this time."

"You wouldn't if you'd been where I've been," said Mr. Hewlett. "My friends here haven't been out in west Texas, Mr. Ordway. I have. They ain't no law out there. My advice to you is, turn around right here and now before you've gone any further. Go home and get started having yourself some more boys. I do hate to discourage a man of pluck, but frankly I think you stand about as much chance as a snow-drop in hell."

"I appreciate your advice," said my grandfather. "But you know how it is. As the blind eye said to the good one, I'd like to see for myself."

"I've got a suggestion," said Mr. Tullamore. "whyn't you take on a line?"

"A line?"

"Line of goods. Sell as you go. Then if you don't find them, why at least the trip won't be a total loss."

"Not a bad idea," said Mr. Webb. "Say something in the farm-implement line. You understand that."

"Well, I've got a much better idea," said Mr. Hewlett. "You just go home and sit tight, Mr. Ordway, and one day about a year from now, after he's been through a drought, a plague of seventeen-year locusts, a dust storm or two and a couple of cyclones and an epidemic of yeller jaunders or something, why you'll see your man coming back down the lane, bringing your little boy with him. If he don't, just look me up—Chester B. Hewlett—and I'll give you one of mine. You can take your pick."

Damn you, Will Vinson! said my grandfather to himself as he undressed for bed in his hotel room that night. *Damn you!* He hoped that a rattlesnake had bitten him. That a tornado had struck him. That he had died a slow death of thirst. That he had been spared none of the hardships which came to his mind when he thought of west Texas. And finally he cursed him for having to take it all back and wish Will Vinson prosperity in his new home—to have to pray, in fact, that Will (until he caught up with him, at least) would have the rare luck to make out in that harsh place. For emptying his pockets for bed and glancing down at the photograph of Ned, my grandfather had a vision of that little dependent of Will's, ragged and barefoot and scrawny from hunger.

To turn around and go back east towards home when the man he was after was somewhere in the west was rather dispiriting, but early the next morning my grandfather returned to Bagwell and began exploring the side roads leading off to the southwest. The Ingrams took him in and gave him board. Mrs. Ingram would put him up some dinner in his pail and he would set off early every morning and try

a different road, returning for supper at night. He would
come to a fork in the road miles from nowhere and would
whoa to the team, would decide to go this way and start
to flick the reins, change his mind and decide to go the other
way, start, stop, until finally he was shaking with indecision
like an old woman on a curb at a busy intersection. For a
day was involved in each choice. A day of jouncing down
rutty lanes, of fording washouts, getting mired in the mud,
getting out to push, often a day of meeting no one even to
ask the time of day, much less whether another fool had
come this way sometime last spring.

And even down these roads, where people lived like the
Swiss Family Robinson, where the passage of a strange cat
could not have gone unnoticed, where his own approach
seemed to have been telegraphed ahead by smoke signals or
jungle drums, so that on the sagging gallery of the general
store he would be met by a delegation of the open-mouthed
and the slit-eyed, the curious and the hostile, of the Vinsons
nobody remembered seeing hide nor hair. He was going
farther and farther out now, leaving the Ingrams' in the
dark of the morning and dragging in after dark at night.
Improbable as it seemed that he would ever find anyone who
had seen them, it seemed equally improbable that no one
had. A loaded wagon with a man and woman, four children,
did not pass like a canoe over the water without leaving a
trace. It must have been seen by someone.

"Are you sure it's not for the best?"

"How's that, ma'am?" said my grandfather.

"Oh, Mr. Ordway!" cried Mrs. Ingram, dropping her dish-
cloth. "Oh, Mr. Ordway, I was only more or less thinking to
myself out loud. I don't mean to go poking my nose into
your family affairs. I was just wondering . . . I mean, if
they're so fond of the child, and his mamma is dead and his
stepmother . . . I mean . . ."

"I suppose," her husband interposed, "that if you was to

die and I was to marry again and somebody was to steal one of yours you'd want me to just let them have him, eh? Why, I'd sooner bury one of them. Yes, I'd sooner bury one of them than know he was growing up among strangers."

Yes, so would he, thought my grandfather. So should any father. But he knew perfectly well that he would not. He wished he had Ned back. But that fierce paternal possessiveness, that deep dynastic jealousy which made a father sooner wish his son dead than growing up among strangers, that was beyond him. No, he had to admit he would sooner Will Vinson had him than that—another evidence of the indifference which had originally cost him his boy. How it shamed him that he should have to be shown by another man the way he ought to feel!

"Ah, dear, dear, it's a cruel old world," sighed Mrs. Ingram as the two men got up from the table. Then lighting her guest up the stairs, puffing at each step, "I guess you're not the first poor widower to marry again thinking to provide a mother for his orphaned children, then discovered your new wife had a mind of her own, eh, Mr. Ordway? Well, good night, and sleep tight."

My grandfather sat on the edge of the bed unlacing his shoes, the picture of Ned along with his watch and change and pocket knife lying on the nightstand at his side. He was rather shaken by this unexpected moral which Mrs. Ingram had drawn from his story. Beyond mentioning that Ned's mother had died giving birth to the boy, and that he had remarried, he had told her nothing to lead her to these deductions. Women all commenced nodding their heads knowingly, however, at the mere mention of a stepmother. In every father married to a second wife they saw a man helplessly torn between the two. He remembered to have been himself the object of such sympathetic sighs and tongue cluckings and headshakes on the part of Mrs. Vinson. And thinking of Mrs. Vinson and that sad sympathetic look she always used to wrap him in, my grandfather suddenly found quite another thought in Mrs. Ingram's words. Had he married Hester without caring for her, merely in order to provide a mother for Aggie's children? Or to express it still more searchingly, not even thinking of their welfare, but merely in order to get them off his hands? He had always supposed he loved Hester. But had he when he married her, and had she believed he did? And the Vinsons, had they thought he married her only for the children's sake, and that she knew it, and took it out on them, especially Ned, and was that what had made them . . . ?

He decided to suppress all mention of Hester in future. No point in exposing her unnecessarily to the censure of strangers.

"Morning, ma'am. Hope I'm not disturbing you. My name is Ordway? I'm looking for a man."

She giggled and said, "So'm I." At least, that was what it sounded like.

"Pardon?" said my grandfather.

"I said, 'Oh, my!' " she said.

"Oh. Well, as I was saying, I'm looking for a man. The man that stole my little boy and run off with him. I wonder if you—"

"That *what!* Stole your little boy and run off with him? You don't mean it!"

"Yes'm, I'm afraid I do. Man by the name of Will Vinson. You see, him and his wife had kids, and we were neighbors, and I would leave my boy with them when I went into town, and that night when I stopped to get him they were gone. I wonder if by any chance—"

"Gone!"

"Gone. Soon as I was out of sight that morning they must have grabbed up what things they could and threw them into the wagon and lit out. I'm not sure they came this way, but maybe you—"

"How on earth did you stand it? And the child's mother!

Why, if such a thing was to happen to me I think I would just—"

"Dead," said my grandfather. "Died giving birth to him."

"Oh, you poor man! Oh, won't you step in?" she said. "Do step in and tell me all about it."

"Well, I ought to—"

"Maybe I do remember some people going past here, now that I think of it. When did you say it was?"

"I didn't say, but it was early May. They were driving a wagon and team of two brown four-year-old mules. I've got a picture of my boy. Here it is."

"No wonder they stole him, a little angel like that!" she said. "You ought to 've known better than to trust that boy out of your sight with anybody."

"Well!" said my grandfather, blushing. "Thank you! Thank you very much!"

"Undoubtably the cutest little tyke I believe I ever seen in my life. Putting aside my own four, you understand."

"Four!"

"Four boys. No more where those come from, alas."

"Your husband . . . ?"

"The same as you, Mr. Ordway. No longer with us. It was last spring a year that poor Eubanks went to meet his maker. He was called in the very Maytime of life, Mr. Ordway, as fine a figure of a man as you'll meet in a long day's riding, though I say it who shouldn't."

"I'm very sorry to hear about it, Mrs. Eubanks."

"Thank you, Mr. Ordway. I know that you will appreciate."

My grandfather then glanced, slightly, so as to bring the subject back around to his personal concerns as unnoticeably as possible, at the photograph of Ned, which the widow Eubanks still held. Seeing his glance, she said, "I declare, this boy sure does look familiar."

"Does he? You don't think—"

"Do sit down, Mr. Ordway, and excuse me for just one

minute. I'll leave the picture here. I want to study it some more. But right now I smell my pie ready to come out of the oven. Just make yourself right at home, I won't be but just a jiffy."

When Mrs. Eubanks returned from the kitchen she was carrying a large tray on which was a coffeepot and service, and, on a dish almost the size of a dinner plate, the biggest piece of pie that Sam Ordway had ever seen. This was yesterday's, she said, and though it had not turned out as she had hoped, she would be hurt if he refused it. He accepted, told her he took two spoonfuls of sugar (she herself took four), and commenced eating. It was very good pie. Pecan.

"Yes, indeedy," said Mrs. Eubanks. "Anybody looking for a boy would sure find them here!"

She took up the photograph and looked hard at it and said, "I would almost swear I had seen that little fellow, sometime, somewheres."

But just as my grandfather, having finally managed to swallow, was about to say what exciting news that was: "Oh, dear me!" she said with a laugh. "Well, I guess I have! He looks just like my own Kermit at that age. Why, you wouldn't be able to tell them apart! No wonder I thought he looked familiar! Can I slice you another piece of that pie, Mr. Ordway?"

"Oh, no, thank you. Thank you, no. I couldn't."

"I'm afraid you didn't care for it."

"Not care for it! On the contrary! It was delicious. But, I—"

"Ah, it does my heart good," said Mrs. Eubanks, though the sigh she fetched sounded as if her heart was breaking, "to see a man eat my baking again!"

My grandfather swallowed noisily, and said the most consoling thing he could call to mind on the spur of the moment, which was, "Awful good pie, Mrs. Eubanks."

"I thought the crust was a little tough."

"No, no! Exactly right."

"Well, it's nice of you to say so, but it's not as good as I generally do. My friends are forever telling me I ought to go into the bakery business. 'You've won all them prizes,' they say." And she indicated with a wave of the hand the row of red ribbons, blue ribbons, white, green, yellow, hanging on the wall behind her.

"You really ought," said my grandfather.

"It's something to fall back on, I suppose. But what would I do with the money? Eubanks left me very well provided for. Clear title to the house and sixty-four acres making half a bale to the acre in a good year. Eight heavy milkers and six heifers. A team and all the farm implements. Not that I mean to brag, you understand. Anyhow, I wouldn't care to do that—take a pie or cake of mine out of the oven and think of some other woman's husband sitting down to it."

"Have you ever thought of getting married again, Mrs. Eubanks?" my grandfather asked.

"Not," she said with a demure downward glance, "up to now."

"Well, it ain't for lack of offers, I'm sure," said my grandfather. "And I'm not just thinking of that half a bale to the acre. A woman that can bake like—" With his fork loaded and halfway to his mouth, he stopped. Something was troubling Mrs. Eubanks's eyes. Suddenly they ceased batting and fluttered open and the look she sent his way seemed to wing over and hover above him and alight like a butterfly upon a blossom.

"What was I saying?" said my grandfather.

"Oh, Mr. Ordway!" she said. "What *were* you saying?"

"I was fixing to say, Mrs. Eubanks, don't hesitate to remarry on account of your children. My two daughters—"

"Your two daughters?" she said faintly. For a moment her eyelids beat rapidly, but recovering herself quickly, she said, "Oh, how I always prayed for some girls! To pass on my cooking to."

"—have got on very well with their stepmother. Oh, I
don't say it's been a bed of roses, but by and large . . ."

He let his words trail off. In the silence which ensued he
took a vow never again to accept any housewife's invitation
to step inside, unless the man of the house was in evidence.
He found himself still holding his fork and laid it down.
Then it seemed that the least he could do, out of common
courtesy, was not to leave that last bite on his plate, gorged
as he was. He ate it, and he felt he had brought the interview
around to about as neat a close as could be expected under
the circumstances, by saying, "Mrs. Eubanks, that was without doubt the best pecan pie I ever tasted." And this, he
fully meant her to understand, was including his two wives'.

Next day, the next road, results the same as the day
before. He was like a fisherman casting over a stretch of
water, beginning nearby and working outwards, and reeling
in and casting again, each cast longer than the last.

On the morning of one of those days, as he went along the
main Paris road he had ahead of him—not much bigger
than a bobbing cork when he first glimpsed it—a wagon
piled high with furniture and bedding, a highboy mirror
flashing in the sunlight, tubs and washpots clattering and
banging against the sides. There was a boy trudging alongside and a little girl holding a baby on her lap sitting with
her legs dangling over the tailgate. Tenant farmers, maybe,
on the move to a new situation; but to my grandfather for
a moment they were the Vinsons, setting out, heading west;
and seeing the slow, ponderous sway of the wagon, creaking
and wallowing like a sailing ship all but becalmed in an
ocean of grass, that broad horizon before them, he felt as
never before the immensity, the hardihood of what the
Vinsons had undertaken.

Overtaking them, he rode alongside. "Hidy," he said.

"Hidy-do."

"Moving?"

"That's right. Yessir, moving. From Oglethorpe County, Georgia."

"All the way from Georgia!"

"Yessir. Been a-coming since around the first of the year. And I ain't there yet."

"Where?"

"Where I aim to get to. But I'm getting near. Look at it! Fur as the eye can see, not a stump. Not one solitary back-breaking, gut-rupturing, plow-busting stump! You could open up a furrow clear to the Psific Ocean!"

"Yes," said his wife, sitting beside him, "but what do you build your house out of? What do you burn in your stove? And whereabouts do you draw your water from?"

"Always complaining," said the husband.

"Well, what do you build your house out of?" she said.

"Sod. Mud and straw. Live in a tent for a time if you have to. Land like this ought to grow you such crops you can send back to Georgia for a load of them damn rocks that come up in the fields ever' spring, and make you a house out of them."

"Yes," said she. "If the rains come. And the grasshoppers don't. And—"

"Why, lady," said my grandfather, "you ain't out west yet at all here."

"Mister, I'm a lot further west than I ever meant to be," she replied. "You mean it gets worse?"

"I swear, if you was ever to find yourself getting low on trouble you would send out to borrow some, wouldn't you, Thelma? Look at this country! It took my old daddy all his life to clear forty acres back home in Georgia, him and three boys. But look! God has cleared the land out here for me and mine. A man can *see* out here!"

"See what?" my grandfather heard the wife say, as, waving goodbye, he whipped up and pulled ahead.

Was it that same day—or had those early days of his search gotten mixed together when he told me the story thirty years later?—that he pulled up late, exhausted, dis-

couraged, covered with dust, thirsty, to a farmhouse of dog-
run construction with a crippled davenport on the front
porch, broken window lights covered with pasteboard, rusty
parts of worn-out farm tools lying scattered about the yard
like the bones of a dried and rotted-apart skeleton, the home
of real puppy-loving poor whites, a pack of some nine to a
dozen of which (dogs, that is) came out from under the
porch to moil about his feet as he made his way up the
path. The man of the house lounged out and leaned against
a pillar grown Pisa-like from such usage. You'd think, said
my grandfather to himself, that he wouldn't have much else
to do but notice and remember anybody that goes down the
road. My grandfather begged a drink. They went out to the
well, where a fresh bucketful was drawn for him. The dipper
was one of that year's gourds and imparted to the water its
own sweet flavor, like new-mown hay. My grandfather flung
out his dregs, then told his story, showed his photograph,
and wearily asked his everlasting question. The mouth was
an organ of perception with this one as with most of them,
and he listened with it all agape, closing it as my grandfather wound up. Then he put his tongue in his cheek like
a quid of tobacco and scratched the beard on his throat.
How many times now my grandfather had seen that train
of gestures! Now he would scratch his nape, ruffle up his
back hair, spit and drag dirt over it with his toe. And now—
yes—he would ask to have the whole thing repeated. Sometime last May, was it? Hmmm. Man about thirty-five years
of age, you say? About that, give or take a year. Four
younguns? Four, yes, running from nine months up to
three years, his own Ned, then Felix, Perry, and baby Grace
Vinson. And this one here in the picture was yourn, you
say? Now he would thrust out his jaw and stare off into
space, would squinch up one eye, put his tongue, like a dip
of snuff, down inside his lower lip, would begin slowly,
slowly to shake his head, and would finally drawl, "Naw, sir.
Naw, sir, I sure wisht I might say yes, but I'm afraid I have

got to say no." Except that what this one said was, "Never had ere big collie dog with em, did they?"

How could he have forgotten Rex? How many people might have answered yes if only he had included Rex in his description! How many dogs there were who stood out in his own memory more vividly than their owners! How much easier to describe, and more memorable Rex Vinson was than Will! He did not forget Rex afterwards, when putting his question to any country man or boy.

Now my grandfather bade the Ingrams goodbye and moved on. But he came to another fork in the road. And having chosen, he came to another fork, and having chosen, another. And now a change came into his little set speech. He no longer ended up with, "I wonder if you happened to see them?" but instead, "I don't suppose you seen them," his own head already shaking.

This is crazy, he would say to himself in whatever farmhouse bedroom he found himself at night, the children having been turned out to sleep on pallets on the floor or in a trundle bed underneath their parents' bed. I can't go from door to door across the state of Texas, especially here where the doors are five miles apart. Why didn't he give up and turn around and go home where he belonged?

Ordinary men were struck with wonder and respect for him, which made him blush with shame. They marveled at his pertinacity. When instead of displaying his affection for his boy or his grief at the loss of him, or flaunting his determination to revenge himself bloodily on his enemy, he said, well, it was the off season, there wasn't much to do around the place just then, and he might as well look a little further, that he wasn't as discouraged as they supposed because he had never much expected to succeed, then their admiration knew no bounds. As a matter of fact, he considered giving up and returning home daily. He could be out on the Paris-Clarksville road in a day, then home in a matter of hours. He was sore tempted. If he kept on going his reasons were precisely those that he gave, and which were put down to his modesty: there was not much to do around the place just then, and though he did not expect to succeed, still he had promised Aggie's spirit to give it his best, and while this might seem to be the end of the world, it wasn't, and he was ashamed to go back emptyhanded and face his friends quite so soon.

Meanwhile he grew more observant of children—with unhappy results. Where before he had never paid much attention to kids, now he looked closely at every one; and where before kids had all seemed to him more or less alike, now he was amazed to discover how different they could be. And in becoming more observant, he could not help remarking how many—alas, almost all of them, he did believe— were so much cuter, and how many so much quicker-looking than his boy.

Poor little fellow. It was not his fault that he was homely. No, indeed. Whose fault that was, said my grandfather to himself, was as plain as the nose on your face. And not only the nose.

What my grandfather could never understand was what the Vinsons had seen in Ned to make them do it. He would look at the photograph where it lay among the things emptied from his pocket on his nightstand, and he never ceased to wonder. Of course, being your own, you loved him —especially when, he thought, catching sight of himself in the washstand mirror, especially when he so plainly *was* your own. But sometimes he almost felt that he had cheated the Vinsons.

Some answered quickly and some answered slowly, but all answered no. Then it was turn around and go back to the last fork in the road and go down the other way. And maybe then go back to the fork before that and take the road not taken there. And so he almost went past without stopping to ask, and collect another no from, the bearded rheumy-eyed old-timer feeding cane to his sorghum mill by the roadside. He did stop, did ask, but did not listen to the reply, heard it only as it echoed afterwards in his mind. He stopped to watch the blindfolded mule hitched to the mill crank plodding round and round and around. Stopped to listen to the snap of the cane as it was fed into the jaws of the mill, the crunch as the millstone bit down on it. Stopped to savor the smell of the running juice. What was that? Said yas, believed he had seen some folks like them. They'd stopped the wagon to eat a bite of dinner. He'd been eating his on the other side of the fencerow. Two little boys, one of them that un there in the tintype, had come on him as they played.

He had become so attuned to disappointment that he was now suspicious of any encouragement, and his manner with this old man resembled that of a policeman grilling a suspect. Whereupon the old fellow supplied him with a description of Will Vinson which he committed to memory to serve him in future, wherever his quest should take him.

"Blink-eyed feller, sandy-haired, medium-complected, stood about five foot ten, pigeon-toed, old carbuncle scar just under his right ear here, had a slow grin and a real hard-working Adam's apple?" In five minutes this old man had noticed more about Will Vinson than he had noticed in five years.

But two days later—and just fifteen miles farther along, such was the character of the road the old man had sent him down—he had encountered not one further word of confirmation, was beginning to suspect that old boy of all sorts of things, including being in Will Vinson's pay to steer him wrong. He had gone through two settlements, two holes in the road, where his approach had been heralded by a squadron of bare-bottomed little sentinels who spied him from half a mile off and ran howling to their respective homes that mamma, mamma, somebody was a-comin—yet of the Vinsons nobody had seen hide nor hair. The third such place, which he vowed would be the last, being still farther back

in the sticks, was even smaller than the first two. The men
on the gallery of the general store, all chewing rhythmically
like a ruminating herd, watched him descend from the
wagon, listened to his story, spat as one, ran their tongues
around their cheeks to collect the stray bits of tobacco, spat
collectively again, and allowed as how they couldn't none
of them recollect no such folks as that. The women rolled
up their aprons and filled their lips with snuff, and the children all shook their heads just about off, and my grandfather was on the point of climbing aboard his wagon,
turning around and going back, stopping only to curse the
old devil who had sent him on this wild goose chase, when:

"I seen em."

Who had spoken? No one.

"I seen em." And from beneath the gallery, like the moon
coming up, rose a saucer-shaped face belonging to a tousle-
headed lad of perhaps fourteen. "I seen them folks," he said.

A number of heads were meaningfully shaken in my
grandfather's direction, and the man standing on his left
whispered in his ear, "Not quite one hundred per cent. We
all humor him." The way he accented that "we" suggested
that it would be taken as a very Christian thing if Mr. Ordway humored him too. So he swallowed down the hope that
had gone sour in his mouth, assumed a smile, and one of
the men, contriving to beam at the boy while shaking his
head sadly at the crowd, said, "Tell us whereabouts you seen
them, Lightnin."

"Seen em rat here," said the youth. "Early in the mornin.
Ever'body asleep but me."

"And I reckon that's true, too," said one man with a hearty
nod. "That boy is always out and doing 'fore anybody else
is up."

"Papa, mamma, and four younguns, just like the man
there said," said the youth, and the locals all nodded at my
grandfather as if they were proud of him—of him, not the
boy.

"And a dog. Just like the man said." And again everybody gave my grandfather an encouraging nod.

"Not quite all there, you understand," said my grandfather's neighbor. "But, Lord, it'll save him lots of heartache, won't it?"

"Boy's daddy, sir," said my grandfather's neighbor on the other side, into the ear which he commanded. My grandfather hoped that the man intended was seated at some distance off, because that whisper had not been any too soft. However, it was not meant to be. It was an introduction, and following his neighbor's nod, my grandfather found himself saluted by the modest father. Meanwhile, raising his voice, the gentleman at his elbow continued, "Pet of the whole place, that boy. Never gives no trouble. Always comes when called. Eats anything you set before him. Don't know the meaning of sass. *There's* a boy that won't never grow up to bring shame on his family. There's *one* boy that'll never come to curse his poor old father, nor leave home to take up with some woman, will you, sonny? No, sir! There's a boy that'll never run off and join the Navy, will you, son? What I say is, the world'd be a lot better place to live in if we had more like that boy. I reckon you ain't much worried what'd become of that boy if anything was to ever happen to you, air you, Dub? Everybody knows which little feller gets the call whenever there's any pans to be licked here in south Saddleblanket!"

"Felix," said the youth.

"How's that, son?" said my grandfather's neighbor.

"Felix. That's what the man called one of them little boys. I jist wusht I had a purty name like that—Felix—'stead of Hubert."

Following that road my grandfather found himself, by a different approach, and three weeks after his first visit there, in Paris, the town through which Will Vinson had been too stupid and too countrified to realize lay his safest passage.

$125
REWARD

for information leading to the recovery of Edward
("Ned") Ordway. 3 yrs old. Blond. Blue eyes.
Slight. Stolen from home near Clarksville, Red
River County, Tex., on May 7, this year, by WILL
VINSON. About 35 yrs age. Medium build. Medium
complexion. Farmer by trade. Fled west by wagon
in company of wife Fern and 3 Vinson children—
Felix (3 yrs) Perry (2 yrs) and Grace (9 mos).
Also large collie dog named Rex. Samuel Ordway,
father of the stolen child, will be at the Ben Milam
Hotel, Paris, on Sat. Oct. 29. All communications
held in strictest confidence.

"Something the matter with it?" asked my grandfather.
"If you catch any mistakes I'd be much obliged to you for
correcting them. I don't pretend . . ."

"No," said the printer. "No, it's all spelled and punctuated
right."

"Then why are you shaking your head?"

"Well, first of all," said the printer, "I can't help wondering at that figure. I mean, why one hundred and twenty-five
exactly?"

That was just what my grandfather had been afraid he
might say. Arriving at that figure had cost him quite a lot
of thought, not to say distress, and he was still feeling far
from sure about it. How much, in dollars, was it worth to a
man to recover his lost child? Impossible to say. Offensive
to try. What did you do when you had to try, had to say? It
was complicated by other painful considerations too. He had
started off by thinking of $100, mainly because it was just
about the most he could think of putting out. It seemed to
trumpet aloud his guilty conscience. His indifference to his
boy, his six months' ignorance of Will Vinson's love for
him, stood proclaimed by that display of atonement, that
bid for public opinion. What was more, another reaction

had to be foreseen. To anger people by an intimation that
his child was worth more than theirs would not help his
cause. And yet there would be others (there would even be
some of those very same ones whom the offer of $100 would
have offended as excessive) who would call him a tightwad
and a bad father if he offered only $50. There really was no
acceptable sum. The trouble with $75 was that it was neither
$50 nor $100. It lacked the humility of the one, it fell short
of the unreserved self-disclosure of the other. How painful
it was, how humiliating, how terribly embarrassing even
though one were all alone, to have to consider the matter
in this way, to have to calculate one's effect and weigh
the public response; yet it had to be done. My grandfather had chosen to stand accused of having learned
too late to value his child, and of overvaluing him now,
rather than of stinting on the price of getting him back, and
decided to post a reward of $100. It was the most he could
afford. No sooner had he put it that way than he was forced
to ask himself, had Will Vinson considered how much he
could afford when he took his boy? Thus, because it was
more than he could afford: $125.

"Well, never mind. Just wondered," said the printer. "Anyhow, you spread it around that you're carrying that kind of
money on you, you're just asking to get knocked on the head
in some back alley one dark night. Furthermore, you got
any more youngsters? Have? Well . . ."

And I was afraid he might say it was too little! said my
grandfather to himself. "What would you think would be
about the right amount?" he asked.

"Well, yours is the first case of a *stolen* boy we have had,"
the printer said. "Get a good many calls for bills for *runaway*
boys. Keep the form in the lock-up, in fact. Hard to say. You
want to get out as light as you can, naturally; on the other
hand you don't want to look chinchy—after all, it's your own
flesh and blood. On runaway boys they generally offer ten
dollars. The last man put up fifteen, but that was for a boy

already working age—nearly twelve. But people like to turn
in a runaway boy. They can put theirselves in the father's
place. You don't have to offer much inducement. I reckon
you will have more resistance to overcome. In your case I
would think you might have to go as high as fifty. That
ought to be a big enough sum to induce the average fellow
to tell you if he knows anything."

"Truth is," said my grandfather, "anybody who gave me
the information I'm after really wouldn't have anything to
fear. I'm not just trying to save money in saying that—
you've seen that I was ready to offer more than you suggest.
But Will Vinson is actually a very mild-mannered fellow—
last man on earth you would ever expect to steal his neighbor's child and run off. But I realize that other people don't
know Will like I do, and would think they ought to be paid
for the risk they would run in—"

"I've got a better out," said the printer. "Don't offer nothing. That is, don't specify any sum. Just say, 'Reward,' and
let it go at that. That way nobody will think you're trying
to get out cheap nor others that you're willing to pay just
anything and try to hold you up. Who knows? When the
time comes you may have to go as high as fifty—maybe
higher. But as long as you haven't shown your hand, there's
always a hope of getting out lighter. It's going to depend on
who you have to deal with. You just may strike some
rounder who'll be happy with five dollars to blow on hooch."

"I begin to see there's an awful lot I hadn't taken into
account," said my grandfather, who as a matter of fact had
once considered offering no reward, but for a very different
reason: he had thought it just might be insulting to any
prospective informant to suggest that he would expect pay
for helping a father recover his lost child.

"This ain't a very full description," said the printer. "I'm
not just trying to run up your typesetting bill, but this ain't
much to go on."

"Here. Here's a picture of my boy," said my grandfather.

"Maybe you can describe him better than I can. You're a man of words. And you know, you never see your own clearly."

The printer studied the photograph, and my grandfather studied him. He kept a straight face; still my grandfather could see that he found it hard to understand why anybody, much less a man with children of his own, should want to steal that boy. "Hmm," he said, "I guess you have said about all there is to say. I suppose they all look pretty much alike at that age." He passed back the picture. "What about the man? Wilson?"

"Vinson. I haven't got any picture of him. He seen to that. He took them all with him when he left."

"Clever," said the printer—a word which my grandfather had not previously thought of in connection with Will Vinson.

"So far as describing him is concerned, though," said my grandfather, "I don't know that it would help much if we did have a picture. Like I say, to look at him Will was just the last fellow on earth you would ever expect—"

"No mustache? A gold crown? Sideburns? Tattoo?"

"Ho, no! Will certainly wasn't the kind ever to get himself tattooed! No, no, you're way off. Unnoticeable! Why, he had lived in and around Clarksville all his life, and yet after this all happened people would come up to me and say, 'Will Vinson. Who is Will Vinson?' And Clarksville, you realize, ain't all that big a place."

"I don't understand it," said the printer. "What do you suppose would make a man do such a thing?"

"Search me," said my grandfather.

"I've heard of men running off with their neighbors' wives, or with money that wasn't theirs, or both, and I knew of a fellow here in Paris once a few years back that run off with his neighbor's bird dog. A Gordon setter bitch, it was. But that's different, ain't it? I mean, you can understand a man coming to think that a certain dog or a certain horse, say,

is absolutely the only one of its kind, and a horse or a dog
is something you can't make for yourself. But this is the first
case that's come my way of a man wanting somebody else's
youngun."

"Well," said my grandfather, "I suppose if some little
fellow just sort of got you . . . came to seem like 'the only
one of his kind.' . . ." He enclosed this in quotation marks
because he wanted to dissociate himself from any such un-
manly sentiments. And certainly he did not wish to suggest
that his boy was "one of a kind."

"I expect his wife put him up to it, don't you expect?"

"Well, Will was always very fond of children," said my
grandfather. Then he wondered why he should feel called
upon to defend Will Vinson's title to master in his own
house. "You think it would help any to say in the bill that he
was sort of blink-eyed, and that when he swallowed his
Adam's apple run up and down real fast? You see, what
worries me about such a loose description is the possibility
that some poor innocent devil might come under suspicion,
maybe even get beat up and tossed in jail, just because he
happens to be a stranger in a place and to have four little
kids. However, I'm counting on that collie dog to help prevent anything like that from happening."

"If he's got any sense," said the printer, "he will have
gotten shut of that dog by now."

"Yes," said my grandfather with a sigh, "I'm afraid even
Will ought to be able to think of that. He was awful attached
to that dog, though."

"Well," said the printer, "not everybody notices the same
things about people. Maybe it's better not to go into too much
detail. He's a white man, at least."

"How do you mean?" said my grandfather.

"Well, we had a case out west of town here last year. Lady
was raped. In broad daylight. Well, nearly raped. They got
up a posse and went out and rounded up all the niggers they
could find. Lady pointed out one—big strapping buck about

two hundred pounds and black as my shoe. ' 'At's him,' she says. ' 'At's the one.' Wellsir, it wasn't a week later that she comes a-running into the house all out of breath and says to her husband, 'I seen him!' 'You seen who?' says he. 'The boy that attacked me,' says she. 'The hell you did!' says he. 'Yes,' she says. 'I must've been mistaken that first time.' Well, so him and a party of friends go looking for this second one, and they take along the lady to point him out. ' 'Ere he is,' she says. And what is it this time but a little bandy-legged runt that wouldn't have gone no more than a hundred and forty soaking wet, and sort of gravy-colored. 'You're sure now?' asks her husband. 'Yes,' she says, 'I'm sure.' 'All right,' says he. 'Just don't come around a week from now telling me you've seen him again, 'cause this is the last damn nigger I'm a-going to lynch for you.' And do you know what she says to that? 'I'm sorry, honey,' she says. 'But you know they all look so much alike.' Now you need two thousand of these by tomorrow afternoon, you say. What time tomorrow afternoon?"

"I would like to have them a little before time for school to let out, if possible."

"We've got a couple of jobs ahead of yours, but they will just have to step aside. Least we can do to help a man find his boy. It's been a pleasure to do business with you, Mr. Ordway, and I wish you the very best of luck."

From the printshop my grandfather inquired the way to the grammar school. On the playground he found a gang of boys, and hired six of them at ten cents apiece to pass out circulars around town on Saturday morning, agreeing to meet them there with the circulars the following afternoon.

The circulars were ready as promised and his boys were waiting for him. My grandfather divided the circulars among them and paid them in advance. They were surprised when they read the text; he was surprised at what they had expected. It was nearing election time, and it appeared that these boys, some of whom had handed out campaign circu-

lars for candidates in previous years, had supposed that he
was running for public office. They were thrilled to be
assisting in a manhunt instead.

"What'll you do with him if you find him, mister?" asked
one open-eyed youngster.

Only later did my grandfather realize that by "him" the
boy had meant Will Vinson. Which explained his look of
disappointment at the answer:

"Why, take him home with me, of course."

Overnight, lying keyed up and sleepless in his hotel bed,
he had begun to have misgivings about this handbill campaign. Informers, tale-bearers, the sort anticipated by the
printer: he could visualize the type, regretted doing a thing
which would bring him into contact with such men. He had
foreseen a slinky, shifty-eyed character sneaking up the
back stairs of the hotel, slipping into his room, mumbling
his sorry tale, holding out his hand—a man to whom Will
Vinson had never done any harm; and he began to feel
strangely beholden to Will, almost ashamed of leaguing himself with such a wretch against him. The morning light dis-
pelled all such gloomy expectations, and now as he lathered
his face my grandfather imagined quite a different sort of
man who would come to his aid. He saw a fellow who,
despite the printer's cynical predictions, rather resembled
himself, reading his bill and saying to his wife, "Mae, you
recall them strangers with that big collie dog that stopped
at our place one day last spring and asked us to boil their
baby's bottle? How many younguns did they have all told?
Wasn't it four? Wasn't it three little boys and that little
baby girl? And the man, you recollect him? What does it
say here—thirty-five, medium build . . . Why, I do believe . . ."

"There's a reward," the wife might say.

"Mae! I am ashamed of you! You can't take money for
helping a man find his boy. How would you like it if somebody was to run off with Lester?"

At half past seven he went down and had his breakfast. Returning from the dining room, he stopped at the desk and told the clerk that if anybody asked for him to send them right up, no questions asked. At the foot of the stairs he had another thought and went back to say that should some second person ask for him while he was still with the first, to keep him waiting, then send him up after the first had left.

. . . That man who perhaps even now was reading his handbill and scratching his memory, and who in a few minutes might come knocking on the door which my grandfather sat watching—he would insist of course that he take money. All the more if the man was the sort to decline it. "I only wish it was more," he would say. Naturally he would not give him the money here and now. But if on the basis of his information he found Ned, he would stop off in Paris on his way home, go call on the man, and say, "See, I have my boy back, and I owe it to you." Then he would say, "You wouldn't claim the reward, but here: you can't refuse this." And he would present the man with a bankbook in his son's name, showing a savings account with a $125 balance.

Musing on that journey home with Ned, my grandfather got out his photograph of him. He laid it face down on the table beside him while he returned his other papers to his pocket. When he went to pick it up he could not succeed in getting his fingernail under its edge. He would almost have it, then it would elude him. He tried sliding it to the edge of the table, but what a ham-handed thing he was! At last, by dog-earing a corner somewhat, he got it—only to turn it back over instantly and slap it down on the tabletop. For in that instant he had had a vision of Ned clinging convulsively to Will Vinson as he tried to pull him away, burying his face in Vinson's neck and crying, "I don't want to go with you! I won't! I won't! Don't let him take me away! Don't let him take me!"

A gasp of amazement at his own fatuity escaped him. He

had been seeing himself all along as Ned's deliverer, had
envisaged a touching scene of reunion. He had imagined
his son pining for him. Had he forgotten the pleasure with
which Ned always anticipated being left with the Vinsons
for the day? He had imagined his son enduring an odyssey
of hardships with the Vinsons on their flight. Fool! Weren't
people who loved him as they did going to cushion him
against every hardship? They would go hungry, would take
food from the mouths of their own children, so that he
might not want. They had sacrificed everything in order to
have him; would they hesitate to beg or to steal in order
to provide for him? Swaddled in such devotion, why should
Ned ever want to leave them? If by now he remembered
home at all, what were his memories? An indifferent stepmother and a father who had been willing to put him off
regularly on the neighbors, a father who (for so a child of
three would see it) had neglected for six months—a lifetime at that age—to come and reclaim him. If right this
minute some man was to walk through that door bringing
news of where he might find Will Vinson and his boy, what
good would it do him?

My grandfather got up and went to the window. He gazed
down the gray empty air shaft, and his mortification was
transmuted into bitterness towards the man whom he
imagined his son preferring to him. He would find him! He
would find him if he had to search to the end of the world.
And if that was what it took, he would tear Ned screaming
from Will Vinson's arms. Blood is thicker than water. He
was his boy, his, and he meant to have him back. And
he would return him to a very different home from the one
he had known before. Hester was changed. So was he. He
would smother the boy with attentions, would let him want
for nothing. Then we would see whether in a short time he
still pined for Will Vinson!

The knock which came upon the door felt as if it were
upon his breast. He leapt across the room. But the door

opened before he could reach it. It was the chambermaid, who said, "Do your room now?"

He swallowed his heart and said, all right. He vacated the room. Downstairs he told the clerk whereabouts in the lobby he would be sitting in case anyone asked for him. After half an hour he judged that the maid would be finished. "I'm going back up to my room now," he informed the clerk.

"All right, Mr. Ordway," said the clerk with a faint smile.

Nine o'clock struck. Nine thirty. At ten he braved the desk clerk's amusement and went down and inquired whether anyone had been in to ask for him.

"I'll send them right up if anybody does, Mr. Ordway," said the clerk.

He remembered having heard of boys hired to pass out handbills throwing half the stack down a culvert or into a vacant lot. He could not believe that his boys would do a thing like that. He left the hotel. The streets of town, the side streets even, such as the one his hotel sat on, were littered with handbills (he remembered then that other name for them: throwaways) as with leaves on a windy autumn day. Surely everybody in Lamar County had seen one of them, had read it, then dropped it to the ground. For everybody in the county, everybody who lived along every road, including the one down which Will Vinson must have gone, was in Paris that day. In the square the streets were like cattle chutes, packed with a milling throng. Men stood along the curbs—no room to squat—spattering the gutter with tobacco juice. Farm women bucked the current, their small fry clinging to their skirts. By this time of day already the cobblestones were so layered with horse dung as almost to muffle the clop of hooves; the wagon beds as they went past rattled and popped. Around the corners of the streets leading off the square there hung upon the air the raw fumes of corn liquor. On one corner stood a big black-brown man, a Negro but with Mexican, maybe Indian blood in him, carrying a large tin-bound box hanging from a strap around his neck, crying "Mollyhot! Hot tamales!" All about him the sidewalk was strewn with the cornshucks his tamales came wrapped in. Whenever he lifted the lid of his box to make a sale he momentarily disappeared behind a cloud of pungent steam. Above the din that reverberated in the bowl of the buildings occasionally there rose the voice of the self-appointed evangelist threatening the crowd out in the plaza with hellfire and damnation.

My grandfather saw one of his boys passing out his circulars. Or trying to. Most men refused even to accept one. Those who did, did so only to get rid of the boy, then, without a glance, dropped the circular to the street. He was even approached by the boy himself. The hour was getting on, and finding himself with such a stack of them still to get rid of, the boy had rather a desperate look. My grandfather accepted the circular, and as soon as he had moved on, dropped it with a sigh. He looked sadly down at it where it lay in the spit and the dung, and saw that it read:

VOTE FOR ATKINS

The one lying beside it read:

VOTE FOR CRITTENDEN

A third which blew by at that moment read:

VOTE FOR WELLS

Also running, for one office or another, were Sayres, Porterfield, Slocum, and Knight, as he learned by turning over others, including several of his own, with his toe. He had chosen a day when circulars had fallen on the town like leaves after the year's first frost. There was to be a political rally in Paris that day, at which each candidate announced that he would speak. Even as he stood there my grandfather heard the distant sound of a brass band striking up, at which signal the square began to empty.

So named because underneath the mightiest of the oaks there the great Davy was alleged to have slept one night on his way to the Alamo and immortality, Crockett Circle lay on the eastern edge of Paris. You approached it through a grove in which now were hitched wagons and buggies and buckboards, the horses' heads drooping, their tails swishing automatically, from among them the lazy *flop flop flop* of dung spattering as it fell. At the edge of the grove, just inside the shade, on long trestle tables, the Ladies' Auxiliary of the Shiloh Cumberland Presbyterian Church were setting out their benefit food sale.

Out in the sunshine the crowd stood facing the speakers' platform, which was draped in red, white, and blue bunting. The day had turned off hot and rather gnatty, a boon to that candidate, one Dewitt O. Porterfield, with whose compliments the ladies had all been given pasteboard fans. It was before the days of universal suffrage, but here the enjoyment of oratory was an end in itself, and knew no sex.

The mayor of Paris finished his welcome to the day's visitors, and introduced the Reverend Cecil Clevenger, who would lead them in a moment of prayer.

"O Lord," Reverend Clevenger prayed, "in time of elections we turn unto Thee. Think not of our deserts but of our sore needs, and send us, we beseech Thee, worthy candidates. Appear Thou unto our good men, inspire them to enter public service as Thou didst inspire Daniel in the lion's den, Shadrach in the fiery furnace, and Jonah in the belly of the whale. Persuade them to run, O Lord, and teach us, that we may know them. Deafen our ears to hollow blandishments. Abandon us not to our own weak judgment, but go Thou with us into the polling booth and guide our choice. With Thy help, O Lord, may the best man win, and once in office, lead him not into temptation but deliver him from evil, for Thine is the kingdom, the power and the glory for ever and ever, amen."

"Amen," said the crowd, and put their hats back on.

The lead-off speaker was the senior U. S. senator from the
Lone Star State, the Right Honorable Clifford Venable, seeking re-election to his fifth term. "Cousin Cliff," as he was
affectionately known ("She's a cousin of mine—a kissing
cousin," he would explain whenever, as usually happened,
his zeal for baby kissing led him to buss the mother too),
Cousin Cliff came shod in those famous old broken-heeled
congressman's gaiters which had been for so long his trade-
mark. "Lord, folks, mah feet are a-killin me! Ain't yawl's?"
he would at some point exclaim at every stop on the campaign trail, and hordes of registered Democratic fellow-suf-
ferers from corns, calluses, ingrown toenails, and fallen
arches would guffaw with pleasure, would poke their elbows
into one another's ribs, and would mentally cast their votes
right then and there. He would invite them to take the load
off their feet, to just squat right down on the grass, and
would himself, with a great mortal sigh, fall into a folding
chair. "Why don't we all just slip the durn things off? We
wasn't born with them on, and most of us, I hope, will go out
with them off. Let's just ease out of them, what do yawl say?
We're all friends here." They would. By the hundreds. And
the atmosphere on a hot day in stump-speaking weather
would often get fairly feetid. And Cousin Cliff would take off
those old gaiters of his, revealing socks with great holes
through which his two big toes protruded. He would wriggle
them, sigh again, and say, "Good gracious, Miss Agnes, don't
that feel good!" In times of dispute on the Senate floor he
had been known to issue the same invitation to the dis-
putants. "Cooler feet mean cooler heads" was one of his copy-
righted maxims, and he had caused to be read into *The
Congressional Record* during more than one filibuster his
documented theory that most of the ills of history could be
traced to great men's bunions and to shoes that fit, as he
phrased it, "a mite too soon."

"Fellow Texans!" Cousin Cliff began.

When the applause finally quieted down, he continued,

"Ladies and gentlemen. Citizens of Paris, the metropolis of the blackest land and the whitest people. Mah frans and neighbors." He went on to say that it was customary, he believed, for a candidate seeking re-election to summarize his record during his term of office. He was not going to do that. In the first place, he himself could no longer recall all the bills that bore his name, reaching all the way back to the Venable Livestock Security Act of 1875, the law which, by putting an obligatory cowcatcher on every locomotive plying Southern rails, had saved from destruction unnumbered family milch cows throughout Dixie, thereby saving from indirect starvation at the hands of Yankee railroad interests whole generations of Southern infants. Coming rapidly up to date, he did not think they needed to be reminded whose senator it was, from what great state, who, during the late session of the Congress, in the struggle to preserve and maintain the sacred institution of the poll tax, when his Southern colleagues and brethren had all sunk one by one into impotent laryngitis, had hoarsely declared, "I have not yet begun to talk!"

No, he was not going to waste their time with these things. They knew them, and besides, he believed he could count on his young opponent to go into his long career at length. He hoped, by the way, that they would all stay and listen courteously to the boy.

The record which Cliff Venable had made during the twenty-four years he had represented them in the Senate of the United States (that federation to which, like it or not, they belonged) was known to every Texan. What he was going to speak about here today was *their* record during that time. He was going to speak of what they, the men and, God bless em, the women, of this great and glorious state had achieved during this past quarter century. Praise to the face was open disgrace, he knew, but he would ask them to restrain their natural modesty (a virtue which Texans carried almost to a fault) and listen unabashed while he told them of the miracle they had wrought.

Twenty-four years. . . . As he looked out now upon this sea of shining faces he was irresistibly brought to mind of that autumn day in the inglorious year of Our Lord 1874 when he first stood upon this spot, beneath this hallowed tree. Long had their beloved state lain under the murky flood of enemy occupation and so-called Reconstruction. Yet in 1874, unbeknownst to the great mass still huddling in the bowels of the ark, a few hardy souls had ventured up on deck, had released the timorous dove, and she had returned bringing in her beak the tender olive branch of hope. Then, like unto the legendary phoenix of old, they had arisen from their ashes, had rolled up their collective sleeves, had spat on their hands, and said, "There is work to be done."

Then it was that he himself had been persuaded by a group of civic leaders to leave, like Cincinnatus, his plow, and add his humble voice to the swelling chorus. To awaken Texas, that slumbering giant, that Hercules in feminine attire, that Samson eyeless in Gaza at the mill with slaves. He well remembered saying as he stood on this spot of holy ground in the fateful November of 1874, "O Texas, cast thy nighted color off!" He remembered saying, "Fellow Texans, we are living *in* this great state, we are living *off of* it, but are we living *up to* it?" "Where now," he remembered saying, "where now is fled that spirit which caused it to be said, 'Thermopylae had her messenger of defeat—the Alamo had none!'" "O Crockett," he had said. "O Austin. O Mirabeau B. Lamar. Thou shouldst be living at this hour. Texas hath need of thee." They had but lost a battle, he had told them. The contest must go on!

How had they responded to that call?

They had fought on! The battlelines had shifted, new weapons been adopted. Swords had been beaten into plowshares; but plowshares were weapons too, every plowman a soldier in the fray. Industrial and agricultural competition had replaced the trial at arms. Above all, the battle had been carried into the very heart of the enemy's camp: the citadel where his very laws were hatched had been breached, and in a series of rearguard actions the equal in brilliance of Lee's Wilderness campaign in the military sphere, Southern statesmen had scored victory after victory in the halls of Congress—for no Yankee who ever lived could match a Southerner in parliamentary maneuver!

How stood the contest now? What report could he bring them back from the battlefront?

During the current campaign he had been privileged to tour once again the length and breadth of this seat of majesty, this other Eden, demi-paradise, this Texas. What had he seen? He had seen the sturdy yeoman tilling his fertile and ample plot, the thriving tradesman at his busy till, the patient blackamoor cheerfully, yea gratefully, restored to his allotted place in God's scheme. It was the harvest season and the good Lord had sent them His sun and His rain in reasonable quantities, and just enough of His boll weevils to keep the cotton prices up. The earth was piled high with His benison. Upon the broad plains he had seen the fatted herds—the ring-straked and the spotted. In the mighty forests he had heard the woodsman's axe, clearing the path of progress. In the rich deltas and savannahs he had seen a land flowing with milk and honey. Were these the wages of defeat?

By way of contrast he was brought to mind of the sights which had met his eyes on his official travels in the cold, unfriendly North. There he had seen the joyless Yankee farmer mortgaged to his rocky hills like Prometheus chained unto his cliff. He had seen the dreary files of listless millhands shuffling to their daily bondage like salt-mine slaves. He had seen their stunted, pale, consumptive children shivering in rags in the crooked streets of crowded, smoke-filled cities. Were those the wages of victory?

He had toured the battlefronts, and this was his report:

the South—with Texas in the van—had won the Civil War!

There was stunned silence for some moments, then the crowd sent up a deafening wild rebel yell. It was minutes before the senator could proceed.

What, he asked them to ask themselves, was the Civil War all about? Was it, as some Southern apologists and historians had long maintained, a conflict of commercial interests? Was it a disagreement over such things as tariffs? Tommyrot! The issue could be stated in a word. The Civil War had been fought over the question of slavery. Now their side had fought for the preservation of that peculiar institution. They were accustomed to think that in losing it, they had lost the War. Well, how many of them had suffered hardship through the manumission of the slaves? Speaking for himself, his old daddy had never owned any slaves. Never could afford them. From youth to crooked age he had done all his dirty backbreaking chores his own self, as did many another back in the so-called good old days. He was not talking now to any born aristocrats there might happen to be in the audience. He was talking to all the rest of you hard-working, never-seem-to-get-nowhere, salt-of-the-earth ordinary just plain folks. What had the freeing of the slaves meant to them?

To answer that question it was necessary to pose another. Namely, what were the slaves? They were the hewers of wood. The drawers of water. The pickers of the cotton. And what did they do now—the nigras, that was to say? Still hewed the wood, didn't they? Still drawed the water. Still picked the cotton. The difference lay in this: who did they do those chores for before the War, and who did they do them for now?

It might not be what their friend Honest Abe had had in mind in promulgating his well-known Emancipation Proclamation, but he was here to state that what Lincoln had done was to free *them*, the white slaves of the South! With one blow the old rail splitter had broken up the detested plantation system, thereby creating a pool of cheap native labor on which all men were free and equal to draw. It was their emancipation! Not for nothing was Lincoln called the Great Commoner. He had taken their greatest natural resource from the greedy hands of the few and given it back to the many, whose birthright it was! He had put the nigra within the means of the common man—"you and me, mah frans, you and me!" No, it might not be exactly what old Abe had had in mind, but they had seen their opportunity and taken full advantage of it. It was a prime instance of spreading the wealth; and if they were against that, then he would ask them to please cast their vote for his opponent, and not for Clifford W. Venable.

"Some talker, ain't he?" asked, or rather demanded, my grandfather's neighbor, shouting in his ear to make himself heard above the roar of acclaim. "You bet he is! Regular spellbinder! And I'm a-going to vote for him, you bet, same as I have four times previous. Don't care what the other feller has got to say for hisself."

The other feller came in now for a passing reference from the senator, who spoke of him as "a young man of promise . . . es." As for himself, well, he had had his say, and now his feet was a-killin him. He would just add this: during the coming term he promised to do exactly what he had done for the past twenty-four years, and that was, to do what they, his constituents, told him they wanted done. To be the inside horse to their team up there in Washington, the clapper to their bell. And in that connection, and in conclusion, he wished to express the earnest hope that they would continue to write him their every wish and command, as so many had done in the past. Just address their cards and letters to Cousin Cliff, Washington, D.C. That would reach him. The postman up there knew him by now. And never mind about the spelling. If it was wrong, why he wouldn't know no better.

Waving aside the mayor of Paris as if to say that he needed no introduction, the next speaker, who had just made a last-minute appearance on the platform, took off his hat and began:

"Folks, I am not a politician."

"Hah!" snorted those in the audience who had heard that opening before.

"I'm not running for office. I'm not on the program of speakers you're scheduled to hear today. In fact, I'm not supposed to be up here any more than any of you all. I wouldn't be if you had read the circular I had passed out around town this morning. I picked a bad day. I didn't know that these gentlemen" (indicating the office seekers at his back, buzzing now like a nest of rattlesnakes) "were coming into town today. But they did, and you all threw my circular away the same as the rest, thinking it was just another politician after your vote."

Now the snorts came from behind him, while the audience, mistaking the guileless smile on the speaker's face for guile, chortled approvingly, and my grandfather (for he it was, rather frightened, but filled as always with trust in the inborn goodness of people and sure of the sympathy which his plight was bound to excite in even the stoniest breast, so that he felt confident of a hearing, and never noticed the two sheriff's men making their way down through the crowd to apprehend and eject him), my grandfather felt sufficiently encouraged to hazard a little joke:

"They stole my thunder, so now I hope they won't mind if I take a little of theirs.

"Folks, you won't object, I'm sure," he continued after a moment, "to giving a few minutes of your time to a poor unhappy father whose little son has been stolen from him, and who comes to you for help in finding him."

A hush fell. Sensing the change of mood, the mayor signaled to the sheriff's men. They halted.

My grandfather introduced himself, spelling his name and

Vinson's, who, however, as he pointed out, was probably going under an alias now, and briefly told his story, winding up with, "From that day to this nothing has been seen or heard of them. The law" (here a tinge of bitterness colored his tone), "the law traced them as far as Bogota—ten miles from home—and no further. I'm hoping, with the help of good people like yourselves, to pick up where the law left off." A murmur of approval greeted this. The crowd was composed of country men like himself.

He knew only that they had come this way, headed west. He described the team, and Rex, and listed the occupants of the wagon. Unfortunately he had no photograph to show them of the man he was after. What was even more unfortunate, he himself was a tongue-tied sort of fellow with no gift of words and unable to supply the lack with any description. About all he could tell them was that Will Vinson was sandy-haired, medium-complected, had a slow grin, was sort of popeyed, and when he swallowed, his Adam's apple bobbed up and down very noticeably. "In short, to look at him, just the last man alive that you would ever expect to do such a thing. Which just goes to show you can never trust appearances."

He did have a photograph of his little boy (he took it from his pocket, and though it was only two by three inches, the entire audience of fifteen hundred craned forward for a look) and would be glad to show it to anyone who thought they might know where to find the folks he was after. My grandfather looked down at the picture and momentarily fell silent. He swallowed and shook his head, and the audience exhaled a sigh. His voice when he spoke again was husky.

"I know," he said, "that you folks will help me all you can, and that a father's everlasting gratitude will be all the reward that any of you would ask. However, I will insist on showing my appreciation. I am not a rich man, and needless to say, I can't put out my hard-earned money just to

have somebody say, why yes, I recall some folks that looked
a lot like that here on the street in town one day six months
ago. But for a lead that really puts me on the trail . . ." Well,
it was hard for a man to put a dollar sign on his own son.
All he would say was, that for the man who helped him get
back his boy he was going to want to do more than just
shake his hand and say thank you.

Now he realized that they did not know him, and maybe
somewhere among them some man was saying to himself
right this minute, well, well! So that new neighbor of mine
down the road is this Vinson, and that one little boy he
calls Ned is not his! You'd never know: he couldn't be a
better father to the child if he was his own. How was anybody
to know that Vinson wasn't doing the boy a kindness? Maybe
this Ordway had mistreated his boy. Who knew this Ordway?
Here he was putting on a big show of wanting his boy back,
but maybe what he wanted was just to lay hands on him
again? Well, he was talking now to that man, if such a one
there was. "I admit," he said, "that I was not always as good
a father to my boy as I might have been. But I ask you, what
man can honestly say otherwise? I believe I can truthfully
say I was never a bad father. And I'll be a better one if I ever
get him back. A thing like this teaches you a lot." He looked
down again at the photograph in his hand, and then, looking up, said, "Did I say *if*? I mean *when* I get him back!"
This earned him cheers.

It struck him then that by way of conclusion he ought—
in as delicate a way as possible, so as not to impute cowardice
—to direct a word to any in the audience who, having the
information he sought, might wish to tell him, yet hesitate
to come forward out of fear. He said, "By way of conclusion,
I'd like to say just a word to anyone in the audience who
might have the information I'm seeking, and wish to tell
me, yet hesitate for fear of Will Vinson taking his revenge.
Don't. I guarantee that you will have nothing to fear."

He meant to go on and explain what a mild-mannered

fellow Will really was, but that was as far as he got. They cheered him wildly, and among their mingled cries the following could be made out:

"Make him eat lead, shorty! Sic him, big boy! We're with you, fellow! You show him, Tex! Make him wish he never was born! You're the one to do it, shorty-boy! Hanging's too good for him! Yea, Clarksville!"

It did not seem the moment for pointing out that what he was interested in, really, was recovering his boy, and that his pleasure in having him back would not be greatly enhanced by the knowledge that he had orphaned Will Vinson's three to get him.

In taking his leave my grandfather apologized again to the crowd, to the candidates, the mayor, and the Reverend Clevenger for butting in. He said he was sure they all had troubles enough of their own without listening to his. He announced that he was in rooms at the Ben Milam Hotel, and vowed that all communications would be held in strictest confidence. Then to loud and prolonged applause he descended the steps and made his way through the crowd, which parted for his passage.

"Mister! Hey, mister! You the man that's looking for your little boy?"

It was a freckle-faced twelve-year-old in overalls and a denim jumper, panting from his run and from excitement. His breathlessness was catching. My grandfather nodded. The boy hopped off the curb into the gutter, poked a thumb and forefinger into his mouth, and meanwhile beckoning with his free arm to someone back down the street, gave out with a long shrill whistle. "Mister," he said, "am I glad to've found you! We must've been just missing each other going and coming—you looking for your boy and us looking for you." He beckoned again more imperatively, and my grandfather saw coming down the street a second boy leading, or rather dragging, a small tot.

This little boy was shaped like a bowling pin and not much bigger, with sloping narrow shoulders down which the suspenders of his overlarge, obviously hand-me-down overalls were slipping, his feet lost beneath the cuffs of his trousers. He was not Ned Ordway—foolish to imagine that he might be. Yet he was about Ned's size and equally towheaded, and if not Ned, he was still a lost boy, and that was enough to melt my grandfather's heart. He was not his, but whose he was was anybody's guess. His face was swollen from crying and so streaked and smudged with tearstains that his own mother would not have known him. He had wet his pants, that you could see now, from fright no doubt, as he was past the age of training, and had fallen down and torn them at both knees, torn the knees too, evidently, for about them, moving along with him in a little knee-high cloud, hovered a swarm of gnats. He had cried himself into the hiccups, his head bobbing regularly and his shoulders heaving. His nose was running. And that was near enough for my grandfather to have to say, "Not mine, boys." Looks of such keen disappointment appeared on their faces that he added, "Sorry. And thanks anyhow."

The two of them looked blankly at one another, then together looked down at their small unwanted ward. One of them said, "Are you sure, mister?"

My grandfather could not help smiling. Then a serious thought disturbed his mind. If ever he should see Ned again, would he recognize him? It was six months already, and might be that long again. And they changed so rapidly at that age. And then a still more disturbing thought: would Ned recognize him?

"Well! Now what are we going to do with him?" said one brother to the other.

"We've just got to leave him here, that's all there is to it. That's how we found him, and we got to go."

"Aw, you can't do that, Bubba," said the other.

"No? Then maybe you've got a better idea? You're the one that found him."

This one looked down at the boy, lifted his shoulders, blew out his cheeks, and said, "I'm beginning to wonder if he has got any folks."

"What's his name?" asked my grandfather.

"Sounds like he's trying to say Wayne."

"Wayne what?"

"That's all he can say. I guess that's all he knows yet."

Oh, dear Lord! Here was another something that he had not thought of. Had Ned known anything more than "Ned"?

"He could say more if he wanted to," said the other brother. "He's just being contrary. Ain't you, boy? What's the matter with you? Cat got your tongue?"

"What would you do with him, mister, if you was us?"

"I told you what we're gonna do. We're gonna just leave him like we found him. We done our best and now we got to get—"

"Aw, you can't do that," said my grandfather.

"Mister, that boy ain't nothing to me. I already done give up most of my fun in town for him. Doggone if I'm gonna spend the rest of the day dragging him around."

"Didn't anybody know whose he was? Whereabouts did you all find him?"

"We found him in a back alley off the square, wandering around lost and bawling his eyes out."

"Oh, poor little tyke!" my grandfather exclaimed. His pitying tone caused the child to burst out in a loud wail, terminated by a violent hiccup.

"Ssh! Hush up," said Bubba. "Ain't nobody hurting you. Buster, hush him, can't you?"

"Me? I can't do nothing with him. Besides, it wasn't me that got him going."

This had a barb on it, which my grandfather felt. He squatted and drew the sniveling child to him. "All right. All right, ole hoss," he said. "Don't cry any more, hear?" He took

the child's thumb from his mouth (it was quite pickled—
colorless and shriveled) and right back in again it went, as
if on a spring, as soon as he let go of it. He was coming
round, though he still glowered up at my grandfather from
under his brows, or where brows ought to have been, mistrustful, skitterish. "There now. That's better. Now let's tidy
you up a bit. My gracious, just look at you! You're about the
blackest white boy I ever saw." He sucked a corner of his
bandana and gave the child's face a spitbath. "Why, if we
was to ask anybody if you belonged to them they would be
downright insulted." He succeeded in whitening the boy as
far back as the ears; the hands would have to stay as they
were: black as the paws of a coon. He held his bandana to
his nose and commanded him to blow. He was a farm child,
of that my grandfather was sure. Something in the countrified way he had of tucking his chin into his collarbone, something in the smell that clung to him—of homemade lye
soap, was it?—in that homemade haircut that overhung his
skull like a miniature thatched roof, proclaimed to my
grandfather that this was one of his own kind. Indeed, now
that he was visible he looked, alas, a lot like Ned.

My grandfather stood up, and he found a subtle but unmistakable change in the demeanor of the two older boys. He
had earned himself a third share.

"Man! He's sure got some pair of lungs on him, ain't he!"
said Buster, hopefully insinuating into his tone a note of
corporate pride.

"Whoa now! Just a minute here," said my grandfather.
"I've got my own to look for. This boy ain't nothing more to
me than he is to you two. Less. You're the ones who found
him."

As if sensing my grandfather's disavowal of him, the waif
recommenced to blubber. It only hardened my grandfather's
heart against him. Compared with his own, this boy ought
to be ashamed to carry on this way after being separated
from his folks for only a matter of hours. Yet as he glared

impatiently at him my grandfather recognized this boy. This was the son of that man whom he had pictured, while shaving this morning, coming to his aid. Who because he was a father himself would refuse the reward money. Whose boy here was the one in whose name he, Sam Ordway, had resolved to open that savings account.

"Gee, thanks, mister!" said Buster. Then, "Say! Maybe his daddy has found yours and yawl can just swap!"

"Come on, fool!" his brother hissed.

"I spent the next two hours toting that little devil around town," my grandfather told me. "First I went to the town constable's office. The constable was out—'out at that political rally, I expect,' a non-voter loafing there said. Well, I just couldn't see myself going back out there and butting in again and saying, 'Folks, here I am back again. Remember me? I have found a little boy only he ain't mine. Which of you does this little man belong to?' So I went down to the market square (I've said you could tell just by looking that he was from off the farm) where the country folks parked their wagons, but nobody much was there, they were all out at that rally too, and those that were didn't know the boy. So I started walking the streets with him. Oh, what a handful he was! It turned out he wasn't trained, and he peed on me and slobbered on me and he howled and he kicked and beat me with his fists. I bought him candy and parched peanuts and he wolfed them down and gave me a kick for thanks. I remember thinking, boy, I just wish Will Vinson had you! And people I stopped to ask if they knew whose he was said, 'Ain't he yours?' One of two old maids that I passed in the street said, 'They ought to take children away from any father that treats them like that!' I stopped to explain the situation to her, and the other one said, 'Come along, Inez, before he says something rude. He's been out at that rally, drinking.'

"Along about two o'clock that afternoon I was sitting on

a curb to rest my feet, the boy sitting alongside of me, when up comes two men. One of them looked faintly familiar. He was the fellow who had been lounging outside the constable's office when I went there with the boy. When I stood up he sort of worked himself around in back of me. The other one did the talking. 'Got a proposition we think'll interest you, mister,' he said.

" 'Proposition?' I said. They knew something about Will, I figured. They looked the type.

" 'That's right. But now before we get down to business there's something you ought to know. There's actually three of us, see? Our pardner is watching us right this minute. You don't see him but he sees us. He knows all that we know, and he is watching every move you make. Understand?'

" 'No,' " I said.

" 'Yes you do,' said the one at my back.

" 'Now we are ready to take that boy there off your hands and see that his daddy gets him back. We will give you the rest of the day to clear out of town before we go to him.'

" 'It's going to cost you,' the one behind me said, and he looked around me to check with the other one, 'five hundred dollars? Five hundred dollars.'

"The first one said, 'Now let's not raise our voices.' I didn't even have any voice. 'There's a mighty big crowd in town here today for this rally. They're already tanked up and just itching for a little excitement. Wouldn't take them a minute to lay hands on a rope. Catch my drift? And just remember, we ain't alone.'

" 'So that's our offer, Mr. Vinson,' says the other one, and when I wheeled around, there was a copy of my own handbill in my face. 'Five hundred dollars and me and my friend here will take this boy and . . .'

"He looked down. The other fellow looked down. I looked down. The boy was nowhere to be seen. I must have let go of his hand, and for the second time that day he had wandered off on his own. We all three just caught sight of him walking in under the swinging doors of a saloon down in the middle of the block.

"When we got there this is what we saw. From the door there was a trail in the sawdust on the floor that his trouser cuffs had made, and at the end of the trail that boy, just putting down, on a tabletop above his head, a beer stein that he had drunk the suds from. Before we could get to him there came a cry from a man standing at the bar. 'Raymond!' he said.

" 'Papa!' cried the boy, and he ran to throw himself into his daddy's arms.

" 'Raymond?' came two more cries. And the two at my side spun and disappeared, leaving the doors flapping.

" 'Boy, where have you been?' the man yells. 'I've been all over this town looking for you!' And he grabs him by one wrist and swings him into the air and lands a series of whacks on his baggy little bottom that sounded like somebody beating out a rug. 'If I've told you once I've told you a thousand times never to let go of my hand in a crowd. Haven't I? Haven't I? You've had me and your mamma half out of our minds! I'll never bring you into town again, hear?'

"Well, I got to laughing. I thought of how I'd pictured the scene, this man getting his boy back and hugging and kissing him and crying over him, and how I would stand there real noble, not letting him know how much like and yet how different my own situation was from his, and how he would say to me, 'You don't know what I've been through' and I would say, 'I can just imagine.' I laughed so hard he turned to me and said, 'What's so all-fired funny? What are you laughing at?'

" 'Myself,' I said.

"He went back to beating his boy. Now I hope I know better than to interfere with another man's way of treating his children. I wouldn't have interfered on that occasion, except anybody could see that the man had lost all self-control. He was going through the same spiel again and the boy's screams just seemed to make him all the madder, and when finally the boy couldn't scream any more then his silence maddened him. In for a penny in for a pound, so I caught his arm and said, 'Here, here, friend. Get a grip on yourself. You've punished the boy enough.'

" 'You trying to tell me how to treat my own boy?' he said. 'This here is my boy, and by God, I'll whup him whenever I feel like it. And I feel like it now! And if I have to whup you first to do it, that's all right with me too.'

"Well, somebody stepped in and took our coats. There's always somebody ready to do that, I've noticed. And somebody else took the boy. We closed, and I don't know who threw who, but we went down and commenced rolling around in the sawdust. He got on top of me and said, 'Holler calf rope. I'll hold you down till you do!' And I got on top of him and said more or less the same. Well, finally I began to get the best of it. What happened was, I sat down real hard on his stomach and knocked his wind out. His eyes rolled back in his head and the whites showed and I thought for a minute I'd killed him. Then all of a sudden I felt a terrific pain in my leg. I twisted around and there was that little boy with his teeth sunk in the calf of my leg and chewing like he meant to chew it right off. I grabbed him by the hair and pried him loose and pulled my pants leg up. The skin was broken with the print of a perfect set of milk teeth and already the whole calf was turning purple. I looked up and saw my opponent hoisting his boy onto his shoulders. The two of them stood laughing down at me. For a moment I thought of getting up and giving them both a good licking. But I sat back down and watched them leave. And right then my leg stopped hurting. That is to say, it hurt worse than ever, only the pain felt good. Blood *is* thicker than water, I thought. Watching that man stride off with his boy on his shoulders I felt that they were Ned and me, and I was Will Vinson."

Back at his hotel, where he arrived limping, still sprinkled with sawdust from rolling on that barroom floor, my grandfather found three men waiting to see him. Two of them obviously belonged to the shady sort he had dreaded meeting, the other one was a preacher. You could tell he was a preacher, he had his collar on backwards.

First in line was a man who embodied the faceless figure that had flitted, or rather had slunk, through his thoughts the night before. This one differed from his imagined informer in one respect only: instead of being shabby he was quite well dressed, as if he was doing well by doing bad. He was one of those forms of life that shun the light and flourish in the shade, and one had the feeling that like a chameleon he could change the color of his blood to blend with any background. "Ten dollars," my grandfather was on the verge of saying, "not a cent more." Luckily he did not, for this turned out to be Lieutenant R. D. (Bob) Loftus, twenty-two years a Pinkerton man, instrumental in solving the notorious Hastings and Alancaster cases among others, recently retired and now at liberty and here now to offer Mr. Ordway the benefit of his wide professional experience. "Father myself," he concluded his introduction, "and know just how you must feel."

That was why he was willing to make him this offer: he (Mr. Ordway) would guarantee his *per diem* expenses for six months. If at the end of that time he had found neither of them, man nor boy, then that was every last cent he owed him. If he found them both: twenty-five hundred dollars.

That was more than enough for my grandfather, right there, and he opened his mouth to say so. However, the lieutenant proceeded, if—and this was a possibility, alas, that Mr. Ordway must surely have considered—if all that was ever found was the kidnapper: two thousand. This was a very fair offer. He couldn't hope to do better than that. Not and get a man with real experience..

What did he mean, my grandfather asked, face the possibility that all that might ever be found was the kidnapper? What did he mean by that?

"Well," said Lieutenant Loftus, cocking his head to one side and slowly shaking it, "it's six months, Mr. Ordway. They panic, you know. Lose their heads. A child is a pretty large and loud piece of evidence to have on you. Lots of bother, too, for a man. And even when they really intend to return them unharmed, they sometimes get frightened at the last minute of a trap. I don't mean to alarm you. You've surely thought of all this yourself. In your case let us hope for the best. But let us be prepared for the worst. For even if you've been paying the fellow off regularly, it's no guarantee, I'm afraid, that he has kept his share of the bargain. Big Ben Alancaster paid out more than eleven thousand dollars to Frankie Thorpe, but when we tracked Frankie down . . . Well," he sighed, "I won't go into the details. You no doubt recall the case."

My grandfather shook his head. "No," he breathed. "What happened?"

"Don't recall the Alancaster case!" exclaimed Lieutenant Loftus. "Why it was headline news every day for months! The search for little Benny Alancaster, sole heir to Alancaster Starch and Bluing? Then pardon me, I'm sorry I brought it up."

"Tell me," said my grandfather.

Lieutenant Loftus fetched a sigh. "Well," he said, "we found him, all right, poor little devil—right where he'd been all the time. It was Frankie himself led us to the spot, behind a prize *American Beauty* in Mr. Alancaster's rose garden. It took six of us to hold the poor old man back. But Frankie got his neck stretched, and so will our friend Will Vinson. How much, if you don't mind saying, has he worked you for up to now, Mr. Ordway, in round numbers? More than you care to remember, eh? Well, small guarantee that it is, I'm afraid, sir, you'd better keep on paying until we catch him."

When first he realized that the man thought Will was holding Ned for ransom, my grandfather breathed again. Then at once he began to worry. Never having been able to comprehend why a man like Will with children of his own should want his boy, he found it all too easy now to believe that gain should have been Will's motive. The fact that he had never received any ransom note did not comfort him. Possibly at the last minute, out of fear of being traced through it, Will had not dared send it. Then to get the child off his hands he had . . . Or perhaps he had sent it and it had gone astray in the mails. And then Will had gone to the spot where he had directed the money to be left, and had found nothing there, and then had waited until the deadline he had set, and then, just as he had threatened in his note to do, he had . . .

All that my grandfather could gasp out was, "I've never paid him a cent."

"Never paid him a cent!" Lieutenant Loftus echoed. "In six months' time?" Lieutenant Loftus had seen many contemptible sights in his career, but now he needed all his protective coloring to hide the contempt he felt for a man rich enough to have his son kidnapped being too tight-fisted to pay—no matter how little hope it held out of ever seeing him again—to get him back. Nevertheless he said, "Well, don't repent yourself, Mr. Ordway. Frankly, my experience has been that it doesn't matter much in cases like this whether you pay or don't pay, and that's the very same advice I gave to Mr. Oscar Hastings. He too refused to pay, and in case you may have forgotten, he was much criticized for it at the time. There were even editorials against him in the newspapers. But Oscar Hastings was not the heartless monster he was made out to be. He cried like a baby when poor little Oscar Jr. was brought up out of that well. I was there and I can vouch for it. It wasn't the money. What did a few thousand dollars more or less mean to a man like Oscar Hastings? He'd have gladly spent any amount if he

had believed it would bring the boy back. And he was proved
right. At Pete Fernandez's trial it was established that Oscar
Hastings, Jr., had been beyond all hope of recall before the
ink on the ransom note was dry. No, sir, I've raised three.
All grown and married now, of course; but if one of mine
had ever been kidnapped, instead of paying the rascal that
took him I'd have spent the money bringing him to justice."

At last the man's deadly tongue fell silent. Then my
grandfather launched into a long and desperately pitched
defense of the man who had stolen his child. Lieutenant
Loftus had heard a lot, but this flabbergasted him. My
grandfather said Will Vinson was no ordinary kidnapper.
He hadn't done it for money. He and Mrs. Vinson were fond
of the boy, loved him like one of their own, better than any
of their own, had almost raised him during that first year
following his poor mamma's death. How probably they believed they were rescuing the child from a stepmother and
from a father who didn't love him as much as they did. How
he had never received any ransom demands from Will. Not
in six whole months. How he was not a rich man by any
manner of means but just a poor farmer and his son not
the heir to anything but eighty acres of not very good cotton
land, and how Will Vinson, his next-door neighbor, knew
how he lived and what he was worth and that you couldn't
get blood out of a turnip. And so on, until he succeeded in
convincing himself, but not Lieutenant Loftus. About midway through this harangue Lieutenant Loftus began to per-
ceive that here was a man who not only would drive some
desperate poor devil of a kidnapper to strangle his son sooner
than buy him back, but that he was working around to
haggling with *him* over his fee, when out of fatherly feeling
he had made him a rock-bottom price. He said, drily, "Sir,
I bid you good day. And I wish you luck in finding your man
on your own. If you should change your mind and decide
that I can be of service to you, here's my card."

My grandfather succeeded in whitewashing over the picture that this man had drawn upon his mind, but it was always coming through and requiring another coat. It was an image of Ned lying dead and buried in a secret unmarked grave far from his mother's side, or possibly someplace on Will Vinson's farm back home, beneath that very soil that he himself had worked. In trying to efface it he was to become Will Vinson's passionate apologist. He reviewed his memories of Will, dwelling with fond gratitude upon the decent and kindhearted actions he had known the man to perform, exaggerating them, in the end even inventing some. The jealousy he had begun to feel of Will's love for his son shriveled in the chill of his dread, and he strove now to recall every evidence of Will's partiality for the boy. Whenever people to whom he told his story on his subsequent travels sought to commiserate with him by attacking Will, he would amaze, mystify, and would frequently disgust them by seeming almost to excuse his enemy. Search on he did, of course, and by day believed that the sun shone somewhere on Ned. But as soon as the lights were out and he lay himself down in another strange bed, his heart rose on tiptoe to await the small mangled ghost that walked nightly in his dreams.

The second respondent to his plea was not the preacher but the other man. Mr. Lindsay Conroy was no retired private investigator—far too conspicuous a man for that; but neither was he the openhearted farmer whom my grandfather had imagined coming compassionately to his aid. Mr. Lindsay Conroy was nobody's father. He smelled of spending too much time in barber's chairs to suit my grandfather's taste: a waft of bay rum and quinine tonic, scented soapsuds, talcum powder. The hand he proffered was boneless and moist and cool as a curd, tender as a mushroom. He seated himself without waiting to be asked, and said:

"I take it, sir, that you have never heard of Lindsay Conroy?"

"Well, since you ask me, frankly, no," said my grand-father.

Instead of displeasing him, this answer seemed to satisfy Mr. Conroy exactly. "In your walk of life you wouldn't," he said. "My work is done behind the scenes. Mr. Ordway, in the absence of any third party to do the honors, you will have to overlook a certain immodesty on my part. I say it who shouldn't, perhaps, but I say no more than any man would say for me who knows the political facts of life in this state. I, Mr. Ordway, have been called 'The King Maker of the Lone Star State.' " He paused to let that sink in, then continued, "I have manageered the election campaigns of some of the biggest officeholders in this state. You are looking at the man who made the Honorable Boyd Ramsey what he is today. In Boyd I saw the senator beneath the hayseed—and I want you to know, in the beginning I was the only one that could see it! Friends said to me at the time I was grooming him, 'Lin, you have put your money on a plug in this race.' I said to them, 'You don't want a sprinter on a muddy track.' Boyd was pure Bull Durham. None of that ready-rolled look about him that is sure political death with the voters in South Bootstrap, Texas. Et his black-eyed peas with his knife. Could milk a farmer's cow for him while talking him out of his vote. I mean *milk* that hussy! Kept his hand in. Still does. I'm real proud of Boyd. But as the poet says, full many a rose is born to blush unseen, and waste its fragrance on the desert air, et cetera. Boyd's got both feet in the trough up there in Washington today; but if he was here he'd tell you hisself that he would be still currycombing cockleburrs out of a mule's tail right today if it wasn't for Lin Conroy. Wellsir, those are my credentials, and now I'll come to a head and tell you why I'm here. Sam (you don't mind if I call you Sam? I have the feeling you and me are going to get to know one another real close), Sam, I have got an entry in this race for lieutenant governor, but I'll tell you candid, I don't believe I'm going to vote for him myself. If you will stand, why I'll scratch him at the post. Sam, boy, you can win in a landslide—with a little coaching from me. Wait. Wait. Don't interrupt me now. I was there and heard you speak today. I felt the pulse of that crowd. You had them eating out of your hand. They was buzzing about you all through the following speeches. In fact, it got to the point that one of the last speakers had to begin his talk with, 'Well, folks, I ain't had none of my kids napped, but . . .' Now wait. Wait. I know what you're fixing to say. It's already October. Primaries are long past. Election time is almost upon us. There's no time left for filing. Never mind. Leave all that to me. Now Hoyt Crittenden had got the governorship sewed up this time around. But the race for lieutenant governor is wide open. And as anybody in the know will tell you, the lieutenant-governorship had got it over the top spot coming and going. The pickings are damn near as fat, and the risks are one hell of a lot less. You're not near as much in the public eye. You ask the average voter, hell, he don't even know who the lieutenant governor is, much less what he's up to. So what do you say, Sam? Take the word of an old handicapper, you are a dark horse if I ever saw one. A political Cinderella. A shoo-in. What do you say, boy?"

"I say," said my grandfather. But what he had been about to say was never known. Suddenly blenching, Mr. Conroy breathed, "Sam. Mr. Ordway. You *are* a Democrat, ain't you?" Then, "Damn me, though, if I don't believe we could get you elected on the other ticket! What an angle! Father searching for his little son far and wide over this broad and beautiful great state of ours, seeking the help of his fellow Texans and fellow fathers in locating his little lost son and heir. It's got everything! Everything! And if you should find the boy! After statewide efforts of public law enforcement officers have failed, father singlehandedly locates stolen son. Shoots kidnapper. Touching scene of reunion. We'll carry the boy around with us, stumping the state. We'll hire us a band and play 'The Eyes of Texas Are upon You' and 'Mighty

Lak a Rose.'" He stopped, held up his hand, and broke into
wavering song:

"Cutest little fella everybody knows.
Don' know what to call him but he's mighty lak a rose.
Lookin at his daddy with eyes so shiny blue,
Makes you think that he-e-ebm am comin close to you.

Sam, not one man in Texas will cast his vote against you.
He couldn't, not and live with hisself afterwards."

"Mr. Conroy," said my grandfather.

"Lin to you," said Mr. Conroy.

"Mr. Conroy, I don't know the first thing about politics,
but—"

Mr. Conroy threw back his head and snorted. "Whew!" he
cried. "Kiss me on the neck, Gus, my mouth is full of snuff!
Boy, you are the greatest natural-born vote getter I ever
struck across. You are a nugget in the raw, Sammy, boy.
It needs a little rubbing up, but you have got it, in the bone.
In the bone. Somebody had to show you what to do with
that thing between your legs, didn't they, but it was hanging
there all the while. Sam, you just get up there and give them
that speech you gave today, about looking for your little boy
and how maybe you wasn't always the daddy you ought to
been but you'll be a better one if—that is, when—you get him
back, and not to worry about Will Vinson, and I'll follow
you and let them know that if they can't help you find your
boy they can write your name in on the ballot. Meanwhile
if it's campaign costs you're worried about, don't give it a
thought. One fund-raising rally, just one, right here in Paris,
and if we don't fill all the hats that John B. Stetson has got,
then I'll eat every one of them, without mustard."

Mr. Conroy could hardly believe it when my grandfather
said he was really not interested in a career in politics, and
he laughed uproariously when my grandfather said he didn't
really believe that the voters of Texas would elect a man
to high office whose only qualification for the job was that

he had had his child stolen from him. Mr. Conroy tried persuasion. He pointed out that as a candidate stumping the state he would be making expenses in his search for his boy, and maybe something over. That as it was now, being a farmer, he was able to look for him only during his off season—through the winter and part of the spring and fall; but if he was elected lieutenant governor, think of the free time he would have! My grandfather, however, did not choose to run.

"Well, I can promise you this," said Mr. Conroy as he put on his hat to go, "now that you've given them the idea some other s.o.b. is sure to do it if you don't."

"Mr. Ordway? Teague. Reverend Dorsey Teague of the First Baptist—"

"Come in, Reverend. Sorry to keep you waiting so long."

Reverend Teague lowered himself into an armchair without waiting to be asked, leaned back, placed his fingertips together, and said, "Baptist yourself, by chance, Mr. Ordway?"

"No, 'fraid not. Metho—"

"Live and let live, I say," said Reverend Teague. "There is more than one pathway to heaven. We Baptists think we are on the shortcut, but even those that take you round by Laura's house all get you there in the end. However, my boy, you may be grateful that the one church in Ben Franklin, Texas, is Baptist."

"I may? How is that, Reverend?"

"Well, excuse me, I am getting ahead of myself. Ah, my son, this is a terrible thing that has befallen you." And he took from his pocket, unfolded, and waved in the air a copy of my grandfather's handbill. "May I offer you," he asked, "a few words of spiritual counsel?"

Oh, dear, thought my grandfather. And he must have looked it, too, for Reverend Teague protested, "Now don't suppose I'm going to give you a sermon about how you ought to regard this as a blessing from God. Had it been a case of outright death, why that is what I would have done. The Lord giveth and the Lord taketh. Suffer the little children to come unto me, for of such is the kingdom. And so on and so forth. But it was not the Lord that took your boy, and he isn't in heaven, he's in Texas. No, sir, I don't know how you Methodists feel, but I just don't believe that the Lord chooses to work through such agents as this Will Vinson, myself. No, what I want to say is this, you are an injured man, an angry man. But we must forgive our enemies. As a man of peace it is my duty to tell you that. We must turn the other cheek. Vengeance is mine—you remember who said that, Mr. Ordway?"

"I don't know about turning the other cheek," said my grandfather. "I'm no saint. But I will tell you something, Reverend, that I wouldn't tell just any man. I'm not aiming to kill Will Vinson. No, I mean it. I can't say I don't bear him a grudge. Thinking about it sometimes I get so mad I say to myself I could kill him. But that is only a manner of speaking. He has sure inconvenienced me and I can't promise not to give him a good thrashing, or" (feeling his fresh bruises) "try my level best, if I ever do catch up with him. But more than that. . . . Well, what I'm after is to get my boy back. I'm not a very bloody-minded man, I'm afraid, and even if I was, let me tell you it's not so easy as people seem to think to hate a man who has wronged you through love of your child. It's a very mixed-up feeling."

"Son," said Reverend Teague, "you have set my mind at rest. Now I can tell you what I have come for. I mentioned the little hamlet of Ben Franklin, Texas. Not familiar with the place, I venture to say. A small community, some twenty miles south of here. General store. Four-grade schoolhouse. One church—Baptist—mine, as I mentioned earlier. A small congregation. A quiet spot, Ben Franklin. There a man might settle down and be lost to the world, far from the maddening crowd and cities' strife. Needless to say, no one ever does.

The Winstons are the first new people to settle in Ben Franklin in—oh, I don't know how long. In all the fifteen-odd years that I've been riding this circuit. However, I can see by your look, sir, that you wish I would stop maundering and get down to business."

"No, no, Reverend! Perish the thought!"

"Bear with me if I seem to be running on about some little one-horse town and folks you never saw."

"Not at all. Not at all. I'll just ask you to excuse me while I open this bottle of Mercurochrome and dab some on this bite on my leg."

Reverend Teague vented a low whistle and, leaning forward in his chair, said, "Christamighty! That looks nasty. He wasn't mad, I hope."

"Pretty mad," said my grandfather. "However, it wasn't a dog, it was a boy."

"A boy! Had he been bit by a mad dog?"

"No, he was protecting his father. But it's a long story. Go on, Reverend."

"Where was I? Oh, yes, the new folks in Ben Franklin. The Winstons. Nice people. Poor but honest. Poor! My, when they first pulled into the place last spring they didn't have nothing but that wagon and team and that collie dog that looked starved to—"

"Collie dog? Did you say collie dog?" said my grandfather, dropping his pants leg.

"And a wagonload of sick kids."

"Sick?"

"They give it out that they all had the chickenpox and couldn't leave the house, not even to come to Sunday school. That was how I first took an interest in them. I went and—"

"How many kids?" asked my grandfather.

"Four. One little—"

"Thank God!" my grandfather breathed. Then, fumbling in his pocket, he found the photograph and thrust it in Reverend Teague's hand. "Was one of them . . .?"

"Little Ted!" the Reverend said. "Then my suspicions—"

"It's him?" said my grandfather. "No mistake? You're positive?"

"Ah," said Reverend Teague, shaking his head sadly, "how that fellow took me in! Winston!"

Happily, yet with just a touch of ruefulness, my grandfather said, "I guess I was right. Will figured he didn't have to go very far."

Still looking at the photograph, Reverend Teague said, "Little Ted."

"Ned," said my grandfather.

"I know him," said Reverend Teague, looking up mistily from the picture, "as Ted. And that is how I'll always think of him. Ah, no one would believe how that little scamp has wound himself around this old heart of mine in just a few short months! Even knowing he's with his own daddy where he belongs won't keep me from missing him."

These words, much as they pleased him, at the same time sent a pang of chagrin into my grandfather's heart. Here was a second stranger who appreciated his child more, apparently, than he himself ever had.

"Mr. Ordway," said Reverend Teague, bringing him back to the present scene, "when I think what that rascal Winston-Vinson has done I could kill him myself. But, as you say, that is only a manner of speaking. As a man of the cloth, I must implore you not to use this information I have given you to bring blood on your head and mine."

"Reverend, I've said it once and I'll say it again, what I want is to get my boy back."

"I believe you. Now listen. You go past the general store and take the first right-hand turn. You go for about two miles and you come to a crossroads and you take a left. Go down that road until you come to another crossing and you take a right. Go down that road and take the first left, and it's the second place after the bridge on your right. I'll be driving out myself a little later in the evening. I preach out there tomorrow. However, who knows? Somebody from out that way may have been in town here today and gone back bringing news of this"—he waved the circular—"little knowing that—"

"I won't wait for you. I'll go at once. But there's no chance of Will himself being in town here today, you don't think?"

"They never come into Paris," said Reverend Teague. "I had noticed that. Now I know why. But I see you're impatient to be on your way."

"Not for a minute yet," said my grandfather. "Reverend, now don't take this amiss. I know that preachers are not well paid and they're human like the rest of us and have to eat and . . . well, I hope you will let me . . ."

"Just stop right there. I don't take it amiss, but that's enough. Ssh! I'm going right this minute and I don't want to hear another word. No, no. I'm the one who ought to thank you, for putting me in the way to help a fellow creature in distress. The happiness this has given me, words cannot express it. No more. Goodbye, good luck, and God go with you." And with that he was out of the door and gone, leaving my grandfather with a lump in his throat the size of a turkey egg.

He glanced at his watch. First to the livery stable, then—

There came a rap on the door. It opened, and Reverend Teague stuck his head in.

"Won't keep you a minute," he said. "It just occurs to me (I almost left without thinking of it—what a pity that would have been) that once you've gotten your boy back you might welcome the opportunity to make a small donation to our Baptist Boys' Orphan Home, of which I am the director. I says the *Baptist* Boys' Orphan Home—it's called that, but of course it's open to orphans of all denominations, including Methodist. Now please don't feel under any obligation. It just occurred to me that if I was in your place I would be wanting to show my gratitude to the Lord for restoring my little boy to me so soon, and what more fitting way than by helping these poor little fellows who will never in this life be reunited with their fathers? Well, again, good luck and—"

"Wait. Reverend Teague, I want to thank you for this suggestion," said my grandfather, taking out his wallet. "Would you be so kind—"

"Well, I suppose . . . Very well, if that's what you would like. I could convey it," said Reverend Teague. Then he said, "The amount, Mr. Ordway, is entirely up to you. Those poor fatherless waifs will be grateful for any little—"

My grandfather had taken four or five bills from his wallet. At these words he took a couple more.

"It's impossible, I know," the Reverend continued, "to express in dollars and cents how much it's worth to get back your lost child." (My grandfather added another bill or two.) "I don't know, of course, how much you were intending to offer as a reward" (he took two more) "but I am sure it will be better spent than on some whom I can imagine bringing you the information you were seeking. With Thanksgiving Day coming along soon . . . Christmas . . ."

To this last appeal my grandfather felt an unworthy impulse to close his ears. He had already dipped pretty deeply into his funds. Yet he had meant to pay a hundred and twenty-five dollars reward, and he had anticipated a longer and more costly search. The stern faces of George Washington, Thomas Jefferson (there were two-dollar bills in those days), Abe Lincoln, and a solitary Alexander Hamilton accused him with their high-minded looks. He took six or eight more bills and added them to the sum. And it was worth it. He felt good all over. Then the grisly apparition which that Lieutenant Loftus had implanted in his mind rose up, and he extracted some more bills and added them to the stack. Then he hastily shut his shrunken wallet.

Reverend Teague did not look down at the money as he took it; he appreciated the amount, though, and his eyes moistened. So did my grandfather's as the Reverend said,

"Sam Ordway, God will bless you for this. You have found yourself more than one son this day."

So wrought up was my grandfather that he was downstairs in the lobby before he remembered his pistol. The remembrance brought a glow to his face. He had known Will Vinson too long to go pointing a pistol at him. Much less that blunderbuss. But suppose Will pulled one on him? This was the thought which struck him now for the first time. Was it possible that Will wanted his boy bad enough to shoot him for him? Painful as it was, my grandfather had to confess that it was possible. And Will would expect him to come shooting. Any man in Will's place would.

He returned to his room. He took his pistol from his satchel. He hefted it, looked at it, and said to himself, how am I going to get out of the hotel with this thing? He tried sticking it in his belt inside his shirt. That did not work. Had it been just a few inches longer he might have passed it off as a walking cane. He could not carry it out in his satchel: they would think he was trying to leave without paying his bill. Pay his bill? That was just what he ought to do. He would not be returning here. He packed his grip, putting his pistol in on top, went downstairs, and checked out.

The town was emptying now as the country people left for home. My grandfather made his way quickly to the livery stable. He settled his bill there and harnessed Dolly and the mule. The stable owner said that Ben Franklin was down south of Roxton, somewhere over in Delta County. Himself, he had never been there.

The streets leading out of town were jammed with wagons and my grandfather lost some little time getting beyond the city limits and out into the country. At last he was on his way. The road was a good one, hard and smooth. Well rested now, the team paced briskly. He began to pass farms. Dusk was settling now and he could hear folks calling their cows and sometimes the tinkle of a cowbell. Several times he was

slowed down by herds of cattle taking up the road. He gave
a ride for a couple of miles to a hunter coming home with
a mess of squirrels. Bullbats came out and circled in the
air, catching bugs on the wing. Lights came on in farmhouse
windows and smoke stood up from chimneys and sometimes
on the air came a whiff of frying meat. Then the road turned
bad. They had had a rain out there during the day and the
road was muddy, and in places the culverts had clogged up
with trash and the road lay under water. The wagon wheels
began to clot with mud, slowing down the team. Towards
nightfall the sky clouded over. It got so dark you could not
see the team. You could hear them, could hear the *slurr-plop*
of their hooves as they drew them out of the mud. It sounded
as if they were wearing rubber boots. Away off in the darkness dogs barked and were answered by still more distant
dogs.

Sometimes the barking was near at hand. Then a light
would flare up alongside the road just ahead. It was past
eight o'clock now and farm folks were in bed. Roused by
their dogs, the farmers came to the door holding the lamp
over their heads and hitching up their trousers and peering
out into the night, calling, "Here! Queen! Here! Spot!" My
grandfather would call out and ask if this was the road to
Roxton, and hearing a strange voice, the farmer would raise
the lamp still higher in hopes of a glimpse of his face. It
was just so—half asleep, half dressed, half blind—that my
grandfather pictured Will Vinson answering his call.

After Roxton, which he passed through at around ten
that night, my grandfather began to fear that he might miss
his turning in the dark. Every few hundred yards he got
down from the wagon seat and walked ahead of the team
for a ways. Twice he slipped and fell; soon he was covered
with mud. Around two a.m. he came to a hamlet. By the time
he entered it the howling of dogs had awakened everybody.
Lights shone in every house.

"This Ben Franklin?" he called to a man in a nightcap leaning out of his window.

"Yes. Who do you want to . . . ?"

"Then I'm on the right road. Much obliged to you, and sorry to have disturbed your sleep."

"Where is it you want to . . . ?"

"Good night!"

Now as his meeting with Will Vinson loomed imminent my grandfather's conscience began to prick him for his indifference to Will's fate. Everybody was expecting him to shoot Will. Everybody. Even Reverend Teague had taken it for granted that he meant to kill Will and felt obliged to warn him against this natural inclination.

For what he had done to him Will Vinson certainly deserved to be shot, my grandfather thought; and if he was to, there was not a man in the state of Texas who would not approve. Not one. That in fact was not the question. The question was, what would they say if he didn't? When friends back in Clarksville said, "So! You got your boy back! Good! Now then" (their faces lighting up), "now then, what about Vinson? What did you do to him?" how could he just smile and say, "Oh. Will. Well, I let him go"?

My grandfather reached under the wagon seat and found his grip. He put it on the seat beside him, opened it, and took out his pistol. In the darkness it seemed to have grown still heavier, still longer. It felt like a plow handle, he said in recalling the moment to his grandson. He held it out before him. "Will Vinson," he said, "if you have got any last words now is the time to say them, only be quick about it."

"I know I deserve it, Mr. Ordway," said Will. "I done you wrong. But I've got a wife and three kids of my own with nobody to look after them but me."

"Too late for that. You ought to have thought about them before you went stealing mine."

"Well," my grandfather told me, "I tried to picture myself

pulling the trigger and enjoying the sight of Will lying dead
at my feet. I knew it was what I ought to do, what any other
man in my place would have done. I knew that if I didn't
I would despise myself to my dying day. It was not only my
right, it was my duty. Why, Will Vinson himself would
despise me for not doing it. Unless I did, little Ned would
grow up hearing people say of his daddy, 'There goes Sam
Ordway. The man that tracked down the fellow that stole
his boy, then was too chicken-livered to shoot him.'"

I interrupted at this point. "Grandpa?" I said.

"What?"

"Never mind," I said. "Go on. Go on." I had been about
to suggest an alternative. That he might have turned Will
Vinson over to the law. Luckily I reflected in time that this
would have been just as shameful as not shooting him, if
not more so, and held my tongue.

"I tried to worm out of it by telling myself that the pistol
probably wouldn't have gone off anyhow. But it was me that
wouldn't go off. I strained and I heaved and I called myself
names—no use: it just wasn't in me. 'Are you a man or a
mouse?' I asked myself. I was glad it was dark and I was all
alone. 'Mouse,' I said, and put the pistol back in the grip
and put the grip back under the wagon seat. I would just
have to live down the shame of it as best I could.

"I'd have shot that Reverend Teague with pleasure,
though, if I could have found the dog," he said.

"What! Shoot Reverend Teague, Grandpa! But why?"

"Because when I had snuck up on that cabin which was
the second place on the right beyond the bridge five miles
(not two—five) after the right-hand turn over the creek and
through the swamp after the crossing beyond the general
store around four in the morning, and this was after leaving
my wagon and team and doing the last three miles on foot
in the mud, not knowing how near the house was and wanting not to give them any warning by the noise of the wagon,
and threw rocks at the door and took off my shoes and crept

along the porch in my stocking-feet and the man came to the door and I slipped behind him and grabbed his arms, even from the nape of his big bull neck and even in that half light I knew he was not Will Vinson and never had been, and that when I let go of his arms I was going to have some mighty tall explaining to do, and that I had come somewheres in the neighborhood of thirty miles on this wild-goose chase and been taken for a fool, much less being out of pocket one hundred and forty-two out of the two hundred and twenty dollars which was all I had to my name. That's why."

"When did you ever see a Baptist preacher wearing a clerical collar?" asked the Lamar County sheriff.

"I'm a Methodist," my grandfather replied somewhat surlily. For already in the hands of these two he was beginning to feel as if he were the suspect, being grilled, instead of the plaintiff.

"Well," said the sheriff with a sigh of deep disgust, "what did he look like?"

"Like a Baptist preacher," said my grandfather. "You'd have said so too. Nicest, kindest-looking old Christian gentleman you ever—"

"How old a man was he?"

"Early sixties, I would say. I could be way off, though. I'm not too good at judging people's ages, it seems."

"Did he by any chance have a mole right about here?" asked the deputy sheriff, touching a finger to his forehead just above the eyebrow.

"I never noticed," said my grandfather.

"Then did you notice this? Did he have a habit of plucking at the hairs growing out of his ears as he talked?" the sheriff asked.

"I'm sorry," my grandfather replied. "Again, I just never—"

"For an amateur sleuth you ain't very observant, are you, mister?" said the deputy.

"Well, tell me this, if you can," said the sheriff. "Did he have a way of breathing sort of heavy and asthmatical, like this" (huffing) "through his mouth?"

"Yes! Yes, he did! Exactly!" my grandfather cried.

"Uh-huh. He also had a mole just over his left eyebrow and a habit of plucking at the hairs in his ears as he talked," said the sheriff. Turning to his deputy he said, "Suds Folsom?"

The deputy nodded. "Sure sounds like old Suds," he said. He got up and went to a filing cabinet, pulled open a drawer and thumbed through some folders, withdrew one and handed it to his boss.

"This your man?" asked the sheriff. And he held out a wanted notice. There, big as life, was Reverend Teague. He was dressed in broad stripes and across his chest ran a sign reading 341-22-0908. My grandfather would have given a dollar to be able to say no, it wasn't; but he had to nod.

"Poor old Suds," said the deputy. "He must be on the skids to make him go after such peanuts."

"Peanuts!" said my grandfather. "Listen, one hundred and forty-two dollars is not peanuts to me."

"Well, you have lost it, my friend. To Suds Folsom. Alias Francis Farley. Alias Fluellen Cummings. Alias Reverend Dorsey Teague. Alias alias alias. Slickest con man in the Lone Star State. You can kiss that hundred and forty-two dollars goodbye."

"You mean to say," said my grandfather, "that you all have given up all hope of ever catching him?"

"I mean to say," said the sheriff, "that as long as there are fools and money in Texas, Suds Folsom and his like are going to go on separating them. And let me give you a piece of advice before you leave, mister. Instead of trying to follow this man that took your boy, stick to following your plow. This is what happens to homegrown Hawkshaws like you that think they can take the law into their own hands."

Now it is a well-known fact that most cases of swindle by a confidence man go unreported, the victim preferring to sustain the loss rather than confess that he had been made a fool. To this rule (as to most rules) my grandfather was no exception. And so the foregoing scene never took place. Not, that is to say, outside of his imagination.

But this scene did take place:

"I thought you told me," said Aggie, "that you would never stop searching till you had found him. This is not the end of the world, Mr. Ordway."

And so, though daunted, my grandfather vowed to search on. Thinking it over, he decided that he had not exhausted all the possibilities with that speech of his. He had been speaking only to the enfranchised. These were the classes of people left largely or altogether uncanvassed:

1. Men without the $2.00 to pay the poll tax.
2. Illiterates
3. Ex-convicts
4. Women
5. Minors and children
6. Negroes
7. Republicans

Minorities, to be sure (except the first, the fourth, and possibly the second category), but when all added together a big enough number of Texans to leave still some room for hope.

And even in the loss of his money there was a measure of consolation, a certain sense of relief. It solved a problem. In future he would have no choice but to offer no reward beyond a father's gratitude, and his appeal would perforce be pitched to the pure disinterested goodness in people. In that general goodness my grandfather still retained his belief. It had received a kick in the teeth, but on examination they proved, though somewhat loosened, to be still all there. That not everybody was good did not prove that folks for the most part were not. And the only sort from whom he might ever have expected any help were the pure in heart. Finally, not to be offering pay for information against Will Vinson (some share of which had been earned off Will's crops) made him feel he was waging a purer fight—and thus one more promising of success—against him.

Saturday afternoon and Saturday night in a Texas town always bring enough arrests so that on Sunday morning there are prisoners in the jailhouse to sweep the streets of the previous day's peanut hulls and melon rinds, horse dung, banana peels, tamale shucks, Dixie cups, cigar and cigarette butts, and pale dry cuds of spent chewing tobacco. The bigger the mess the bigger the crowd that left it, and the bigger the crowd the more drinking and fistfights, thus the more arrests; so the streets are always fresh and clean for families crossing the square on their way to church and Sunday school.

Prisoner's garb is reserved for those committed on more serious infractions and in for a lengthier stay, and these, being liable to sudden desperate breaks for freedom, are exempted from service on the broom squad, regardless of race, color, or creed. The crew of sweepers are the disturbers of the peace, the vagrants, the drunk-and-disorderlies, et cetera, and they are mustered out in their civvies, their crumpled, slept-in, dusty, often blood- and vomit-stained Saturday-night finery, in loose-knotted neckties and unlaced shoes, sporting shiners and billy-club bumps, bruises and cuts around the cheekbones and jawlines, their own knuckles often skinned and raw, and fingers that wrap stiffly around a broom handle. They blink painfully at the sun and breathe the fresh air as though it stings; but an hour with a broom is good tonic for that morning-after head, that furry tongue.

In some of the older counties the Sunday street-cleaning gang is composed exclusively of Negroes, but as you go west Negroes grow less plentiful, and in some towns they are not encouraged to linger long enough after nightfall to get themselves into any trouble. Such towns, though there are always rumblings about it, are obliged in the interest of public sanitation to integrate the broom squads. Under the watchful eye of the deputy with the sawed-off riot gun the races sweep in harmony, and in step. It is noticeable that the best sweepers are the whites. This arises not so much from superior aptitude, as from the fact that they are eager to get the job finished before they are seen at such work and in such company by other whites on their way to divine services. The ignominy of it is enough to keep even the most incorrigible, who are as a rule the ones most conscious of their racial superiority, out of trouble, or at least from getting caught, for sometimes as long as a fortnight.

They were sweeping the streets of Paris that Sunday morning when my grandfather got back from Ben Franklin. By that hour ordinarily the job would have been finished, but the crowds in town the day before had been large and the streets were left a mess. With liquor flowing and politics in the air, however, the jail had been filled. By the time my grandfather had checked back into his hotel and had his breakfast and returned to the street, not a handbill, political or paternal, was to be seen littering the gutters.

Orphans' home?

It was while eating his breakfast that those words, that question, popped into my grandfather's mind. He was as busy thinking as a one-man band, playing three instruments at once. The lead, or harmonica part, of his thoughts was what has already been set down: the conclusion not to report his deception to the authorities, the determination not to give up and go home and endure the derision of his friends but to stick by his vow to Agatha and search on, extracting what consolation he could from his predicament. As an accompani-

ment, to this, the guitar of his mind was upbraiding Reverend
Teague, saying, *The amount, Mr. Ordway, is entirely up to
you. Those poor homeless little waifs will be grateful for any
amount, however small.* Saying, "It's not so much because
it's me, personally, that I resent it. It's the principle of the
thing. A poor distracted father in search of his little stolen
son!" Meanwhile down in the rhythm section his thoughts
were still contending with that Lieutenant Loftus. The beat
was the same as before. That Will was not the criminal type.
He and Mrs. Vinson were simply overfond of his boy. Had
probably, not without some reason, almost come to think
he was theirs. He had never received any ransom demands.
Slim-witted as he was, even Will Vinson knew that he, Sam
Ordway, was not the man to pick when you went kidnapping
somebody's child for anything more than love. And even if
Will did send a note which he never got, and the deadline
passed, he still wouldn't harm the boy. Slow, yes, he might
be slow, but never cruel. He might threaten to do something
horrible, but when the time actually came . . . Not Will. Not
good old Will Vinson, softhearted, gentle, sweet-natured old
Will Vinson.

This was the moment when his thoughts struck the
chord:

Orphans' home?

He imagined Will in Paris. Desperate, on the run, his
bridges all burnt behind him, his ransom demands unmet,
saddled with this boy. He saw a tree. Saw Will skulking
about this tree day after day, long past the deadline he had
set for the money to be left in the hollow between the roots.
Then he saw him leading Ned by the hand through the
streets of Paris. They entered an alleyway. There, slyly dis-
engaging his hand, Will Vinson stole away, abandoning the
child like an unwanted kitten. He saw Ned wandering lost,
wailing, finally found by a pair of boys. Unable to locate his
folks, they turned him over to a man who in time turned
him over to the sheriff.

"What's your name, sonnyboy?" asked the sheriff.

"Ned," said Ned.

That they might have checked in their files and found, or at least suspected, that this was Edward Ordway, stolen from home near Clarksville on May 7, this never entered my grandfather's mind, so complete was his contempt for the law, or rather for the law's interest in the affairs of a poor farmer like himself.

"Well," said the sheriff to his deputy, "I'm afraid there's only one thing to do with him."

"Looks that way," the deputy agreed.

"If you're thinking of adopting one of them," said the man to whom my grandfather gave a ride in his wagon (for the Paris orphanage, non-denominational, was a few miles outside of town), "you want to pick a young one." A farmer, he had the contract for the orphanage slops. Though Lord knew his hogs wasn't getting very fat off of what them poor little devils left on their plates. "Be a longer investment 'fore you get him up to where he's any help to you, or to your wife if what you're after is a gal for her, but it pays off in the long run. Thing is to get them before the place ruins them, teaches them bad habits and dirty talk, makes them tough and shifty. Hamlin Underhill, he's tried three. The first one run off with all the money in the house and they haven't caught him yet. And what do you reckon the second one done?"

"What?"

"Took him a ball peen hammer and smashed all the furniture to a flinders, then set fire to the outhouse!"

"My goodness! What did the third one do?"

But there they were. Behind tall cyclone fencing, a compound of barracks like an army outpost, with short intersecting streets, a church spire rising over it all. On the field which the wagon now drew alongside of, a band of the orphans were playing soccer.

"Oh, but . . . they're all girls!" said my grandfather.

"Them ain't girls," said his passenger. "Them's boys. They keep them in them smocks up to about ten years old, or twelve. Easier to make. And to launder."

"Oh, yes," said my grandfather. They were nearer now. "Yes, I can see now that they're boys." And he shook his head. What he could see were their fuzzy close-cropped polls, like coconuts.

"Them's the girls," said the farmer. They were passing a second soccer game, separated by a fence from the first.

"Where?" asked my grandfather.

"There. Them's girls. They crop their heads same as the boys'. Have to, they say. Only way to keep down nits, ring-worms. Well, this is the gate. I'll get out here. What do I owe you for the ride? Much obliged to you. Hope you find one that takes your fancy. Remember what I told you about picking a young one. Younger the better. You won't re-gret it."

"Mr. Ordway, I hope you won't take exception," said Mr. Marchbanks, the director of the home. "I know that to a father his child is like no other. But in a job like mine," he said, tapping the photograph of Ned against his thumbnail, "where you see over six hundred every day . . ."

"Six hundred!" my grandfather exclaimed. "I never knew there were that many orphans in the whole state of Texas!"

"Oh, my dear sir! In addition to the district and county homes, like us, there are all the various denominational homes, there is the State Orphans' Asylum down in Corsi-cana, the lodge and fraternal organization homes, Woods-men, Masons, Oddfellows, et cetera, the privately endowed homes, the homes for the blind and the deaf-and-dumb and the insane and the colored and—"

"Think of that!" said my grandfather. "That many poor little children that have lost their parents!"

"Or never had any. Or never had any, Mr. Ordway. Much

the commoner case, I assure you. Oh, no! Dont talk to *me* about your pure, unspotted Southern womanhood!"

"Six hundred!" my grandfather repeated. And he was afraid that he smiled. He could not help it; among a number that large his chance of finding Ned was multiplied beyond his hopes. Anyhow, for him to pull a long face over it was not going to lessen the number of orphans in Texas.

Mr. Marchbanks was saying meanwhile that although it had gotten so he could hardly tell one child from another (and small wonder, thought my grandfather, remembering those boy-girls and girl-boys, those uniforms like cotton-sacks), Mr. Ordway was welcome to tour the home, and if his boy was there, then of course he would be able to pick him out. My grandfather was not so sure of that, as he tried to picture Ned with his hair cropped. At this point Mr. Marchbanks returned the photograph, and, looking at it, my grandfather was shocked to find how little difference it would make in Ned's case.

They went first to the infirmary. "Now we will hope we don't find him in here," said Mr. Marchbanks. "But since it's on our way we will just peek in."

Passing a door, my grandfather thought he heard the cry of an infant, a newborn baby. So he had. Of more than one. "Do you get them here that young?" he inquired.

Mr. Marchbanks stopped. "Mr. Ordway," he said, "we have found them not more than a few hours old lying at the gate when we went out to unlock it in the morning. We found one there one raw day in February that had its cord still attached. Its mamma had given him a doughnut. Can't you just picture her? Probably all of about thirteen years old. The things I have seen, Mr. Ordway, the things that I have seen! One morning—this was not in my time but during the administration of my predecessor—they went out to open the gate, and there lying on the ground outside was a young woman just giving birth. The matron and the cook delivered her on the spot, with nothing more than a paring knife and

a broken F string from a banjo, which luckily the cook
happened to have in his pocket at the time. Now a lieutenant
j.g. in the Marine Corps, that young fellow. I get a card
from him every Christmas. Care to look in for a moment?
Pleasantest ward in the whole place, the nursery. So long
as you don't let your mind dwell on what the future has got
in store for them."

They went in. Every crib was occupied and the floor alive
with babies on blankets. "So many!" my grandfather exclaimed.

Mr. Marchbanks nodded. He nodded and nodded. Which
manner of orphans these were, his expression left no doubt.
He nodded eight or ten times more, and said yes, they were
so overcrowded they had recently had to add another night
watchman to the staff. Patrolling the fences to keep the
ones inside from trying to break out, one man could not also
guard the gate to keep the women from leaving more there.
And not only women. Men too had been caught sneaking
away after leaving babies at the gate, after the mothers had
left them on their doorsteps. Yes, men. And though he
named no names, some very highly placed and respectable
men around the town among them. Caught sneaking away,
leaving their little bundles of joy to be brought up at the
expense of the county taxpayers. Forced to come back and
pick them up and take them off. At the picture which this
conjured up my grandfather could not help smiling. Mr.
Marchbanks couldn't either, though he quickly wiped his
off (my grandfather followed suit) and said, peering down
at the mass of babies squirming on the floor, "I leave it to
you, sir, to judge the state of morals in northeast Texas."

Only this morning they had caught a young hussy making
off after leaving hers at the gate. Big, strapping, rawboned
country gal, perfectly capable of working to support it; but
if she didn't make another try tonight, he would be very
much surprised. Well, he said with a comprehensive look
around, they couldn't catch them all.

Mr. Marchbanks paused for a closer look at the occupant of one crib. "This young gentleman here," he said, "I've got my eye on him." He pursed his lips and shook his head. "Something tells me he is not going to be with us much longer."

"Oh, really!" said my grandfather. Peering in, he saw a fat, rosy-cheeked baby. "Gee, he sure looks healthy enough."

"It's not his health I'm watching," said Mr. Marchbanks, "it's his complexion. I suspect that boy may have had a passing swipe of the old tarbrush. Too early to be sure; but he is definitely a shade darker than he was the last time I looked. If he keeps this up, why he will have to be sent down to the other place, of course."

"It must be awfully hard to be sure in some cases," my grandfather observed. "I wouldn't want your responsibility. Don't you worry sometimes that you might have made a mistake?"

"It is hard to be sure sometimes," said Mr. Marchbanks. "I can recall babies that had the board of trustees in here hanging over the crib for as long as half an hour shaking their heads and trying to make up their minds. There have been cases where they never did. Whole board split right down the middle. There are eight of them. I'm the ninth— honorary—and in case of a tie I cast the deciding vote. It is, as you say, a responsibility, and I do worry sometimes that I may have made a mistake. For this reason, whenever there is the least shadow of a doubt I always cast the black bean. You can't be too careful."

Mr. Marchbanks pointed out the large number of women attending the children. They had found, he said, and not only they but other orphanages as well, that up to the age of one year, without the attentions of a foster mother children just died. From plain lack of affection.

Next they went into the sick ward, a long room with rows of beds along the walls and an aisle running between. The sick boys lying or sitting up in bed all turned towards the

door when it was opened, but their faces did not light up
as the face of a child expecting its mother to come to the
sickroom would have done. Down the aisle they went, then
back up it again, while my grandfather inspected the patients. Boys of all ages they were, in identical nightshirts,
beneath identical gray blankets, with bed tables on which
stood identical water bottles and tumblers. None of them
was Ned, though it was disconcerting how many of them
reminded him of Ned. My grandfather found himself smiling
a frozen fatuous smile at them, which they returned coolly.
In their eyes all natural childish curiosity had been snuffed
out; instead they looked out upon the world with a cynical
indifference. Or was it, my grandfather asked himself,
simply the lonely self-preoccupation of children with no
one to think of but themselves and no one to think of
them?

The day being Sunday and the weather fair, the boys
were all out of doors. All, that is, that were allowed out;
some were confined to quarters for misbehavior. They toured
the dormitories for a glimpse at these, and were glowered
at like visitors to a zoo. My grandfather felt pleased and
proud to find that Ned was not among these.

From there they went out into the yard in front of the
church. Services were just about to begin. The orphans stood
in the yard waiting. Mr. Marchbanks pointed out some of
the more interesting cases. He had said he could hardly tell
one from another, but he did distinguish two types, the
well-born and the troublesome. These two types were sometimes united in one inmate. "Take that boy there," he said,
indicating one who had already caught my grandfather's
eye, and whom he had taken to be a little girl suffering
from her hideous haircut. "His daddy would have been
mighty surprised to be told, as recently as just six months
ago, that his son and heir would soon be in the orphans'
asylum and he himself in his grave with his own bullet
in his head. Mr. Stanley Blankenship, he was, a big man

in local affairs, chairman of the board of directors of one of the banks, officer in any number of county corporations, treasurer of his church funds. Got to dabbling in west Texas oil rights. Found himself short and mixed his accounts with his church's. The auditors came in at just the worst possible moment. A familiar story. Put a pistol to his head one Tuesday morning. The shock of it carried off his wife, ruined any number of investors in his various enterprises. Now there's his boy. An only child and spoiled rotten, as you might imagine, and don't take to his new life here at all. I look for trouble from that boy.

"And over there now, that red-headed one" (my grandfather was a little at a loss to find hair enough to identify its color), "now there's a boy with a history, Mr. Ordway. Remember the Earlham case of a few years back? No? Well, maybe it didn't reach Clarksville but it was big news here in Paris. This Marylou Earlham caught her husband two-timing her with her own sister and killed them both. Caught them in the act and stabbed them both with a saddle awl. Well, she couldn't get herself another husband after that, and she couldn't support the children herself and the one she had killed was her only sister, so here they are. The boy's twin sisters are those two over there by the steps—always off to themselves. Now then, you see that boy over yonder. That boy's daddy was hanged for armed robbery and murder. He's much looked up to on that account by all the other boys and it's gone to his head, and if he don't come to the exact same end himself, then I'll be very much surprised. And now over there is one who . . . No, over there by that tree. That boy . . ."

The moment was inopportune, but something which Mr. Marchbanks had dropped had been weighing heavily on my grandfather's mind, and he interrupted now to say, "You spoke of a home for insane children. I guess I had never realized that there were insane children. Feebleminded, yes. But you don't mean that? You mean insane?"

His imagination was already busy answering his own question. Insane children? Yes, of course there must be. If the minds of grownups buckled and gave way beneath their troubles, why not the softer and more exposed ones of little children? One with no mother, for instance, and who suspected (for even the youngest were terribly sharp in such matters), who suspected that his own coming had been the cause of his mother's death. Suspected perhaps that his father resented him on that account. Suspected that his stepmother would sooner not have him around. And would it not unhinge a child's mind to be whisked away from home and familiar sights and faces and share the harried life of fugitives on the road? Maybe to have the man who had taken you begin to regret the madness of what he had done, or what he had let his wife talk him into, and turn mean and cruel, finally abandoning you, turning you loose to wander alone and lost in the streets of a big city, being found and passed from hand to hand, questioned by policemen in uniforms, put into a dormitory with a gang of tough, dirty-talking boys, hazed and tormented by them, your head shaved, your . . .

"Haven't seen any yet that looks like yours?" Mr. Marchbanks inquired.

"No!" said my grandfather. "No!"

"Well, don't give up hope yet," said Mr. Marchbanks. He looked at his watch. "Services will start soon. Attendance is required. Just stand right here and you'll have a chance to look them all over. Too bad this neighbor of yours didn't know about us. If it was a boy he wanted he could have come here and had his pick."

"Yes, well he had boys of his own," my grandfather replied. "He seems to have taken a particular fancy to mine, I don't know why."

"Yes," said Mr. Marchbanks, though with his job-lot attitude towards boys he seemed to find it hard to credit.

As one by one the orphans filed past him into church a

change stole over my grandfather's feelings. As they went past in their shapeless garments, their high-top shoes and dirty-brown cotton stockings, their cropped heads (which had the effect of making their eyes enormous), and my grandfather searched their faces without discovering Ned among them, he grew more and more anxious. But his anxiety was not lest the next one should not be his, but that it should. And once again his mind was defending his enemy Will Vinson, magnifying his fondness for the boy, convincing himself that no matter what, Will would never have abandoned him, turned him loose to be picked up and brought to this place. When the last bunch had passed by and gone inside and the yard stood empty, so great was my grandfather's relief that when Mr. Marchbanks said he was afraid that was all there were, he heaved a loud sigh of thanks. Mistaking this for a sigh of disappointment, Mr. Marchbanks said he was sorry. He had been hoping for once that they *did* have a child, he said.

Singing broke out inside. Mr. Marchbanks invited my grandfather to stay and attend the services. Their choir was very good, he said. My grandfather replied that he would like very much to, only he had not gotten any sleep that night, and he was having a little trouble with one of his legs. He thanked him for all his help, and assured him again that he was not too disappointed. He really had not expected to find his boy here, it was just something he felt he ought to try. Mr. Marchbanks seemed not to be attending. He was studying my grandfather from out the corner of his eye. A picture took shape in my grandfather's mind of Ned being examined by that board of trustees, all eight of them shaking their heads while Mr. Marchbanks stood off to one side, weighing his decisive vote and cautioning himself that you couldn't be too careful. He wondered if he hadn't ought to ask where the "other place" was. A shake of Mr. Marchbanks's head, as though dispelling his own self-doubts, did not altogether quiet his mind. He thanked him again and left, followed by

the piping of high thin voices praising God, from whom all
blessings flow.

Now my grandfather realized that he was in for a long
search, and accordingly outfitted himself. He had hoops
made for his wagon, bought a tarpaulin and covered it,
bought a pair of blankets and a few pots and pans. He
called it his bachelor wagon. I have a photograph of it with
him standing alongside before me as I write. Underneath
the bed can be seen the rawhide sling for throwing in any
bits of wood found in the course of the day's travel, for you
could not count on finding a supply waiting for you at whatever spot you stopped to make camp for the night. In the
picture the tailboard is down, horizontal, supported by a leg.
This was the kitchen worktable. By his own account, my
grandfather's cooking was elementary. But at least he could
push on now, not be forced to stop early because the next
settlement was too far to reach before nightfall. It was comforting to hear the jangle of his own housekeeping vessels
as he rode along, especially as there was nothing much else
to hear.

When darkness overtook him he looked for a place where
there was water and bedded down for the night. He wished
instead of that pistol he had brought his old shotgun. There
was plenty of wild game. Along the road he often saw prairie
hens and whole coveys of quail and, at dusk, doves settling
in trees to roost as thick as leaves. As it was, he opened a
can of hash, fried a pan of bread, boiled a pot of coffee, and
had what never failed to seem the best meal of his life.
Night fell, and when he had washed his utensils he would
pile his fire high, and to stave off loneliness and homesickness he would get out the little French harp and play to
himself for an hour. Since the instrument had only eight
notes, his repertoire was at first severely limited, and the
unresolved chords were maddening. But it was surprising
how much you could do with eight notes, and before long his

inner ear transposed the octaves and he was hardly conscious of the lack. The tunes he played were from the prisoner's repertoire, as the instrument was the prisoner's instrument: "Birmingham Jail," "If I Had the Wings of an Angel," "Hand Me Down My Walking Cane." The moon rose and the stars came out to shine, his fire blazed and crackled, and beyond it, just inside the encircling darkness, bright pairs of little eyes glinted curiously. From time to time out of the darkness came the contented whinny of old Dolly, tethered nearby. The nights were chill, and when he turned in he would stretch out in the crisp, clean-smelling straw and pull the blankets up to his armpits and put his hands behind his head and lie counting the stars until he fell asleep. And as he was drifting off, it seemed that he had been set down among the stars with the task of finding a certain one lost among the millions all alike.

My grandfather was like every farmer in not feeling much affection for animals. They were his natural enemies, on whom he was dependent. Cows were mainly good for kicking over the milk pail, swatting you in the face with a cowpiss-soaked tail. Mules were contrary brutes, would balk, would not budge though you beat them till your arm dropped off. So you did not beat them. You knew they were more efficient if contented, knew they were contented only if given their own way in everything, knew they would have their way whether you liked it or not. So you treated them with care; you had money in them. But now he grew genuinely fond of old Dolly. Slue-footed, clumsy, spiritless old nag that she was, she was a tie with home. They had plowed many a furrow together. The mule, too, seemed to sense that they all had to stick together out here, and shed some of his reserve, becoming the first mule in Ordway memory to pardon us that old injury of Ella's to his kind.

The roads were silvered with rime these mornings, and the drainage ditches coated with thin ice. Syrup making was finished and farmers came out to meet him now wearing

tow-sack aprons smeared with blood tied round their waists
with baling twine. Carcasses of pigs hung head down from
the limbs of trees, waxen white, scalded and scraped hairless, their hind legs spread by a singletree and the body
cavity standing open red and steaming. Once—the man
suffering from an injured wrist—he offered to help. Donned
an apron, and as the pig was stuck, slit the hocks and bared
the hamstrings and attached the singletree and grabbed the
rope and swung the pig up still squealing, and afterwards
stayed to supper and shared the backbone and sweet potatoes
and the hot fresh cracklin' bread.

After outfitting his wagon, and after another couple of
weeks of exploring the byways of Lamar County, where the
people hardly spoke, much less read, English, he was low on
money. It was the off season and work impossible to find.
And even if work could have been found it would have
meant an interruption to his search. Remembering the suggestion made by those three traveling salesmen, he invested
ten dollars in a stock of cow-bag balm, only to find that just
the month before another peddler had gone through and
every farmer in the country had bag balm enough to last
him for years. *He* had eight dozen half-pound cans of the
stuff. Meanwhile among the social orders on whom he now
pinned his hopes he was encountering no more encouragement than he had among their betters. It was November.
The prairies turned brown and the dry grass sighed in the
wind. To the rare trees clung a few discolored wind-vexed
leaves. For farmers it was that cozy, indoors, rocking-chair-
by-the-fire time, when they came forth only to kick clods,
stand with their hands in their pockets. Hunters were to be
met now with gun and dog going along the road in the early
morning. Ducks down from the north, and sometimes big
wild geese, arrowed high overhead, honking, flapping. In the
thick smoke from farmhouse chimneys you could smell the
sap, and in your homesickness could almost hear it sizzle

from the logs. So matters stood when my grandfather came one day to the town of Enloe.

"In for the big show, are you?" asked the first man he met. "Folks been flocking in since before sunup. Was you at the parade? No? Oh, that's a pity! They had the steam calliope going and the girls in spangled tights and clowns turning somersets down the middle of the street. Made me feel like a kid all over again!"

And so:

Dear family [said my grandfather's next letter home],

I have joined the circus. No I am not the man on the flying trapeze nor the wild man from Borneo, who is really from some place called Terry Hoat Indiana and quite a likable old sot. No what they have got me doing is running the shooting gallery on the midway—me that could never hit a bull in the you know what with a paddle! But are you not supposed to be looking for Ned, you may ask. That is what I am doing. The way I was going at it was awful slow so I thought the thing to do is to draw Will to me. Only how? I could not think. Then this opportunity came along and I jumped at it. The circus I mean. Think for a minute. What draws kids like a circus? We play a different town every day. If he is anywhere in this part of the world then with three of them pestering him to take them even if he did not want to go himself it will be hard for Will to keep away. Meanwhile I am making expenses.

Yr. loving husband & father,
Sam. Ordway

P.S. Running the shooting gallery I know now why none of the boys could ever knock over any of those ducks when we tried it at the Red River County Fair. It could not be done with a sledge hammer.

P.P.S. I started this letter three days ago but have been on the run so never got a chance to mail it and already in that time I have lost my job running the shooting gallery. The last fellow that had it before me had let the sights on the rifles get all out of line. Well yesterday Mr. Dickey who owns the circus stopped by my stand to see how my stock of prize dolls were holding out and just to be doing something picked up one of the rifles and shot at a balloon and busted it. But I am still with the show and will tell you about my new job next time I write.

Circuses, in my grandfather's view, were like that purple cow: better to see than be one. "Perhaps you have sometimes considered leaving home and joining the circus?" he asked. I admitted that the notion had once or twice crossed my mind on hot days. "Then listen and take warning from me," said my grandfather.

He said there had been a boy just about my age traveling with Dickey Bros. at the time, who had run away to join the circus from the very orphanage he had visited in Paris. When that boy learned that he had been to the orphanage, and knew Mr. Marchbanks, he got real homesick, my grandfather said. He had thought it was an awful place while he was there, and had hated old Marchbanks, but now he just wished he was back. He had learned his lesson. He didn't want to be a circus hand any more. What did he want to be? Well, being an orphan, and having his own way to make in the world, that boy had given lots of thought to the choice of a career, and he was being very farsighted about it. It looked like steamboats were going to spell the end of piracy. Cattle rustling, from all reports reaching him, was getting to be just too crowded a field. Stagecoaches would soon be a thing of the past; holding them up didn't seem a very promising line for a young man to go into. There were still banks and trains to be robbed, but for them you needed a gang, and nowadays where were you going to find two or three boys you could trust? All these had had to be ruled out. Now he knew for sure what he wanted to do. That was, to run an orphans' home, preferably the very one that he himself had escaped from. He ought to be real good at that, having been through it himself. My grandfather agreed, applauded his putting aside those other ambitions, and said that having suffered himself as an inmate of one, he would be able to bring to the administration of an orphanage a new broom that would sweep the place clean. Yes, he would certainly make some changes when he took over, this beastly boy agreed. "The first new rule I mean to make is, they have to salute when I go by and stand as stiff as pokers. Any boy caught smoking—confined to quarters for a week. Any complaints about the treatment—bread and water for a month! The girls—I've worked out a whole special set of punishments for them. Oh, they think they've had it tough with old Marchbanks, just wait till they have me to deal with! I know all their tricks. I've played them all myself. Just let one of them try to get out when I'm in charge of things. I'll hunt him down and drag him back by the ear. Yes, sir, it's just what I'm cut out for, and if I ever just get a chance to run away from this awful circus I'm going back and start working my way up to the top of the orphanage ladder."

My grandfather had traveled with the circus another month after lining up the sights on those .22 rifles, but in his other letters home he never did get around to saying what his new job was. "I didn't want to alarm your grandmother unnecessarily," he confided to me. Mr. Dickey had been so disgusted he had ordered him off the lot. "You're just not circus," he explained. My grandfather pled so hard to be kept on in any capacity whatever that Mr. Dickey's suspicions, and therewith his guile, were aroused. Seeing a chance for some captive labor, he offered my grandfather the job as assistant to the circus's elephant handler. His suspicions were confirmed when the offer was accepted. "I pretended to be unhappy about it, but I could hardly keep from laughing. It was like Br'er Rabbit begging not to be thrown in the brier patch. It might be the lowliest job on the lot, but Topsy—that was our elephant's name, Topsy—was what the kids wanted most of all to see, and that would give me a closer look at them than running the shooting gallery ever would. At Will too—in case he should come to the circus. Will was not the marksman type.

"Topsy was an African elephant standing twelve feet high and weighing around seven tons. There are, as you may know, two varieties of elephants, African and East Indian. African ones run about half again the size of Indian ones. For this reason they make a bigger attraction, and so you may suppose that the circus which had Topsy was quite a high-class one. Other considerations enter into the matter. Being bigger, African elephants eat a lot more. They are also more dangerous. So actually they go cheaper on the elephant market. It's like secondhand cars. We couldn't afford Topsy, but we couldn't afford one any smaller. For Dickey Bros. was what is called in the trade—oh, how I came to hate the term!—a mud show. Well, Topsy was not economical, and what she may have been as a heifer I can't say, but by the time I got to know her she was about as dangerous as a Jersey cow. You just had to mind out not to let her step on you, as she had grown rather longsighted. She would no more think of hurting anybody than an iceberg. But you know how women are.

"Red (what his last name was, I never did learn), Topsy's handler, reckoned her age at between fifty-five and sixty. She looked it. She was a mountain of wrinkles and her fur—"

"Fur? Grandpa, elephants—"

"That's all you know about it! They have fur, all right, and every single hair of it is to hair what an elephant is to—well, the point makes itself. The reason you don't know about it is, they shave them regularly. To feel of an elephant in need of a shave is like running your hand over a cut cornfield. Topsy had to be shaved oftener than most, so as to keep her from showing her age; otherwise she would have looked like what in fact she was: a white elephant. Circus people love to fool newcomers, and the first time Red told me we were going to give Topsy a shave he had me believing we were going to whip up a barrelful of lather and use the tent for a hot towel. Actually it was done with a blowtorch. The smell was like a fire in a mattress factory. Twice a day

Topsy had to be swept. You put a ladder against her and climbed up on top with a broom and dusted her off up there, then you went down the ladder a rung at a time and swept off her sides. If you have ever painted a barn you will have some idea of it. Once a week she had to be scrubbed down. Every so often she had to be rubbed down all over with neat's-foot oil. What a greasy mess I was when I got done with that job! Then her toenails had to be pared. Let me tell you, nothing is more deceitful in appearance than an elephant. They're bigger than they look. And everything about an elephant is to scale. Water, for instance. Seventy-five gallons a day Topsy had to have. Remember, this was before the days of water mains and running hydrants. Those were the days when fires still had to be fought with hand pumps and bucket brigades. We had the bucket brigades—boys in the towns who earned passes to the show by toting water to the elephant; we had a hand pump too: I pumped it. Then there was the matter of food to be scrounged up. Two bales of hay a day. A sack of mixed grain. A bushel or two of greens and not too rotten fruit. This in addition to the cotton candy and popcorn and parched peanuts and candied apples and pink lemonade and cigars and chewing tobacco and all the other trash that people fed her. And like a chicken, she had to have gravel, roughage. Correction: a chicken needs gravel, an elephant requires paving stones or brickbats or scrap iron or a laxative on that order. (Needless to say, what went in had to come out—in fact, it seemed to me that more came out than went in, for one of my chores was disposing of the product.) In the towns we played all of these items were hard to come by in such quantities, nothing more so than the water. Topsy was not our only animal. In addition to the menagerie (one sleepy old toothless lion and half a dozen flea-ridden monkeys) and the performing horses, we had two dozen big heavy Clydesdale draft horses, and in some of those dry little prairie towns half the population got into the show on passes for hauling water to the

circus lot. All the same you couldn't help but grow fond of
Topsy. It wasn't her fault that she was so outlandish. I would
get awfully impatient with her sometimes, but whenever I
did I would just remind myself how much entertainment I
had had out of her. There is nothing like an elephant for
keeping you from brooding.

"Not that there was much time to brood. For although
I have given you some little idea of what was involved in
being Red's assistant, the fact of the matter is, that was
really just a diversion. I had to steal time away from my
duties to look after Topsy. A circus when not on the road,
which is most of the time, is either coming up or going
down. As the towns we played were only big enough for a
one-day stand, we used to wake up (if we had gotten to bed
that night) in a new place every morning—though what we
saw of them they all looked pretty much the same, our lot
being always on the edge of town in some cow pasture that
went by the name of the Fair Grounds. Everyone was up at
break of day and out of doors for a look at the sky, hoping
for fair weather and praying against wind. Wind is the
circus's worst enemy. Not only does it make the animals
edgy, there is always the fear that the tent might blow down.
Early as it was, the lot would already be swarming with boys,
for school was let out the day the circus came to town. They
used to follow around at our heels like puppies, panting with
wonder and excitement and ready to faint with joy if one
of us spoke to them. They never knew what sorry low-down
rascals some of them were that they idolized. Not all, you
understand; but it is true the circus does attract some pretty
shiftless specimens. We used to eat our breakfast on our
feet outside the cookhouse, a mug of sweet coffee and a
cruller, then to work. The first thing to be done was put up
the tent. To bring it out of its wagon and unfold and spread
it on the ground took all the hands we could muster, including those who later in the day would blossom out as the
Bearded Lady and the Alligator Boy. Then the stakes were

driven. Then we crawled underneath and raised the outer poles all around. And then Topsy was brought out to do her bit, and from that moment on I, along with Red, was the biggest *human* thing on the lot as far as those kids were concerned. As assistant bullhand (that's right, Topsy was a lady, but around the circus all elephants are 'bulls'), I was got up in pink pants and a yellow silk sash and a pea-green majordomo's jacket with shoulder boards and gold braid and tassels and a bandolier and a red fez with more tassels. Up close it was all pretty tacky, but you had to be grown to see that. Topsy and Red and I would go inside the sagging tent and pretty soon the quarter poles commenced to rise and then the center pole and the bale rings were raised and the tent tightened like an umbrella and drummed in the wind and the stake ropes stretched and hummed, and then we came prancing out, and sitting up on Topsy's head in my get-up I would think, if Ned could see his daddy now Will Vinson wouldn't stand much of a chance!

"After that, Topsy brought the ring sections and the seats were laid up, and by then it was dinner time, hers as well as ours. And after dinner the sideshows and the midway stalls were put up, and it began to look like a circus, and to smell like a circus, with the fresh sawdust and the sweat and the animal odors and the dust in the air and the cotton candy being spun and potato chips and doughnuts frying in the wire spiders and—well, the way a circus smells. The performers were getting into their costumes and on the sides of the vans mirrors flashed in the sun while the clowns put on their paint and everybody was tense and curious to know how big and what kind of a crowd we would draw. None was more interested in the gate than I was. It didn't matter that the day before I had been just as hopeful, and there had been no sign of Will or Ned. This was today, and a new town.

"My head used to reel with looking at so many faces. Not that we drew such great crowds, but it was more people

than I was used to at one time, except once a month
on Saturday afternoon in Clarksville. And these were all
strangers. After a time I began to fear that I had forgotten
what the man I was after looked like. Especially as, Will
being a rather common type, as I've said before, so many
men did remind me of him. Fortunately he was not the
type to come up and say, 'I don't like the way you're staring at me'—though I did have that happen a couple of
times. And sometimes it would seem I was seeing Ned
in every little cotton-headed boy I looked at. I had not
seen him for some while, remember, and it got to the point
that I would sometimes have to sneak a look at the photograph I carried of him, and compare it to some little boy
I'd seen coming through the stile ahead of his folks, so as
to know whether or not to get ready to jump the man standing at the window of the ticket wagon counting out his
money.

"The first thing everybody did was come to see the elephant. I would stand beside her trying to see over the faces
in front to catch sight of Will or Mrs. Vinson among those
in the back before either of them should recognize me.
Meanwhile I had to answer questions. 'Yes, ma'am, that is
right, there is a secret elephant burial ground where they
all go to die. Yes, sir, live to be around a hundred and twenty-
five to fifty. No, sir, never forget a thing.' And then the little
blank cannon went off that announced the performance
time and for me it was another day like the one before, another town with no sign of what I was searching for, and
I would have to begin thinking of tomorrow and hoping it
would be different. Then the show was over and the people
went home happy and the seats had to be dismantled and
stowed away and the tent taken down and folded (Topsy
being put to work again: she pulled up all the stakes with
her trunk) and the sideshows and all the stalls, and at last
we pulled away, leaving just a ring of sawdust that made a
pale circle as evening came on, like a pond in the moonlight.

"A sight more pathetic than a rained-out circus, unless it be an ice-cream cone melting on the sidewalk, I don't know. I had been with Dickey Bros. less than a week when we had our first rainy day. We'd gone through all the work I've described, plus a lot more that I haven't mentioned, while the clouds piled up and blackened overhead all morning. We just about had the tent up when it began to drizzle. 'Maybe it'll blow over,' we said as we put up the sideshows, all of us drenched to the skin. By performance time it was sweeping across the lot in waves and sputtering on the hard-packed ground like grease in a skillet. The tent shuddered and shook. The canvas began to sag and water gathered in the dips and the streamers hung down limp as union-suits on a clothesline and the walls of the sideshows flapped and showed that they were only made of painted muslin stretched on laths. Soon the grounds were muddy as a hog wallow. A few country folks splashed around the booths, but we drew a small house that afternoon and the show fizzled out like a damp firecracker.

"After hauling down and folding the wet tent and getting packed and off the lot we had twenty long miles to make that night to get to our next stand. It was then that I first learned to appreciate that term 'mud show.' Dickey Bros. traveled in a dozen wagons (plus the one my joining the circus had added to the number), tall, heavy enclosed vans with heavy-duty wheels, drawn by those big Clydesdales— underfed and rawboned like everything else, animal and human, connected with Dickey Bros. To draw the biggest wagon of all, Topsy's, took six of them. On the best of roads and in good weather our top speed was about four miles an hour. That night we had a taste of what we were in for right away. One wagon got stuck in the mud before we were even off the lot: Topsy's. Gross weight with her in it of that wagon was close to ten tons. She climbed the ramp, the driver whipped up the team, the wheels turned half over once, and sunk up to the hubs. Not even those six big horses, damned

near the size of elephants themselves, could pull it out. We
had to uncouple three more span of horses from other
wagons and harness them to the six already there and get
out in the rain and get our backs against the wagon while
more of us pushed on the spokes of the wheels and strained
and slithered around in the mud and grunted and cussed
and threw brush under the wheels and brought poles to lever
it with. That was the beginning. It rained nearly every day
for the next three weeks and I reckoned once that I had
helped push that seven-and-a-half-ton elephant and that one-
ton wagon for three hundred and some odd miles.

"Why not have brought Topsy out and made her walk?
you may ask. Why not, in fact, have hitched her to one of
the wagons? So we did. The first time was one night, or
rather morning, around two a.m., when we bogged down
on a back-country road miles from nowhere and tried with
all the horses and all the men and made about one hundred
yards in two hours, and decided at last to let Topsy pull
her own weight. Even then, Red was against it, and sure
enough, we no sooner had her out than she raised her trunk
and sniffed and set off cross-country. She pulled up about
fifty feet of the barb-wire fence at the roadside, pulled up
wire, posts, and according to Red the postholes as well,
stopped long enough to eat all the apples in a farmer's
orchard, then moseyed on down to the millpond that she
had gotten wind of, knocking down six or eight apple trees,
not out of any mischief but just because she couldn't see
them. She drank about half of that millpond, then when she
had slaked her everlasting thirst she got in to take a bath
in what was left. We threw rocks at her and she threw them
right back at us. She squealed and trumpeted and squirted
us and sprayed herself and frolicked about, and all the while
the farmer, who had been roused from bed by all the hulla-
baloo and come running out with his shotgun, stood threatening to shoot us if we didn't get that elephant off his
property that minute. She was the playfullest old idiot

around water, you couldn't help but laugh, and me being amused made the farmer all the madder. Around six o'clock Topsy decided she had had enough and started to climb out. She couldn't make it. The banks were too steep and too slippery. She managed to hook her trunk around one tree and got about halfway out, then the tree came up, roots and all. We finally had to bring down the main tent cable and fourteen horses to haul her out. After that episode it was a good while—more than a week—before we got desperate enough to let Topsy out again. Meanwhile the rains came down and the crowds stayed away and the roads ran liquid and our transportation problems multiplied. Our own particular problem, Red's and mine, could have been solved only by a span of elephants—the East Indian kind, maybe— to draw Topsy with.

"Back-road bridges were never built to carry the likes of Topsy. One morning around six o'clock, after being on the road all night long, we came to one that looked too flimsy to support the empty wagon, let alone the elephant. We had lost so much time that night and fallen so far behind schedule that the rest of the show had gone ahead to get started setting up, leaving me and Red to follow with Topsy. We came to that bridge. Being late and worn out and having no idea where the nearest bridge was nor any reason to expect that it would look any stronger than this one, and the creek being shallow and only about twenty feet wide, we decided to swim Topsy across it. Red got on the far side to call her and coax her out, if necessary. She didn't need any coaxing. I led her out, she lifted her trunk into the breeze, waded across the creek in two strides and up the bank and past Red, who was not even watching her but seemed to have his nose in the air too, and set off down the road at about forty-five miles per hour. By the time I got across the bridge she was five hundred yards down the road with Red about a hundred yards behind, and gaining steadily on her, while I brought up the rear. In time Red caught up, passed Topsy's tail and then her mid-section and drew up alongside her nose, and for the next hundred yards or so it was a dead heat. Then Red went ahead. ''Attaway, Red!' I yelled. 'Head her off! Turn her! I'm right behind you!' But Red never even turned himself, he just went out in front and kept on going until he had taken a hundred-and-fifty-yard lead. He turned around once then to see how far ahead he was and put on another spurt. Very shortly, however, he commenced to fade. He was winded and Topsy closed the gap. She caught up with him, and again it was neck and neck for a stretch. Then Red fell back alongside her middle and back to her tail and Topsy passed him and took the lead. When she reached a certain point she turned off the road, struck across the field, and headed for the woods. I caught up with Red, who was still giving it all he had, and I started to slow down, for I was pretty winded myself. 'Run!' he panted. 'Catch her! Damnation! There won't be a drop left!' I ran. Crossed the field and into the woods. To trail Topsy there wasn't hard, she had cleared a path. But by the time I got there it looked like Red was right—*there* being this moonshiner's still in the woods—and Topsy had already drunk all of the current run and was starting in on the open vats of mash, and if we had been much slower she would have found the bottled stuff. Judging by the wet level in the drum where the finished stuff dripped out of the still, she had drunk between eight and ten gallons. There was nothing to be done but camp there and wait for her to come to. Took her thirty-six hours to sleep it off. What a hangover that elephant woke up with! Matter of fact, we were all three in pretty sorry shape. We brewed black coffee all around and choked down a hair of the dog that bit us and on Wednesday, traveling by night and day, we managed to catch up with the show, all of us still looking mighty seedy, five towns further on. Red and I got back on keel after about a week but poor old Topsy was never the same again, never re-

covered from that last big toot she went on. She was entirely too old to be carrying on that way. Besides, that
whisky was enough to kill anybody. Real rotgut. Her digestion was upset and she went off her feed. She developed
the shakes, her eyes were bleary and bloodshot. Finally she
caught a cold—elephants are highly susceptible. She had all
the symptoms, magnified: runny nose, sneezing, coughs,
fever, and worst of all, constipation. Epsom salts, castor
oil, prune juice, Black Draught, Milk of Magnesia, Fletcher's
Castoria, Syrup of Pepsin, we tried them all, by the bucketful. Finally we gave her an enema—no use. She just dragged
around, and at last, in the town of Zodiac, old Topsy came
to the end of the line. She was a long way from home, I was
thinking, a long way from that secret burial place where all
elephants go when they feel the end is near. And that led me
to wonder just where we were going to bury her, when out
came Mr. Dickey to see how his star attraction was faring.
No sooner had he heard the sad news than he said, 'Raise
a tent over that animal.' No sentimentality to that man—
he was show business all the way. We had posters printed
up and fanned out around the countryside posting them on
sides of barns and picket fences and telegraph poles, and
people came from miles around. 'DEAD ELEPHANT. LIMITED
ENGAGEMENT,' the posters said. Luckily there had come a
cool snap, and the weather held, and Topsy held, and we
did the best five days' business during all my time with the
show, though in my own case it still didn't draw Will out.
At the end of those five days the weather took a sudden
shift. It was perfect circus weather. Out came the sun we
had been praying for and not a breath of wind was stirring.
After about one hour of it the entire population of Zodiac
was down on us. They came out carrying guns and wearing
bandanas over their noses—looked like a townful of des-
peradoes. 'Get that thing out of here, and be quick about it,'
they said. By then the sky was clouding over with turkey

buzzards. We all fell to digging in shifts but by the middle of the afternoon the temperature had risen to the high seventies and our hole still not nearly big enough for one of those East Indian ones, if Topsy had been that kind, much less for her. We were all wearing bandanas by then too. Meanwhile the citizens of Zodiac were cocking their guns. 'Men, this won't do,' said Mr. Dickey. 'We've got to find another way out.' So we all sat down, some distance out of range, and discussed the problem. 'If only we could find a dry well,' somebody suggested. 'Dry coal mine, you mean,' said somebody else. Another was for putting her in her wagon and going down along the road until we found some place to dump her. 'That's seven and a half tons of dead weight you're talking about loading into that wagon,' someone else pointed out. One fellow suggested setting up a cannery, cooking Topsy, and selling it for dog food. But it seemed we had waited too long for that. Somebody else was for stalling the local men till dark, then pulling out, but it was plain that they had already thought of that one too, and now had their guards stationed all around, within sight, but out of smell, or as near to it as you could get. Well, I hadn't said anything and they all turned to me. I had nothing to offer. As a matter of fact, however, I was the one who found the solution. I can't take any credit for it, though."

"How is that? If you solved the problem, Grandpa, then why can't you take the credit?"

"Because I wasn't thinking what I was saying when I said it. I wasn't thinking of anything. I was just sort of mumbling to myself as I walked around the problem, so to speak. When it came my turn, I said, 'Well now, what is the situation? The situation is, we have got fifteen thousand pounds of very high dead elephant here where it's not wanted. Now then, either we get this dead elephant away from this town, or . . .'

" 'Or what?'

" 'Or we get this town away from this elephant.'

"Well, I didn't know I was going to say that, and the minute I heard myself, I wished I could find a hole with a top to crawl in and pull the lid down. I tried to laugh, to turn it into a joke, but it was no time for joking, and besides, I couldn't laugh. The others all sat there looking at me with their mouths hanging open. Mr. Dickey looked like he was having a stroke. I remembered then that Jesus Christ says somewhere, it is by his idle words that a man will be judged. 'By God!' Mr. Dickey managed to say at last. I tried to find words to apologize. While I was still looking for them, Mr. Dickey said, 'By God, sir! Now that is what I call circus!' Then I really felt awful. There was no higher compliment in that man's power to bestow, and I not only had not earned it, I hadn't even been thinking what I was saying.

"Well, the town folks fairly jumped at my suggestion. All of them had been dying for a change for years. Topsy was welcome to the damned old townsite as far as they were concerned. As for us of the circus crew, dismantling Dickey Bros. daily meant that this was all in a day's work for us. We found a spot about fifteen miles to the leeward of Topsy where the water didn't taste nearly so much of rotten eggs, and there we relocated Zodiac. Afterwards, on Thursday, Mr. Dickey announced that he was going into winter quarters and asked if I wouldn't like to go with them, come back on the road the following spring. From the look he gave me it was plain he meant to offer me a hideout. He still believed I was running from the law, as he had ever since I took the job as assistant bull handler. I thanked him but said I had other business to attend to. As a parting gift he gave me a bonus of fifty dollars for the suggestion I had made. I tried to decline it, knowing how little I deserved it, but he insisted. Old Topsy's bones lay out there on the bald prairie until just a few years ago, when they were carted off to the Museum of Natural History in Dallas and there they may be seen today mounted on a stand and labeled 'Prehistoric Mastodon.' "

Christmas 1898 fell on a Sunday. The Saturday before, Dallasites doing their last-minute shopping stopped in the streets to stare at a man wearing a sandwich board on which was painted:

HAVE YOU SEEN
MY LITTLE BOY
?
MY NEIGHBOR
STOLE HIM
AND WENT WEST
FOR
FURTHER
DETAILS
PLEASE STOP
AND ASK
THANK YOU
AND MERRY XMAS

Up Commerce Street from Houston all the way to Harwood, then down Main to Houston again, then up Elm all the way to Deep Elm (or Ellum, as everyone there calls it) and along the principal cross streets he went, passing several times in the course of the day his colleague, the shuffling, stoop-shouldered old stumblebum wearing boards advertising a loan shop, from whom he had adopted the idea, and attracting comment everywhere. Outside Sangers' and A. Harris' and the other big stores (there was no Neiman-Marcus in those days) the shoppers stopped to read his sign and discuss it among themselves, and some to ask for further details.

It worked. At five o'clock that afternoon on the corner of Elm and Akard streets a man from out in Grapevine, Texas, in Dallas for the day, approached my grandfather, asked to hear his story, examined the photograph of Ned, and told of a meeting with the Vinsons in his home town some months previous. And so the big city, where the trail looked most hopelessly lost, provided the lead which set him on Will's track again. Staked him to continue his quest, as well. For by that hour of the day he had collected a total of $62.50, which the good people of Dallas, filled with Christmas spirit, had pressed on him; and this was after he had refused the first half dozen or more who had tried to give him something.

The man from Grapevine also set my grandfather off again on an inward path of self-discovery, by reminding him of the obligation he lay under, and which he was as yet so woefully inadequate to fulfill. My grandfather had hardly begun his story when the man exclaimed, "The *what*?" Then darting a glance to either side, satisfied that no one had overheard, drew my grandfather off Elm onto Akard Street and lowering his voice, he said, "Let me give you a word of advice, Mr. Hathaway. Just keep that part under your hat. Don't let on to nobody that you have had the law working on this for you. I'll overlook it myself 'cause you're a stranger and don't know no better. But hereabouts you get the law out after a feller, why folks that never even liked him before start pulling for him. Out here in Texas folks do look down on any man that goes to—"

"Well, I know that myself. I went to them before I realized that it was personal—if you know what I mea—"

"Why, hit was a johnny come out to our town from up north someplace and before he had time to catch on to our ways he had a falling out with one of our local citizens. Hit all started over a woman. Well, hit was the northern feller's wife, in point of fact. She up and littered a pair of twins that didn't look no more like their daddy than the man in the moon. Spitting image of this other feller, both of them. This led to hard feelings and things went from bad to worse and 'fore long they had a falling out, like I said—hit was over a Poland-China boar—and the northerner he up and went to law. Well! He'd been making out pretty good till then. He'd opened up a little grocery store and worked real hard and folks'd got so they didn't hardly mind him being a foreigner—but oh me oh my, he sure come a whopper when he went to law over that hawg! His trade fell off to nothing, his kids didn't hardly have no more'n a rag to cover their nekkidness, it got so people would cross over to the other side of the street to keep from wishing him good day. Well, to cut a long story short, somebody finally took pity on him and wised him up and he called the other party out and they shot one another up a right smart and shook hands and become the best of friends. After that his trade picked up and now he's doing right well again. But let me tell you, that poor man like to of ruined hisself just through plain ign'rance. So believe me, if you ever want to see that boy of yours again, you'll take my advice and not let on that you've brought the law in on it. Whereabouts did you say you was from?"

"I didn't say, but . . . Arkansas."

"Yes, I guessed you must come from some place like that. I believe that's where this other feller come from too. Well, I'll overlook it, as I say; but do as I tell you, hear? Don't breathe a word of this to nobody else."

And so my grandfather began schooling himself in the universal belief that getting back his boy was more or less incidental to settling his score with Will, and on the way he began rehearsing for that encounter.

So, Will Vinson, you dirty dog, I've got you at last! You're mine! Yell all you like. Go ahead. Nobody will hear you here. No, I won't make it quick. I'm in no hurry. I mean to enjoy this. First I'm going to work you over a bit, pay you back a little for the merry chase you've led me. Save your breath, you'll need it to say your prayers. How's that? Hah! What's that to me? I wouldn't care if you had a dozen. It's the orphans' home for them!

It used to be that he got no further than that, when, remembering with a shudder the orphans' home which he himself had toured, he would relent. No more. Now he saw the thing through unflinching to the end. *You didn't know the man you had to deal with, Will. It's us quiet ones that when the worm turns, he turns. I'm not easily riled. But when I am riled, then watch out! And you have riled me. There! Take that! That's for being cheated out of my money. And there! That's for that little jaunt to Ben Franklin and what I had to take off of that fellow I thought was you. There! That's for all those muddy miles of pushing that derned elephant which you never brought the kids to see. And there! And there! And there! And now, time to say your prayers, Will. Be quick! All right, that's all. Now may the Lord have mercy on your soul!*

Season of peace on earth, good will to men notwithstanding, by the time he reached Fort Worth my grandfather had killed Will Vinson seven, maybe eight times. He was killing him at least once a day, regularly after lunch, and sometimes before breakfast. He killed him in Grand Prairie and again the same day in Arlington. He last left him dead in a thicket just outside Fort Worth. Proceeding into town, he was promptly pointed out by the man who had been gathering pecans on the edge of that thicket, arrested, and clapped in jail.

The cell they put him in was the veritable Sistine Chapel of jail cells. On the ceiling and along the walls were depicted, in lead pencil, the scenes from the Old Testament which Michelangelo had hurried over, beginning with Adam and Eve playing Apple Core, Baltimore. Then was illustrated the Book of Begats, so many old patriarchs multiplying you couldn't count them all. The bigamist Jacob was portrayed keeping the peace in his irregular ménage. A Saturday night in old Sodium (Sodom?) when it was a wide-open town on the plains was the subject of one panel, and in the adjoining one the daughters of Lot were shown doing their filial bit to keep the name of Lot alive. The impotent elders were represented peeping out from behind the bushes and slobbering over Susannah. Onan was pictured doing unto himself. One entire wall was devoted to the shenanigans of the degenerate David clan, with that sweet psalmist the king himself in state, or rather in a state, watching his neighbor's wife taking her bath, then that business between his daughter and that one odd brother of hers, and finally the goatish antics of old Judge Solomon, that chip off the old block, with his harem and his libertine lyrics.

And of whom was all this the work but my grandfather's old friend Reverend Teague! Yes, of course he remembered Mr. Ordway. Did he ever find that boy he was looking for? He even volunteered to pay back that little loan which Mr. Ordway had made him. However, he withdrew the offer when the other prisoner woke up, rubbed his eyes, saw my grandfather, and leapt from bed crying, "Lefty! So they caught you at last, you old horse thief you!"

"My name is not Lefty, and I never saw you before in my life," said my grandfather.

"I thought you was dead!" the man continued. "How in hell *did* you ever get out of San Antone alive?" Turning to Reverend Teague, he said, "You know what this little son of a bitch done in San Antone? He—"

"I have never set foot in San Antone," said my grandfather. "I don't know you and you don't know me. My name is Ordway. Samuel Ordway. I'm here looking for my little boy. Ask him" (indicating the Reverend). "What I am doing in this jail, I don't—"

"Looking for your boy? Well, that's a good story, Lefty. Stick to it, hear? What name did you say you was going by now? So I don't forget it."

"Look here," said my grandfather. "I'm not even left-handed. Give me that pencil," he said to Reverend Teague. He wrote on the wall, "Samuel Ordway." Then he scratched it out, not wishing his name to be seen in such a place.

"Write some more," said the prisoner, whose name was Rags. "Write, 'Thirty days hath September.'"

"Remarkable!" said Reverend Teague. "I've seen men learn to talk Mexican or to play deaf and dumb and never once slip up, but this is the first time I ever saw one learn to write with his other hand."

"What's even more remarkable," said Rags, "when I used to know him he couldn't write with his left hand either."

"Tell me, just what kind of racket was you trying to work with that story about a lost little boy?" asked the Reverend. "Oh, all right then. Keep it to yourself."

Five weeks the Reverend Teague had been in jail, one for each book of the Pentateuch, and it began to look as if he would come to the Last Judgment before he ever came before an earthly judge. He was in for breach of promise.

"To think," said Rags, "you could just marry your way out of here!"

"Her heart is set on vengeance now," the Reverend sighed. "She would sooner have me rot away in this place."

But his was nothing to the case of poor Rags. He had really had the book thrown at him. He had been given a year on charges of trespassing.

"A year for trespassing!" exclaimed my grandfather. (What he wondered, was he himself in for?)

Well, they had added on other charges, as they always did when they had it in for you. Vagrancy. Disorderly conduct. Profanity. Drunkenness. Violation of the sanitary code (he had spat where spitting was forbidden). Disturbing the peace. Resisting arrest. Insulting an officer. Contempt of . . .

"But those are minor offenses," said my grandfather, "and even all put together not enough to keep a man in jail for more than a few nights."

"And treason," Rags said.

"Treason! Growing out of a trespassing charge?"

Well, he had been drinking at the time, it was true. And he was without fixed means of support. And he had spat in the officer's face who arrested him, no getting around that. But when they tried to tack on all those other things, then he had told them just where to insert their lousy government and threatened to emigrate and renounce his citizenship, and that was how the treason charge got stuck on. Then they really got their backs up and started prying into his private life and booked him with trigamy—

"Bigamy," said Reverend Teague. "Bigamy."

"I can count," said Rags. "And so can they."

—fornication, adultery, desertion, gambling, corrupting minors, multiple balloting, consorting with persons of known criminal record (though how he was to avoid that he didn't know, short of turning his poor old mother out into the street), receiving stolen goods (a Christmas present —shirt studs—from the same parent), cruelty to animals, indecent exposure, loitering, and when he got done serving time for all those things he faced a charge of attempted petit larceny. "Never go trespassing," he concluded, "in a bank vault at three in the morning."

There was more in the sequel to the Reverend's story too. Having recalled that he already had a wife and five children, he had backed out of a hasty promise to marry a widow woman in the town. She objected less to that, however, than she did to the fact that when the time came to return all the little gifts they had exchanged, he was unable to recollect where he had mislaid the three thousand dollars she had entrusted him to invest in her name.

Punctually at half past five the jailer came bringing the supper tray. A surly-looking brute, he was a lesson in the deceptiveness of appearances. "Gentlemen," he said with a hideous but well-meant smile. "How are you all this fine evening? Everything to your satisfaction? How is that nasty whitlow coming along, Mr. Brown?" (By which name he seemed to mean Reverend Teague.) "That poultice of my wife's do it any good?"

They replied that they were very well, thank you, and

that they had just one complaint to make at the moment. Would he be a pal and take away the bucket? He did so with a compliance which surprised my grandfather, for as he observed once the man was out of hearing, he had not expected such politeness towards prisoners on the part of jailers. Nor such excellent stew.

They said he ought to have been there before. Before last week, that was. The chili con carne had meat in it now but formerly it was just plain old chili con carne. Up until last week the jailer had used to come banging on the bars and growling, "Here it is, you scum," or words to that effect.

New jailer? my grandfather inquired.

Same jailer, but he was a changed man, and the whole regime had been reformed, owing to a riot they had staged.

To protest the food, asked my grandfather, or the abuse?

Neither, actually. Both admitted having eaten, as well as been called, worse, in as well as out of other jails. It had come about in the following manner: some while before, they had been given a new cellmate . . . The jailer returned at this point, with the bucket emptied, scoured, and sweetened with Lysol. Would that be all for now? he asked, and on being told that he might go, wished them each and all a hearty appetite. New cellmate, as they were saying. Fellow brought in on charges of having passed a lead half dollar, although he swore he was ignorant of the fact and that if it was counterfeit then he had been done out of a day's wages; and it was true that he had no others like it, or for that matter unlike it, on him at the time of arrest. He had seemed at once not only a decent, but what was more, a particularly likable soul, a very sporting loser at three-handed stud (they played nightly, low man to do the chores around the cell next day, such as making the beds, mopping the floor, et cetera), quite content to take thirds on the bucket in the morning, and the longer you got to know him —and some three weeks went by with no sign of his case coming to trial—the better you liked him. To be useful to others was a pleasure to him, so that in time they gave up the nightly poker session and just left the housekeeping to old Bill. The man had a gift for finding things when they went on the street-sweeping detail on Sunday mornings, and always insisted on sharing with them. All the better-quality cigar butts that he picked up he passed on to them, saving only the two-fers for himself—said Havana leaf upset his digestion. Once he found a two-dollar bill, and what do you think he did with it? Sent out for a fried-chicken dinner for all, and swore when it came that the gizzard and the pope's nose were his two favorite pieces and left the rest for them. Bill—Bill O'Shaughnessey—was a positive ray of sunshine. One of those easily-put-upon fellows that don't know how to get mad. Would give you the shirt off his back. Would do anything for a friend and didn't have an enemy in the world. One of those . . .

"I know the type," said my grandfather.

"Mr. Ordway, I doubt you do," said Reverend Teague, "for he was not what he seemed to be."

"I first begun to get suspicious," said Rags, "when he insisted on calling me mister. 'Mr. Rags, here, let me polish them shoes for you—I'm good at that. Mr. Rags, would you mind swapping with me? This here is more pudding than I can eat.' And so forth. 'Just plain Rags will reach me, pardner,' I said. But no, he—"

"To cut a long story short," said Reverend Teague, "one day at dinner Bill draws a long breath and says, 'Gentlemen, I can't go on like this no longer. I cannot take advantage of your trust and kindness no more. Every day of this deception adds to the load on my conscience. Gentlemen, for three weeks now I have enjoyed your company, your hospitality, your friendship—company too good for me, hospitality to which I had no right, friendship I did not deserve. Oh, gentlemen, I waited for you to see the truth for yourselves, but no, you are too trusting, too goodhearted. It never occurs to you that others can be any less open and aboveboard than yourselves. Gentlemen, look at me! Now do you see? No? Oh, Mr. Rags, Mr. Brown, for three weeks now you have unknowingly shared your bed and board with . . . Oh, how can I break it to you? Gentlemen, I am but fifteen-sixteenths Irish. The rest of me . . ."

Well, the mayor and the entire board of aldermen and the county sheriff, the town constable, the whole shooting match had all come to apologize. Nothing like this had ever happened in their jail before and they could promise it would never happen again. It was an honest mistake, the sort that anybody might make, for the fellow was only one-sixteenth, after all, and it wasn't always easy to spot them in cases like that. Well, apologies were all very well, but such a blow to a man's self-respect was not to be healed by a few words, nor even a few scraps of meat in the chili con carne. It was Rags's lawyer's hope that by entering a plea of police brutality he would go scot-free on his charge of armed entry.

"I thought all along that son of a bitch was awful friendly and obliging for a white man," said Rags.

"Well, he took me in, I don't mind admitting," said Reverend Teague. "I just thought he wasn't any too bright. But he was as light-complected as Mr. Ordway here."

My grandfather assured them that he was what he seemed to be, at which they pshawed and said they had never doubted him for a moment. Privately he resolved to be a little less pliant and easygoing than he suspected himself of being ordinarily, so as to give them no cause to question their confidence in him.

"Got to keep them in their place," said Rags. "Let them in here, next thing you know one of them's married to your sister."

After supper they played poker. My grandfather lost. Then the daylight faded and they made music in the gloaming. They sang of Lilian the dog-faced lady whose bark was worse than her bite. Of that hometown gal we all used to know who now was selling huh-what she used to give away-hay. Of the growing girl who to the tune of "Turkey in the Straw" swore she wasn't gonna do it for a nickel any more, wasn't gonna be just an ordinary whore, fifteen cents was gonna be her new price—give her a quarter and she'd do it twice.

After turning in that night my grandfather heard from the bunk below a *hssst!* followed by, "Listen. It goes without saying that you never saw me before either. Tit for tat, eh, Lefty, old pal?"

"Deal me in on that too," said Reverend Teague from across the room.

However, they came the very next day—the county sheriff, a Texas Ranger, and a U. S. marshal—with a dossier on Mr. Brown identifying him as the notorious Suds Folsom, and hauled him off to Austin, there to answer for his crimes.

They came also that same day to interrogate the prisoner Ordway.

"Tell them," Rags counseled, "you won't speak a word without a lawyer."

But my grandfather responded to their very first question.

"What body?" he cried.

He was remanded in custody and returned to his cell, charged, until such time as the corpus delicti should be found, with suspicion of murder.

My grandfather's court-appointed attorney, Mr. Sully Parker, was a man in his late nineties or early hundreds. Leaky with rheum, he was constantly hawking and spitting and blowing his nose, and his eyes were as liquid as a brace of oysters. He had lost all command of his voice, which sounded like a faulty long-distance telephone connection, choky and faint one moment, startlingly close and piercing the next. Printed, HIS conversATION WOULD have LOOKED LIKE this. In the course of his long legal practice he had heard as much as an elderly priest, and it was a question which Mr. Parker despised the human, or at least the Texan, animal more for, his law-breaking or his law enforcement.

In the case of Texas vs. Ordway he was not encouraging. Not encouraging at all. He listened to his client's protestations of innocence, and advised him to plead guilty. He too was curious as to the disposal of the body. My grandfather finally managed to convince him that he had not killed Will Vinson . . . yet. But then he went on to confide that all he wanted, really, was to recover his son. He went so far as to hint that it would be a source of remorse to him, enough to detract from his pleasure in later years as he watched his Ned grow to manhood, to have it on his conscience that he had orphaned Will Vinson's three children. "ALL RIGHT, son," said Mr. Parker. "No need to LAY IT ON." He reminded his client that he had been overheard in that thicket, and that they had his pistol in evidence. He said he could just conceive the possibility of a jury accepting a man's sworn statement that he intended not to kill a fellow who had stolen his wife, say, or a daughter. And perhaps had Mr. Ordway been from out of state, or even a local colored man, a jury might be suborned to believe that so long as he recovered his boy he would be content to let Will Vinson off with a good pistol-whipping. But to expect twelve idiots to believe that a native-born white fellow-Texan was not going to shoot the man who had stolen his first and only son was asking too much.

But after a week's search had failed to disclose any corpse, or any telltale evidence such as bloodstains on the suspect's clothes or human hair on the butt of his unfired pistol; and as the state's principal witness had only heard, not seen, a killing committed; and as the accused man stoutly maintained his innocence despite hours of questioning, the grand jury refused to hand down an indictment for murder. Instead he was charged with intent to kill, illegal possession of firearms, carrying a concealed weapon, disturbance of the peace, and interference with justice.

My grandfather was brought before the presiding judge
and bail was set. Five hundred dollars. But to the disappointment of the court's hopes that he would make it, then skip
(for Fort Worth in those days was quite a humble and back-
ward place. Now, of course, all this has been taken care of,
but in my grandfather's day it stood in need of a good few
civic improvements, such as: pavement, street lamps,
sewage disposal, fire truck, water tower, dog pound, relief
fund for sheriffs' and tax collectors' widows and orphans,
et cetera, et cetera, and the town's budget was sunk in
arrears), the prisoner refused bail.

Came the day of the trial. That he might make the worst
possible appearance, though the reason given was that he
might overpower the barber and seize his razor, the prisoner
was denied a shave. Rags wished him luck, giving him a
wink and a broad grin as he called him "Mr. Ordway." He
was then escorted under guard to the courtroom. There was
a good crowd. Mr. Parker had a large following, so did Mr.
Shively, the prosecuting attorney, and a match between the
two always drew well. On a table to itself lay my grandfather's pistol, a tag tied to the trigger guard. His Honor the
judge arrived and court was declared opened. The veniremen
were called and the opposing counsels used up their per-
emptory challenges on them. Then twelve good men and
true, and without preconceptions in the case, were duly
sworn and seated. The prisoner under advice of counsel pled
guilty as charged. The sheriff was called by the prosecution
and deposed the details of his arrest. The nut gatherer, one
Dewey Tutwiler, recounted what he had overheard that day
in the thicket. Three farmers, four housewives, a miller, a
blacksmith, a wheelwright, and a surveyor were called to
the stand, deposed that the accused had approached them
seeking to learn the whereabouts of a man named Will
Vinson, of whom he had grimly declared himself to be in
pursuit. A witness who identified himself as Eber Smithwick,
resident of Tarrant County, was called. He deposed that on

October 29 of the preceding year he had been in Paris, Texas. Yes, he had seen somebody there that day who was now present in the courtroom. He pointed a finger at my grandfather. Where had he seen him? It was at a stump-speaking. He then recounted more or less accurately my grandfather's unscheduled speech of that day, concluding with his guarantee that anybody who gave him information leading him to Will Vinson would need fear no reprisal.

After each of these, "Your witness, sir," said the prosecutor.

And each time, "NO questions," said Mr. Parker.

The defendant was called and sworn. The prosecuting attorney got to his feet with a loud sigh, as though saddened by the prospect of the perjury before them all. He strode past the witness stand three or four times, nodding at my grandfather in passing, contriving thereby to suggest that he had seen him in that seat on former occasions. At last he stopped pacing, wheeled on the witness, and said:

"Your name, please. Remember, you are under oath."

"Ordway. Sam . . . Samuel Ordway. That's O–R–D—"

"Place of residence—if you have one?"

"Clarksville. Well, Mabry, actually. That's over in Red River—"

"Well? Which is it?"

"Mabry."

"All right. Now we've got that cleared up, I hope. And now will you tell the court your version of what has brought you so far from home?"

"I'm out here looking for my little boy."

"Looking for your little boy? Ran away from home, did he?"

"No, sir, he did not run away. He wasn't but two, going on three years old."

"That is young to run away," the prosecutor agreed.

"He was stolen from me. My neighbor took him. Will Vinson."

"Ah-hah!" said the prosecutor with a look meant to speak volumes. "And when did this occur?"

"The seventh of last May."

"You reported it to the authorities at once, of course? I'll have to ask you to speak so that you can be heard, please."

"Well, shortly. Not at once. After two or three days."

"Thank you. Now in future please face the jury and speak up when responding to questions. This child that was stolen from you, he was your only child?"

"No."

"You have other sons?"

"Sons, no. Three little girls. Another child on the—"

"Ah, daughters. The stolen child was your only son, that is correct? Fair to assume, I suppose, that he was his father's favorite?"

"No, sir, it's fair to assume no such thing. I'm one father that tries not to play favorites among my children."

"You wish the jury to believe that you valued your only son exactly as much, neither more nor less, than his three sisters?"

"Well, if anything," said my grandfather, "I'm afraid little Ned was sort of neglected. You see, I . . ."

"That is a very interesting admission," said the prosecutor. "In other words, it took a man to steal your boy to teach you to appreciate him?"

"I can't say I'm proud to have to admit it, but as I'm under oath, there is something in what you say."

"A very interesting admission. Thank you. I ask you now," he said, taking up the pistol from the table, "to look at this. Have you ever seen this weapon before?"

"It's mine."

"Did you purchase—or in whatever way acquire it— recently? With this trip in mind?"

"No, I've always had it."

"You have always had it?"

"Yes, it was my mother's."

"Your mother's! Well! Did you say your *mother's*? Hmm. Perhaps we will go into that later. In any case, you brought this weapon from home with you? You took it with you in setting out on your quest? With what object in mind?"

But my grandfather had seen this question coming and promptly replied, "I thought I ought to have one. Traveling out here with money on me."

The courtroom erupted with a mixture of hilarity and out-raged civic pride. Now he had the audience against him, and from the looks on their faces he had cooked his goose with the jurors.

"Tell the court," said the prosecuting attorney with a smirk, "exactly where you were between the hours of twelve noon and one p.m. on last December twenty-ninth."

"Well, I was where he" (indicating Mr. Tutwiler) "said I was, in that thicket here on the edge of town. Only . . ."

"And did you or did you not say while in that thicket, as the witness has testified he heard you say, and I quote, Will Vinson, prepare now to meet your maker? Unquote."

"Well, yes. But—"

"And did you or did you not say at the same time, quote, You thought I'd never find you, didn't you? But I was too smart for you. Not all the Texas Rangers could find you, but I found you, and now you won't get away. You have come to the end of your trail. Unquote. Did you say that?"

"Yes," said my grandfather, very red in the face.

"And did you also say on that occasion . . . ?"

But my grandfather could hardly bear to recall the rest of his own words which the prosecutor had quoted at him. He had to sit there and listen to himself boast and rant and rave and threaten and pretend to beat and stomp and murder Will Vinson, then had to confess to a crowded court-room full of men that he had been all alone in that thicket, and that he was (had to say this three times before the prosecutor was satisfied that everyone had heard it) "just practicing."

And with that the state rested its case.

The judge directed Mr. Parker to proceed with calling his first witness.

"Your HONOR," said Mr. Parker, "the DEFENSE will call NO WITNESSES. We REST OUR case."

The judge had to pound his gavel and threaten to clear the courtroom. Then he said, "Mr. Parker, the bench, mindful of your long experience before the bar, hesitates to instruct you. However, we would be remiss in our duty did we not point out to you that you may be putting your client in jeopardy by your—"

"IF my client WISHES OTHER counsel he is free to SEEK IT," said Mr. Parker. "Meanwhile, I shall CONDUCT HIS DEFENSE in my own MANNER."

The prosecuting attorney began his summation to the jury. He said that in a case of murder accompli, so to speak, it was necessary to establish a corpus delicti, to prove that somebody had existed, and had, through violence, ceased to do so. To establish a motive and to prove the accused guilty of the crime. In a case of intent to kill it was necessary to provide a prospective corpus delicti. This they had in the corpus of one Will Vinson, present whereabouts unknown. The accused's motive for the crime had been amply established. The murder weapon, or the intended murder weapon, had been introduced in evidence, the prisoner had acknowledged it to be his.

To accuse a man of intent to kill, said the prosecutor, was to accuse him of intending the gravest sort of murder. For the law, he said, distinguished three kinds or degrees of homicide. The gentlemen of the jury were not lawyers, but no doubt they knew, as it was common knowledge, that first-degree murder was the most severely punishable and third-degree murder the most leniently punishable, with second-degree murder standing midway between. In third-degree murder death was held to ensue upon a chance encounter between the two principals, to have been committed in the heat of ungovernable passion, and with whatever weapon lay to hand, whereas first-degree murder was premeditated and done in cold blood. Roughly speaking, if two men had a falling out on a downtown street corner and came to blows and one of them tore up a paving stone and hit the other over the head with it and the victim died of the blow, that was murder in the third degree. If they parted and one fellow then whipped out his knife and took out after the other and caught him down in the next block and stabbed him then and there, that was murder in the second degree. But if he went home and brooded on it overnight and next day loaded his gun and took a streetcar and rode across town and took aim and shot his victim through the window as he sat eating his breakfast, then that was murder in the first degree, premeditated and with malice aforethought.

Now the defendant in this case had been brooding for some nine months on his revenge. He had come halfway across the state of Texas on his grim mission. He had brought with him from home a fully loaded weapon merely to heft which required premeditation. He had been overheard and had confessed to rehearsing in preparation for his act of retribution here in the purlieus of their own peaceful and law-abiding community. This was surely intent to murder in the first degree, and for such determined bloody-mindedness nothing short of the maximum penalty under the law was thinkable: a stiff jail sentence, a heavy fine, an order of restraint, a bond to keep the peace, confiscation of the man's weapon, and payment of court costs.

He cautioned the jury against any attempt on the part of the counsel for the defense to claim for his client the extenuation of "cooling time."* That the accused was an injured man no one would deny. To steal a man's son was no

---

* "Cooling time": a line of legal defense, peculiar to Texas courts, in which it is held that if a man kills before he has had time "to cool" after receiving an injury or an insult he is not guilty of murder.

light provocation. But nine months was time enough for any
man to cool down, especially one who had admitted on the
stand that it had taken the theft of his son to teach him to
appreciate him.

He also foresaw and warned against the possibility that
counsel for the defense might take a different line, and raise
the question of the posture and attitude of the intended
victim at the moment of the commission of the act of which
his client stood accused of the intent. In other words, he
might suggest that it was reasonable to doubt that Will
Vinson was just going to stand and let his client shoot at
him like a bottle on a stump. That what his client was
guilty of at most was intent to kill in self-defense. This, he
cautioned the jury, lay in the realm of pure conjecture. None
of them knew Will Vinson. None could predict what he
might or might not do. They were not there to try Will Vinson. Moreover, on the basis of the evidence and the testimony
which they had heard, there was no reason whatsoever to
suppose that Samuel Ordway was the sort of man to give
Will Vinson a fighting chance to draw and defend himself.
This was not the way of the Samuel Ordways.

"Let us," he said, "enact this intended, this as yet uncom-
mitted, this still-preventable murder. Time: we'll say six
months from now" (an estimate at which my grandfather
could scarce repress a groan). "Place: a small town on the
Texas–New Mexico border" (another near groan from my
grandfather). "Towards nightfall a man stands looking down
from a bluff onto the town where he has reason to believe his
long, long trail has come at last to its end, its sanguinary
end. Bearded and in rags, his eyes glazed with an animal
hatred, steadily mumbling to himself, does he, on entering
the town, report the suspected presence of the man who has
wronged him to the local authorities? No, gentlemen. There
is not enough disrespect for the law in Texas but this Samuel
Ordway has got to add his bit. He has come a thousand miles

for this one moment. He has not eaten in days. He is afoot, having sold his horse to continue his mad quest, and walked the last seventy-five miles over burning sands. Through rain and shine, blizzards and tornadoes, through hunger and thirst he has come. Now he takes out his pistol." The prosecutor picked up the pistol. "He checks the cylinder. It is fully loaded. Five shots. And he intends to use them all. He smiles a cruel, a pitiless smile. He hardly remembers any more the original cause of his quarrel with the man he seeks. That he has a little boy, he has all but forgotten that. Now he finds his way to the home of his victim. He creeps to the wall of the house. He peers through the window. There, unsuspecting, unarmed, sits the object of his hatred. He takes aim. He cocks the pistol." The prosecutor suited his actions to these words. That is, he aimed the pistol at the window. But cocking it gave him some little difficulty. He tried again, repeating, "He cocks his pistol." No go; the hammer was stuck. With both hands he tried again, saying between clenched teeth, "He cocks his pistol." By now out of at least a hundred hip pockets pistols of every caliber had appeared and were being waved in the air. "Here, Ed, try mine!" "Hurry, goddammit, 'fore the bastard gets away!" "Here, have a shot at him with mine, Ed!" voices cried.

Boom! There was a shattering roar and the prosecuting attorney disappeared in a cloud of smoke. He came staggering out, coughing, pistol pointed towards the ceiling from the recoil. There was a moment's silence. Then from the rear of the courtroom came, in a disgusted voice, "Hellfire, Ed. You missed him a country mile."

Mr. Parker's defense was brevity itself. A famous jurist of the state, he began, had said that in a Texas murder trial the first thing to be established was whether or not the deceased ought to have departed. He believed, he concluded, that the same principle should apply in cases of intent to kill.

The jury, out ninety seconds, returned a verdict of not guilty, plus a pool of thirty-six dollars to be presented to the acquitted with which to buy himself a more reliable firearm.

Dallas is the capital of East Texas. Cotton town. Market for dirt farmers' crops. Fort Worth, just thirty miles away, is the capital of West Texas, a stock breeders' and cattle ranchers' town. Men in Dallas are much like men everywhere. They wear shoes. Those in Fort Worth wear high-heeled boots and walk bowlegged. "Where the West begins," is the way Fort Worth advertises herself. There you leave the blackland prairies and launch upon the plains. Looking back, you can see the sparse low timberline receding like a shore, like a continent's end. Looking ahead, you can see nothing.

Onto the plains you issue as onto a lighted stage, and with that sudden sense of isolation and exposure. The farther behind you leave the now-familiar prairie, the fewer people you see, the stronger grows the sensation of being watched. The silence sharpens the ear, the emptiness the eye. An ambiguous, double sensation comes over you: you feel at once taller, a very tall man, and smaller, a very small creature. The changeable winds pass and repass over the dry grass with a sound like shifting sands, and running before the wind, the grass turns its nap, first this way then that way, like velvet pile when a hand is run idly back and forth over it. Flat as a marble floor, the land stretches away empty and endless as the bare boundless sky above. The eye strains ahead for a landmark, a rooftop, a spire, a tree, anything vertical, anything that thrusts above the brown level monotony.

Looked at long enough—and once embarked upon it, you look for a long, long time—the land will seem to exhibit that phenomenon called *seiche*, to rock slowly from side to side like the wallowing of a lake. That, and the absence of objects to relate yourself to, bring on land-sickness. Even the sun gives no direction, but hangs straight overhead all day, as if uncertain of the way. Under moonlight the plain whitens like an arctic snowfield. When you do see a man you first see him at such a distance that he is like a fly crawling on a tabletop. There is no horizon. Rather, there is horizon everywhere. The horizon is created whenever something or somebody stands up somewhere in the landscape. Then where a rooftop rises, the barren eye eagerly draws all lines towards it. You see clouds underneath the belly of a cow, see the sky winking between the legs of a walking man. It is a place without perspective, and things thrust themselves up isolated, unsurrounded by any of the close familiar objects by which one judges distances and size; and so the eye, as if out of focus, cannot judge, cannot relate it: is that a child nearby or a man far off, a haystack or a hummock, an insect or a bird—or nothing at all, a mirage? And because you have any landmark or person for so long in view, nor ever lose it, or him, under a hill or behind a bend, you seem to take forever getting there, and time hangs suspended and unreal. And yet when you finally reach the place no time has elapsed, for across that unarched plain of a sky the sun inches along and it is noon all day. Across the plain west from Fort Worth the road runs straight as the line left when a woman pulls out a thread to cut a piece of cloth along.

In such a landscape to come upon an anthill was a welcome diversion. One day riding along, my grandfather came upon about a thousand anthills. Beginning at some distance from the road, they covered a large tract of land, so thick it looked like a field hilled up for planting table corn. My grandfather stopped for a look, stood up in the wagon bed, and stretched his neck. As he did so, dozens, hundreds of hitherto motionless and invisible little furred animals, their pelts the same ginger color as their dirt mounds, stretched themselves up for a look at him. The next instant, as one, as if all the target animals in a shooting gallery had been popped off with a single shot, they flipped over, the dusty white soles

of their hind feet flashing as they somersaulted, and disappeared. It was a feature of the West that he had heard of:
a prairie-dog town.

Inquisitive creatures, they were already poking their noses
out of their holes again as my grandfather approached what
might be called the city limits of their settlement, where he
meant to sit down and watch. Instantly they drew in again,
like turtles withdrawing into their shells. Soon, however,
their curiosity brought them back out. From where he sat
my grandfather could see that the town was intersected with
beaten paths. Some were main thoroughfares, others side
streets, still others mere back alleys. Comically humanlike,
two or three of the creatures would collect on the front stoop
of one of their neighbors' houses and gossip, their heads
bobbing in solemn agreement, jerking up all together at anything untoward happening down the street. Now and again
a spat would develop among their children and with a burst
of yelps they would break off and dash over and separate
them and box their ears. Sometimes a truant youngun would
scamper down the block for home ahead of a scolding
mother. Others meanwhile appeared repeatedly at their holes
like an industrious housewife coming out to the front porch
to shake out her dust cloth or her mop. Quick, nervous, ex-
citable, they could not keep still for a moment. With their
queer little bark and their humorless, almost petulant expression, they appeared to be destroying reputations and
always lecturing one another, and constantly taking offense,
abruptly turning their backs on their interlocutor and going
off in a huff into their holes. Rumors seemed to fly through
the town. One would say something to another, then duck
into her hole, and out of three or four neighboring ones inquisitive heads, as at the windows of a house, would pop up,
whiskers twitching, as if they had been told to go have a look
at what was going on out outside, and believe it if they could.
My grandfather had been so entertained that when he rose

to go, and looked at his watch, he found he had wasted the better part of an afternoon.

Five days beyond Mineral Wells my grandfather saw another feature of the West.

Seen from a distance, the town had looked like a mirage. Up close it looked still more unreal. He was not sure he was seeing it when he first saw it. Lying along the horizon, colorless, close to the colorless earth, it appeared and disappeared, throbbing in and out of vision like heat waves. Across the plain the only movement was an occasional restless and lonesome tumbleweed. As he rode into the main street he sensed an eerie quiet, as if it were a town in quarantine. He thought at first that he had entered by the bad end which every town has: the first places he passed were stores that had gone out of business years before, a little grocery on one side of the street, its sign dangling drunkenly from off the building's high false front; across the street a place, no knowing what it had been, the porch roof of which sagged in the middle like an awning full of rain water. It was an old town, with board sidewalks, and in this end of it the walks had rotted and caved in and an occasional plank stuck up crazily in the air. The stalks of weeds poked up through cracks in the walk and in the street itself weeds grew in clumps. Not a sound was to be heard. Then he heard the plaintive creak of something, something wooden, swaying and rasping in the wind: a signboard, a loosened shutter, or the rocking of an unsteady wall. The source of that sound he could not discover, but the lonesomeness of it he never forgot: a thin rusty wooden creak in the wind, audible at noon in the street of a hushed town. Past more abandoned stores he drove in the deepening silence. Now he could see the other end of the street, could see where the plains recommenced—indeed, the grass had overgrown the road and ran a way into town, tall prairie grass growing between the last few buildings. He came abreast of the tallest buildings, those which rose three stories, and looking into one on his left, he saw that the interior was lighted, and saw why, how: the roof had fallen in. The wind soughed and the old, paintless, dry walls groaned. HOTEL said the dim sign which hung above the building across the street, BLACKSMITH said another on the side of the building and below it an ectoplasmic hand with a finger pointing down the alley. Silently reining in his team, my grandfather sat and looked around. Where there were windows you could see nothing inside the buildings, so beclouded with dirt were they, but where the windows were broken you could see inside. The walls were tattered and peeling and on the floors a layer of dirt had grown weeds from seeds blown in by the wind.

"Welcome!"

My grandfather bounced on his seat, spun about, and saw down on the ground alongside the wagon wheel an old man with a dirty white beard and flowing long white hair, dressed in rags and camped under a tentlike hat.

"What place is this, uncle?" asked my grandfather. "Or was it?"

"Why, this here is what they call a ghost town," said the old man, chortling. "I'm the head haint. Pretty spooky, ain't it?" This sent him sputtering off into a fit of bronchial laughter. "Don't know where you're at?" he said when he had recovered, and this sally sent him off choking again. "Wellsir, suppose I tell you that right here"—and he hopped with unexpected spryness onto the board walk—"on this spot Pat Garrett stood one day and just stomped his foot at a man that'd just been threatening to whup any man in town, and that feller turned tail and run and was never seen here again?" He unexpectedly lifted his foot and stamped his heel. The echo seemed to search out every cranny in the empty town, reverberating, echoing upon itself. The old man, obviously demented, cackled with laughter. "There," he said, pointing up the street, "that was the Silver Dollar Saloon. One night in there I seen a man lose eighty-six thousand dollars at three-card monte."

"Pat Garrett?" said my grandfather. "Wasn't that the man that killed Billy the Kid?"

"He wasn't the one that killed Cock Robin," said the old-timer, and went off into another peal of laughter. "You look like an all right feller. I'll let you in on it. This here"—he put his hand to his mouth, rolled his eyes in both directions, and whispered hoarsely, "this here is old Fort Griffin. Don't tell nobody."

Fort Griffin! Famous frontier outpost. Scene of the great Comanche Indian Wars. Cattle drovers' town. . . .

"They was all here," said the old-timer. "Pat Garrett. Billy Dixon. Bat Masterson. Jesse Chisholm. Charley Goodnight. Care to see the place? Here," he said, hopping back into the road and holding out his hand, palm up, empty, "here's the key to the city. That'll unlock all the doors. Be my guest."

When they had walked up and down both sides of the street and gone into several of the buildings, my grandfather said, "These were the places of business. Where did the people live?"

"Nobody stayed long enough to call it living. Them that did was single men that lived for the most part in little shanties made of hide. Wasn't much else to build out of and it never mattered if they didn't last. Like to know what become of all them shacks?"

"Yes," said my grandfather. "What?"

"Guess."

"Rotted away."

"Wrong!" His eyes watered with amusement. "Guess again."

"Blew away."

"Wrong! Try again."

"I give up."

"I bet you do. I bet you do! Wellsir, I'll tell you. I et em. That is to say, I et all of em I could before the coyotes et em, and then I et the coyotes. And let me tell you, they tasted good that winter of eighty-six! Bet I'm the first man you ever met ever et a town, ain't I?" And he laughed till he choked.

This was the history of Fort Griffin. The soldiers came to kill the Indians and make the place safe for human habitation. The job done, the troops were ordered farther west, the post abandoned, and the town, with nothing left to live for, died. The hide hunters came while the soldiers were there. They exterminated the buffaloes, and moved on. Some stayed on a while to gather the bones which littered the plains, as if that barren soil had grown a crop, the great cages of bleached ribs, held together by sinews which in that dry heat hardened into glue, sticking up like the branches of some ghostly plant. When the bones were gleaned the pickers pulled out, leaving then only the old, the crippled, and the crazed.

Early one cold windy Monday afternoon my grandfather drew up before a naked little house floating on the plain like a solitary chip on the ocean. It hardly deserved the name of house: a low little shanty, new and raw and yet already shabby from neglect. The window lights were already frosted from the driven sands and the blistered paint was peeling from sunburn. The surprising thing, here, however, was that it had ever been painted. It was the first habitation my grandfather had come upon for miles and miles, and he was glad to see it, to see any sign of humanity, anything, glad, as he went round to the leeward of the house, to find some shelter from that stinging wind if only for a moment.

As he stepped out from the shelter of the wall there crashed against his eardrums a series of cracks like shots from a repeating rifle. There was a wash hanging on the clothesline (so dingy that even a man must be struck by it) and the wet heavy bedsheets were whipping and popping like loosened ship sails in a storm. Out of one of them came, fighting and flailing to extricate herself, a woman, her hair streaming, her skirt blown full of wind. She bent to her basket and brought up another sheet, spread it, and was lifted off her feet by a sudden gust that inflated it and dragged her along like a ground-crewman trying to anchor a balloon. *Crack! crack!* went the wash on the line. And suddenly the clothesline broke. The line of wash was raised on the wind and hung fluttering like the tail of a kite—towels, union-suits, dresses—then in a momentary lull fell to the ground and tumbled over in the dirt. In the lull the woman was just gathering in the sheet she was clinging to. Then she turned and saw her wash on the ground all muddied. She just stood there looking down at it with a wan impassivity which to my grandfather spoke of the hours bent over the washboard, of the difficulty of heating the wash water in this land so scarce in firewood, scarce in water too, and of the number of previous times this very same thing must have happened. She did not cry or curse, she just looked down at the mess with a numb and weary resignation, almost satisfaction. Then, still without any sign of emotion, she deliberately dropped the sheet she was holding.

My grandfather dashed over, lifted his hat and jammed it on again, and said, yelling into the wind, "Let me help you, ma'am!" and began gathering up the clothes and the line.

It was only after watching him struggle with it alone for a minute that she volunteered to help. Starting at the other end, she too began gathering up the clothes, line and all. They met and stood up and she said something but he could not hear. She carrying one part, he the rest, connected by the line, they made for the house. When they were inside the kitchen he said, "DOES IT ALWAYS BLOW LIKE—" And then with a laugh, "Does it always blow like this out here?"

"No," she said. "Sometimes it veers around and comes out of the west." Then, nodding at the clothes, "Just throw them in the corner there. I ain't going to do them again today."

My grandfather began his little spiel. He got no further than "I'm from Clarksville."

"I'm from Red River County too!" she cried.

"Fancy that!" he said. "The two of us meeting away off out here—" He was about to say "in the middle of nowhere," and only just stopped himself.

"I'm from Box Elder," she said.

"Is that a fact!"

"And you're from Clarksville! Mrs. Blainey, my neighbor, is from Clarksville."

"Blainey? I know the Blaineys in Clarksville. That is, I don't know them—much too high-quality for me—but I know of them. Very well-to-do people, the Blaineys."

"Yes. My Mrs. Blainey is one of them."

"I didn't know any of them had come out here," said my grandfather.

The lady knew of something to help him in his search. Not down her road—in fact, nearly fifty miles away—but some people who might be the ones he was after had passed through some months ago. It had reached her because news of strangers traveled far, if slowly, out here, and these particular ones were said to have come from somewhere back in their parts. She had regretted bitterly not meeting and talking with them. Now she asked, she almost begged my grandfather not to hurry off. "You don't know what it means to me to see somebody. Somebody from back home, I mean," she said. "If you would only sit and talk a while, tell me about things back there, you would be doing a charity."

"Well," said my grandfather, "I'm afraid I don't know Box Elder. I've never been there."

"Oh," she cried, "Clarksville is near enough to Box Elder to seem like home when you're away off out here in the middle of nowhere."

So, putting aside his vow never to enter a house when the man was absent, my grandfather allowed himself to be shown into the parlor (the sand on the rugless floor gritted underfoot like spilled sugar) and sat down while she went out to the kitchen to heat the coffee. She hoped he didn't mind condensed milk? From out in the kitchen she suddenly dashed back in. She did not say anything, just stood looking at him, as if she wanted to make sure he was still there. She smiled a nervous smile. Then she caught herself smiling and dashed back out. From the kitchen she called, "I can hear you from here. Tell me all about Clarksville."

"Well, I don't know how long it is since you last seen Clarksville," said my grandfather. "However, I don't expect it's changed much. Same old creek still runs through it— about two feet across in the wide places. A big new confectionery has just recently opened up on the west side of the square, about in the middle of the block, run by a nice young Greek fellow named Athas. From Greece, he is." He looked up and to his surprise found her standing in the doorway.

"Oh," she said, "I wish I had knowed you was coming! I am so ashamed for anybody to see this house. So ashamed! Such dirt, such untidiness! I hope you won't think I was brought up no better than this. I grew up in a nice home, Mr. Ordway. My mother taught me better. I myself kept a nice house in De Kalb for the first year of our marriage, before he brought me out here. I had flowers and shrubs. Everything. All so neat. You had such a lot of fresh water to wash things in back there. Here I just can't seem to keep ahead of things. Its only the two of us, but I don't know, I don't know . . ."

She returned to the kitchen, came back with cups and saucers, then made another trip for the coffeepot.

"Been out here long?" my grandfather asked when they had begun to drink. She could not have been there very long; she was quite a young woman.

"Yes," she replied. "Nearly two years."

"I see," said my grandfather, hiding his smile in his cup.

He almost dropped his cup at the violence of her next exclamation. "Oh, I hate this place so! When we come out on these plains and I caught my first sight of them I said,

'I'm not going any further.' But I did, and we come on out here and I swear to you, Mr. Ordway, I cried without stop for three months. I don't think I'll ever be able to cry again over anything. I haven't got any tears left. I hated it the minute I set eyes on it and I hate it the same this minute. Always alone, but yet never private. No trees, no flowers, nothing but earth and sky. I always did love flowers so! I tried to grow a few little bushes but the poor things just wilted and died. I went without bathing to water them plants, Mr. Ordway, but the poor things just turned brown and dried up and I watched them going and couldn't do anything to save them and I felt like I was losing all the friends I had in the world. Oh, give me a home," she said in a sudden change of voice, "where the buffaloes roam— except there ain't even any of them any more, and I ain't seen no deer nor antelopes playing either—where seldom is heard a discouraging word, or any kind of word, and the skies are not cloudy all day. Oh, what I wouldn't give to see one of them big creamy white clouds back home, a great big cool white thunderhead floating on the skyline. And songbirds. Oh, if I ever do get home again I want to lie in the shade of a green tree and listen to the mockingbirds singing! I'll wear a whole bouquet of flowers in my hair— none of these burnt-up odorless prairie flowers, but sweet garden flowers, roses, carnations, gardenias. I was quite a nice-looking girl just a few years ago, Mr. Ordway. Almost pretty, though I don't expect anybody to believe that."

Squirming with discomfort, my grandfather said, "Why, you're a very nice-looking young woman now."

"Oh, you don't have to say that to me. I don't even care any more, that's the trouble. I've let myself go just like I've let the house go. My husband's tired of me and I don't blame him. Poor Phil. He's beginning to let things slacken too. A man without a wife pulling right along with him out here is like a one-armed man. But I haven't the heart for it. But

I'm sorry! Burdening you with my complaints, when you have got such much bigger ones than me."

My grandfather was about to ask if she had had no children, when she said, "Children haven't come. It's a blessing. This is no place to bring up children." Then she burst out, "Do you know what I yearn most to see? A woman! How I long to see another woman!"

"What about your friend Mrs. Blainey?" asked my grandfather.

"Oh, yes," she said. "Yes, she comes over when she can. Of course, she's older than me. But she's real nice. She has such nice hair, nice soft hands. She keeps herself so neat. I don't know how she manages it out here. Yes, we talk. We talk about her children, and patterns, and recipes. Yes, I don't know what I would do for company if it wasn't for Mrs. Blainey."

My grandfather set down his cup and saucer.

"Don't go!" she cried. She did not even try to cover over her astonishing plea. She was almost weeping. "Don't go."

"Well," said my grandfather uneasily, "well, if you've got it there already in the pot, why maybe I will take just another half a cup."

They chatted for a while. She asked him questions about his family life, his wife, his other children, and more about the Vinsons and the missing Ned. Then again she said, "How I yearn to see a woman! One with a big soft bosom I could lay my head on and cry."

"Ain't your friend Mrs. Blainey the kind you can tell your troubles to?" said my grandfather. "Don't you all ever have yourselves a good cry together?"

"Oh, Mr. Ordway!" she then cried, almost screamed, "there ain't no Mrs. Blainey! I made her up!"

She had gotten so lonesome, she said, by herself in the house all day long with no one to talk to, listening to the wind blow. She had fallen into a make-believe. She invented

a neighbor for herself, a woman from back home, someone
from a real nice family; that was how she had given her
the name Blainey, for she remembered there was a real
high-class old family back in Clarksville by that name. "She
would come over and visit with me in the afternoons and
we would talk, lady-talk, you know—about fashions and
cooking and flower gardening. Oh, it got so I even give her
a made-up daughter at school back in the east and she
would come over and read me her latest letter from her
daughter. But I'm not crazy, Mr. Ordway. I know there is
no Mrs. Blainey. Sometimes we'll be talking, she and I, and
a storm blows up and the window lights go dark and I
catch a glimpse of myself in the glass, talking to myself in
an empty house, and I think, you're losing your mind, there's
nobody here but you. But I'm not losing my mind, I'm just
so lonesome! I look at that chair, the one you're sitting in
now, and I can see plain enough there's nobody there.
There's no Mrs. Blainey. Oh, how I wish there was! It would
make all the difference to me. I sit by the window all through
the afternoon—I ought to be cleaning up this dirty house,
trying to fix a little different supper for poor Phil—but I sit
here looking out, looking at nothing and listening, and I
start seeing things out there: houses, streets, lawns of grass,
wagons and teams and people. It's only make-believe, I
know, but I keep looking and I see it all, people coming to
call, and I hear them laughing and talking. Then it all
vanishes. It's all a mirage, and the sound I hear is nothing
but the wind. . . ."

In the letter he had been writing home these past few
nights my grandfather had said, "I like it out here. The
towns are all new, some would say raw and ugly, but I just
say new and leave it at that. They look like children's alphabet blocks bunched together on the floor." He enjoyed the
sense of being present at the beginning. Like every son, or
every son of a son of the old South, he had had enough
history. The less history a place had, the happier its past.

The cemeteries out here were not yet crowded. Nobody seemed to have any ancestors out here, they were the first. "But," he added, in closing his letter that night, "it is a hard life on women."

It was a hard life on an a man too; or at least it was on him, as he soon began to feel. Like St. Anthony in the desert, my poor grandfather, during those days and nights he spent alone on the desolate West Texas plains, was beset by all seven of the deadly sins, come to tempt him from his vows. Gluttony. How he used to long, as he sat eating sardines and Vienna sausages out of little tins, for some of my grandmother's good home cooking! Sloth. How he yearned to be back home beside the fire in his old rocker, wearing his old run-over felt carpet slippers, waited on by his wife and daughters. Avarice too. He really ought to be home. Here it was now into February. Every day he wasted out here not getting ready for spring planting was costing him money. Despair. He would never find Will Vinson. That was perfectly plain now. He would never see his boy again. There wasn't a hope left in the world that he would. Envy. The sight of other men (the few men to be seen out here) with their little boys holding their hands made him gnaw the dry bone of envy. Lechery, above all. For though his desires were perfectly licit, the temptress who came to him by night intent on weakening his resolution and turning him aside from his quest being his own lawfully wedded wife, this only made her all the harder to resist. Against all of these things he had to struggle, and since he had never been very strong in his faith, it was uphill all the way.

"Watch him, Jake! Watch him, boy. He's slippery. Oh, look out! Look out! Oh! Oh! Oooooh! Well, all right, come on, get up. All right now, go for him. There! There! That's the way, Jake, boy! You've got him down, now stomp on him!"

It was a real good fight. Two heavyweights, and very evenly matched. It would have drawn everybody in Clarksville, and here they had not even brought it out of the back alley. It was being fought behind a disused shed on the edge of town, and only two men were watching. Only one of them was doing any cheering.

"Which one you for?" said he to my grandfather, apparently ready to start another bout if he did not like the answer he got.

"Oh, why, I'm a stranger here," my grandfather replied. "I don't know either of them."

"Hell, that don't make no difference, you can still enjoy yourself. The one on top right now is named Jake, and the other one's name is Chuck. Root for Jake. Give it to him, Jake! 'Attaboy! Hold him down till he hollers hogtie!"

"What's it all about? What are they fighting over?" asked my grandfather.

"Him," said the man, pointing to the other spectator, a smooth-faced youth who stood to the side, looking on the fracas with a placid, disinterested gaze.

"Why, what did he do?"

"Oh, he didn't do nothing. They're fighting over him."

"Well, why?"

"Tell you when it's over. Oooh, Jake! Didn't I tell you to watch that left of his? Keep your guard up, fool! All right now, close in on him! Why ain't you rooting?"

"Why, I can't take sides without even knowing what it's all about," said my grandfather.

"Well, stranger, I'll tell you. It's what they call a triangle. He was Jake's friend, his boy friend, and Chuck tried to steal him."

"You don't mean . . . ?"

"Yes, I do mean."

"Well!" said my grandfather. "Well! Hmm. I'd heard of that, but frankly I never believed it."

"Oh, it happens all right, and not uncommon out here on

the range. No women, you see. And then some of the boys seem to acquire a taste for it and come to prefer it to the real thing. And if you was to see some of the women that's available you wouldn't hardly wonder. Incidentally, I'm married. Get him, Jake! 'At's the way, Jake, boy!"

My grandfather shook his head. Strange places bred strange ways. But he had learned in his travels to be circumspect in criticizing the customs of people he fell amongst, so he confined himself to the observation that this was not what he had always thought of when he thought of cowboys. "I suppose," he said, "that one of them sort of fellows must come in for a good deal of bullyragging from the other men?"

"Ya-as," his new acquaintance drawled, "if you'd like your jaw broke, why, just sashay over there and wag your wrist at either one of them."

My grandfather regarded the scene. The two were charging one another and colliding with a leathery thud, like two range bulls locking horns over a heifer.

"I wouldn't jump to the conclusion if I was you," said his friend, "that either of them boys is any pantywaist."

"I see what you mean," said my grandfather.

After the fight was over and Chuck and the contested youth had ridden off together into the sunset, my grandfather was told over a drink in the saloon by his new acquaintance, "Mister, you've come to the wrong place to look for a man on the lam. Everybody more or less is on the lam out here.

"Let me give you an illustration of what you're up against. See that fellow down there at the far end of the counter? About as close a friend as I've got. Name's Bill. Bill what? Couldn't tell you. Where's he from? Well, I've been riding with Bill for going on ten years now, but I don't know nothing about him. Never asked. You ask him about me he'll tell you the same. Now it just happens that I was born about ten miles north of here. I never come out because I had to.

I haven't got anything in particular to hide, and I wouldn't mind telling Bill my surname. It may be the same with him for all I know. But he's never going to tell me his name and I sure as hell ain't going to ask him. Out here a man's name is his business. So there's a very good chance your man is in these parts, but finding him is not going to be easy. We got lots of Will Vinsons of one sort or another out here, and they all stick together."

So my grandfather began to wise up. He grew a disguise, a beard as kinky as karakul and a big soup-strainer mustache. "Guess who this is hiding behind the shrubbery?" is written across the back of a photograph which he sent home from out there at this time. A good question. It was not Sam Ordway, it was Samuel Hathaway hiding back there. Or Ridgeway. Or Holloway. Or Sidney Latimer. Or Thomas Mabry.

Or Sam Vinson. . . .

Come Saturday he tried always to find himself in a town, for that was the day the farmers and ranchers and cowhands flocked in from the surrounding countryside. He would check into the hotel, if the place had a hotel, on Friday, giving as his name one of the above, and he would pass the afternoon and evening seeking out drummers, surveyors, railroad men, peddlers, buying postage stamps he did not need and drinking alkaline coffee so as to strike up conversations with waiters and postmasters, all whose work brought them into contact with people. He was out in the town early the next morning, hanging around the market square as the country folks came in, or the depot, if the town had one, or the stock auction ring or the saloon or the domino parlor or on the curb of the courthouse, wherever men collected, posing as a cattle buyer or as a man scouting out the land for a place to settle in. When he overheard men speaking of some community that he had missed, he would break in boldly, saying, "Excuse me, gentlemen. I couldn't help overhearing you all mention Scattercreek. You all from out that way, I take it." They would look him coldly up and down and would answer not a word. He was already on thin ice. He talked fast. "I'm trying," he would say, dropping his voice to just above a whisper, "to locate my brother."

"What's your brother's name, mister?" one would ask.

He would look pained, would stammer, would glance furtively about, lower his eyes, and confess that he did not know. "He's about my size, maybe an inch or two taller," he would say hurriedly, "and just two years younger than me. Wife. Four younguns, running from about so up to so. Medium-complected man, hair the color of—"

But how was that? Just a minute. Hold on. How was that? Not know your own brother's name?

He would study their faces. They looked like understanding men. . . . Well, his brother had gotten mixed up in a little trouble back east. Never mind what. He was innocent, and besides, the other two was every bit as guilty as Will and, the skunks, they had put the whole thing off on him. *His* name was Vinson, but what name his brother was going under now, he didn't know. . . .

Or, he would say that his brother had had a quarrel with their old father and left home, and now the poor old man lay at death's door with but one wish to keep him alive, and that was to see his younger son once more and make it up with him before he died. He had traveled far and wide, searching high and low, and now he was beginning to think that his brother had been so mad he had thrown off his father's name and taken some other. . . .

Or, that their old daddy had died, leaving money to be divided between his brother and him, and a reward to anyone who could locate his wayward son. Or, suddenly: "What? What town did you say? Not Fat Chance, Texas! Let me see, where did I put that letter? Fat Chance. . . . Why I do believe this is the very town my cousin Everett's boy Will come out to. Fellow about my age. Wife and four

younguns. Big collie dog. Where *is* that letter? Got it right
here. Got it somewhere. Well, never mind. I'm sure of it:
Fat Chance. No? Don't know him? Just come out. Fellow
about my build. . . ."

Or sometimes he would introduce himself as Dr. Samuel
Hemingway of the State Board of Health, and say, "Now
don't go spreading this around, 'cause we don't want to start
a panic. But if you do see this fellow, take him into custody
immediately and send for me. Just to be on the safe side,
I wouldn't touch him if I was you. However, don't be
alarmed. You probably won't catch it unless you actually
drink from the same cup."

"For God's sake, Doc! What is it? What's he got?"

"Leprosy, poor devil. But keep this to yourself, hear?
Some folks, they just have to hear that word and they go
into conniptions."

And as he was strolling away he would hear, "Holy smoke!
You know what I just heard? Be on the lookout for a feller
with four collie dogs and a wife and kids! Only don't touch
him if you value your life. Hold him off with a gun and run
for that man there. He . . ."

But in order to get his mail c/o General Delivery my
grandfather had to show identification, to use his own name.
There were letters from home awaiting him in Cisco. Said
the clerk brightly as he passed them through the bars, "Any
relation to *Will* Ordway, from somewheres back in your
parts?"

"My brother," said my grandfather. "And if you can tell
me where to find him I'll be much obliged to you. I'm
ashamed to confess it, but I've lost touch with him. To tell
the truth, Will and me had a falling out, as brothers sometimes will, you know. The dispute was all my fault, I realize
that now. I'm out here now looking for him, to make things
up. Blood is thicker than water."

It was not presence of mind which prevented him from

crying out or cursing aloud; it was dismay, chagrin. He had thought he was so clever, taking Vinson's name. Will had outsmarted him at his own game. Ordway! It was the cleverest, the most impenetrable alias he could have adopted, the last that anybody would ever have thought of. But my grandfather's consternation was soon elbowed aside to be replaced by another emotion. Just what it was would be hard to say, for it went beyond mere anger, went beyond umbrage. Not content with stealing his son, the man had taken his very name!

My grandfather returned to the scene to hear the postal clerk saying, ". . . and nobody knows where they went to. I've expected to hear from them, 'cause being neighbors, even though it was only for a short while, we got quite friendly, especially Mrs. Ordway and my mizzus. But they haven't wrote. What a shame! If only you'd been three months sooner."

"Three months," echoed my grandfather dully.

"Yes, well anyhow you'll be glad to know that your brother was looking very well."

"Was he? Yes, I'm very glad to hear that. Thank you. And the children, my nephews and my little niece?"

"All fine. All in the pink of health, last I seen of them."

"Little Ned, how was he?"

"Ned? Let's see now, which one was he?"

"Ned's the one that takes more after me. I guess that's why I'm partial to him."

The clerk studied my grandfather's features. However, it did not seem to help him distinguish Ned. "Well anyhow," he said, "they were all fine. Well, probably you'll catch up with him before I hear from him," he concluded. "Tell him when you do that we'd enjoy getting a postcard, will you?"

"Yes, I'll do that," said my grandfather.

Around midnight that night there popped into my grandfather's mind a new and altogether different explanation of Will Vinson's having adopted his name. He had lain there until that hour rigid with indignation, when suddenly he realized that Will had not done it as a ruse. Indeed, Will had not *chosen* to do it at all. My grandfather visualized a little scene. He saw the Vinsons on their flight, perhaps somewhere near the very outset, forced to stop for something, food, water, and saw Ned momentarily slip the leash and saw a stranger, just as Vinson was on the point of retrieving him, chuck Ned underneath the chin and say, "What's your name, sonnyboy?"

"Nedordway," piped Ned.

And then and there (pretty quick thinking for a stupid man) Will Vinson had become Will Ordway.

And my grandfather had the answer to the question whether his boy had known his family name before being taken from home.

He had known it, all right, and had bestowed it upon his foster father. For on reflection it must have seemed to Will (1) that he needed an alias; (2) that this one could hardly be improved upon; (3) that such a declaration from Ned was bound to recur and that he could then either (1) try to persuade Ned that his name was not Ordway, but Vinson, or (2) that he could bring up his own as yet unconscious younger two under whatever name he chose, and that he could more easily persuade his own, less intelligent, Felix, if Felix was even aware of a last name, to a change, than he could persuade Ned.

My grandfather sat up in bed. His anger had vanished. Will Vinson would be forced to go through life (assuming that he did not succeed in tracking him down) and to bring up his children with *his* name! Oh, no, he was not angry at him for taking it any longer. He wished him joy of it. What triumph! What unimaginable retribution!

He pictured another little scene. He saw Vinson introducing himself to a man—preferably one a little hard of hearing. Heard the man say:

"Pardon me, but I'll have to ask you to speak up. I'm a

little deaf. I didn't catch your name. Would you mind repeating it?"

"Ordway."

"How's that again?"

"Ordway. ORDWAY. ORDWAY!"

"Mind spelling it, please?"

"O–R–D–W–A–Y. ORDWAY."

"O–R–D–W–A–Y. ORDWAY? Oh, yes! Ordway. Of course.
How do you do, Mr. Ordway. And this is Mrs. Ordway?"

"Yes. My wife."

"Come again?"

"I SAY, YES. THIS IS MY WIFE. MRS. ORDWAY."

"Very pleased to make your acquaintance, Mrs. Ordway.
And what is your name, little man?"

"Felix Ordway."

"You'll have to speak louder, sonny."

"FELIX ORDWAY."

"Oh, yes! Well, how do you do, Master Ordway? And what
have we here? Two more little Ordways, I believe."

My grandfather knew how to relish this. Having traveled
himself under Vinson's name (with this difference: that he
had chosen it, not had it forced upon him, and knowing that
he could drop it and reassume his own whenever he pleased,
that his was a name that did not have to be kept hidden),
he knew what it was to have to answer to your enemy's
name. Even temporarily, even when practiced out of guile,
it was galling. Between the two cases there was this further
difference, that he was beholden for nothing to the man
whose name he had appropriated. On the contrary, he could
despise the name Vinson as belonging to the man who had
wronged him. What must it be like to have to answer to the
name of the man whom you had wronged? Moreover, my
grandfather knew how hard it was to remember, how even
after weeks of it he still had to remind himself constantly to
remember to answer to that assumed name. And he had
had nothing to lose if his deception had been disclosed,

suspicions aroused. Imagine having to remember to answer to the name of all names that you wished to forget! And imagine having your children answer to it.

My grandfather could almost see Will standing at the foot of his bed, those eyes of his that would always widen with the effort to comprehend any new thing, appealing to him to explain what had happened to him. What had he gotten himself into? Forced to go through life as his creature. His conscience in his enemy's hands. The child he loved never, no matter how long he might have him, never really his, but the other man's, with the other man's features, the other man's blood in his veins, and now his very name forfeited, that of his wife, his own children. No, he had not assumed the name Ordway; it had assumed him. It had consumed him.

Sometime during the night my grandfather was shaken out of a troubled sleep. He awoke to find the hotel night clerk bending over him, shaking his shoulders.

"You were having nightmares," he said. "Talking in your sleep. Yelling. You've woke up everybody in the place."

"What was I saying?"

"You was saying over and over again, 'You damn fool, you brought it on yourself. I never asked you to take him.'"

So now he had to say to people—oh, how queer it sounded!—"I'm looking for a man named Ordway." And they began to say, "Yes, I met up with a man of that name. Your brother, was he?" And one even said, "Yes, I can see the resemblance."

In the town of Tuscola, just south of Abilene, Will Ordway had worked for a man named Bryant.

"He come here looking for a job," said Mr. Bryant. "I needed a hand, but I told them the only house I had for them wasn't much of a place. They looked poor enough them-selves, but decent, and I was ashamed to show them that house. We ain't choosy, the man said. If it keeps out the weather. So I took them to look at it. I could see the wife turn kind of sick when she seen it, and he went kind of green when he looked at her. But she said, well, go bring the wagon. From what you tell me I guess she must have known they wouldn't be stopping here long, but that never kept her from doing what she could to fix the place up pretty. And he was a worker, mister, that brother of yours!"

My grandfather tried to look proud but not too proud.

"The way he worked and the time she put in on the house and yard I took for granted they meant to stay on. So when he come to me one day after just two months and said he was moving on, I couldn't understand it. Was something bothering him? I asked. No, he had no complaints. Was his wife unhappy? No, but he was moving on. I made him the offer of a raise in pay—highest wages I had ever offered a man. He turned it down. I asked, wasn't that enough? It was more than he sometimes cleared farming for hisself, he told me. Not many men would have admitted that, I thought."

This tale of the privations which the Vinsons had endured, of Will's industriousness and his honesty and the loyalty he had inspired in only a short time in his employer, all made my grandfather extremely uneasy. Meanwhile he had to pretend to be gratified by it.

"Nothing would hold him. I'd seen it before, and I knew what was itching him. They get it, some men, like others get the drink or the gambling fever. It's a disease. Where you going? I said. West, he said. This is west, I said. Not west enough, he said. What ain't it west of, I said, California? I guess he was thinking it wasn't west enough of the home he had left behind him. He drawed the pay he had coming and I made him take a loan of twenty dollars to help him on his way, seeing as he was bent on going. He sent five of it back to me. I mean, it must have come from him. I can't think of nobody else I would get an envelope with a five-dollar bill in it from."

"Postmarked from where?"

"Well, I remember," said Mr. Bryant, "because it was such an odd name. It come from a place called Utopia, Texas."

Seeing as it was his own brother, and him so very hard up, my grandfather felt obligated to pay Mr. Bryant the fifteen dollars still owing on Will's debt.

After poring over his map for a solid hour that evening my grandfather concluded that Utopia, Texas, must be too small a place to be shown. He studied the Sweetwater area, the Abilene area, the Big Spring area, the Lubbock area, the San Angelo area, and spaces intervening; he unfolded his map all the way out to El Paso: no Utopia.

He began to trace back his own path. The X's marking his wanderings had turned the map into something resembling a stitched sampler. How many towns he had been in, he who until now had never been anywhere! Lake Creek, Howland, Broadway, Charleston, Cunningham, Ladonia, Klondike, Birthright, Peerless, Cumby, Brashear, Campbell, Weaver, Sulphur Bluff, Hagansport, Bonanza, Cash, Cut Hand: all these (and many more) during his time with the circus. Weatherford, Millsap, Mineral Wells, Breckenridge, Lusk, Throckmorton, Olney, Graham—the list ran on. Honey Grove, Paris, Detroit, Bagwell . . . his eye idled back towards home. It seemed he had been gone forever. He began to count the months. Doing that made him realize afresh how near it was to the time of Hester's confinement. And that, despite all he could do, turned his mind to thoughts of Agatha's death in childbirth. He relived that terrible day.

It had been a long one, beginning early, at breakfast, when, getting up from the table, Agatha gave a startled cry as her water broke, flooding down her legs in a scalding gush. But this was known sometimes to happen (although it had not her two previous times) and, once the surprise was over, was nothing to be alarmed about. Shortly afterwards she felt her first pain. He harnessed the team and drove into Clarksville for the doctor, stopping by the Vinsons' to leave Bea, and to ask Mrs. Vinson to meet Winnie when school let out and bring her over also to spend the night at their house.

The doctor, in his wire-wheeled buggy, overtook and passed him on the road coming back. When he arrived home Agatha had taken to bed. The doctor allowed him only a moment with her, then, jovial and bawdy, shooed him out. On the table outside the bedroom door stood three stiff white bands, the doctor's shirt collar and cuffs.

For the next couple of hours, during which time nothing happened, he busied himself puttering about the barn and the barn lot. Before putting herself to bed Agatha had set out a lunch of leftovers and at two o'clock he and the doctor sat down and shared it. There was a cake which she had begun before breakfast and which before going to bed she had filled and iced. The last cake she ever baked, he had thrown it out days later, uncut, the icing gone hard and crystallized and cracked. Just as he was about to slice it came a moan from the bedroom. He knew that sound, that unanswerable plea, that undeniable reproach; he had heard it twice before; still it shook him, shamed him. He was to hear it again, and yet again, and again; after this time, up to the last, he cringed from it as from a blow in his organs of manhood.

The doctor, getting up with a smile, said, "That sounds like she means business."

But hours passed and still the baby did not come. Twice he went and knocked timidly at the bedroom door and was let in and went and stood for a moment at the side of the bed, feeling useless to help, and each time she gave him a rueful little smile and shook her head at herself, as if to say she was ashamed of taking so long, of making such a fuss over nothing. From time to time as he came up to the house in the course of doing his evening chores he heard her cry out. He slopped the hogs and gave the chickens water, scattered

oyster shell for them, though it was plain that she herself
had done so only yesterday, fed the dog, milked the cows,
fed the cats, prolonging each task in an effort to distract his
mind and to deceive himself as to the hour. Coming up
from the barn just as twilight was beginning to settle, he
was frozen by a sudden scream from the house. As he stood
trembling, it rose to a shriek, seemed to pass beyond the
realm of hearing. Until now he had been able to tell himself that it had been like this, or very nearly like this, those
other two, successful times. But nothing like this had he
heard before. This was not what the doctor described as a
good healthy, angry, fighting cry. This, and the broken
whimpering which succeeded it as he ran towards the
house, were sounds hardly human, wrung from a body
tortured past endurance.

As he went through the back door another groan commenced, animal-like, unearthly, something to make the
scalp prickle, rising again, louder than before, to that intolerable shriek. He bounded through the kitchen and into
the hall and down the hall to the bedroom door. As he
reached for the knob that terrible shriek abruptly broke off.
He faltered, his breath coming in sobs, and as he stood
there, irresolute, he heard the wail of an infant. Weak and
trembling with relief, he grasped the knob, opened the door,
and went in. The doctor, his broad stripe-shirted back bent
over something live and kicking at the foot of the bed, did
not look up. The baby commenced to squawl. His wife
lay unconscious. A last tear ran from the corner of her
closed eye and into her ear, over which her hair had been
drawn back. She lived for another hour, regaining consciousness only at the very end, and then only momentarily,
and whether in that moment she had recognized, or even
seen him, was impossible to tell. Her lids fluttered open and
an expression of pain began to gather about her mouth.
Then suddenly the color drained from her flushed and
swollen face, leaving it pallid and glistening with a mist of

fine cold perspiration. Her lids fell open wide and in the depths of her eyes the light went out as though behind them the shades had slowly been drawn.

For some while my grandfather sat staring at the map spread before him, his own eyes glazed and turned inward, fixed upon that image of his dead wife. Then, just as the color had paled from her face while he watched, so now her face paled from his mind. There was no recalling it; he soon ceased to try. He sensed that his life was about to take a new turn, to close a phase and enter another one. "I must put you out of mind," he had said to Agatha at her graveside; now belatedly that renunciation was accomplished, and Agatha passed over into that region of his memory where all his dead lay lastingly at rest. "Hester is my wife now," he had further said to Agatha, and now Hester took her place. Rather, Hester at last took her own place. Her appearance now in his thoughts caused him a moment's confusion, so altered did he find her. He set his mind to visualize her more clearly, to recall her as she really was. But this was a new Hester, different from the former one, nor would she reassume her old shape. Outwardly she was unchanged, yet in some important but indefinable way she had been transfigured. My grandfather did not know this yet, but it was not Hester who had changed; it was himself. A new love for his wife entering into his heart had made him a different man; it would require a period of adjustment to this new self which had replaced his old familiar one.

Meanwhile his first, his immediate impulse was to get up and harness the team and start for home, for her, that very night, that very moment. With a longing so intense it passed into conviction, he saw himself arriving unannounced and saw Hester opening the door, surprised, overjoyed, standing back until the girls freed him, then falling into his arms. No words were spoken. Between them passed a new understanding which rendered words unnecessary. And then they stood back from one another and he surveyed

her figure and saw its swollen condition and in upon his
reverie broke a shiver of apprehension and dread. Calculat-
ing rapidly the date she was due to deliver, he vowed to be
with her when that time came, to let nothing, nothing, de-
tain him.

This resolution sent him back to the map still spread
before him to search again for that town—what was it
called? But all he saw now was a tangle of lines in red, blue,
and black, creases and penciled crosses and blank unlined
gaps. He was tired. He had better give it up for the night, he
decided, and began folding away his map, and then his
eye dropped down—down practically out of the United
States and into Mexico—and there it was: Utopia. It was
not to the west of him at all, but away down in deep South
Texas, not less than two hundred miles away. His heart
sank. Two hundred miles! That would put him six hundred miles from Clarksville.

He rebelled. He would not, he could not go. There were
other claims upon him. He must get home. He was needed
at home. He felt certain that could she have been appealed to,
Agatha would have agreed that his place now was at home
with his wife. And with Agatha's two other children, dependent upon him for support. It might seem callous to turn his
back upon a place where Will was known definitely to have
gone. But what reason was there to suppose that the chase
ended there, that Will had stopped in Utopia any longer
than it took to mail Mr. Bryant his five dollars? The trail,
so far as he was concerned, came to an end right here.

He emptied his pockets for bed: his watch and chain,
change, pocketknife, his billfold, and what proved to be a
lone loose jujube, so fuzzy with pocket lint that it resembled
a cottonseed. And the photograph of Ned.

He had last shown the photograph to a man just a few
days before, and asked his old question, whether he had
seen a little boy who looked like that.

"Like what?" the man had said.

It was then for the first time that he had seen how creased and cracked, how dog-eared and tattered the picture had gotten in his travels.

He had not seen this at once, though. "Like that," he had insisted, and looked at the photograph himself. Only then had he learned that when he looked at the picture now he no longer saw it. He saw instead an image in his mind, an image which, oddly, seemed to have grown sharper as the picture faded and peeled.

How many hands had handled it now!

He remembered when he was just starting out, one of the first men he had shown it to, the joker in Paris, who, asked had he ever seen a little boy who looked like that, had replied that he had never seen any little boy who didn't look like that. Well, he had seen many little boys now who looked different, many who, though seen for only a moment, were no doubt better-looking than his, quicker-looking too. How was it that the Vinsons, people with children of their own, children whom obviously they loved, had been so captivated by that quite ordinary little face, had endured what they had for his sake? He still could not understand that. A little thing, short for his age, scrawny. All legs, like a newborn calf, and feet that were forever in his own way. Hair of no particular color, eyes, like his father's, set too close together. A nose that was not cute, not anything, just a nose. Not by any means always a good boy, but often willful and stubborn as a mule, with a look in his eyes as if the whole world was against him, a tremor in his chin. . . .

And there his child all but stood before him, and my grandfather knew at last why the Vinsons had been unable to give him up.

Reminiscing on his quest in after years, my grandfather recollected this final southern expedition with a vividness surpassing all the rest.

Torn between two calls, two longings, he set off down

there with this plan in mind: to go just as fast as his foot-
sore and sorry old team could carry him, to search up to the
last possible moment, then, with Ned or without him, to
sell his wagon and team, wire Hester for the balance if
necessary, and buy passage home on the train, arriving in
time for the birth of her child. So, pointing himself about,
he drove south into another landscape, another season, another world, finally into another age.

For the first hundred miles, or in other words for the first
five days, he traversed more of the same country with which
he had grown familiar: flat, treeless, boundless plains swept
by a steady cold north wind often snow- and sleet-laden,
differing here from the land behind him in being divided
between cattle range and stretches green with winter wheat.
Swedish Texas, this was; a country of tall, thatch-topped,
pale-eyed people with fair freckled complexions like butter-
milk, hearty, laughter-loving, heavy eaters themselves and
prodigiously hospitable. Then he came to the Concho River.
He had crossed the Colorado, and would later cross the San
Saba, the Llano, the Frio, the Nueces; but the Concho in
particular my grandfather remembered because there he had
been astonished by an unexpected, an awesome sight. The
river there was banked by steep rock cliffs and along the face
of one of these cliffs, near the top, in the shelter of an overhanging cornice ledge, ran a frieze of hundreds of savage
figures painted in red, black, orange, and white, so uniform
as to seem to have been stenciled on the rock, or as if in
addition to serving as art they served also as the alphabet of
a primitive tongue. They depicted stick-figure men chasing
animals, throwing spears, running, and dancing a dance in
which their limbs were flung out in X's. Though their colors
had retained their strength, their great antiquity was felt
nonetheless, felt powerfully in the wild stillness of those
surroundings. Closer inspection revealed others so very ancient that they had faded almost away. Revealed too a story:
the coming of a more sophisticated race, bringing with

them their creed, and with it the passing of the people whose artists had scaled these walls to paint these pictures as their ancestors had always done. By the relative vividness of the pigments one could trace a great span of time between the earliest and the last, but in all that while no change had been made in their content or their manner. For centuries they had simply added more of the same stick-figure men chasing similar buffaloes. Then, in a manner crudely imitative of white man's art, appeared a mission church, a priest in a cassock, and a Christian devil with pointed tail and a pitchfork. After that, bare rock.

There at the Concho River the plains ended below brown hills in ranges piled one atop the last, and from that crossing overwatched by those painted figures the road wound up among the rocks. This section which my grandfather now entered, called on the maps the Edwards Plateau, was, and still is, a rugged, wild, and beautiful place, dry and barren, covered with scrub oak and low olive-dun-colored cedars, broken by rock-walled canyons in the beds of which rush clear, cold streams strewn with boulders. There may be seen armadillos, deer, and the clownish chaparral bird or roadrunner, and though seldom seen, there may be heard by the camper at night the scream of panthers, the howling of wolves, and when he awakes early in the morning, the gobbling of wild turkeys. Among those silent hills as he rode along one day my grandfather heard a man singing, in Spanish, a sad and lonesome lament, forlorn as the cry of a muezzin, accompanied by the tinkling of bells. It was a goatherd, a Mexican with a face like leather, wrapped in a cape, shod in sandals, and his flock of silky long-haired Angoras. It was a sound and a sight which seemed to awaken in him some deep-buried memory, something retained from earliest childhood, perhaps the memory of Sunday-school days and lithographs of the Bible lands, or possibly not a personal memory at all, but some inherited sense of what the world was like in the childhood of the human race.

Undiscovered country: that was how my grandfather described that region, or described his feeling on passing through it. Some days he had driven from sunup to sundown and seen not one human being. From the crest of one of those bare hills he had looked in all directions and seen not a single habitation. Then he would go down into one of those canyons, along a road of sorts, just wide enough for the wagon, but which looked like a game trail that had been there forever, down alongside one of those bounding, clear, cold streams between narrow, steep rock cliffs, and he had the feeling that from up there his every move was being watched by slit-eyed sentinels in war paint and feather bonnets, but otherwise he was the first person ever to venture there. At first, seeing it with the eyes of a farmer, my grandfather had been put off by the desolation of that country. He had found it unproductive, therefore unlovely. Even to him the high plains had seemed drearily monotonous, but he was a native and lifelong resident of the prairies, and his first hills gave him claustrophobia. But by the time he quit the place he had come to love it, and now as he recalled it he sighed to think that he would never see it again.

The perhaps somewhat over-enthusiastically named town of Utopia lay down in the southernmost range of those hills. It was quickly canvassed, and as my grandfather had suspected, Will apparently had stopped there just long enough to lick a postage stamp. He must have had his own stamp, for any stranger buying one from the postmistress anytime during the past ten years would have been remembered.

From Utopia, lacking directions, there were two ways to go, west or south. With no clue to point him in one direction or the other, my grandfather elected to go south. That was the way which, had he been Will, he would have gone from there. To the west rose more of those rocky brush-covered hills over which he had just come; to the south the land opened up. One way the living looked hard, the other way it looked easy.

South of Utopia, just when it seemed that those hills were going to go on forever, they came abruptly to a stop at the edge of a precipice below which for as far as the eye could see stretched a rolling, fertile plain. The Balcones Escarpment, that natural wall is called; it rises above the valley of the Rio Grande like a sea cliff. Below that cliff the tide of Spanish America, in its long withdrawal southward before the advance of the gringos, came finally to a stop. Down onto that plain and into that other world my grandfather next went, and conscious though he was that every mile would have to be driven back over, enchantment led him on as far south as Uvalde, Crystal City, Carrizo Springs, to the river itself and the border with Mexico. Enchantment, not evidence. Few enough were the people even to ask, and most of those spoke only Spanish; but if he received no encouragement to believe that Will had in fact come this way, his senses told him that this was the place to which all men yearned to come. The spell he felt was that which everyone feels in places blessed by yearlong sun, but which a dirt farmer, whose one crop a year was watered with his sweat and then was pinched in the bud by a belated winter blast, or dried up by drought, or drowned, or flattened by hail, would feel as few other men could. Here one did not wait helplessly for rain which came too late, or else washed away one's labor in a flood; here one brought water from that mighty river where and when it was needed. Here the weather was not a man's enemy but his friend, and in that rich alluvial soil beneath that gilded sky grew not one but two and even three crops per year. The winters here were green. This was citrus land, banana-palm land, where fruits grew for the plucking which he knew only as treats at Christmastime.

Down there in that old hot country where the tempo of life made even that of Mabry seem hurried and changeful, among that settled and traditional people, my grandfather felt, even in the anxiety of his search, made all the more

urgent by the earliness of the spring, a mood of peacefulness
beginning to steal over him. Even while it defeated him, this
land reconciled him to his defeat. He sensed there a different way of feeling about life, about time, about fate.
Seeing those dazzling little low white adobe towns crowned
by their brown weathered mission church, from the twin
towers of which at evening bells as soft as the cooing of
doves throbbed upon the purple air, those slow-moving, big-
eyed, copper-colored women in their fringed mantillas carrying their water jugs balanced gracefully on their heads, the
priests in their soutanes, the men in the fields dressed in
their white pajamas working at their leisurely pace, beneath that clear sky, he felt not only better reconciled to
the loss which life had recently brought him, but felt himself eased of some lifelong, some inherited deep, dull ache.
This land, because it lay outside your own bloody national
past, and you were ignorant of whatever bloody past it had,
seemed, despite its great age, strangely new, fresh in its
very antiquity. The hatred, the dissension, the fratricide of
America had not reached this corner of America. Blood had
been shed here, no doubt, since blood has been shed everywhere; and since it never stops, no doubt it still cried out;
but it cried out in tongues which there was no one left to
understand. Exposed daily to this hot sun, that old unhealed
historical wound seemed at last to dry up and to cease to
ache.

The days were getting longer. Warmer too; and sometimes as he was walking up a flower path (here already
abloom with color) wading through the yapping dogs to
knock at yet another door, he would find himself in shirt-
sleeves and have to go back to the wagon for his jacket to
make himself presentable. The skies shone with a hard
polished gleam. It's getting on, he said to himself; then said
instantly after, but it's not too late. There was still time.
Still hope. Perhaps in the next settlement, at the next house,
perhaps from the next man he met on the road . . .

One day he drove all afternoon to reach the only habitation visible in the landscape, a hut, a *jacal* of willows daubed with mud, in the dirt yard of which fat brown babies, scrawny chickens, and hairless black dogs frolicked in equal profusion, where he was greeted by a walnut-colored man with a gap-toothed smile and a barefooted woman who shook constantly with laughter, between the two of whom and him not one word of communication was possible. When he showed the man the photograph of Ned, the man slapped him on the back and pointed to his yardful, and when he made motion to go on his way he was dragged down off the seat and made to come in and have something to drink which tasted like turpentine, every sip of which one followed by sucking hastily on a lemon, then made to stay for supper off one of those chickens and then to sleep in the only bed in the house while the family stretched out along with the pups in the yard. This experience was repeated, and while he enjoyed the hospitality, he was forced to ask himself how he could hope to get anywhere in a place where no one spoke his language. Here Will Vinson had not only fallen out of sight, he had fallen out of English.

He was following a lead picked up in the hamlet of Catarina. Hardly a lead: a half hint, a maybe. But he was following it, as he had so many, because he had no other. One morning first thing on awaking he saw a robin perched upon the tailboard of the wagon, head cocked, round button eye shining, a wisp of grass in his bill, green grass, eyeing the straw upon which he slept. True (as he was constantly reminding himself), things here were ahead of things back home; but there too the robins would be coming back and nesting before much longer.

Such observations only made him drive himself, and the weary old team, the harder. As the days lengthened and his time ran out, and as the trail disappeared into the blank uncolored areas of his map like trickles of water in this dry soil, he told himself that here was just the sort of un-

likely place where success was most probable, and that the
eleventh hour was the time when everything always happened. A nod encouraged him now, an expression of the
face, even a hesitant "no." He had reached that state of
hopelessness when hopes shimmer ahead like a mirage.

There came a blazing dry day when by two in the afternoon, having been on the road since dawn, he had not seen
a single soul, no sign of life, only signs of death in the
buzzards which patrolled the wide, hot, empty sky. Desperate by noon, he had not stopped to eat, and now the team
was dark with sweat and he himself looked like a tired
baker, with brows and nostrils caked with floury white dust,
eyes heat-glazed, face flushed as if reddened at an open
oven door. At last, topping a rise, he saw below him one of
those sudden cool green valleys scored with brown irriga-
tion ditches, and in it saw a man plowing. He stopped to
watch. The man was just opening the field, the plowshare
set to run deep. He meant to wait for the man to reach the
end of the row and come back, then speak to him. But the
rows were long out here and the man simply plowed over
a rise and out of sight while my grandfather sat watching
the firm earth curl back along the furrow in an unbroken
strip like an apple peel and smelling the fresh damp smell.
That brought him to himself, and he turned around and
headed back north, still searching up to the last, as he made
his way to the nearest railway town.

Although unaware of the fact, he was actually on a different search now. He had ceased looking for Ned some days
back, when he began trying to imagine him at the age of
six, as a boy of twelve, as a young man; attempting, without
much success, to fit him into the background of this country.
When he had wondered whether that Ned would retain any
memories, however vague, of him, of home, the red
hills and the terraced green valleys and the tall blue sky
answered: no. He was looking now for a place to stop looking. Some spot so trackless, so untamed that he could

say (not to Agatha; she had long ago released him from his vow) to himself, "Beyond this point there is no going further. This, for me, is the end of the world."

Somewhere west of the Nueces River, east of Del Rio, north of Uvalde, south of Sonora, where the Balcones Escarpment rises sheer as a rampart above the hot plains of the Rio Grande Valley, he found it, recognized it: the spot where he could say, "If I had to lose him, if I just had to lose him, I'm glad at least to think that Will made it to here." It was a land of strong contrasts, of bright sunlight and deep cool shadows, of dry rocky hills and lush verdant valleys. A land so old it had come round new again, lost its records, forgotten its age, and started over. Whose battles had been fought in forgotten tongues by vanished races over dead issues, where the bitterness of old divisions lay buried in unmarked graves. It was good country to grow up a boy in. My grandfather's last regret was that Will would never know how hard he had tried to find him. He hated for him to go on forever thinking that he had cared so little for his son. But there was nothing could be done about that, and so with one last lingering look at the country he was leaving him to, he bade Ned goodbye and turned the team around and started on his long journey home.

PART FOUR

Family Reunion

MY UNCLE Ned Ordway was a little boy in a picture in a flowered pewter frame which stood next to the ivory-faced marble clock with the spidery numerals on the mantelpiece in my grandfather's room, a boy much younger than I already was, when I first became aware of him, and inherited his story. Once having heard it, I was not long in learning to dislike that picture, nor much longer then in persuading myself that it was not a good likeness. For just as the photographs of me accorded not at all with my own picture of myself, which is to say with my notions of the great deeds I was to do and the fine man I was to become, so that sad-looking, pinch-faced, whey-colored little boy with the tow hair parted in the middle and so thoroughly wetted down that he appeared to be bald, was not my Little Ned. Such a wretched boy was not worth stealing and running off with into the Wild West. Or maybe he had looked like that before he was stolen, but certainly not for long afterwards. For Ned had been taken to a land where surely even mothers grew sensible and no longer wetted down one's hair, a land where it never rained and there were two Saturdays a week instead of Sunday, and there he must have blossomed like a desert flower, overnight acquired a big, lean, loose-jointed, muscular frame and a mustache as black and thick as a shoe brush, a rangy gait like a mountain lion on the prowl, skin the color of a new saddle, sharp steady eyes the color of a western sky which seemed to notice nothing while taking in everything, and a ready broad smile instead of the frightened pucker on that little boy's face as he sat for the itinerant photographer that day long ago.

He was my constant companion. Despite the photograph he was the elder of us, and on our expeditions was always the leader. This phase passed, and though I went on calling him Little Ned, he was no longer a boy in my mind, he was a grown man, only without all those depressing anti-children, or more particularly anti-boy attitudes which all other grownups seemed to have been born with. At about this time I began to go to the picture shows, and my image of my uncle took definite shape. That is to say, his costume and his character took shape; his face underwent regular weekly change. One week he would be a dead ringer for Johnny Mack Brown. The following week he looked more like Buck Jones. Or Hoot Gibson. Or Ken Maynard. Or Fred Thompson. Or Tim McCoy. Or Bob Steele. It all depended on who had starred in the preceding Saturday's feature film. The image stuck with me pretty well through a week of long division and sentence diagramming, as I was always first in the line at the old Capitol, waiting for the ticket window to open at a quarter to ten, with my lunch in a paper bag, and in the front row of seats I stayed until my mother came and dragged me out at half past six that night, dazed, half blind, and still clutching the bag with my lunch, which I had forgotten to eat.

I felt no disloyalty towards my father (Earl Ordway, third of the ten children of Samuel and Hester) for wishing sometimes that I had had another. The one I would have preferred was his own brother.

Little Ned! How glamorous to me it was, that name! Not
a name, not just something to answer to when roll was
called or sign on checks, like Archie Ragsdale or Luther
Haines, but a title, an appellation, like Wild Bill Hickok or
Indian Jim Bridger or Lone Wolf Gonzales. The "little" would
be, of course, in a country of tall men, a way of signaling
his towering height. A hard man, Little Ned Ordway, but
with a fondness for small boys, especially if related to him.
He spoke little, and then in a quiet commanding drawl, like
Randolph Scott's, never raising his voice, not even when
riled, especially not then, though the quietness then had a
different ring, like the three mild little clicks which the
hammer of a pistol makes on being cocked, or the initial
premonitory rattle of a rattlesnake. He wore saddle-whitened
blue jeans, a clay-colored Stetson sombrero, a fringed buck-
skin jacket, and a pair of hand-tooled Nocona boots. There
clung to him the smell of horse sweat and leather and campfire smoke. When not riding herd or making a drive up to
Dodge City or Abilene, he was in the saddle night and day
rounding up the cattle, lassoing and branding dogies, bronc-
busting. Then there was vigilante duty and gangs of rustlers
to have to catch, necktie parties to have to attend, towns to
be cleaned up and establish law and order in. A wanderer,
or as they said in the pictures, a drifter, constantly saddling
up and moving on to avoid the gratitude of the lovely
virgins whose fathers' ranches he had saved from the de-
signs of a villain in a black hat and a flowered waistcoat
named, invariably, Kincaid. For me my western uncle was
Kit Carson, Buffalo Bill, Pat Garrett, *and* Billy the Kid. He
was, under a thick coat of moral whitewash, Cole Younger,
Sam Bass. Sometimes on rainy days when I could not go out
he was the young cowpuncher on the street in Laredo, all
wrapped in white linen and dying that day.

I have said that I was sure my father would not have
minded had he known (supposing of course that I could
have come and visited him and Mamma often) that I would

really a little sooner have been his nephew, the son of his
brother Ned. That is true, yet there was one thing which
disappointed me in him—that was his impatience with me
sometimes when I asked questions about Little Ned. Of
course my father had never known Ned any more than I
had, and could not give me any new information. But it
was not this that made him impatient; besides it was not
new information that I was after. I knew everything there
was to know, and by then the addition of any new bit to the
lore of Little Ned which I already possessed would probably
have been upsetting to me. I just wanted to hear the same
old things over and over again. How the family had gotten
ready to go into Clarksville early that Saturday morning,
the seventh of May 1898. How Aunt Flo (who must have
been the grimmest-faced baby, with that one paralyzed eye-
lid stuck halfway up, poor thing, like a balky window shade)
had cried all the way over to the Vinson's. How they, the
Vinsons, had behaved no different from any other day, and
all the while they were plotting to steal our Ned and run off
with him. How the family came back in the wagon late that
afternoon and drew up at the Vinsons' gate. How Grandpa
had gone to the door and called "Hello!" and his voice came
echoing back from the empty house. How he had gone west
and searched and searched, and how . . .

I simply did not know what to think, not only of my father but of his whole generation, the first time he indicated
that all this, which after all he was much closer to than I,
was not as endlessly fascinating to him as it was to me. And
all my aunts and uncles were the same.

By my time just about the only aspect of the tale of Little
Ned that was kept alive by his brothers and sisters was the
cautionary one. I, along with all his other nephews and
nieces, was kept on a very short leash, and warned daily
against accepting rides from or speaking to or even smiling
at passing strangers. At the time of the Lindbergh kidnapping, long after the other mothers of Clarksville had re-

turned to their senses and realized that their offspring did not present nearly the same temptation as the Lindbergh child, I was still hardly allowed out of the house. "Remember Little Ned," I was told.

Did Little Ned remember us, Grandpa and Grandma and Aunt Winnie and Aunt Bea—without, that is, knowing who and where we were? Or had old Will Vinson fooled him into believing that he was his own flesh and blood? Did he ever wonder who he really was (as I myself often did) and did he sometimes speculate, as he sat in the saddle out riding the range, on a lost father and mother, and maybe an unknown nephew, back east? Had they, I once wondered in one of the blackest moments of my young life, even changed his name, and was he not, to himself, Little Ned, our Little Ned, but something disgusting like Duane or Ferris or Troy, or some such Vinsonish given name?

And how had Little Ned gotten along with his foster brothers and sister? Had one jealous one (that Felix Vinson, maybe) told him that he was a waif and a maverick and a stray, something found in the rain barrel, found in a pig track, something the cat drug in? Did they all gang up on him and tease him and pinch him and trip him whenever their parents' backs were turned?

Sometimes as I lay in bed waiting for sleep at night, or on a summer day lay in my hideaway, a cave formed by rattan vines in the thicket down behind our house, then it was not Little Ned but I myself who was stolen by the Vinsons and carried off into a perilous wild country far from home. I saw myself waving goodbye to Grandma and Grandpa, who, younger, greatly resembled my own mother and father, and lying very still in Mrs. Vinson's fat imprisoning arms, watched them out of sight in the wagon. I knew what they did not know, that we would never see each other again, and even greater than my own sorrow was my sadness for them. Then I pictured the feverish haste in

the Vinson house, and I confess I rather basked in such
admiration as could lead a family to pull up its roots and fly
to unknown wastes for love of me. Then I saw us all jouncing
along in the wagon, hurriedly thrown together, and I saw
Will Vinson, a stout, red-faced, silent man, bloodshot of eye
and needing a shave, whipping up the horses and cussing
them for their slowness, and I saw the countryside trans-
form. My imagined flight with the Vinsons took me through
a flickering badlands in dim black-and-white and the fleeing
Vinsons in my reverie moved with that frenzied jerkiness
as of an overwound toy which characterized the motions
of Tom Mix, Rex Bell, and Yakima Canutt. Behind us, in
grim but vain pursuit, came Grandpa. I would wonder how
Little Ned had felt on awaking that first morning after, and
sensing his distress at not finding Grandma, I would begin
whimpering for my mother. And when my mother came I
would ask how she would feel, and whether she would have
another boy to take my place, and if she did, whether she
would ever think of me, if someone was to steal me from
her and take me far away; and indulging myself in in-
consolable self-pity, I would sob myself to sleep in her
arms.

For a long time I was shy with my grandfather, because
I loved him so. Too, he was a silent man, always deep in
thought, sad-seeming now that watery-eyed old age had
come upon him, and so when I went to spend my first summer on the farm he was still a kind of beloved stranger to
me. Nor did it seem at first that our acquaintance was likely
to improve much that summer, even being in the same house
together. With the constant craving of old folks for silence
I had been thoroughly impressed before leaving home—
more impressed than I believed I was given credit for, so
that, to prove myself, I was practically mute. To the few
remarks my grandfather addressed to me my replies were
almost idiotically monosyllabic. I felt that he had only

spoken to be nice, and I was conscious that I had nothing to say which would interest a man who had seen so much and who had such a lot on his mind. I watched him from afar going about his chores, and I would have liked to offer to help, but I hung back. The stoop in his shoulders as he brought in the milk pails or carried slop to the hogs excited my deepest sympathy. I saw him sitting unrocking in his rocking chair on the front porch, gazing over the fields, thinking his heavy thoughts, and I wished I could comfort him. At night I prayed, "Dear God, have pity on poor Grandpa, for he lost his son just like you. And, dear God, please let him take just a little notice of me."

The answerable half of my prayer soon was, and beyond my wildest dreams. One day at dinner, eating my glass of cornbread crumbled in sweetmilk, I felt someone watching me and at the same moment heard my grandfather say, "Bless my soul!" I looked up to find his eyes on me, and I realized that I had been scraping the dribble from my chin with my spoon after each mouthful, a fault my mother was always correcting me for at home. I burned red. Then Grandpa said to Grandma, "For a minute there I would have sworn it was Ned come back just as he was."

Now my grandfather had never seen Ned at anything near the age which I had reached. In all likelihood he was confusing both me and Ned with the childhood of one of his other sons. However that may be, I had reminded him of Ned, and on my side I did not feel I was being likened to that miserable boy in the picture, but to the cowpuncher of my fond imaginings. The resemblance to Ned which he fancied he saw in me was strengthened when my grandfather discovered the secret cult I had made of my missing uncle. The topic was no longer painful to him, and so, out of my grandmother's hearing, for he supposed it was still painful to her, he began that summer to tell me his adventures in search of his son, and over them we drew close. As certain family traits will sometimes skip a generation,

passing over the children to reappear in a grandchild, in
my grandfather's case and mine it was Little Ned and the
West.

Reading over what I have written, I see that I have made
it seem as if I spent every hour of my boyhood mooning over
my lost uncle. Needless to say, I did not. Nor did I suppose
that my grandfather had nothing else to think about. He
had twelve other children, for one thing, and I had often
seen him in their midst on Christmas and Thanksgiving Day
and on his birthday being quite thoughtless and gay. I had
gotten over thinking it was unfeeling of him, after Ned's
abduction, to have had other children. But as Little Ned was
never far from my thoughts in those days, I assumed that
he was even less often absent from my grandfather's. As a
matter of fact it was I who had brought him back, after long
and almost total absence. I, and the onset of old age.

When I came along it was many years since 1898. Many
years, many bales of cotton, many children. His wife was
old and his children gone from home, the friends of his
youth dying off. His work was done, and now as the restlessness of old age came upon him his mind turned to the
great adventure of his life, flooding it in a blaze of remembered light. The palette of his memory was spread with pure
prismatic colors and the pictures he painted were of a land
of perpetual summer, of sweeping yellow plains on which
herds of cattle moved in a slow red tide, of brown hillsides
sprinkled with white sheep like mushrooms, green valleys
lying below red hills where melons grew in winter, hot to
the touch, like sunned rocks; crimson bursts of poinsettia,
bright lemons, glowing, incandescent amid their dark leaves,
huge aloes with curling arms like tentacles, like some great
octopi of the desert, creature-like geological growths of red
sandstone carved by the winds which seemed to whisper
a language around them; a sound heard once and never
forgotten, like wind rushing in a cavern, as a thousand sheep

cropped the grass in a hidden and windless valley; lilac-blooming almond trees and purple bougainvillea, alligator-pear trees and banana palms with their tattered leaves like great feather dusters stood on end, and over it all a bright blue cloudless sky. I in the restless longing of childhood for my life to begin, he in the fretful climacteric of its close, beguiled ourselves with his remembrances of that hot, free, unrestricted land; and out of the landscape of our vision, shimmering like a mirage, rose the figure of our son and uncle, the personification of the place, of our dreams and our regrets, with eyes the color of that clear sky, skin the color of that burnt earth, a smile as radiant as that bright, bone-warming sun.

I learned now why my aunts and uncles and my father were bored with the story of Little Ned, and although I never shared the feeling, I understood how it might be so with them. My grandfather had tried at first to keep alive the memory of their lost brother in Winnie and Bea, to instill a feeling for the brother they had never known in the ones born after-wards. They had not been bored then; they had listened, had listened with bated breath, they had cried hot tears. He thought they were crying for their poor little brother; he realized at last that each was crying for himself. He saw that their interest was the fascination of terror, and he saw that each felt obscurely ashamed of not having been kid-napped himself. He saw that each felt himself loved less than the child who had been stolen. They were only chil-dren, they were not to blame. He was. He had been a fool. He would be one no longer. And so he put Ned away in the attic of his mind as he had put away his clothes and his toys in the attic of the house.

And then time took its effect. The other children outgrew their childish fears, their childish jealousy, and the two who had known him simply forgot Little Ned, and the rest who had not sometimes forgot that they hadn't, and he became a story, and then became an old story.

At first he had tried to tell his wife of his adventures. They would settle down before the fire after supper at night. Selecting an opportune moment, my grandfather would clear his throat with a reminiscent chuckle. Never a penny was he offered for his thoughts. After a while he would try again, upping his volume a bit. She went on knitting bootees. Finally he would have to say, "Did I ever tell you about that time in Waxahachie when I—hah!—when I . . ."

Now in relating any story about himself, my grandfather, after the immemorial fashion of country men, would always cast himself as the butt of the joke; only in this way could a story in first person singular be rendered unegotistical. My grandmother missed this point. So when he had wound up a long and intricate and lovingly embellished tale of what a rube he had been taken for in Waco, or what a fool he had made of himself in front of strangers on a streetcar one day in Dallas, or what he had been caught by his waiter doing with a certain unfamiliar dish in the dining room of his Fort Worth hotel, she would offer comfort in these words, "Well, never mind, dear. It's all over now and you can just forget it. You're home again where you belong and you needn't ever go away again."

Her new child had turned out a boy, and my grandmother was a much more contented woman. Rather more contented than my grandfather felt she had any right to be, forgetful of Ned and her share in the loss of Ned. Relations between her and her stepdaughters had improved in his absence, partly through his absence, which had brought them closer together, and now even more through her greater content-ment in having a son of her own. The girls were crazy about their little brother Ewen. You would think they had never had a brother—a brother of their own, my grandfather caught himself thinking. Oddly enough, the one he felt closest to at that period was little Florence. Not so very odd, really. She did not disappoint him as Bea and Winnie did; she was excused in his mind from the loyalty towards

Ned which he felt they ought to show. And she appealed to him because of the neglect she now suffered, or that he thought she suffered, through her mother's absorption in Ewen. Meanwhile it was not that Hester tried to force the baby on his notice; or if she did, naturally she never thought of it as forcing. But to my grandfather it seemed that she was campaigning to make him forget Ned. So towards little Ewen his original impulse of resentment began to harden into rejection. Too happy to notice this, my grandmother would say that the boy looked just like his father. To my grandfather what he looked just like was Ned. At night when it was his spell to walk him when the baby was colicky and cried, he would pray, "Oh, Lord, teach me to love this child of mine. He is a fine boy and I ought to thank you for him. He can't help it that he's a boy. It's not his fault that his brother was stolen from me and not him. A man can have many sons and love them all. Only why did you have to make this one look so much like the other one, to remind me of him a thousand times a day? I know you sent me this boy, Lord, to console me, to take the other's place. But I didn't want to be consoled—at least not just yet. I didn't want another boy. I just want my boy back."

That spring the tax assessment on Will Vinson's house and land was sent to Samuel Ordway, and he went into Clarksville, to the courthouse, and paid it. Thus was the place of the man who had stolen his son, and whereon he had raised and harvested a crop, tacitly acknowledged to be his. He installed a tenant in the Vinson house, brought over one of Vinson's cows and gave him the milking of her, for he had a peaked and stringy little boy about Ned's age who could do with a drop of milk, helped put the now listing chicken house to rights, and agreed with his tenant to share work on the two places. Being already behind, he was out of the house at dawn, in the fields until after dark, could not even come home for his dinner. My grandmother would bring it down to him. She would come carrying the baby

and would yodel to him and he would stop plowing and come
to the fencerow. She would give him the baby to hold while
she spread his dinner on the ground. Amused at what she
took for his clumsiness, his timidity, she would say, "Not that
way, goose. You'll drop him for sure. Hold him close to
you, like this. I should think you would know how by this
time."

For some years afterwards, with the first breath of cold
weather in the fall, a change would come over him. He
would be picking or weighing in a sack, and would pause,
lose himself, not know where his mind had been. My grandmother knew. It was like a seasonal instinct, like that of
migratory birds; and as the fields were stripped of their
whiteness, leaving the brown empty hulls of the cotton bolls
to rattle drily in the wind, as the frost tingled in the air
and ice as thin and clear as a watch crystal appeared on the
cow tracks, he would pause, bemused, and as though at
some instinctual stirring in his blood, insensibly turn to westward. Across the prairie, heading out, the train hooted and
cried, and the smoke left a trail on the air. Then as to birds
there comes, after weeks of restlessness, a day of decisive
frost, the last bale of cotton was ginned, the last cane of
sorghum was pressed, and the vague prompting in his heart
rose, a clear call, into his mind. This time he would go just
a little farther, go just beyond where he had turned back
before. . . . And then Hester would announce that another
child was on its way. The coming of others, among them
other boys, took from Ewen the onus of being the sole
interloper, and my grandfather accepted him, and grew to
love him.

Then there were two Little Neds, the one I shared with
Grandpa, and the one I shared with no one. Grandpa's and
mine had fixed features, though they had come to be fixed
somehow without ever being discussed. But when we fell
silent and together stared off in Ned's direction, when we

had conjured him up and, as I think back on it now, must
have felt we were gazing into his eyes, we were both con-
centrated on a spot about six foot four off the ground. I
never wanted us to differ, and so I was never sure whether
this Ned still boasted the bushy black mustache he had acquired so early in life. On my side he did, and I left it at that.
It went without saying that Ned's handshake was a real bone-
crusher. This Ned had ceased to roam and settled down and
now had about four thousand mixed head of Hereford whiteface and Santa Gertrudis cattle on his ten-thousand-acre
spread. And someday I was going to go out there and pick up
the trail and go just a little farther west from where my
grandfather had turned back, and find him. The second Ned,
my own, was protean. He changed with me, and I changed
with the weather.

My grandfather retained the old fashion of saying "sir"
to boys. "Do you know what this is, sir?" he would often
ask, and I, even when I knew very well what it was, would
answer, "No, sir." In one such instance, on a memorable day,
though I felt he would hardly have asked unless the answer
had been less obvious than it appeared, I could hardly help
answering, "It looks like a French harp, sir."

"It is," said he. "What more can you say about it?" And
he handed it to me.

I could have said it wasn't much, as French harps went,
and I almost did. That was the judgment of a boy who just
the past Christmas had received a Hohner chromatic and
who had already mastered (as nearly as he was ever to
master any music in his life) "La Cucaracha," "Old Rattler,"
and "The Cowboy's Lament." Possessed of just eight notes,
it was a baby's toy, and it was anything but new. In fact, it
was green with age. I hoped my grandfather was not fixing
to make me a present of it. "Sure is a small one, isn't it?" I
ventured.

"Bought for a small boy," said my grandfather. "I got
that for Ned. Picked it up in town the day he was stolen,

meaning to give it to him that night. When I went looking for him I took it along, to show him I hadn't forgotten to get him something that day, should I ever find him. Well, Ned never got his play-pretty. It's yours, if you think you can find a use for it. You'd be surprised how many notes you can get by without in playing a French harp if you have to." Instantly my gaudy note-bloated Hohner became a thing of dirt and indifference to me. He took it from me and rendered a few bars of "Red River Valley." He said it was "Red River Valley," and of course after he said so, why I could hear that it was. It became doubly precious to me when he told of playing it to himself at night on the plains in front of his campfire, and what a comfort to him it was in his loneliness. My preference for Ned's French harp to the fine one she had given me puzzled, and I am afraid hurt, my mother. No doubt she would have understood if I had told her that it was Ned's, or intended for Ned; but I did not tell her, not even her, for it was my secret, mine and Grandpa's.

So I would spend the summer on the farm, and after dinner, in the heat of the day, we all took a nap. Dinner was the big meal of the day, as it is on a farm, and we could scarcely rise from the table. Grandpa would stagger off to his room, Grandma to hers (for he snored so loud they slept apart), and if there were any cousins of mine, other grandchildren, staying on the farm, and often there were, we shared a bed—not for lack of space, far from it, but for company and fun. The dogs slept underneath the porch, popping their chops and munching in their sleep, or yapping and twitching sometimes as they ran rabbits in their dreams. The cats curled up inside their fur and disappeared. The pigs snoozed in the shade, what shade was cast beneath that blazing sun which hung directly overhead until late in the long afternoon, and the occasional clucking of a hen or the rusty creak of one of Grandma's drowsy-headed guinea fowls out in the yard sounded like a person talking to himself in his sleep. The flowers drooped on their stalks like umbrellas in a stand, and even the houseflies stopped buzzing and dozed on the windowpanes. Only the honeybees worked through the heat, and their intermittent hum as they hovered about the clematis outside the windows and doors was like the sound of regular deep breathing and made your brain reel with heaviness. The windmill creaked to a stop. Occasionally a locust snored, a sound like my grandfather's whistle as he turned over in his sleep. We kids were always determined to stay awake. But you would watch a housefly on the pane rubbing its head and stretching, and your face would grow hot with drowsiness. Looking out, you saw the gourds sagging on the vines and the chinaberry tree hanging limp, and you yawned, sighed, and passed out.

On one such afternoon, lying half awake, alone in my bed and listening to the breathing of the house, I heard from a great ways off the buzz of a car engine. It pulsed and faded and seemed to stand still and seemed to have been going forever and never to have been going at all and then it was hours later and I heard it, or dreamed I heard it, outside the gate. Then I heard a car door slam and a man's voice call out from below:

"Mr. Ordway? Mr. Samuel Ordway?"

"Yes? Yes, Samuel Ordway—that's me."

"Then I have come to claim kin with you. Seems I am your son and not who I always thought I was at all."

"Now, sir, before we go any further I want to say that I won't hear a word said against Mr. Will Vinson. It's true he done you wrong, and I reckon he wronged me too. But he was always good to me, and I will thank you to cuss him when I'm not around. Begging your pardon, sir."

This speech (which shocked me—I was upstairs looking down on their heads) pleased my grandfather, warmed him instantly towards the man. "When did Will pass away?" he asked. And there was nothing in his tone to have offended any child of the blood of Will Vinson.

Sensing which, and softening his tone, Ned replied that Will Vinson had passed on that spring. That it was with his dying breath that the man he had thought was his father had confessed the truth of his birth. "He told me," said Ned, "if I found you alive to ask you to try to forgive him."

He had forgiven Will Vinson years ago. He did not know that he had, until now. More than that—this too he realized only now—between him and the man who had stolen his son there had been a kind of bond, and far from exulting now at the death of an enemy, he felt as if he had just been told of the death of an old, old friend. No, nearer than that: as if word had been brought of a death in the family. No, nearer than that: he had lost his old, familiar, only enemy. Something had gone out of his life. Something which, to be sure, he had not known was there until it was there no longer, but which had been there nonetheless, and the loss of which left a vacancy, and left him feeling old. Will Vinson was dead. He could see him in his mind as plain as if he stood before him. Now he was dead. The last link with the years of his prime had just snapped. Certainly it was not affection he had felt for the man who had wronged him. It was a feeling he could not put a name to. But it was real, for all that; a bond more real than this flesh-and-blood stranger, this cowpoke, standing there and claiming to be his flesh and blood.

He started from his reverie. He put out his hand and Ned put out his. Then my grandfather's eyes filled with tears, he opened his arms, and embraced his son. Then embarrassment overcame him and he said in an offhand manly tone, "Well, the climate out there seems to have done you good."

He'd have come sooner, I heard Ned say (he spoke loudly, apparently thinking that his father was somewhat hard of hearing), but first he had had to wait until after the shearing, and then . . .

As every American boy knows, the enemy, or rather, since that term confers a certain dignity, even almost an equality of status, the pest, the plague of the cattleman was the squatter, the nester: the sheepherder. And just as the cowman, horsed on his mustang, booted and spurred and six-gunned and sombreroed, that hater of barb wire, champion of the open range, derived his costume and his outlook and his glamour from the noble beast he drove, so too the sheepherder took his qualities from the creature he tended. Object immemorial of the cowman's scorn, the sheepherder was tame and timid and anonymous and woolly as his stupid, blatting, cowardly flock. A veterinary barber. A ewe midwife. A pedestrian. A colleague of Little Bopeep. No picturesque trappings on him. No swagger. Imagine a sheepherder saying with a cold glint in his eye, "You want to smile when you say that, pardner"? True, that noblest of cows, the longhorn, had, like the buffalo, like so many noble things, gone to greener pastures by my time. But memory was there. And for present-day consolation there was the proud and independent whiteface, the cantankerous and exotic Bramer. They might not be longhorns, but you would never think of counting them to bring on sleep. Having gone to such lengths to show my contempt for sheep and all they stood for, it will hardly be necessary to add that it never occurred to me that my Uncle Ned might be a sheepherder. Well, he wasn't. Oh, how glad I would have been, when I learned the awful truth, if he had been!

"Shearing?" said my grandfather. "Sheep?"

No. No, what Ned raised were to sheep what sheep were to cows.

"Goats?" I heard my grandfather say. And I thought he checked an impulse to turn and look up at my window, hoping to find that I was safe asleep.

Goats? Raise goats? I never knew that anybody raised goats. I thought goats just grew. On garbage dumps. In vacant lots.

"Angora goats," said Ned. "Three thousand of them."

He was not the Gary Cooper of my daydreams. Instead of

tall, dark, and silent, he was average, florid, and talkative.
He was not proud and dangerous, hair-triggered, but (like
both his fathers) incapable of anger, likable to a fault, a
grin of unruffleable good nature always on his lips, the sort
of fellow that dogs turned belly-up to and little old ladies
asked to run errands. Petted by those people who had doted
on him to the point of criminality, yet denied material in-
dulgences by the roughness of life out there, he was a happy
man and kept a summery disposition in all sorts of weather.
A perennial boy, restless, prankish, barely housebroken, he
had never married and never would. He seemed to have
been on holiday all his life, including the time he had helped
old Jack Pershing in his scuffle with Pancho Villa. I held
out against him for about an hour. No boy could resist him
longer than that. On consideration I found that the West
which my uncle represented was not so very different after
all from the one I had pictured to myself, only maybe more
fun, and certainly a good deal safer.

My grandmother's reaction to Ned's return was watched
closely by all. Though it lightened the burden of her old guilt,
it brought her fresh misgivings too. How could this help but
reawaken all her husband's tender memories of Agatha, his
youth with her, and his sad memories of her death? How
could it help but blow into flame his old resentment of her
for the loss of his and Agatha's son? Suppose Ned had
turned out well: would this not make the years of his
absence all the more painful? Suppose he were a disappointment to his father: would he not think this the fault of his
upbringing by strangers, and blame her all the more?
Dormant for so long, while she was busy with raising
twelve children and the house rang with their clamor, this
guilt of my grandmother's had revived in the time since
silence had fallen on the house and her mind and her hands
been overtaken by idleness. Her own thoughts having re-

verted to those early days, she supposed that her husband's thoughts had too. His avoidance of the subject, which she had always attributed to consideration for her, she now began to find suspicious, oppressive. Was it still so painful? Did he still feel too unforgiving to trust himself to mention Ned's name to her?

At least Ned's coming broke this silence. The man himself was nothing that his father need feel ashamed to own; that much was evident on first inspection. This Ned, Agatha's son, her own mistreated or at least neglected stepchild, this as yet abstract Ned, had done well—better, for that matter, than any of his unstolen brothers. Life had not treated him badly out there, no need to torment herself on that score. Nor had he himself any regrets for what had befallen him. He made it pretty plain that he would not have traded places with any man. As it had turned out happily in the end, he looked upon himself as doubly lucky; he had had two fathers, one to step in exactly on the death of the other. In himself he saw nothing to sadden anyone for losing him. After all those years of not being able to mention the subject, my grandmother was startled, but very agreeably startled, when he said, "Well, ma'am, I reckon you are about the luckiest woman I know, to have had somebody take me off your hands."

In fact, she was beginning to regret not having had the pleasure of rearing such an agreeable young man. Not the least of her reasons was her belief that she could have done an even better job of it than had been done.

All these things I have listed up to now only prepared my grandmother to welcome Ned—any Ned; not necessarily to like him. This particular Ned, whom no one could dislike, my grandmother soon began to like very much. In fact, he soon had her eating out of his hand. She liked his rowdiness, both for itself and because it contrasted nicely with the polish of the sons she herself had brought up—a con-

trast which did not, she believed, go unremarked by their
father. His simplicity appealed to her. She did not like him
one bit the less for being able to look down on him a little.
The immaturity of his ways made her feel young. He flirted
with her and he flattered her flagrantly—and flattery was
one good thing of which my grandmother could hardly have
too much. He noticed, and in the week he spent there,
patched up and mended things for her around the house
which my grandfather had been going to get around to one
of these days for years. He observed that, being rather above
average woman's height, my grandmother was forced to
stoop over the kitchen sink, where so much of her time was
spent, and while she was out one afternoon he raised it.
When she realized it (two days later) she cried. The back-
ache of which she had complained for years was never
again mentioned. And Ned knew when to stop. Before she
would have had to compare her own sons unfavorably to
him, to reproach them in her mind for having neglected
her. Finally, she admired his loyalty to Will Vinson and
defended it against his half-brothers' and half-sisters'
criticisms—not, I truly believe, only because she wished
my grandfather to have to share Ned's love with another father. But even more was she predisposed in Ned's
favor by his loyalty to Mrs. Vinson (who, I have omitted to
say, had died a year or so before her husband). For men
who never married, my grandmother cherished a particular
regard. Her secret hope had always been that one among her
own sons would choose to stay single, remain at home. A son
whom no other woman could make to forsake his home,
which is to say his mother, and cleave unto her, was the kind
of son my grandmother admired the very most.

"I kind of feel that my new brothers and sisters would like
it better if I was to disown Mr. Vinson, so to speak," said
Ned to my grandfather once, after he had been back a few
days. "I can understand their feelings, of course. I hope, sir,
you don't think . . ."

"My boy," said my grandfather, "whatever I may once have felt about the man, it was all a long time ago." It was also a lot less vehement than this left implied. But to that day my grandfather had retained his sense of apology for the weakness of his resentment against Will, and while he knew that Ned had loved the man, and that for him to have said he once meant to do him harm would have pained him, he felt too that to say he never meant to harm him would be painful, and would lower him in his son's esteem. "A long time ago, and now all I can think of is that he told you about me before he died. I'm not sure I would have done it in his place. It means a lot to me to have all my children near me once again, here towards the end. You must not think that I expect you to change your feelings about him. I don't expect you to love me overnight as you love the man who was a father, a good father, to you all your life. I don't hate Will myself, and I certainly don't expect you to."

Ned stayed a week, during which time all his brothers and sisters, with their children, came home to meet him, singly and in pairs and all together for a grand family reunion. On Sunday we went in a body to church. Though it was not Mabry's day, the preacher came out specially for us. To celebrate the occasion he preached on the text: "And Israel said unto Joseph, I had not thought to see thy face" (Gen. 48:11). Which, considering its overtones, was perhaps not the happiest choice he might have made. After church my grandmother took my grandfather aside and suggested that Ned might like to visit his mother's grave. Ned, of course, had evinced no such desire. With all the new knowledge of himself which had recently been revealed, he had trouble remembering about Agatha Ordway. He had learned that his mother was not his mother; to have to bear in mind that his father's wife was not his mother either was rather like learning the same thing a second time. "I am sure he would welcome the suggestion," said my grandfather. "And all the more if it came from you."

"Well, if you think so," said my grandmother, "then I'll speak to him." She had of course meant from the start to be the one. Having by now succeeded in convincing herself that Ned had come back expressly in answer to her prayers, she felt a proprietary interest in him, and she intended to offer him up at his mother's grave in discharge of her old debt to Agatha. She would have liked to conduct him there personally. Restoring her lost son did not settle the issue between Agatha and her, to be sure; but it cleared it up considerably, and greatly reduced her disadvantage.

"I expect he would have asked himself," said my grandfather, "but for consideration of you."

"He needn't have—"

"Of course not. But he can't be sure of that, you see. So it will be better if you suggest it. And then . . . well, maybe I ought to be the one to take him there? What do you think?"

"Yes, I think so," said my grandmother without batting a lash. "Unless . . ."

"Unless what?"

"Unless you think he might rather be alone with his thoughts?"

"My dear," said he, patting her hand, "count on you. You always think of everything."

The time came for Ned to return home. He invited his entire family to come down and visit him on his ranch. All said that would be very nice. Ned said, good, let's go. They had not understood that he meant right then, that very day, with him. That was impossible. School was out and the children free, true; but that many people could not just pick up on the spur of the moment and set off seven hundred miles, be gone from home for two or three weeks. Men could not just take off from their jobs, shut down their businesses. My grandfather said nothing. Neither did my grandmother. When they were turned to for appeal against this madness, it was evident that she wished to go, never having been anywhere, and that try as he might to take no sides, my grandfather would like to go back out there once again. Another time might be too late for him: that thought could be read in his eyes, and that decided it.

There were sixty-two of us, all told, and we went in a caravan of fourteen cars, Ned and Grandpa and Grandma and I in the lead—Grandpa and I together in the back seat, Ned and Grandma in front—then Aunt Flo and Uncle Cecil, Uncle Ewen and Aunt Jewel, Uncle Ross and Aunt Edith, Aunt Winnie, Uncle Herschell, and so on down the line.

Roads then were not what roads are now, and neither were cars. We had that first day alone no fewer than five blowouts among us, three boiling radiators, a broken spring leaf, a stripped rear axle, and a burnt-out coil. In those days, though, every car carried a spare car in parts, and every driver was a shade-tree mechanic. Ned's car was new, a new Ford, a sedan, marvelous to me because it was his and because it was new and because the horn, with which he was wonderfully liberal, went *ah-oogah! ah-oogah!* Behind us Uncle Ewen percolated along in a 1927 Moon, and though I now forget just who had which, I recall such other defunct marques as a Durant of dim vintage, a Whippett, and a Star. This last was the caboose of our train, belonging to my Uncle Malcolm, the baby of the family, and as we made a long curve I would hang out the window and wave back to my little cousins Dorothy and Matt.

Down through Jefferson and Marshall we went, through Henderson and Lufkin, and Grandpa, beside me in the back seat, thinking of Will Vinson and his pursuit of him, kept musing aloud, "Del Rio! So that's where Will was!" He seemed to lack only one thing now to make his enjoyment complete; that was to have Will himself there to share it all with him.

What with car troubles and carsick children and frequent stops to go behind the bushes and the business of meals and getting through towns and stopping for soda water for all the children and stopping at roadside cafés to ask them to boil the babies' bottles and frequent herds of cattle taking up the road and detours where the highway was under repair, we were able to make only about a hundred miles a day. Which of course was about ten times better than Grandpa had done in his old wagon, and as we went through Kilgore at dusk, or rather at the hour of dusk, for the thousands of blue gas flares roaring upwards from alongside the derricks prevented night from falling, he asked what town this was, and when he heard, responded with a look of delighted disbelief.

We saw oil wells in the middle of main streets in some of those towns, the traffic flowing unconcernedly around the derrick. We saw whole forests of them, like trees blackened and branchless after a great fire. We saw them by the hundreds standing amid the cypresses in bayous, up to their knees in water, the men who tended them, a special breed of men, burly and blackened, going about their work in motorboats, the water thick with a greasy scum, so that it looked like a lake of crude oil, which it very nearly was. We had always in our ears the steady pounding of the pumps, the rattle and clank of the drilling rigs, the constant grinding of heavy truck gears. We saw capped wells working away in cottonfields that were sown right up around the pumps, derricks in front lawns on city lots, in schoolyards, towering like skeletal spires over greasy churches. Oil was everywhere. The roads were black with it, slick with it, from the drip of the convoys of tank trucks. Pools of it stood like mud in the fields, and roadside ditches ran black. It was in the water you drank (at a dollar a gallon some places) and in the food you ate. Touch something, anything, and your fingers came back to you oily; touch nothing, they were oily all the same. It clouded your eyeglasses like a spray. The very air seemed oily. You could taste it, couldn't not taste it.

It was a world on fire. The smoke turned the day into night and the fires turned night into day. A garden of flames, like species of flowers: the pointed blue smokeless gas flares roaring upwards against the night like blowtorches; the blue intense heatless glow of the sulphur fires; the leaping yellow and red and orange of the crackling oil flames, billowing vast black rolls of smoke; near fires with men silhouetted against the flicker like busy demons, distant sputters like a match struck in the dark, small far-off steady flames like candles burning on the ground.

Towards nightfall I rejoined my family in our car, for in the matter of a place to sleep for the night priority went by seniority. The lead car, Ned's, took the first tourist home that offered, peeling off like a plane dropping out of formation, the rest drove on and the then lead car took the next, and so on. The following morning, starting out from the rear, Ned came down the line gathering up the van, and we were on our way again. Meals, after the first day out, were a picnic. For although anxious mothers had started off insisting on dull balanced diets, this was at once found to be impracticable, and afterwards we gorged on baloney and crackers and pickles and weenies and Vienna sausages and potato chips and buns and bottled pop and bananas and peanut butter and sauerkraut and marshmallows and other ready-prepared and portable poisons. The men of our clan had all pooled their home brew, which we transported in tubs of ice in the trunks of several of the cars. For though national prohibition had recently been repealed, our men scorned near-beer and three-two, which was all you could get at that time, and you could not get even that in dry areas of local option. Ice notwithstanding, it traveled poorly, and as many bottles blew up as got drunk. Every once in a while one or two or even three of them at a time would let go, and it sounded as if the car was backfiring. Those in the rear of the van said they were

not much worried about getting lost, for we laid down a trail
of scent like a brewery, and going through towns we were
often sniffed at by lounging locals.

And so we made our way down through the state, taking
turns, we cousins, in one another's cars, stopping in some
town in midmorning and buying out some little grocery
store, stopping to picnic at some pretty roadside spot just
whenever we felt like it, singing songs, waving and shouting
to everybody we passed, and playing Alphabet, getting separated and put into different cars when we quarreled, and
instructing our parents on the historical associations of the
places we passed through.

Lovely old somnolent Jefferson, that one-time inland port
on lotus-choked Big Cypress Bayou, with its crumbling
wharves where gaudy stern-wheelers had docked in the days
when the Red River ran navigable down to the Mississippi
and New Orleans. Where we crossed Trammel's Trace, the
old Indian trail over which Sam Houston and later Jim
Bowie on his way to the Alamo had entered Texas. Marshall,
stately and plantational. Fragrant, floral Nacogdoches, se-
date old Nacogdoches, so improbable a brawling ground and
yet the scene of six revolutions. Then Navasota, where
La Salle was killed by his own men. Huntsville, where old
Sam Houston died, disregarded, dishonored, and despised.
Washington-on-the-Brazos (off the route, actually, so that
when, at the junction of highway 6, Ned signaled for a turn,
everybody began to honk. So Ned signaled for a stop and
pulled over to the side of the road and everyone else pulled
in behind us. All the drivers piled out and came to the head
of the caravan, saying, "What'd you turn off here for?
You've made a wrong turn. We want to stay on 190. This
goes off to—"

"You don't even know where it goes off to, I bet," said
Grandpa.

"Well, it goes off the route, that's for certain."

"It goes to Washington-on-the-Brazos," said Grandpa.

"And do you want us to pass this near to the spot where the Texas Declaration of Independence was signed and not have our children see it? We can't do that. Can we, sir?" he said, turning to me, who had shrunk into my corner, seeing what a to-do I had caused.

"How far out of the way is it?"

"Never mind that," said Grandpa. "It's educational."

So although at first, like all Texans behind a wheel, we had thought we were in a hurry to get where we were going, we realized that we were not. My grandfather was enjoying the sights, and even before that detour to Washington-on-the-Brazos he kept putting on the brakes. It was a wonder we did not have a dozen fourteen-car pile-ups, the way he was always saying to Ned, "Stop!" so he could get out and have a look at a creek which he maintained was running north, or a mare and her foal in a pasture, or to strike out across a field and satisfy his curiosity about the workings of a new-fangled farm implement in use there, and only by deception and distraction could he be gotten past any state historical marker. When such ruses failed and he had his way, he would get out and go over and read the plaque, every word down to the erected-during-the-administration-of-governor-so-and-so, and would come back and take his seat without a word. "Well?" someone would ask. "Oh," he would say in surprise. "I thought you-all weren't interested." And he would leave it to me to tell them that Anson Jones had slept there. Anson Jones? Just the last president of the Republic of Texas. And trying not to look too smug, he would indicate that we might now proceed.

It came over us all that we had as much time as space, and after dinner we would take a short siesta, the older folks and the infants napping while the boys and girls romped and played and explored the neighborhood. On one of those days, after noon, while the women were shaking themselves awake and beginning to gather up the leftovers and tidy up the grounds and the men examined tires before proceeding

and measured with sticks the gas levels in tanks, suddenly
Marie, Uncle Ewen's married daughter, said, "June? June?
Where's June?" (Not a girl, but William Junior, aged three,
called June.)

At that the women all raised their heads as one, like a
flock of sheep, and instantly began to echo the call:

"June? June? June! Where's June?"

By this time Cousin Marie was darting distractedly here
and there, looking behind rocks and underneath cars, and
all the other mothers, first making sure of their own children, were joining in the search.

"One of the children is missing," Grandma was explaining
to Grandpa. "June. Marie's boy, June. Ewen's Marie." And
he, still full of sleep, was saying, "What? Missing? What do
you mean, missing? Where is he?"

Now the men had left off their chores and joined in.
Various ones were trying to bring some system into the
search, others were trying to calm the women. Just then up
strolled Ned with June riding on his shoulders. Ned was
wearing the broad grin without which he would have looked
undressed. "Hello, everybody!" he sang out. "Have a good
nap? Ready to hit the road?" From that time onward the
Ordway women were less hysterical about one of their children repeating that old scare story of our family's.

Then we became strangers in our own home state. We
began to see Mexicans. Once Ned stopped to buy fruit from
one. Ned spoke in Spanish. My grandfather listened in amazement. That a son of his could speak a foreign tongue astonished and delighted him. At Castroville, west of San
Antonio, we saw a European village, settled by Alsatian immigrants in 1848, who survived Indian raids and droughts,
grasshopper plagues and cholera, and whose strong old
fachwerk houses with their peaked dormers and long upper-
deck galleries still stand, and whose descendants still speak

a mixture of French and German with a strong Texas twang.

West of San Antonio we entered another world. A spiny land, all pointed and prickly, with plants like those sea animals that look like plants. Weird growths with names, reeled off by Ned to our gaping admiration, as twisted and fragrant and exotic as the things they signified: huisache with its lacy blooms, its dizzying scent, ocotillo, and maguey, yucca, greasewood, mesquite. Then we headed into the Valley, where, right on the border of Old Mexico, Ned had his ranch.

It was a real ranch, like the ones in the pictures. It had a big adobe hacienda, square, flat-roofed, white as a lump of sugar, with the butt ends of the rafters sticking out of the walls, which were two feet thick, and little round-arched windows without any panes. There was a corral with horses in it. There was also a pervasive and rutty odor of goat, and to everything, much like cotton on the weeds and wires back home, clung strands of goat hair. We were put up in bunkhouses, ate our meals out of doors. Grandpa followed at Ned's heels, and I at his, beaming at the way he talked Spanish with the hands. One day while we were there one of the goatherds, a Mexican wrapped in a serape and wearing a big-brimmed sombrero, came down from the hills bringing on the rump of his horse the mangled carcass of a kid. He and Ned talked for a while and then Ned said, "With all these extra hands here, it's a good time to get rid of some of these pesky coyotes." So there was a big coyote roundup and all the men got to shoot one and the dead coyotes were hung up in the trees and on the fenceposts to scare others away. One day my grandfather expressed the wish to visit Will Vinson's grave. It turned out that the Vinsons were buried right on the place, a common practice out there still, as it had once been around Clarksville, where the ranchers lived too widely scattered to maintain a community cemetery. They went down back of the house and along an arroyo, over a rise and down again into a little

draw where, in a cleared spot among the creosote bush, overhung with mesquite, were three graves, Will Vinson's, his
wife's, and their little girl Grace's. On the graves of the latter
two were stones on which only their given names appeared.
So the question which had drawn my grandfather there
was still unanswered, and he had to put it directly to Ned.
What name did he intend to put on Will's headstone? Vinson
or Ordway?

Ned said he had spoken to his two brothers—meaning
Felix and Perry (one of whom lived in Laredo, the other in
Corpus Christi)—about this. They themselves intended to
go on using the name they had grown up with. For himself,
of course, there was no problem. But as for his . . . as for
Mr. Vinson, he was puzzled to know what he would prefer.
And now there was someone else to consider.

"Who?" asked my grandfather.

"You," said Ned.

"Oh, son," said my grandfather, "I'm not jealous of my
name, and if you think Will Vinson would want to lie under
it, it's his for the rest of time, insofar as it's mine to give
him. I was only born to it, he earned it the hard way. But
if you think he would want his own back now, then for
God's sake and mine give it to him. It has been a burden on
my mind for years. I never signed my signature without
thinking that somewhere in the world was a man—never
mind how he had wronged me—who bore my name like a
brand."

When we had been there a week there began to be talk
of our returning home. Ned announced a barbecue. A truck-
load of half-grown goats were brought in from the range and
placed in a pen. A Mexican ranch hand would grab one of
them, deceiving it with a soft murmur of Spanish the while,
and holding it between his legs, would slit its throat, sever-
ing its terrified bleat in half, cursing it at the last moment
so as to work up a righteous feeling in himself. They were
hung, the hind legs spread by a stick, and skinned. The

carcasses drained bloodlessly pale, almost white. Twenty of them, they hung like a day's bag of game. I vowed I wouldn't eat any of them.

Fires were kindled the following morning and over the coals were stretched grills of cyclone fence wire. The goats were thrown on the grills, basted with sauce. The smell spread on the air and we were all drawn nearer and nearer. Somehow the carcasses now looked as if they had been born that way, dressed to eat. The barbecue sauce was pure fire and to put it out much *cerveza* and *gaseosa* was needed.

When we had begun to recover from our dinner and to sit up and breathe once again, we felt the stirrings of another appetite which our family reunions always aroused. We children, when we saw the first of our fathers come alive, would be already aflame with excitement. We would have to contain ourselves yet a while, though. We understood, young as we were, that grown men, at childish moments, must be spared having to liken themselves to children.

One of the men would get to his feet, stretch, and as he flexed his arms and felt his biceps ripple, the cords of his neck bunch up, and looked about at the assembled men of his clan, he would feel swell within him a sense of his own singularity, a challenge to all his brothers, those who once had bullied him and those whom he had bullied in his turn (and who now thought perhaps that they were ready to shove him aside?), and that other crew, the ones to whom at all times he felt himself superior, his sisters' husbands. He—whichever of them it happened to be—did not then say aloud, "I can run faster (outwrestle, jump higher, shoot straighter) than any one of you." He quietly went and picked up a horseapple and heaved it. He watched it fall with seeming indifference—lest it be thought that he had put all of himself into that one—but drew a line in the dirt with his toe to mark the spot he had thrown from, just in case somebody else should feel called upon to throw a horseapple.

Now a horseapple is a heavy thing, and it takes a good

arm to throw one. For the benefit of non-Texans, it looks like a rough overgrown green orange (in fact, the tree is called the Osage orange, though we call it the bois d'arc, pronounced "bore dark") and to pick one up is to get your hands covered with a sticky white sap which quickly turns black and which nothing short of turpentine will take off. Nevertheless you cannot resist a horseapple; it lies there, a perfect handful, just waiting to be picked up and chunked.

But now, that one thrown gauntlet of a horseapple would lie where it fell, disregarded, and nobody went to pick up another from the pile beneath the bois d'arc tree. Only after about five minutes would a second man rise and hitch up his trousers and saunter over and look down at the toe mark and out at the thrown horseapple, and say, if he bothered to speak at all, "Nice throw." Then he too would pick up one, or first pick out one, as critically as if he were choosing one to eat. And he would play with it, tossing it into the air like a boy skipping home after school with his lunch-box orange. Then, stepping quickly to the toe line, he would rear back and heave.

By then there would be a squad of juvenile umpires officiating down near that first horseapple, and the moment the second one came to earth up would go a yell—cheers and jeers—no getting it straight for a time which of the two was the better throw. When it was settled, "Best two out of three," the loser would demand, and the winner would reply, "Many as you like. Go ahead. You've got a throw to beat already." By then too a crowd had gathered, everyone cheering, taunting, the men egging one another on to challenge the winner. A chair was brought for my grandfather, who liked nothing better than watching this annual rite, delighting in the strength and skill of his sons as they engaged one another in trials. Soon word would reach the women in the kitchen ("What're they doing out there?" "Oh, showing off, them fools") and they would come flocking out, shaking their heads and pursing their lips in disapproval, but with their eyes kindling with excitement, hope, pride in their own men. All of them, like my own mother, country girls who, having left the farm and acquired townish notions, affected to find these old-fashioned amusements countrified and embarrassing. Actually what they were embarrassed by was their pleasure in them. For whether as participants or as spectators of the men's events, once the going got good they quickly shed their superciliousness.

Yes, we had contests among the women too. Only among the children was competition discouraged that day. They were such spoilsports and graceless losers they were apt to ruin the fun. But we children did not mind. Footraces and such among ourselves were everyday; only once a year, or rarely twice, did we get the chance to see our parents cut up. And nothing tickled us like seeing our mothers kick off their shoes and shake down their hair, their faces aglow with girlish fun, poise themselves on the mark and run a footrace. And nothing thrilled us like seeing our fathers peel down to their hairy chests and wrestle with our uncles. We were excused, of course, from the impartiality which was expected of the grownups, and we shouted and groaned, and sometimes we wept hot hidden tears of filial chagrin, along the sidelines, and sometimes we got into fights among ourselves, disputing the outcome of one of our fathers' matches. I never loved my mother so much as when, red-faced, panting, laughing, she fell on the grass and rolled with me in a hug and I felt the blood racing in her strong young body and she laughed at herself for being so childishly pleased at outrunning her sisters-in-law at the annual Ordway family reunion.

By now it was pretty well established in the family that certain ones excelled at certain things, and were expected to win. But it was a decathlon, with all expected to participate in each event. Besides, nothing was ever conceded. Time brought changes. Champions were made of flesh. And now a new contender had entered the lists—one of us, yet not one of us: Uncle Ned.

My grandfather, when it was a contest between two of his own children, always cheered the underdog. When it was between one of his own and a son- or daughter-in-law, he always cheered against his own. My grandmother was incapable of this detachment. At such times she preserved a kind of swollen silence, and when required to congratulate a victorious son-in-law, did so with what was called in the family her persimmon-eating smile. "You didn't have to root so hard against Ross," I had overheard her say to my grandfather when they were alone together later at night.

"What? What are you talking about? When did I root against Ross?"

"When he and Edna's husband Ira were wrestling."

"Oh. Well, he won, didn't he?"

"Not with your help, he didn't, poor boy." This poor boy was six feet tall, weighed two hundred pounds, and was the father of four.

"To listen to you anyone would think he'd lost."

"No, he won, all right! But not with any help from his father, poor boy."

To her children my grandmother's predilection for them over their brothers- and sisters-in-law had long been a source of amusement, affection, and embarrassment. That she should not betray her bias that time the family games were played down on Ned's ranch concerned them every one. They feared that, win or lose, Ned was sure to feel her displeasure, and this was sure to be felt by their father. All were relieved when Ned, conscious of being something of an outsider, as well as being the host and the eldest son with a dignity to maintain, placed himself *hors concours* and took a seat alongside the old folks to look on.

But Ned was never cut out to be an onlooker when any

sort of games were being played. Dignity fitted him like a hand-me-down, and the diadem of seniority had sat for only a brief while on his unruly curls before it began to slip down over his eyes. He could not even be an aloof spectator, but must loudly take sides in every contest, his favor going sometimes inside, sometimes outside the fold, with himself in consequence seesawing in my grandmother's favor. In between events he put on an exhibition of Western rope tricks that would have done a cowboy proud. Finally the running, the jumping, the weight-lifting and the rifle-shooting had been settled. Then, despite pleas from the women and a positive prohibition from my grandmother, they began to wrestle. Ned could sit on the sidelines no longer. He was matched against none other than my grandmother's favorite, Uncle Ewen. No one could watch them for watching her. When the third straight fall was scored for Ned, my grandmother rose to the occasion by emitting a cheer. It was not the loudest cheer ever raised, but falling as it did upon a silence fraught with some uncertainty, her thin, cracked old woman's voice carried and was heard. The two contestants, naked to the waist, bathed in sweat and streaked with dirt, got up to take their bows, saw that the applause was not meant for them, and joined in it. My grandmother received the acclaim with mixed feelings, smiling yet frowning to find her frailty so generally known, at having attention called to her unusual generosity. But as the clapping swelled she accepted it gracefully, and shared it with her husband. He sat glowing with pride in his strong bare-breasted sons. Loud and long was the applause that day for the man who had fathered them and the woman who had borne them and brought them up.

Early next morning (the men all stiff and sore) we left for home. On saying goodbye to him I gave Ned his French harp, and told him its history. The cars were lined up pointing east. There were promises to write and to come back soon and to visit together often. But it was a long way from Clarksville, no matter by what means you traveled, and as I waved back to my Uncle Ned and watched him grow small, I knew in my heart that it would be a long time—that I might even have to be my own man and could come out by myself—before I saw him and his part of the world again, and so I was.